Long Time Gone

Anne Meisenzahl

Relax. Read. Repeat.

"We cannot escape our origins, however hard we try, those origins which contain the key—could we but find it—to all we later become."

— James Baldwin, Notes of a Native Son

LONG TIME GONE
By Anne Meisenzahl
Published by TouchPoint Press
Brookland, AR 72417
www.touchpointpress.com

ISBN-10: 1-946920-81-9
ISBN-13: 978-1-946920-81-2

Front cover layout: Erin Meisenzahl-Peace
Cover photo: Christine Quinlan
Cover Design: Colbie Myles, ColbieMyles.net

First Edition

Printed in the United States of America.

For all the Frankies and all the Crystals

Part One

Lord I been a longtime gone
Lord I ain't had a prayer since I don't know when
Longtime gone
And it ain't comin' back again
—*Darrell Scott*

1

January 1, 1998

G race Schreiber stared at the manger scene in the center of the kitchen table. Its plaster baby Jesus, tiny arms open, lay in a cardboard cradle on a few brittle pieces of straw. Mary and Joseph knelt beside him. The donkey's tail was broken, and the cow was scratched. Oblivious to the animals' flaws, three wise kings genuflected outside the stable, gripping gold-painted gifts. In the darkness of the descending night, a candle's orange light sputtered, and the holy scene seemed to glow.

As a child in snowy Buffalo, Grace had adored Jesus and the manger. She and her mother decorated the polished dining room buffet with this same nativity scene every December. Her older sister dragged her outside in the afternoon to make snow angels in the yard and then back inside, toes and noses tingling, to drink cocoa while familiar Christmas tunes played on the stereo. Every Christmas Eve, her dad roused her from sleep to go to Midnight Mass, and in the morning, the girls woke up to gifts under a small tree.

That life, those simple celebrations, seemed distant now. The battered crèche was the one memento of her childhood Grace still possessed. At the tail end of her forty-third year, deep in her sunny southern California lonesomeness, on the first day of a new year, she found in the scruffy little manger a tiny bit of nostalgic peace.

Grace looked at the new calendar she'd thumb-tacked to the wall a week ago. January 1, 1998. Tomorrow her so-called vacation would be over. She would have to leave her self-imposed isolation and return to her teaching job in the heart of Compton. She'd have to face her motley band of students and confront, once again, her inability to help them. Her heart

3

ached when she thought of how many lonely nights would be filled with memories of Jake.

She'd fallen head over heels in love with him, stayed with him for a year and a half, then, five months ago, he dropped her like a dirty sock to self-actualize with somebody else.

Then she'd left San Francisco for Los Angeles after accepting a job at the Cesar Chavez Adult Education Center, eager for something important to do that would take her out of her small, aching self.

Grace let herself be comforted by the candle's mesmerizing flickering. Her headache was not going away. She lay down on the sofa, pulled a pillow over her head, and drifted into a fitful sleep.

The phone's jingling startled her awake an hour later.

Her arm grazed the candle as she reached for the phone, spilling wax and flame across the tabletop and singeing Mary's plaster gown.

Grace scrambled off the couch and doused the fire with water from the sink. Now the animals were charred, and the wise men were in a jumble. She picked up the phone and cradled it between her head and shoulder.

"Yes, hello?" Grace said, wiping down the wet stable and its overturned occupants with a towel.

"Happy New Year, LA girl," her sister said. "Have a wild night last night?"

"Hi, Gloria. Not exactly." Grace sighed. She hadn't talked to her sister in Denver or her dad in Buffalo since Christmas. In fact, after the obligatory calls, she had unplugged the phone for the week so she wouldn't have to speak to anyone until she could adequately fake a lilting tone.

And here was her sister's voice in her ear an hour after she'd plugged the phone back in.

"New Year's Eve was…nice. Nice and quiet."

"You okay, Holy Girl?"

Her sister always insisted on taunting her about her religious youth. Her sister had the same early Christmas memories, but unlike Grace, Gloria had resisted the religiosity of the season. She'd nose-dived instead into presents and cookies, ripping open packages and crying if she didn't get what she wanted.

Even as a young child, Grace loved trying to be patient while surrounded by brightly wrapped gifts. She wanted to prove to her mother and father and

4

God that she could be a very good girl. But that desire had passed long ago. In spite of the miniature manger scene she planted in the center of her table every winter, there was no danger of returning to that phase.

That's all it had been–a phase.

She gave the tabletop one more wipe and gently repositioned each actor in the sacred scene.

"Of course. I'm fine." Grace worked to keep her voice even.

"Having fun in La La Land? Laying back? Lolling around?"

Talking to Gloria required her to rally all her defenses. Grace unscrewed the lid off a bottle of Tylenol. She uncorked the white wine she'd opened at eleven the night before, leaving her half-drunk and snoring before the ball dropped, popped the pills into her mouth, and took a swallow.

"Yup. Life is just fine. Happy New Year to you too."

2

Sheaves of worksheets lay askew on a table. All the pencils needed sharpening. Grace sighed at the mountain of work ahead of her. She swigged the last of her cold cappuccino as she prepared for her six o'clock twice-a-week night class. She had to pick a language assignment from her workbook to write in yellow chalk on the board.

She'd had a rough day. Her first class had been packed with new students, each one needing to be registered and oriented and tested. After a rushed lunch break, she returned to the classroom to teach a class packed with talkers. She found it hard to think straight enough to encourage them to listen. Her hour break after her afternoon class was useless, and at five-thirty she was back at it, utterly unprepared.

She looked around the cluttered room and shook her head. How did she get here? After years of odd jobs and private school tutoring, here she was in a dilapidated old building in a dicey part of town, working herself to exhaustion, and all to escape San Francisco. And Jake.

Grace had fallen for Jake on the day they met. It had been early February over an unexpected cup of coffee which led to a meandering walk in the park. On the walk back, he told her he appreciated her rough loveliness, her head of curly red hair. He admired her green eyes, her long body, even her freckles. During the hazy months that followed, he made her feel both sensual and spiritual. He'd helped her begin to reconcile those two essential parts of herself which until then she'd thought would always be at odds. Choose one, lose the other.

He was thirty-four years old. Seven years younger. But she loved that he was free-spirited and youthful. Intense and unfettered, he was her opposite. He encouraged her to meditate and practice yoga, detoxify and give up caffeine, make love under a canopy of trees.

She let herself get snookered by his high-mindedness and his praise, especially that first night in her bed when he polished every inch of her skin with warm oil and cooed, *You don't know your own beauty*. He fed her mango and papaya slices, shared a ceramic bong-full of what he called "transcendent weed," and told her, *I think you are blind to your own power.*

Eighteen months later, she came home to find a bundle of sage burning in a clamshell on her kitchen table. A note beside it declared that he was in love with their yoga instructor and asked her to bless him on his new journey. He hoped, he wrote, that the sage would cleanse her home of whatever negative energy she might feel since he was moving in with this Linda Starflower into an ashram a couple of miles away.

She had called and called, leaving messages full of pleading sobs. Later, anger seized her, but she hadn't had the heart to scream at him. She was so hurt and embarrassed at letting herself get baited and hooked, more disappointed by her own naïveté than angry at him.

He never called her back or asked her to meet him for tea so they could talk. He just ditched her.

In a blur of despondency, she planned her escape. She quit her tutoring job, responded to every teaching ad outside of San Francisco that didn't require a certificate, and kicked herself for never having jumped through the bureaucratic certification hoops. She had needed to find something to do far away from San Francisco that would occupy all her time so she wouldn't fall back into indulging her rejected self. So here she was in the sad, musty classroom where she'd landed.

At fifteen minutes before six o'clock, a young man walked in, startling her. No one was ever early. His good looks made her reflexively inventory her appearance: black jeans, low cut blue tee moist with sweat, hair loose, eyeliner probably smudged.

"Evening, ma'am. I'm Frankie Morales. I'm ready to join this class. I need this. Could I start tonight?"

He extended his hand. She set down the chalk, brushed her hands on her pants, and shook it. She smiled when she recognized the sincerity in his gentle black eyes.

She already had thirty-five students on her roster, which was the limit. New students were supposed to go to the office to enroll before they could begin her class, but she felt like making an exception.

"Yes, of course. Welcome. Come in and have a seat. We'll start in a few minutes."

"This is a big change for me. I want to finish something for a change. I want to get this right, you know?"

His long hair was combed back with mousse, and his mustache and goatee were neatly trimmed. A black stone sparkled in his earlobe. His arms were inked with intricate maroon and black images of Jesus on the cross, angels, and snakes. The mouth of a howling wolf opened on this elbow. *I love Jesus and Marisol* was tattooed on his neck.

Frankie's concentration never wavered over the next hour and a half as Grace taught a lesson on commas and conjunctions. His musky cologne surprised her as she leaned over him to show him how to find the pretest in the Language Arts book. He nodded, pulled out a new notebook and a sharp pencil, and set to work.

Frankie smiled when he came up to Grace's desk at the end of class. "Can I tell you something? I know I'm too old to be here. I should of done this a long time ago. But I got to get my diploma."

"That's great. You're not too old. It's never too late."

"And I want to be a writer, and I want you to push me, to keep me on this."

"Okay," she said. "I will."

Her students rarely approached her. The older ones shuffled in and out quietly; the young ones laughed or screamed after class, intertwined with each other, uninterested in her.

"Thank you. For teaching us. For helping me reach this goal of mine."

"Well, I think it's a good goal. Why do you want to be a writer?" Grace had given up on her pipe-dream of becoming a journalist after her freshman year of college. She could arrange words on a page pleasantly enough but doubted how much she had to *say*.

"I want to start diggin' deep. You know, writing my autobiography and all. I been through a mess of stuff, and I want to understand it better. I started when I was locked up, and then I had to stop to work and have a baby and all. But now I want to start it up again."

"I'm happy to help," Grace said.

Grace thought about her new student while she waited outside for the security guard to walk her and the other teachers to their cars. He was so focused, and that neck tattoo intrigued her. What did Jesus mean to him? Who was Marisol? What stories glowed inside him? As different as they were, something about him reminded her of herself when she was young. He seemed ravenous, innocent even, full of simple longing.

On the drive home, she fantasized calling Jilting Jake and telling him she never thought about him anymore. She had an interesting life without him.

She imagined him sitting cross-legged as they spoke on the phone, admitting he'd screwed up, begging her to let him come live with her in LA. She rolled her eyes at the image. He'd never apologize, of course, but if he did, she wondered if she'd be cool enough—after five months of distance—to not succumb to his charms.

She didn't stop to think when she got the job offer from Chavez. She'd packed up and left San Francisco without a backward glance, immediately immersing herself in their neglected adult education school program. The first time she saw the school building, she couldn't help but think that it looked even sadder than she felt.

Its low buildings and scattered portables were overwhelmed by colorful, indecipherable graffiti. Patches of brown grass hugged the broken asphalt of an unused basketball court. Her classroom was a grey box, its windows high and smudged, cluttered with old-fashioned desk chairs crammed into disorderly rows. Dusty dictionaries and textbooks with ripped binding appeared to have been thrown onto the sagging shelves.

No one was happy to be there. Most of the teachers had no credentials and very little training. There weren't enough workbooks or pencils for all of her students. When she brought this up with the program's director, he told her that she'd have to make the best of the situation. "We're doing what we can on a tight budget," he said.

She'd realized her first day on the job that she had way too many students to give any of them the attention they deserved. Unlike the private school children she'd worked with on and off for years in San Francisco, these students ranged in age from sixteen to sixty-five.

Many of them could barely read. Five of her teenagers were pregnant or had infants at home. Most of the young men had spent time in jail. Two of them were arrested and whisked away halfway through the last semester. Thanks to family problems and work schedules, lack of bus fare, and illness, few students completed a whole semester.

The neighborhoods surrounding the school looked particularly bleak in the waning light. There were no sidewalks and no posted speed limit signs. Children ran in the street, followed by tired-looking women pushing strollers. Young men hung around in clusters under streetlamps. Garbage bins overflowed on the corners. Every third or fourth house was boarded up; every fifth house was protected by a menacing iron gate.

All the houses, orange now as the sun sank, looked bedraggled and beat up.

By the time the forlorn neighborhoods of Compton gave way to the primly manicured streets of Gardena, it was dark. Grace pulled into her driveway and sighed. Her quiet house waited for her with nothing but emptiness and yesterday's dishes. She set her piles of student work and lesson plans on the kitchen table, pulled off her clothes, and crawled into bed.

3

"Listen, Amazing Grace," Gloria said. Grace had answered the phone against her better judgment. She was already late for class. "I just got back from a run. I was jogging at Inspiration Point this morning at the crack of dawn, looking out at the mountains, and I got an inspiration—of course."

"Hi, Gloria," Grace answered. Her sister was uncharacteristically perky today.

"Early morning running is my New Year's resolution!" she'd informed Grace in their last conversation.

Apparently, it was working out great. It left her husband David to deal with her teenagers' grumbling, got her to her café before the other staff tumbled in, and put her in a way better mood.

"Do you want to know what it is?" Gloria asked.

Grace heard metal clattering in the background. She could envision the long cord wrapped around her sister's shoulders, a *Take a Break Café* apron tied around her hips, her hands covered in flour.

"Okay. I guess." Grace stuffed her students' papers into a bag and tossed back her last gulp of coffee. "But I'm late. I have to go."

"Here's the plan. You move here. You live with us and work at the café while you job search. And then you find a boyfriend. Maybe even a husband! Tons of handsome men walk in here on a regular basis. A coffee shop is a great place to meet someone."

Gloria had it all worked out. Grace would pack herself up and give herself over to the adventure of living in a sprawling suburban house with talkative Gloria, her taciturn husband, and their two surly adolescents. She'd let her sister find her a nice job and a perfect mate. What could be easier than that?

"That is quite the inspiration," Grace said.

"I know, right? Promise me you'll think about it."

11

"I will. But I have to go now. Love you. Bye!"

Not in a million years, she chuckled to herself as she slipped out the door and turned the key in the lock. *Not for a million bucks.*

Fifteen minutes before her evening class was supposed to begin, Frankie poked his head inside her classroom door. Grace had finished straightening up from the frantic chaos of the day and was just sitting down to review her lesson plans. Essay assignments still needed to be scratched on the blackboard.

"Hello, Miss Schreiber. How ya doin' tonight?" Frankie's smile was broad, his teeth perfect.

"I'm fine. Thanks," she answered. The truth was she worn out from three arduous days in the classroom and not enough sleep "How are you?"

"Good, good. I'm excited. I'm ready. I ain't been in school, on the outside, I mean, for a long time." He smoothed his mousse-slick hair and winked. He tucked himself into a desk, pulled out a notebook, and wrote in silence as the rest of the students trickled in.

Grace showed the class how to compose a basic five-paragraph essay and gave them a few sample prompts. Frankie chose the second prompt.

Our world views, our values, and our beliefs are often influenced by our experiences. Describe an event that influenced your beliefs and explain how it has impacted your life.

He continued writing after everybody else left then tore three pages out of his notebook, walked up to Grace's desk, and handed the pages to her.

"Could you read it and tell me if it's good?" His dark eyes were wide, and Grace noticed that his hands were shaking. "I used to write a lot, poems and stuff. But I wanna get better and start to write for real."

"Sure. I'm going to read everybody's essays this weekend. I'll talk to you about it when I see you next Tuesday."

"Thanks. That's great." He reached out his hand and shook hers. His palm was calloused and dry. "G'night."

Grace smiled, imagining herself opening her front door at home, cracking open a bottle of white wine, turning on the gooseneck lamp, and starting in on the essay.

When Grace arrived at her classroom the following Tuesday, sandwich and coffee in hand, Frankie's muscular frame was slouched against the wall outside the door.

He straightened when he saw her walk toward him. "I know I'm early. I know you probably have stuff to do. But I wanted to talk to you about my story. Is that okay?"

Grace nodded, unlocked the door, and set down her things. She looked steadily at the young man who'd foisted himself upon her. She didn't have time to talk to him, but his presence was both commanding and gentle. She didn't want to disappoint him.

"Pull up a chair. Let's review what you wrote."

She rifled through the pile of essays until she found his. She laid it on the desk between them, flattening a bent corner. The red slashes and circles she'd made looked like bloody cat scratches on the page.

"Ouch," he said. "Pretty bad, huh?"

"No! It was good, interesting. Great stuff." She was embarrassed now by her corrections. She wished she could wipe them clean. "Ignore all the red marks. Let's just talk about the content for now. Read me what you wrote."

"Hello, my name is Frankie Morales."

"You don't need that," Grace said, more adamantly than she meant to. "But don't worry about it. Go on."

"I would like to say that I'm a nice guy, or at least that's what they tell me. I was born November 3, 1968, so I am twenty-nine years old. I have brown hair and brown eyes, and I am five-foot-eleven inches tall. Some people say I'm good looking and I look like Javier Bardem. He is that actor in Spanish movies. But I don't think so. He is not Latino. He is from Spain, and that is very different. And because he is a famous millionaire actor you can tell that his life experience has been very unique from mine."

Grace nodded. "You like that so far?"

"Yeah. That's me. It don't sound too sophisticated, though. I want to make it more college sounding."

"Okay. Keep going."

"I have a baby and a good wife," he continued, "who changed my life forever, which will never be the same again. Mine was not a childhood of richness. I have decided to tell my story because I sincerely believe that

13

our life experiences has a big influence on who we are. And because if people do not tell their stories of where they come from they will explode. I believe that this is a true statement for me."

"Frankie, that's good. See? You have an introduction right here." She picked up a pencil and circled the paragraph he just read. "The corrections are easy to fix. Being clear about what you want to say is the key."

"It's not bad?"

"No. I like what you said about how important it is for people to tell their stories."

Grace paused, wondering if she believed her own words. She had never told anyone her story. Nobody knew why she moved to California from Buffalo so many years ago. She'd developed the ability to repress her heartache over her mother's death into an art.

She respected people who wanted to tell their stories. But that wasn't her.

"Keep going. I thought the next part was great."

Frankie bent forward, eyes scanning his words. He pressed his palms flat on either side of the page and read, "I grew up in the roughest part of Los Angeles which some people have called the City of Angels. The only angels which ever inhabited my part of LA was the kind that you see flying around your head after an overdose lands you in the back of an ambulance. The ones that take you to your final resting place, not the kind that watches out for you on earth."

"That's nice, Frankie. Interesting way to make your point."

"I like writing this real life stuff."

"You're being honest," she said. She knew what was coming because she'd read the essay three times the night before, curled into a corner of the sofa. It had made her miss her mom so much she'd had to turn on a stupid TV show to block the sorrow.

"The experiences you have in your life does influence what you believe. I was a smart kid who loved to read books, especially the ones with lots of pictures of kids in big houses that had tons of money and big adventures. They solved mysteries and crimes and stuff even though they was only kids.

"My mother was a wonderful lady who told me to keep learning because that was the way we would have a better life. She fought against the odds of a neighborhood that was trying to do everything it could to keep me and the other kids from thinking we could be something. She pushed against the pressure. She said Holy Mother of God Parish School was a peaceful place to be, away from the bad life on the streets, and that the Sisters and Fathers there was looking out for your back."

"Your school," Grace interrupted, "sounds almost like a sanctuary."

"Yeah. It was." He looked up from the paper and studied the clock on the wall. "Those first four years at Holy Mother of God from kindergarten to third grade was some of the best years of my life. They taught us kids we were smart and gave us a chance in life.

"They did a lot of Mass and religion classes and all that, but that's okay. The Mass was boring, but I know they tried. There was crosses everywhere! They was trying to teach us how to act right and sit still and pray."

Grace felt herself shudder as Frankie read about his memories of church. Could she have kept a tighter grip on that security, that innocent faith? Would she be less of a wreck if she had? Grace's dad had wanted her and Gloria to attend Catholic school, but her mother balked at the idea. She'd insisted they have a public education so they could mingle with a wider variety of kids. Would Grace have held more tightly to her erstwhile faith if she'd worn the uniforms, been nurtured by nuns and steeped in the Catechism? Been allowed—encouraged even—to pray every day?

Frankie lowered his voice and read the last paragraph quickly as students began to file in. "I know that Jesus died so we could live and that God was watching us, trying to show us to how to be good in this world that is full of the temptations I would succumb to in the later years."

Chairs creaked around the room as the students settled in.

"I am a man determined to make sense of my life and all the things that has happened to me, all the things I got from my family and from the Church. I need to understand everything. The good and the bad things. The fair and the unfair parts. What I did and what they done to me."

Grace nodded and tapped the paper with her index finger. "That's brave, Frankie. Keep writing."

4

1970

*W*aking before daybreak was the hardest part. Her head cloudy with disturbing dreams, fifteen-year-old Grace pushed back the covers of her bed, reached over to her night table, and picked up The Lives of the Saints *and the dog-eared, yellow-highlighted New Testament,* Good News for Modern Man. *Heavy-eyed, she stepped onto the cold floor and sneaked over to her dresser. She tried not to wake her sister as she pulled open the squeaky drawer to retrieve a pair of socks.*

*"No regular person wakes up early to pray," Gloria had hissed as she clicked off the lights the night before. "Normal people sleep late. Nuns get up at four a.m. and waddle off to church. Sane people do not. Are you practicing for nun*dom*?" She had emphasized the "*dumb,*" then turned her back to Grace.*

Grace turned the comments over in her head as she slipped on her socks and padded past her mother's room. The door was closed. A hand-lettered Do Not Disturb Please Thank You *sign was taped near the handle. It has been there for over a year since the day before Grace's birthday when their mother had declared that henceforth Gloria and Grace would be sharing a room and she'd have this one to herself, thanks to "these horrible headaches and this dreadful insomnia."*

In the face of the mangled sign, Grace felt herself sink into the fear that something slippery and impossible to hold was wrong with her mother. Grace longed to clutch a handrail of purpose and peace. She thought of the nuns in Mother Theresa's Homes for the Dying Destitute in Calcutta. They rose early to wash and dress in white and blue saris and pray together. Nobody snickered at them as they cooked huge pots of rice to share with the lepers they brought in off the street; nobody questioned whether they were normal.

She calmed herself by imagining the interior of St. Joseph's downtown where she and her father attended Mass. Its simple but elegant altar. Its unadorned walls. The statue of St. Joseph holding the baby Jesus, both their heads encircled by halos of gold.

In the kitchen, she moved gracefully through the routine she'd practiced over the past few months. Since she decided to cleanse her body and spirit, she'd had truly blissful moments. She'd felt her spirit lift above her mother's sadness, all the petty daily preoccupations that bring everybody down, all the weighty wanting. She'd known joy, the sparkly joy of not-wanting, the dizzy glee of prayerful single-mindedness. It felt like a bird fluttering inside her chest, especially after a day of eating nothing but broth and juice.

She knew what to do, what to eat, what to think. She set the water on to boil. Watching the water heat up, gurgle, then roll, she whispered her morning prayer.

"Lord, free me of sinful desire. Help me to rise above."

When the water was ready, she measured out a half cup of oatmeal and poured it into the pot, watching the steam rise. She breathed in the thick odor of the cooking cereal then pulled an orange from the fridge to squeeze into her special glass. It is was golden and cold; she'd have to make an effort to not gulp it down all at once.

She needed take it slow this morning, not like yesterday when she couldn't stop herself from eating an apple and a cookie for lunch even though she wanted desperately to fast all day. She would read a line from St. Paul before each mouthful. She would train herself to find fullness in the ordinariness of the day.

5

race read her students' essays with the television on, scribbling
vague comments on each. *Good job. Nice writing. Keep going.*
She got up to stretch, poured her second glass of wine, snuggled
into the sofa, and began to read Frankie's latest installment of his story.

*In fourth grade was when the worst thing ever happened to me. Even
though I said their was no angels in LA it's a lie because my mama was terrible
sick and died and she was an angel. The best kind of loving angel ever. It was
like something got taken out of me, like an organ or something. I don't know
how to say the words for the hole that was left when she died.*

*Like I had a place in me that couldn't be filled by anything else no matter what
I tried. Like I was used to being loved and safe and full of kisses and hope. And then
it all disappeared too young for a child to have any comprehension at all.*

Grace had the sensation of ice cubes tinkling down her spine. She
unwrapped herself from the sofa and began to pace to keep herself from
crying. She was amazed at the synchronicity of their stories. Both of them
had felt comforted and protected by the Church during their childhoods.
Grace, like Frankie, had sought solace in the rituals of the Church when
her own mom got sick. And Frankie had also lost his mom.

Grace was fifteen and a half when her mother was diagnosed with a brain
tumor. After all these years, she still recoiled from thinking about her mom's
illness—her nauseating headaches, the debilitating sleeplessness, the worried
way her father watched her after they learned she was living with the
malignant intruder.

Its sudden blossoming had blindsided them all. When her mom died in her sleep six months later, in the middle of a harsh Buffalo winter, everything changed. Grace, her dad, and her sister were left alone, hollowed out, bereft.

Like I had a place in me that couldn't be filled by anything else no matter what I tried. She knew the sorrow that gripped Frankie's heart and left him without words. She knew what it felt like to be left, to be lost.

I tried to be brave and all for my mama who would of wanted me to stay strong. But I didn't do a very good job at it. I went from my small clean place which had books and stuffed animals and clean blankets and blocks in it which I had with my mom and love, love, love to the crowded apartment in the projects where mi abuela lived. I stayed with her and the cousins she was already taking care of because my uncle was a drug addict, and his wife died too.

My abuela was a old lady who didn't read or speak english but worked real hard to teach us the right path even though it was hard. But when she had got sick with diabetes, she had to go into the hospital for swollen ankles. The state said she can't take care of us no more after her amputation. So all my cousin's and me went away again to foster homes and group homes and some was good and some was terrible bad.

"Frankie, I'm so sorry about your mom," Grace said in their quiet alone-time before the next class. She'd asked him to read his paper out loud again. His voice was thick with emotion.

"That's a lot to go through."

She wanted to tell him she understood but knew the thought was ridiculous. His life had been much harder than hers. She had Gloria, and they both had their dad. Gloria was judgmental and demanding, and her dad was a curmudgeon. They hadn't been very supportive or communicative, but they still cared about each other. She tried to keep irregular tabs on them both. That was something, wasn't it? It's not like she had lost everything.

19

"It kills me a little every day, even after all these years," Frankie said. "I would of been a different person if she stayed alive. I believe that."

Grace nodded, lost in her own thoughts. She stood up and pushed in her chair then readied herself for the rest of the class to enter.

Frankie handed Grace another three or four pages of tight and careful script, double-spaced in pencil, after every class for the next five weeks. Each time he asked politely if he could come in fifteen minutes early and go over it with her.

"Yes, of course," she always answered.

She felt at times as if some mysterious force had drawn them together.

They would sit at her desk. As he read his words out loud, his voice grew more measured and confident. She asked questions, pointed out phrases she liked, and praised him for being honest and specific and brave. She caught herself noticing his bulk, his easy laugh, his caramel-colored skin, his tattoos like finely inked inscriptions on a lacquered pot. She hoped it wasn't affecting her behavior, but there wasn't a moment when he was in her presence that she wasn't aware of his beauty.

Ever since they started working together at Cesar Chavez, Janeen had been Grace's mentor. She encouraged Grace to give her students relevant writing activities and create anthologies of their published work. She reminded her on a regular basis to give her students lots of encouragement because they'd been wounded by a system that failed them. Once a week, she visited Grace before class or sat in the back to observe.

"Give them your all! Celebrate your students!" She whispered her motto to Grace before she began her lesson.

Grace had started at Chavez with low energy, and then the students sucked out of her what little she had to give. The young ones especially wore her out. After a long day of dealing with their needs and demands, she didn't feel like celebrating anything.

Two months into the semester, Grace invited Janeen to meet for a drink. She wanted to tell her about Frankie. The occasional after school drink they'd shared since she started teaching at Chavez usually loosened Grace up enough that she revealed her worry that she couldn't do the job. It was a relief to finally feel proud of herself. For once, there was air in her tires, and she had a positive teaching experience to brag about.

They sat at a corner table at El Terremoto Café. Grace nursed a Dos Equis as she watched Janeen read Frankie's essays.

She nodded when Grace asked, "Isn't that amazing?"

She twisted her short, gold-tipped braids with long fingers as Grace described his eagerness to write, his inability to stop when class was over. "Isn't he an interesting man?"

"He is," Janeen said. "But they all are."

"What do you mean?"

"You seem infatuated by this guy. What's that about?" Janeen leaned in and fixed her eyes on Grace.

"Very funny."

That was not the reaction Grace had expected. She wanted praise for a change. Why would Janeen conclude that she was 'infatuated' with Frankie? He *was* attractive, but Grace had never let herself ruminate on anything other than their student-teacher bond. She was fourteen years older, and he was married. But if she *were* younger, and if he'd shown the tiniest bit of interest...she knew she would have been smitten.

She shook her head and frowned. "He's a kid. But...he's different. He's serious. It's refreshing."

"Maybe devote yourself to your other students a little bit more so you can see how special they all are too?" Janeen sighed and took another sip of her margarita. "I don't mean to be harsh, but I've never heard you talk about them the way you're fawning over this guy."

"I know. I don't know why I'm..." Not attracted. That wasn't the word. "...entranced by him. Do you want to eat something?'

"No, I'm fine," Janeen said. Grace slipped out of her chair and walked over to the counter. She asked the owner to bring them more chips and salsa and ordered a tamale.

"I think you need to look deeper and figure out what the hell you're doing, Grace," Janeen said when she returned.

"What does that mean?"

"Find your mission! Find the thing in life you want to give yourself over to. What's your passion? What's the thing that sucks you in and takes hold of you? You seem like you're kind of floating here." Janeen's eyes were slits as she studied Grace's face. "I don't think this is your calling."

"I know." Grace nodded. She felt her eyes sting. "But I don't know if I've ever been sure if I was doing the right thing. You know, like my purpose in life." She groaned. "It's such a bore."

Janeen shook her head and chuckled. "I was offered a position in Seattle as Assistant Principal for a middle school starting in the fall. It's exactly what I've been waiting for. It's my dream."

"You were? Wow. I'm happy for you." She hugged herself. Now who would she complain to?

"Me too," Janeen said, smiling and twirling her braids. "It's what I want to do with my life."

Janeen's confidence felt like a stick poking Grace in the ribs, pushing her deeper down into her slippery, muddy confusion.

Grace arrived earlier than usual, hoping for a little more time to straighten her classroom and get organized before mid-semester reports were due. Time was moving fast. It was already late March, and she wasn't sure—except for her work with Frankie—if she'd accomplished much of anything at all.

She gasped when Frankie walked in. His left eye was bloodshot, and his eyelid and cheekbone were swollen purple.

"Sorry about the eye."

"Frankie, what happened?"

"My girl," he said, his voice excited. Nervous energy coursed through him as he jammed himself into the chair alongside her desk. "She was walking with the baby back to our crib. She had a grocery bag in her hand. I was working on her car. I heard her curse out this stupid kid from around the block. I seen him before. He was tryin' to grab the bag, so I ran over and jumped him. He punched me. I grabbed him and told him to give the fuckin' groceries back. Excuse my mouth."

He punched the air.

"But I didn't hit him. I told him he's a punk, and he coulda got locked up if I decided to seize his ass, but I didn't want him to go there. You know what I'm saying? I know about that road, and I told him he better fly straight cause I know where he lives and he said sorry."

Frankie laughed, crinkles forming around his good eye. He seemed light-hearted and energetic in spite of his injury. "I have this black and blue eye to prove I put the past behind me. I ain't harming nobody never again. I don't care. Especially a hurtin' young brother. I am so proud of myself for not slammin' that kid! 'Cause I know what's in his head. That kid is just like me ten years ago. Kids these days is seriously messed up, and they need some serious help."

Most of the time standing in front of the class, Grace felt ill-equipped, as if she were putting a Band-Aid on a battered woman's bruises. But she worked until she was blurry-eyed anyway, devising lessons and correcting papers and checking quizzes. She wanted to give her students hope even though so many forces determining their lives were outside of their control.

She never knew who would be in class the next day or who would suddenly drop out. She didn't know if she was reaching any of them. Janessa was pregnant with her third child at seventeen. Teresa had been kicked out of her mother's house and was living in a shelter. Briston couldn't read. Rodney hadn't said one single word, no matter how much she cajoled.

Her mature students sometimes surprised her with small expressions of gratitude that buoyed her flagging faith that something worthwhile might be happening here. Taneka donated pens and paper. Lydia offered her small homemade tres leches cakes. Jerry bowed and said, "Thank you, ma'am," as he slipped shyly out the door. But even the motivated students missed a lot of days.

Frankie was never absent. He was the most focused student she'd ever had. He presented her with another segment of his evolving life after class. This one explained how he fell in with a gang, got caught up in a botched store heist at seventeen, and was sentenced to ten years in prison for second-degree robbery and attempted murder. He was released after eight.

He wrote about how he felt grateful for the time in prison, as stultifying and bleak as it was, because it forced him to grow and change. He'd had to come to terms with the heroin addiction that would have taken his life if given a chance. He'd learned auto mechanics and carpentry and began studying for his high school diploma. He'd been given time to reflect, to praise Jesus for giving him a second chance, to stay out of trouble, to reform himself.

"Miss Schreiber." Frankie tapped his knuckles on the pages of his latest confession. "I know this sounds crazy, but I want to make this into a book. I want to help young brothers by telling them to hang tough and not give up."

"That's a great goal. You have some powerful stories to tell."

"I feel like I got so much to say. I can't get my pencil to move fast enough to get it all out."

Grace had written about her own life in thick white sketchpads, but she hadn't read those journals in years. She was sure what she'd find there would mortify her. She had been so naïve. "I'm impressed that you're being honest. I hope you keep going."

"It's like a...how do you say it? Like a river that wants to burst right out of a dam. I get home, and after I play with the baby, all I wanna do is write. I never had this much urge in me before."

Grace needed him to keep writing. His words were a rope tossed over the side of a boat as she flailed in the water. She wasn't marring his words with red inkings anymore. She just let the story progress and tell itself, errors and all. She understood—though she wasn't proud of it—that she relied on his revelations to get her through the day.

Janeen's insightful and slightly annoying comment, "Find your mission, the thing in life you want to give yourself over to," kept replaying in her head.

Frankie had found his mission. What was hers?

"Well...thank you, ma'am...for not...I'll see you next week. Five forty-five on the dot!"

"Wait!" Grace turned and picked up a stack of books. *Manchild in the Promised Land, Down These Mean Streets, I Know Why the Caged Bird Sings, The Autobiography of Malcolm X*. She'd bought them for him the night before at a used bookstore.

"Read these," she said. "These are some pretty truthful writers. What you're trying to do is very similar to what they did."

He thanked her and said he would. He left class with a shy smile on his face and the stack of worn autobiographies under his arm.

6

The light on the answering machine flashed. Grace set down her heavy bags and played it.

"Hail Grace full of Mary. Call me."

Gloria picked up on the first ring when Grace called her back as if she'd been waiting by the phone. "Dad fell," she said.

"Oh, my God," Grace whispered. "What happened?"

"The hospital called. He put both of us down as emergency contacts, but they couldn't reach you. He fell down the stairs and sprained his foot. He has to use a wheelchair till it's healed 'cause he can't put any weight on it. Somebody has to help him put a compression dressing thing on it every day for a couple of weeks. Then he'll have to wear a special shoe. And he might get bad arthritis from it. He can't go up and down stairs anymore."

"Sounds bad."

"I talked to him today. He got a neighbor to set up the sofa bed so he can sleep in the living room. And he had to order a commode because the bathroom is on the second floor. A nurse is going to check on him three times a week for the next week, but that's all insurance will cover. He needs somebody to go and take care of him and—yuck!—wrap his foot."

"So...what should we do?"

Grace waited for her sister to say it. She knew her older sister so well she could always anticipate the self-serving advice or criticism about to tumble from her mouth.

"He needs help, Grace, and I think maybe you should go stay with him. That's fair, right? I'm swamped at the café. You're single, and you get a lot of breaks, right? Can you stay with him till he can walk independently again? If you're not too busy, that is."

Grace ignored her sister's mocking tone. Gloria had no idea how busy she was. "Sure. I mean, yeah. Of course."

She hung up and called her dad.

"Dad, Gloria told me. I'm coming home."

Her father groaned. "I know you love your life there, but I'm going to need a lot of help."

"I'm glad to do it." She hoped he couldn't hear the frown in her voice. She dreaded the prospect of spending time at her father's house. She hadn't been there in three years.

"Whatever you do, Grace," her father said, his voice low and thick, "don't grow old."

The old house looked weary from the work of holding itself up. Its blue paint had wilted, and its grimy red shutters hadn't been washed in many months. Patches of brown grass poked out between clumps of melting grey snow. The once bright home appeared to be sinking.

Grace pulled the rental car into the driveway. Lingering in the car, she surveyed her childhood yard. The basketball hoop her sister had once begged her dad to put up sagged above the garage door. The giant maple tree with its open-hand-like leaves still tented the lawn. She had loved to climb that tree when she was young and lie in its shade reading as a teen.

She made herself take a deep breath as she put her hand on the metal handle of the screen door. "Anybody home? Dad?"

She found him in the living room under a heavy blanket embroidered with a green American eagle. He was sitting in his favorite TV-watching chair, his wrapped foot elevated on an ottoman. An ache seized her. Fine threads of hair covered a scalp mottled with brown spots. His cheeks were sallow and sunken.

Her father's eyes blinked open as she studied him from the sofa. "Aren't you pretty," he said. "You look just like your mother."

He'd told her this before, and every time it moved her. To be told she was pretty still surprised her. To be reminded of her young mom and how much her dad had been drawn to her stirred in her a tiny firefly of happiness. Her green eyes and overlapping bottom teeth were her dad's genetic gift, but she had her mother's curly mop of auburn hair, her long, freckled nose, and her full lips.

"Nice to see you both," he said, amusement in his tired eyes.

They spent the rest of the evening reconnecting. He was surprisingly good-natured about having to get in and out of a wheelchair to keep the weight off his foot. It'd be at least another week until he could walk, and then only with a walker.

He let Grace take him out to the Greek diner on Kenmore he liked. Why had it been so long since she'd been back? It distressed Grace to think about how little effort she'd made to keep in touch with her aging father. She'd had this melancholy overtake her before, when she realized she'd missed something, been too distracted by worry to enjoy a meal, too overwhelmed with work to enjoy the weather, too busy watching her feet on a hike to notice a hawk as it wheeled across the sky. Where had her mind been all these years?

Maybe, she thought, as she prepared to sleep in her mom's old queen-sized bed, she could somehow make amends for the time she'd spent away from him by starting fresh, listening to his stories, paying attention. *Every day is a new day*, her mother used to say.

Grace dutifully sponge-washed her dad's foot and wrapped it in an Ace bandage daily. He always thanked her. She went for long walks and read a couple of paperbacks from his bookshelves. Much of the time, he slept. She made him easy suppers, and they spent the evenings chatting and watching TV.

By the end of her week-long stay, he was strong enough to walk with a walker or a cane. He'd adjusted to his new orthopedic shoe. Grace smiled when she watched him hobbling around the house. She felt good about her selflessness. She appreciated the break from work, but she was eager to return to Frankie and read what he'd written while she was away. She asked her father twice if he thought he should look into an assisted living senior facility. He growled at her both times.

"Don't ask me that. Ever. Do you understand? That is something I will never do."

She almost risked mentioning it a third time when she hugged him goodbye but decided instead to keep the parting moment sweet. "I love you, Dad," she whispered in his ear. "I'll come back to visit again soon. I promise."

Frankie stood by her desk as the other students sauntered out. He was gripping a dense stack of pages folded into a tight square. He stood staring straight ahead.

She'd sensed that something in him had shifted. He wasn't his usual

27

playful self. He didn't eagerly hand over his writing or plead with her to meet before class next time.

"Um, hey, Frankie." Grace put down an armful of workbooks and walked toward him. "You gonna share those with me?" She touched his arm lightly and smiled.

He pulled away and looked down. "I gotta go. Listen. These are private, okay? And I don't want to do it no more. Meeting and talking and everything."

"What…what do you mean?"

She had shared his essays with Janeen without asking his permission. Did he know that? Was he mad at her for leaving? Maybe he resented her for withdrawing her attention, if only for a week.

"I gotta go," he said, jerking his head toward the door. "I ain't got time to talk."

"Oh…Okay." She felt the blood rise in her cheeks. "Um, do you…I mean…"

"I gotta go." He passed her the clump of pages then snuck out of the door with the crowd.

Grace stood motionless and surveyed the cluttered room. The recycling bin was overflowing again, and all the chairs needed straightening.

Her encounters with Frankie over the past few months had been healing. The hours she put into teaching in this raggedy room felt worth it because of the bond they had built. And now he was pulling himself away from her, and she had no idea why.

Finally home, she dropped all her belongings inside the door and retrieved Frankie's wad of papers from her purse. She fell into a kitchen chair and read his essay under the fluorescent overhead light, her elbows grinding into the tabletop.

I can't tell the whole story of my life if I keep a secret. That would be like telling a lie. And I can't have a clean heart with the lie in there.

The way to have a clean heart is to take all the garbage out.

The way to clean out a brain that is full of stinking junk is to dump it out.

Maybe writing it on paper like Claude Brown is the way to sweep it clean. I don't know.

Their is garbage in my heart that was put there by some terrible people, but if I hate them. I am giving the hate to myself and carrying all the bitterness inside of me so it is me who eats it.

The secret is that mi abuela told me to go to the church after school because they will keep you straight and free from the life that ain't no life, the life of the streets, and I trusted somebody to help me be a better person and fill the pit my mother dug when she died. His name was Father Santiago at HMG cathedral. He took me on trips and promised me he would help me get money to go to college if I did my homework at the rectory and was a personal assistant to him.

He said he cared about me and listened to all the problems we was having with mi abuela being sick and my foster moms hitting me and all that. He took a special interest in me, and I know I needed that, but then he tells me he had something very important to teach me and because he was a priest it was okay. He kissed me flat on the mouth and then made me touch him even though I pushed back and pushed away. I was mad because I loved him so much and now I couldn't love him no more.

This was when I was twelve, and then it happened again when I was thirteen. I knew there must be something wrong with me because he said there was and because why else would he pick me. Why would he take me in my altar boy clothes that was suppose to be holy and kept all perfect and rape me behind the altar like its not a holy place and then tell me that was a sick thing I made him do. But I didn't make him do it I don't think.

If I ever publish this book like Piri Thomas or Claude Brown I will have to burn this part. Miss Schreiber is the only one who ever heard this. Please Miss Schreiber, I am begging you. Do not ever tell no one about this sad chapter of my existence that came before I made the changes and gave up bad things and became a man for real the right way by having a good woman and a baby.

Grace's forehead sank to the table. After all the nights of reading Frankie's essays in the lamp-lit corner of her sofa, delighting in his openness and optimism in the face of all he'd been through, looking forward to listening to him read, now this.

Panic rose inside her. She felt as if a crow were banging its wings against the inside of her chest. It was much too terrible to imagine what Frankie had endured, the shame he must have experienced, the betrayal. He suffered at the hands of people he expected to protect him, in a supposedly sanctified place, in the Church. The Church where she'd learned to kneel, to open her mouth and heart to the Body of Christ, to beg for forgiveness, to gaze with pity on the long-suffering Christ, to feel heartened by the Resurrection. Santiago was evil, the worst kind of criminal. No wonder Frankie had been so reticent when he shared those final damning pages.

She stood up and walked over to the counter to pour herself a glass of wine. She paced around the room with her glass in hand.

Why did he share so much with her then beg her to keep it a secret? She knew that was wrong. Something *had* to be done. But what? Was there somebody you were supposed to go to in situations like this? Should she go to the Cathedral and demand to see a priest? Go with Frankie to confront them? Maybe Santiago had left the priesthood, or better yet, had died. Can you even call the police about a crime that happened fifteen years ago?

She took a cold shower then crawled into bed. For hours, she wrestled with her hot pillow and jumbled covers. Thoughts, questions, and images raced through her brain. There was nothing to do but feel miserable as she waited through the weekend to see Frankie again.

But the following Tuesday, he didn't show up. It was the third week of April, the first time in fifteen weeks that he'd missed class. After he didn't appear on Thursday either, she found his phone number on his registration form and left eight messages asking him to please return her call. In desperation, she located his address on a map and drove by his house three times, each time finding it quiet and shadowy, almost cloistered. It didn't make sense that he would stop coming to school without saying anything to her. They were almost friends, weren't they? He had entrusted her with close to a hundred pages of confessions. He had unveiled his tragic secret to her and no one else and then vanished. People were such a mystery.

She left a note on the front door and drove away, feeling deflated.

Call me so we can talk about what you wrote. I'd like to try to help.

7

"He did it seven times, all in different secret places, and there was blood in my pants that I had to lie to my foster house about and get a beating." The words came out fast and hushed, like trapped air finally released from a valve. "I was too scared to quit because everybody would say, 'Why, Frankie? Why did you quit being the altar boy? It's a good thing for you to stay off the streets.' So I never told nobody. Not even Victoria. She's too good and loves church too much."

Frankie looked down at the linoleum tabletop as he spoke. His hands gripped a porcelain coffee mug as if it were about to be yanked away. Ten days after Grace left her note on his door, he called her and asked her to meet him at Ray's, a diner at the other end of Compton, far from his neighborhood, nowhere near the school.

"I'm glad you're telling me, Frankie," Grace said quietly. She was shivering. Her stomach was a maelstrom of disgust, sadness, and relief. He was here. He was talking to her again.

"I don't want to talk about it," he said. "But I feel like I got to, or I'll die."

She nodded. She wanted to say something reassuring but didn't know what to say. *Just listen, for God's sake,* she thought.

"Father Santiago told me I was bad and a tempter and a travesty against God for luring him there."

Frankie pressed the heels of his hands against his closed eyes and rubbed so hard Grace was afraid he would hurt himself. She cringed and waited as she watched him struggle. She realized that of all the things he had admitted to in his life, this might be the hardest.

Frankie removed his hands from his eyes and clenched them into tight, angry fists. "He told me I would go to juvie for years if they found out what I made him do."

His voice was stronger now, harder.

"I thought and thought about it for many, many nights, but I couldn't think of how I made him do it." He grimaced, staring at the wall. "Except maybe I did. I was only thirteen and stupid about life. I still don't know. Did I tell him something like I love you…but I didn't mean that kind. It was more the father I didn't never have or the big brother kind of love. I was only thirteen."

Grace studied the cold coffee in her own mug. She knew there was nothing she could do to lift his spirits and make him feel good about telling his story the way she had in the beginning. She wondered if all this was her fault. Who was she to pry into the psyche of a vulnerable and openhearted person she hardly knew? Her throat seized up at the thought that she might just be using Frankie and his evolving story to relieve her own pain.

"I wish he was dead because it is very hard to go to Mass with him there acting all pure. And I wish I was dead sometimes."

He turned to face her for the first time since they sat down.

"But not really, because I have a new life." His voice cracked. "And my girl, Victoria. I can't do that to her and my baby girl. I have to be strong."

Fat tears welled in his eyes and dripped onto his shirt. He didn't rub his eyes or wipe his face. "Sometimes I want to go to Mass for the peace I felt there. But I can't never go there. I won't ever step in there again, and I still ain't told Victoria why."

Grace blinked to keep her own eyes from welling up. "I'm glad you're telling me all this," she whispered, looking around at the few patrons hunkered over their plates in the diner. "I can't believe Father Santiago is still there. Don't you think we should do something?" She leaned forward and studied his familiar face. "What do you think we should do?"

"Nothing," Frankie said, his voice cold. "Please don't do nothing. I'm done. I'm done with it all. *Done.*" He put two dollars on the table, stood up, and left without saying goodbye.

Two weeks later, the phone's shrill ring jerked Grace awake. She'd fallen asleep atop a pile of newspapers and a rumpled quilt. "Yes?" she breathed into the phone.

She didn't recognize the voice on the other end of the phone, mumbling something plaintive in Grace's ear.

"Excuse me, what? Who is this?"

"This is Victoria. I'm Frankie's girl. He told me a buncha times how you helped him write and pass his tests. You were his teacher, right?"

What did she mean—you *were* his teacher? Where had he gone?

"Yes, I'm his teacher. Is he okay?" Grace sat up and pressed the receiver to her ear. "He hasn't been back to class. He just disappeared."

She didn't know if Victoria knew they'd met at Ray's. She didn't know if Frankie had told Victoria anything.

"He disappeared for good now. Me and him were doing a good thing, raising our baby." The woman's voice broke into sobs and gasps.

"What do you—"

"He's dead. My Frankie's dead."

"No! You're *kidding*!" Grace cried. Her shoulders shook from the cold and shock. "What happened?"

She stared at the melted wax ruining the finish on the bedside table. Every night for the past two weeks, she'd lit a candle by her bed and prayed, or wished—she didn't know what to call it—that Frankie would call her again.

"I'm keeping it private. What happened. It's between Frankie and me, why he died."

"Well, did…did he…was he sick?"

"No, it was an accident." Victoria gasped.

"Was he hit by a car? What happened? Can't you tell me?"

Victoria paused to blow her nose. "No. I'm not tellin' nobody."

"I don't know what to say." Grace clutched her stomach. She felt queasy. She lay back down, gripping the receiver, and curled into a ball.

"He talked about you a lot. What you done for him. There's going to be a Mass at Holy Mother of God Cathedral next Sunday if you wanna come."

"Yes, of course. Thank you for telling me. Of course I'll come."

Grace ducked quietly into the back pew, hoping no one would see her. It had been twenty-five years since she'd craned her neck to gaze at a gilded ceiling or knelt in a wooden pew or heard the ethereal choral voices. She was a child the last time she'd studied the depressing drama of the

Stations of the Cross and taken the fragrant musk of incense into her lungs.

The mourning family came in together, ten or twelve of them, wearing black and clutching tissues. *So that's Victoria*, Grace thought, watching the short, plump woman at the head of the group. She was wearing a tight black dress, black stockings, and spike heels. A lacy black veil covered her hair and face. She leaned against the shoulder of an older gray-haired man. A middle-aged woman followed close behind carrying a doe-eyed Marisol in a flowered dress with puffy sleeves. Tiny earrings dangled from her earlobes.

Grace gasped when she read in the program that Father Santiago would be officiating the Mass. Her throat constricted as she watched five altar boys, maybe ten, eleven, thirteen years old, wearing blousy white embroidered vestments over long red gowns, walk down the aisle. Her stomach churned as the silver-haired priest entered behind the procession of altar boys wearing a purple velvet-striped cassock with flowing sleeves. His hands were pressed together near his heart.

Grace couldn't take her eyes off the boys as they performed their choreographed routine. One was pudgy with a sweet face. Another was skinny and pimpled. All of them were unbearably innocent and cute and intent on their holy tasks. They swung the smoking incense bowls, exchanged gilded plates, snuffed out candles, and held the Bible for the priest to read, his hands open in supplication.

She hardly heard a word of the generic homily or the rote, sad Mass. Most of it was in Spanish anyway. She slunk out before Communion was over and hurried to her car.

"Not Father Santiago," she said aloud, head pressed against the steering wheel. "No, God. Please, no."

She let herself sob, let herself gasp and wail, for herself and her lost faith, for those beautiful and guileless altar boys. For Frankie, poor Frankie, so much braver and stronger than she was. Frankie, who had given her so much, who had saved her, who was gone.

8

Grace hadn't done anything but work and obsess about Frankie for days, so for once, Gloria's call was welcome.

"Dad fell again. This time it's his hip."

That was all she needed to hear.

There were four weeks left in the semester, and she'd committed to teaching in the summer. She had planned—when she could gather up the courage—to strut into the Archdiocese with Frankie's stories and shove them under all their faces, demanding action. She was determined to call the police and demand they investigate Father Santiago, but a small, embarrassed part of her was relieved to have something else to worry about.

"I'll call Dad right now," she said.

This was not a good time to fly back to Buffalo. She didn't know how long it would take to yank her father out of his house by the roots and drag him against his will to a senior facility of some sort. She would have to take a long leave of absence because now, as Janeen would say, she had a mission.

Grace walked into the director's office the next day and quit. She explained that she had a family emergency, and she didn't know how long it would take to handle it. The director told her he wished that Grace didn't have to leave, and he would consider hiring her back when she returned, whenever that might be.

"I'll be there after you get out of the hospital," Grace said when she called her dad to tell him she was driving home. "We can pack up together. I'll help you figure out how to sell the house. I've started researching online for places to move. It'll be a fresh start."

"But what if I'm not ready to give up the house?" he said, emotion pinching his voice. "What if I don't want a fresh start? Did you ever think of that?"

"Dad," Grace sighed, thinking about the upheaval she was about to visit on her own life. "I don't think you have much of a choice."

Grace packed her car and locked the door to her house. She rolled up the windows of her Honda and blasted the AC as she rifled through the tapes and discs she'd bought for the trip: Dylan, Ani DiFranco, *Wide Open Spaces* by The Dixie Chicks.

She tore the plastic off *Hejira*. Janeen had given her the CD before she left for Seattle. Janeen had called Grace a hippie on more than one occasion and had snorted when Grace told her she'd tried to use *Big Yellow Taxi* to teach alliteration. The album was intended to be ironic; together they mocked its earnestness.

Before she sped out of the city, she headed for Cabrillo Beach. She walked along the sand, already littered with blankets and the bronze bodies of sunbathers, dreadlocked teens, and huddled, sleeping men. She tied her hair up in a high ponytail and jogged along the concrete pier.

By the time she reached the end of the pier, her chest hurt. She stared at the sparkling sea. The same sea, calm and glistening, that had drawn her to this coast twenty-five years ago. Its vastness still made her feel transfixed, small and in awe. She'd stood at the water's edge countless times and imagined flinging her worries into the incoming waves and watching them sink into the ocean's depths.

She took ten deep breaths. After all this time, what did she have to say for herself? What had she accomplished? A year after she arrived on the west coast, she enrolled at San Francisco State. She was drawn to Journalism, imagining herself exposing the My Lai massacre or the Watergate break-in. But the courses were too technical, too fixated on grammar and fact-checking, and she was too shy to confront all those powers-that-be.

She changed her major to Education but never took the tests and classes necessary to get certified to teach in public schools. But she'd done a decent job teaching English to spoiled rich kids in private schools. And that counted, didn't it? She had a plaque that read *Thanks for being such an important part of our unique learning community* to prove it.

A soothing wind caressed the back of her neck. So little of her time lately had been spent reflecting on what she'd done with her life. She felt like all she did now was react. When she was in her early twenties, she'd fantasized about becoming an artist, but just like her dream of becoming a writer, nothing ever came of it. She'd never made the time or space to paint more than the occasional random tree.

What had she actually ever *done*? She canvassed for donations at night for Bay Area Women Against Rape, cashiered at the food co-op, and overnighted as a home health aide. *Things could be worse,* she'd repeat to herself while pulling socks on the feet of a woman who'd fallen and cracked her spine.

She'd collected signatures on petitions in the Mission District, half-learned Spanish, half-learned to play guitar. Tripped and fell on her face through a series of failed romances. She taught privileged kids. Tried to help these poor folks in Compton get a bit of an education. Struggled to pick up the pieces of her shattered heart.

Face to face with the ocean, inhaling the salty air, she could keep it all in perspective. She could even laugh at herself a little.

"No one's perfect," she said aloud, then jogged back down the pier.

Everyone makes mistakes, and she had made quite a few. That's how you learned. She felt seized by a momentary sense of possibility as she walked briskly across the sand back to her car. She sang along to the whole of *Hejira* as she headed out of town.

Miles of gleaming metal pressed against the horizon on the way out of the city. Grace felt the muscles of her shoulders tighten until she realized this would be her last hoorah in LA traffic for a while. She decided to loosen her grip on the wheel and notice the shimmering beauty of it all. For half an hour she inched along, studying all of them so separate and together, in line to who-knows-where.

And then it broke. After the slow crawl to San Bernardino, the metal river flowed into tributaries, and everybody roared on to their next phase. Her route took her through the expanse of southern California desert, a gradual ascendancy of red rock. Entering it felt like an exhalation of breath. She was off. And the path was stunning.

Grace drove seven hours the first day. The melancholy of the past few days began to lift. She was leaving the sadness of Compton behind, at least for a while. She was on a road trip. The thought made her chuckle.

Feeling adventurous, almost giddy, she checked into a motel near Flagstaff and walked across the black expanse of parking lot to the Burger King next door. She brought a large bag of greasy fries and a dry chicken sandwich back to her room.

If she got up early the next morning and drove straight for six hours, she could be at Mesa Verde by two o'clock. She had decided not to drop by her sister's house in downtown Denver even though Gloria had asked her to and it was on the way. If she stopped, she'd kick herself for interrupting what she understood could be a blissfully solitary meditative trip. This was the first time in months she'd allowed herself to feel delighted.

She fell asleep at eight o'clock and slept straight through until six in morning, waking to find a French fry salty and mushy against her cheek.

As she continued her eastward march through Arizona, jagged pink and red striped rocks gave way to snow-crusted mountains, stark against parched orange earth.

Grace stopped at Bo's Desert Diner for a soda. She hesitantly approached an old metal payphone that appeared ready to fall off the faded wood of the wall. She entered her calling card code and looked up at the weathered sign on the diner announcing *Steaks Chops Fries Tacos Burgers Shakes*. She craved a crisp salad and a strong coffee.

"Hey, I was expecting your call," Gloria said after two rings.

"You know…I think I'm going to keep on going," Grace said. The words came out measured and slow.

"You have *got* to be kidding." Gloria's voice was shrill.

"Don't be mad. I just feel like driving without stopping." Grace imagined herself as Neal Cassady in a white t-shirt, speeding down the open road with one tanned elbow sticking out the window and the other hand on the wheel. Only Jack Kerouac wasn't sitting in the passenger seat.

"You're not going to sleep?"

"Of course I am."

"Sleep here. Don't you want to see your niece and nephew? And David and me? Everybody was excited that you were coming."

Grace knew it was a lie. The last time she visited three years ago, the kids were off swimming in meets most of the weekend, and when they weren't, they ignored her. David was awkward and withdrawn. He usually spoke in short phrases while looking down at the newspaper or a book. Gloria told her in a follow-up email that he'd been jealous when the two of them stayed up late talking over piña coladas and mushroom canapés from Gloria's café. The thought of being pulled between Gloria's judgmental questions and the rest of the family's aloofness exhausted her.

"I just want to keep going on alone is all. Nothing personal."

"It is personal. And it doesn't make any sense."

"I need to spend some time alone before foisting myself on the old man."

She wanted to drive through to whatever this next phase would bring. There was a feeling of a fresh start to this small adventure. Visiting her sister would mire her in the sludge of history, familiarity, and old assumptions. She closed her eyes against the scrutiny of the afternoon sun.

"God, you're so difficult. The one time you drive right by my house, and you won't stop."

"I know."

"I think you're being kind of selfish." Grace thought Gloria sounded on the verge of crying, which was decidedly out of character for her sharp-tongued sister.

"I'll call you when I get to Buffalo. And I'm sorry. I am."

The phone clicked. Grace stood there for a moment, staring at the rough wood of the restaurant wall. She decided against a soda and headed back to the car.

9

The long road into Mesa Verde National Park was scattered with juniper and pinion trees. She'd read that Pueblo women used juniper berries as contraceptives and that the pinion nuts were nutritious and delicious, but they looked stark and scratchy, scrub brushes on curly sticks.

Grace climbed out of the seat and leaned forward to touch the ground. She stretched her back and neck, trying to release tension after sitting for hours in the car. The sign said she needed to be part of a tour, so she waited with the other straggling visitors in the shade of the scruffy pinion trees.

She wished she could amble up the path to the cave dwellings on her own. The idea of living on a cliff overlooking the forested expanse filled her with surprising desire. What would it have been like to live so tenuously yet so entwined with air and trees? To make fire high up in the sky? To live among people who worked and prayed and chanted in the wind?

She imagined that in the cliff dwellings, women didn't live to be forty-three without a mate, if they lived that long at all. They probably got pregnant easily and early, spent their days weaving reed baskets, boiling corn over smoky embers. She imagined them chattering, nursing naked babies, and spending their nights making love on the rough clay floor, animal skin soft beneath their backs.

The park ranger arrived, interrupting her musings. The Anasazi, or Ancient Pueblo people, he explained, had lived here for over seven hundred years and then moved on, disappeared. He told the group about the importance of roads to the Ancient Pueblo people, especially the Great North Road, which may have been used for pilgrimages, agricultural ceremonies, or solstice rituals.

"Many archeologists believe that for these ancient people, roads were religious. Modern Pueblo people say that this road connects to *shipapu*, the spiritual place from which the ancestors emerged. Spirits stop along this road as they journey toward the world of the living. It's as if the road is a connection to another dimension."

Grace trailed behind the group of tourists as they walked to the Mug House and listened as the park ranger explained how the Ancient Pueblo people had constructed the cliff dwellings in shallow caves under rock overhangs along the canyon walls, how they gathered in kivas for sacred ceremonies invoking dead ancestors as intermediaries to the gods.

"I often think about how different our experience of community is now than it was for the Anasazi people," the ranger said as the group peered into one of the bare round kivas. "How much of our daily existence is spent alone. We're raised to think we are—or should be—independent. The Anasazi understood how interconnected we all are and how much our survival depends on working together. The spiritual, one could say religious, experiences of the cave dwellers were intensely communal."

The ranger described the cliff dwellers' reverence for kachinas, spirits which might have represented anything in nature. There might have been kachinas for thunderstorms or for sun, for corn or for bugs. He ran his hand along the smooth rocks. "The people who lived in the cliff dwellings understood that they had to respect these life forces or they would not survive."

Grace stared up at the jutting mesas imagining the men farming above them under a bleached white sky. She gazed down and pictured herself descending the rough ladder into the dark ritual space of the kiva. These people were never alone. They slept together in a fire-lit room, their lives and the world interconnected.

How many times had she felt isolated, divorced from genuine communion with others? Hadn't she always, even when she was working with people, even when she was with Jake, felt unconnected, untethered, preoccupied with her own small self?

Grace walked back to the car with slow steps. She inhaled the warm afternoon air and studied her feet as they crossed the dusty path to the car. She wanted somehow to carry the images of Mesa Verde with her into this new uncertain phase of her life. She longed for connection and community, though she had no idea where to find it.

Remember those dark kivas, she admonished herself. *Remember how the cliff dwellers listened to the spirits, connected with the earth and the sky, cared about and depended on each other.*

She took a long, deliberate breath and felt her face muscles relax as she slid back into the car.

Grace spent the night in a motel near Mesa Verde. She got up early, grabbed breakfast, and drove straight for six hours until she hit Colorado Springs. It was so dangerously close to Denver she feared she might get caught. Gloria and a minivan full of swimmers might run into her in a Subway parking lot. Grace would have to apologize and follow her, chastised, back to her mountain house. The idea was silly, of course, because Gloria didn't know where she was. But to be safe, she pulled into a McDonald's. Gloria would never allow her little athletic league to eat such unhealthy fare.

"What'll you have?" the woman behind the counter asked while Grace studied the long list of inexpensive burger options on the illuminated menu.

"Just an orange juice and a coffee."

"Coming up," the woman said. Grace envied this pleasant-looking woman in her mid-fifties. She'd probably lived here all her life, hardly noticing the mountains resting like sleeping women all around her. She imagined she was content to play with her grandkids, watch TV with her husband, go to her job every day and serve fried food, not wishing she was somewhere or someone else.

"That's two dollars and fifteen cents, honey."

Grace sat on a red plastic chair and stared out the window at the slumbering mountains. She had always wished she was someplace else. When she was fifteen, she longed to live in a convent in India with Mother Theresa or in a rural Catholic Worker community tending goats and serving coffee to the ragtag residents.

When she was sixteen, after her mother died, she couldn't stand the sadness that seemed to seep from the walls of her home. She dove headfirst into fasting and Bible reading and prayer. She spent every hour she wasn't in school volunteering with handicapped kids or serving hot meals to the poor.

In spite of her strident efforts to be good and her prayerful pleas to Jesus that she be freed from the body's desires, one of the cool boys, a pock-marked, long-haired, guitar player, invited her to a dance. She was eighteen years old, and it was her first date ever. She let him kiss her behind the gym. Just one kiss. That was alright.

She didn't say anything when he had crushed her breasts with his hands. She had wanted to feel something, needed relief from the numbness of loss. But he didn't stop at that. She didn't resist when he lowered her down, slipped her underpants to her ankles, and wrenched her knees apart. His weight pressed her against a sharp stone in the grass.

She felt her mind leave her body. The pebbles and sticks under her back, wet lips on her mouth, the swelling and breaking of waves—it all crashed over her, leaving nothing but white blankness inside her head.

He pushed himself against her like heavy rain. She remembered it as a thunderstorm. She was laid low by it, stunned by its ravenous wind, but she didn't resist.

She got pregnant, of course. The humiliation and confusion of it came flooding back. She was sure, back then, that no one would understand. Certainly, no one would know how to help her. It was, after all, her fault.

Her father would be furious if he found out what she had done. He would have thrown her out of the house. The Church couldn't help her. Her few friends would judge her. Gloria would mock her. She knew she had to leave before the consequences of her fornication began to show, before she lost her resolve. She had to lie.

She told her dad she wanted to go on a road trip and she would call him when she arrived on the west coast. She had no idea what else to do. After so many months of practicing rising above like a dove, all she knew how to do was fly. So she flew. She left her dad and her home.

Oblivious to the dangers and possibilities of setting out for a new city with a little fish inside her, she had bought herself a bus ticket and traversed the country alone. Remembering it now, twenty-five years later, she couldn't believe she'd done it.

She'd arrived in San Francisco in a stupor, fascinated and repulsed at once by her pregnant self. Her girlhood beliefs seemed meaningless and trite in the face of her long solitary pregnancy, her disappointment in herself, her inability to be the good girl she wanted to be. Her prayers felt vacuous. She started questioning everything about which she'd once been so sure. But despite all her doubts, the Church's power over her lingered, and she continued to be enveloped by shame.

She'd walked around detached from the busy, big city with its hills, moody skies, and bright houses. She became entranced by the luminous photos of floating fetuses in the library book *A Child is Born.* Her conscience wouldn't allow her to consider an abortion, though it had been made legal the year before. She found a clinic in Berkeley offering free prenatal care, which in turn referred her to an adoption agency.

Grace swigged the last of her cold coffee and sighed. Of all places, in the mountains in between the coasts, in McDonald's, she had let herself be ambushed by memories—the agonizing release of pushing out the baby, the regretful surrendering—and everything that changed as a result. She hated it when her thoughts reverted to those relinquishment papers, that metal room and the masked nurses, the wrinkled pink infant they placed in her arms then unceremoniously removed, the milk that kept dripping.

She jogged back to the car and the solace of the road. She longed to be speeding again under a crisp cerulean sheet of sky, trucks roaring beside her.

Dylan's gravelly voice, wailing about the brokenness of it all, somehow brought comfort as she zoomed down the highway toward what used to be her home.

10

"Hey, Dad. I'm on my way. How's your hip?"

Grace stopped at a gas station to buy a drink then pulled out her calling card. She balanced the receiver between her head and neck while she opened a can of Pepsi.

"Where are you?" Her father's voice was hoarse with disuse.

"Burlington, Colorado. A couple of hours outside of Colorado Springs."

"Gloria called and said she wants you to visit."

"Um, well…I decided to go past Denver this time. Just, you know, enjoy the solitude of the drive."

A fly buzzed as it circled her head, like a zipper opening and closing, then settled itself on her nose.

"You should go to Denver. She's your sister."

"I don't know. We'll see. I'd have to backtrack."

"And I've been thinking. I'm not sure I want to move after all."

She brushed the fly away and took a swig from the can.

"I know. But I don't think you have a choice. You can't use the stairs anymore, and there's a chance you could fall again. And we made an appointment to look at the senior living, you know, the assisted living place, when I get there. They have a one-bedroom apartment with a little kitchen, remember? And a balcony? And somebody comes in and cleans for you once a week?"

She'd found the website for Cherry Lakes Senior Living Community before she left. She'd already called them and asked what was available and discussed it all with her dad.

"But I don't want to live around a bunch of old people. It makes me depressed just thinking of it. All that drooling."

"Oh, Dad!" Grace chuckled. "They won't drool."

"It's an asylum." Her father insisted on describing Cherry Lakes as an asylum, an old folks' home, an old coots' joint, an institution for the infirm.

45

"It's a senior apartment complex." The residents in the photos on the website all looked much younger than her father, who, when Grace last had seen him, was thin and bent over, a wisp of his former self. "And you said you liked that they were all Catholic. Did I tell you the woman I spoke to on the phone told me one of the residents was a priest?"

"Truth be told, I'd rather live with young Protestants or middle-aged Jews than old Catholics."

"I don't think that's true. Last time we talked you said you wouldn't mind living there at all."

"Well, I was only being polite. I'm sure all the inmates use canes and walkers. I don't want to be surrounded by walkers! Talk about a fire hazard!"

"I think it'll be great. They'll check on you if you fall or if you don't go down to dinner, but otherwise, you're on your own. And besides, you'll be living around people with common interests. You'll have a community."

She flashed on images of Mesa Verde and its many busy inhabitants, all working together to bring in the crops and care for the babies.

"I don't want a *community!* The one privilege of growing old is freedom to do what you want. Now they want to take that away from me too! And what kind of a place is called Cheery Lakes, anyway?"

"Oh, Dad." The fly returned to its zipping. "I need to get back on the road."

"Why didn't you fly?"

"I wanted to have my car. And I wanted to bring a lot of stuff since I'll be with you for at least a month."

And I wanted to leave all my possibilities open, she thought, for the first time aware that she might not want to go back to...What would she be going back *to*, after all? To Frankie's ghost, to that sad sack school? To her disconnected life in the big city with its omnipresent sun?

"A road trip. How nice," her father muttered. "It's as if you're Dorothy on the road with Bing and Bob."

Grace smiled as she remembered donning her mom's fancy long gloves, wrapping herself around a pole in the basement, and lip-synching along with her father's Dorothy Lamour records on the stereo. "I like the image."

"Well, you be safe. And visit your sister. You're in her neighborhood."

"Bye, Dad."

"Bye. Have a nice time with your sister."

"Oh, God," Grace said aloud as she slipped back into the car and unfolded the map over the steering wheel. "I have to go back."

Her father was right. She should suck it up. Do the right thing and visit her insistent sister even though everything about her sister reminded her of all the things she wanted to forget. Annoyed with everyone, including herself, she shook her head and took off.

Grace pulled open the door to the café and stood there for a moment, letting the cool AC wash over her. Sade's voice floated liquid and hot in the background. It was four in the afternoon, and all the tables were cluttered with half-eaten goodies and coffee cups. People chatted, drank espresso, laughed; silverware clinked against ceramic plates. Gloria stood behind the counter with her back turned toward the door.

"I'll have a cappuccino," Grace said to the spiky-haired young man at the cash register. "What pastry do you recommend?"

Before he could answer, Gloria swung around. Her straight dark red hair was short, clipped, and styled, so unlike Grace's long mass of ringlets. They had the same nose, though, and the same full lips. Gloria wore a chic lime green scoop-necked blouse that showed off her fit, full figure. Grace glanced down at her jeans and thrift store t-shirt, wrinkled after a long day on the road.

She smiled awkwardly at Gloria, not sure if her sister's face registered happy surprise or irritated shock.

"So, you just show up? What happened?" Gloria asked in a throaty whisper. The young man half-smiled and stepped aside.

"I decided to surprise you," Grace said, glancing at the man's stiff hair then looking back at her sister.

"Well, you did." Gloria rolled her eyes, put down the metal tray of pecan tarts she was holding, and picked up a dishtowel. "Have a seat. I need half an hour to finish up here."

Back at the house, Gloria prepared pasta with scallops, garlic salad, and bruschetta. She insisted Grace shouldn't help. When dinner was ready, the family tripped in, laden with swim bags and jabbering about practice.

David kissed Gloria on the cheek, gave Grace an uncomfortable "hello" and sat at the head of the table. Tall, redheaded Jenna and pink-cheeked, pimply-faced Peter mumbled a greeting then resumed talking amongst themselves.

Before they all arrived, Grace and her sister had each swallowed two tumblers-full of Cabernet, so every sentence out of Grace's mouth during the meal came out as an overly effusive question.

"What grade are you guys in now? How's the swimming going?"

She didn't remember where her brother-in-law worked but placed her bets on asking, "How's the office, David?"

The responses to her queries were brief and shy. Grace was unsure what to do in the awkward silences that followed. It had been such a long time since she'd visited that her niece and nephew hardly knew her. Nobody asked her anything about her life, her road trip, her radical uprooting, or her dad. Then the family disappeared, leaving Gloria and Grace alone with the dishes.

"Thanks for dropping by, Holy Girl," Gloria said, bumping Grace's hip with her own as she scrubbed the dishes and Grace toweled them dry. Grace still had a hard time knowing when her sister's tone leaked sarcasm and when it was sincere.

"I'm glad I did. This is a long drive! It's nice to take a break. Dinner was great. And I haven't seen you in a while."

Gloria rolled her eyes. "It's been three years since you visited us here."

"I know. I've been super busy with work."

Gloria wiped soap suds off her hands with a dishtowel and turned to look at Grace. "You've been busy? For three years?"

"No, Gloria. I mean lately."

Gloria sighed. "Well, I appreciate what you're doing. Moving King William out of that house." She poured both of them another glass and pulled two bowls of creamy chocolate mousse out of the fridge. "Let's sit."

They settled into the sofa. The whole downstairs was empty of family life. Even the two dogs were gone as if Gloria and David had made a secret agreement to clear everybody out.

"I'm glad it's you taking care of things and not me," Gloria admitted.

"You have a lot going on here. And I quit my job, so I'm free."

Gloria hesitated, her full spoon halfway to her mouth. "Why'd you quit?"

Grace described how ill-equipped she felt to teach such struggling students. She'd been pretty good at teaching reading and writing to receptive, giggly middle schoolers in a high-priced alternative private school, but the needs of her students in Compton were daunting. She told her sister she felt burned out and frustrated by her inability to help anybody. She swallowed three huge spoonsful of mousse then scraped the glass bowl clean. She stifled the urge to lick it.

"And one of my students was raped by a priest."

"That's sick! You reported it, right? To Child Protection?"

"It happened fifteen years ago. He wrote about it." She was afraid she might cry if she admitted how much Frankie had meant to her.

"That's another reason why I hate that oppressive, misogynist, medieval, backward Catholic Church. I read how stuff like that is happening a lot, and they cover it up. You know, they move them around so they can abuse more kids."

Grace nodded. She closed her eyes.

The sisters sank into silence and nestled deeper into the velvety sofa. It was right that she had come after all, Grace thought. Gloria was a caring person, cynical, smart, and familiar. It felt good, at least for a moment, to be known.

"Gloria," she ventured, "do you miss Mom? Do you ever feel, like, abandoned?"

"Every day. Some days it gets pretty bad. It makes me angry after all this time." The sisters rarely talked about their mother's death, but Grace knew it pressed them both down like a wool blanket, scratchy and damp. "There are times I'm so mad because I can't call her and ask her advice or tell her about my day."

"Me too."

"The kids never knew their grandmother. And I could have used help when they were young. It's not *fair*."

"My student—Frankie, the one who was abused—lost his mom when he was in fourth grade."

"It's never a good time, Grace. They say losing a mother when you're a teenager is one of the worst losses anybody can go through."

Grace sighed. "I know."

Gloria straightened. "You should think about moving here. Like I told you before, you could work at the café while you look for a nice suburban teaching job. I could introduce you to some cool single men. It's a great way to meet someone. No past. Fresh start."

"I don't know what I'm going to do. I feel kind of in-between."

Gloria stretched her legs out on the coffee table. She raised her arms above her head and arched her back. Grace glanced at the faint trace of a scar on her forearm.

"Too bad your in-between has to be in the kingdom of Buffalo in the court of his royal highness."

"Gloria, why do you hate Dad? He's not an easy person; I know that. But he's not *that* terrible. And it's not his fault mom died. I mean, he's been all alone for twenty-five years."

"I don't hate him exactly. I just…I can't stand all his antiquated religious dogma," Gloria said. Her lip curled in distaste. "His religious superiority."

"You know he really wanted me to come visit you, don't you?"

"He probably wanted you to check to make sure I was praying the rosary at my Jesus is the Way Café."

Grace snickered. "But, no, I mean it. Why did you leave so soon after mom died?"

She set her glass on the coffee table and rubbed her arms. Wasn't there a blanket somewhere? She looked away from Gloria's face. Her whole early history stared back at her from those familiar green eyes.

"I would have loved having you around a little longer. But you disappeared."

When their mom died, Grace still had two more years left of school. Gloria had a few months before graduation. She stuck around to finish, and then she bolted. Grace wasn't sure if she would have loved having her bitter sister around during the ensuing years, but somewhere inside her, she knew there was truth in it.

"Everything would have changed if you hadn't taken off."

"I couldn't stay one more minute after I finished high school." Gloria arched her neck and looked up at the ceiling.

"But why? What was the big rush?"

"Let's just say I couldn't stand him and leave it at that. He was horrible to me. He screamed at me. He was mean, okay? It was such a hard time. Mom dying...everything ending. I don't want to talk about it. You left right after high school too. It wasn't only me."

"True," Grace said, aware that her secret defined her. If she told her sister about the pregnancy and the adoption, they'd have to reconfigure all their entrenched ideas of each other. Full of wine and chocolate, halfway between her old life and her uncertain new one, she wasn't up for all that work. "I don't want to talk about those days either." She uncurled her legs, reached for her drink, and turned to look full on at her older sister. "Resolved, then," she laughed, lifting the glass in the air. "Nothing deep."

"You said it. Nothing deep," Gloria echoed, raising her glass high.

11

Kansas was a flat green cloth, the sky an empty canvas, but Grace couldn't appreciate the acres of verdant farmland. Her feelings were a muddle. She was glad she'd doubled back and visited her sister but sad by how much they'd left unsaid.

What if they had seized the opportunity to share their secrets with each other? Grace imagined painting the word *truth* in ebony ink across the blue sky. Someday she'd tell Gloria what happened to her at eighteen, about the forces that lured her, too, away from home.

Or about how, a year after she gave up the baby, she gingerly entered the dating scene. Gloria knew almost nothing about those years. Eager for a relationship but clueless how to find it, Grace had catapulted into a disastrously unfulfilling affair with a United Farmworkers labor organizer who also happened to be a married man. She toyed with the risky flirtation for over a year. She liked the adventure of sneaking off with him after a rally, the built-in barriers to actual connection. But soon she started to hate herself for hurting another woman and stopped it before it went too far. She resolved never to stoop so low again.

For years she looked for someone to love. She dated many men, each one dedicated to some movement or other; she couldn't remember them all. Months unspooled themselves in between her exploits, which sometimes lasted little more than a night, a week, a few months. She was relieved when she broke the spell and fell into a comfortable groove with Drew.

She met Drew while volunteering at a local food co-op. She liked him well enough, but she didn't love him. They strung each other along for over three years before she finally asked him to move in and try to make a family. She was thirty-two and felt like she was walking sideways down a slippery hill. Maybe a husband and a baby were what she needed to not feel like she was grasping at branches to keep from sliding.

He said no, of course. *Whatever gave you the impression that's where we were going?* Shortly after he married a woman from the Philippines he'd found in a personals ad.

A couple of years later, she fell into an affair with an environmentalist named Marcus, who announced he wanted to marry her on the condition that the marriage could be open. He wanted the freedom to explore, and he would grant her the same freedom. She was floored. Roberto seduced her with oily massages and stories of how he'd overcome his myriad addictions but then left her to be with a woman he met in AA.

Gloria, on the other hand, met David soon after she arrived in Denver and maintained a normal relationship with him from the start. They dated for two years, got married, and had two kids.

Each of Grace's relationships seemed embarrassing by comparison. As far as her sister knew, she'd dated a few guys over the years, but she hadn't had any serious relationships. At forty-three, childless and husbandless, Grace knew Gloria saw her love life as an intricate jigsaw puzzle that needed solving. She was intrigued by the random cut-out snippets of stories Grace occasionally shared. She was the big sister. She knew best. She could fix everything.

Grace obsessed about relationships or her lack thereof with similarly angst-ridden single friends over the years. She knew full well what she was doing wrong. She ignored any interest shown to her by decent, ordinary guys while becoming bewitched by the unavailable ones. Every man she dated had a triumvirate of traits: devotion to some Big Belief or noble cause, head-turning good looks, and a neon light flashing from his forehead advertising his inability to commit. What had made her unable to let herself relax into normal, reciprocal love? She was capable and smart in many ways but still a teenager when it came to love.

And then, like a savior, Jake parachuted in. Surfer-blonde, seven years younger, thin and golden, azure-eyed, serious and refreshingly sincere. Jake, who invited himself into her bed one gloomy day after they met at Bright Eyes Café on Telegraph Avenue.

He was standing in front of her in line. He ordered a yerba mate; she ordered a latte.

"We rhyme," he said.

He motioned to her to sit with him. He flirted with her shamelessly and made her feel interesting and attractive. They sauntered through People's Park as he expounded on his spiritual evolution, on his desire to be pure.

He made himself a regular presence in her lonely routine. He cooked with her, teased her, taught her about Hinduism and reincarnation and relaxation. He encouraged her to get high on hash with him while he played guitar. Under the haze of her infatuation, she began to believe that love might be possible after all.

She let him consume her to the point of annoying her girlfriends. Some of them accused her of betraying their solidarity, their single-girl bond. But she hardly noticed. Jake held her heart in his hands like a ball of wet clay. He formed it into something beautiful and fired it with the intensity of their exploring.

Then, after almost two years together, he dropped the clay bowl of her love and shattered it, leaving the shards on the floor.

Linda, whom they'd both met on a yoga retreat, was his "sexual and mystical ideal." Linda lived just down the road from Grace's place, but she was on a different plane of existence. She helped him "clear his monkey mind."

A note, that's all he left her.

He thanked Grace for understanding his need for spiritual growth and wished her harmony and light on the path. Without intending to, he pushed her, sideswiped by surprise and brokenhearted, to the City of Angels. And now she was leaving it behind as well.

After a day crossing the prairie, Grace parked in downtown Topeka and walked the wide boulevards. She breathed in the cool evening air settling over the stately buildings and manicured parks. She stumbled across Prince of Peace Church and its boastful marquee: *The Largest Catholic Church in Kansas Welcomes You.*

In front of the prim brick church, a white stone statue of a serene Virgin Mary stood on a pedestal of cement encircled by pink begonias. Grace trod up the broad stone steps and strained to open the dense wooden doors. She ignored the voice in her head that said, *You don't belong here,* and ducked inside.

A polished pinewood Jesus drooped on a plain cross on the wall. An altar adorned with a white cloth and gold candlesticks stood in front of the crucifix. Yellow banners with blue and green felt letters proclaimed *He Is Risen* and *He Dwells Among Us*. Her dad had stopped their car in front of many such churches during the road trips of her youth.

Her mother had always sighed with impatience, anxious to return to the road and get where they were going. She'd sit in the car, head back against the vinyl seat, eyes closed, while her dad motioned the girls to get out, pulled open the heavy doors of the strange church, and stepped into the cool darkness. Her sister would pout or complain about how "stupid" it was that he always made them stop.

Grace slid into a pew in the back. She used to love feeling the smooth wooden pew beneath her legs as she sat in a Catholic church, its stained-glass windows glimmering in the summer sun. She loved to light the votive candles nestled in sand. Grace was her dad's ally; she understood his longing to enter quiet sacred spaces. How many times had she followed behind him obediently, protecting him from her sister's annoyance and her mother's indifference?

She stared at the naked wooden chest of Jesus gleaming in the multi-colored sunlight and remembered how deeply she had longed for a savior. She remembered, too, how holiness had turned to hollowness as she struggled to find her way in the world. The Church had invited her into the water, but it had refused to teach her how to swim.

After a night in a motel, she drove another eight hours then followed signs for Indianapolis. She checked into a Holiday Inn. One more full day of driving lay ahead of her before she arrived at her dad's house. She was worn out and ready to stay put for a while.

She turned on the TV and stretched out on the bed to watch the news. Linda Tripp testified before a grand jury that she'd taped possibly illegal conversations with Monica Lewinsky. A strike at a General Motors factory in Detroit shut down five assembly plants, leaving hundreds of workers panicked.

Boston's Cardinal Bernard Law stood in the rain, his snow-white hair under a red skull cap, microphone close to his mouth. He sounded sincere, grandfatherly, as he told the reporter that the priest, Father John Geoghan, had been laicized.

"On the face of this earth, he will not be known or act as a priest ever again," he said. "He has violated the trust people had in the priesthood, and a priest by his very nature invokes trust."

Grace stiffened, her fingernails digging into her palms.

According to the reporter, Father Geoghan had been accused of abusing at least fifty, possibly a hundred, boys over the past two decades. He had been transferred from one diocese to another but continued to have unrestrained contact with children. Finally, after the priest's archdiocese had paid millions of dollars in lawsuits, Pope John Paul II approved the defrocking.

Supporters of the Church called the move "drastic and unprecedented." A spokesman for the advocacy group Priest Abuse Information Network expressed fear that the Church was trying to "buy the silence of victims" to make the scandal disappear.

"I hope this act can bring peace to some," Cardinal Law said. The Suffolk County District Attorney, the reporter said, was considering criminal charges.

Grace stared at the screen. The TV blasted an ad for McDonalds' chicken nuggets with four new dipping sauces. A swirl of grief and fury gripped her as she thought of Frankie's accusations, Victoria's devastating phone call, that terrible May afternoon in church.

She turned off the television, pulled Frankie's essays out of her suitcase, and cocooned herself under the comforter as she read one of her favorite passages again. Before Frankie's death, she'd found it lighthearted and buoyant with hope. Now, she only found it tragically, hopelessly sad.

I am free to play with mija, my baby girl, my precious baby girl. I would give the world for her. The way she puts her little hands on my face and stares in my eyes like I am the picture of love melts my heart. I am free to walk down a city street in the sun and don't have nobody telling me you have to walk in a line, you have to wake up at four am and mop the filthy floor, you have to eat nasty slop inside of the concrete box of the big house and stay there for ten years. I am free to feel the heat of the summer sun on my face. That is the most blessed feeling in the world that nobody ever ever ever again will take it from me. I have something to live for. I love Jesus and Marisol and Victoria and LIFE.

Part Two

Be not forgetful to entertain strangers:
For thereby some have entertained angels unawares.
—Hebrews 13:2

12

hy did she think her dad would want her to descend on his life? It was one thing to visit for a weekend. It was one thing to help out like a visiting saint for a week. It was a whole other thing to move in for months, interrupt the old man's life, and force him to move out of the house he loved.

Grace tried to pretend that it wasn't a big deal. He needed her. She could help him. And she did need to feel useful.

Finally, she had arrived. She was exhausted from the drive, relieved to be done but hesitant to go in just yet. She began to unload bags and boxes from the back seat, setting them on the picnic table in the backyard, then took her time cleaning out the car. She stuffed water bottles, sticky gum-filled wads of paper, disposable coffee cups, and chip wrappers into plastic bags and set them on the ground in front of the garage.

She opened the garage door and found the rakes and brooms that normally would be hanging on their nails on the wall laying askew on the floor. The metal garbage can, full of rotting food, reeked when she opened the lid. She'd have to take care of that.

She left her car garbage sitting outside on the driveway, yanked the garage door shut, and walked back to the picnic table. She gathered her first load and studied the back door of the house. The screen door was shut, but the wooden door was open wide.

Should she knock? Should she walk in? Would she have to get herself a key? She sighed as she thought about what she was getting herself into. Little prickles of heat tickled her neck, and her cheeks felt flushed. She imagined herself repacking her car and screeching out of the driveway. She'd wait until she was an hour away to call her dad and say it was all a mistake. She and Gloria would just pay an aide to help him stay at home. She was exhausted and achy, but she was seized by a longing to be back on the road, alone, not settled, unattached to anyplace. But she knew it was too late for that.

Grace drove her dad to the appointment she'd made for him at Cherry Lakes Senior Living Community and sat quietly as he asked questions about the meals, the activities, the other residents' ages and interests.

Was there a priest on the premises? Did they have Mass? How much privacy and autonomy would he have?

He was pleased to learn that Cherry Lakes did indeed have a resident priest who led daily meditation in their chapel. The adjoining skilled nursing facility, Immaculate Heart of Mary, had a full-sized church which offered Mass every Wednesday afternoon and Sunday morning and a van that would drive him there.

Because they also had a jitney that would take people to the store and doctors' appointments, many folks found it more convenient to relinquish their cars. He agreed on the spot to move in after his house was sold and signed all the papers.

They spent the next week preparing for his transition—that's what the Admissions Specialist had called it—to Cherry Lakes. Grace ran up and down the stairs a hundred times, collecting things in a box and bringing them downstairs to be separated into piles. Things he would need. Things that had sentimental value. Things that he could live without. The last pile was largest since he'd no longer have an attic or a basement to stockpile ancient stuff.

Grace found herself actually having fun. She had expected her dad to be sullen and grouchy the entire time, but he seemed cheerful and light on his feet, in spite of his still achy hip.

Every morning after a full four hours of packing, they drove to Dunkin' Donuts or Starbucks for a coffee and a quick bite. Her dad's memory for directions wasn't as sharp as it once was. He got flustered if she asked for directions, but Grace soon learned that if she just let him talk, he could make his way to most places.

He still managed to guide them to the imposing statues in the knolls of Forest Lawn Cemetery, past the houses where he was raised, down to South Buffalo to the magnificent Our Lady of Victory Basilica and the dense, lush smelling interior of the art nouveau buildings of the South Park Conservatory. They drove to Lackawanna and the crumbling monstrosity of the empty steel plant, its giant silos, coal bins, and coke ovens like rusty roller coasters on the shore of the lake. He told her stories all along the way. He seemed accepting of his more vulnerable state and grateful for her return.

At the end of the first week, standing at the kitchen table without his walker, he cracked.

"I can't do it. I won't! I've lived here for almost three decades. And I don't want to live around a bunch of old coots!"

His voice got breathy and high-pitched; even from the living room, she could tell he was crying. Grace had been surprised by how easy the past week had been and worried this moment might be coming. But she was still unnerved by his sudden outburst of feeling.

She walked toward the kitchen, a damp dust rag in her hand. "I think you'll make friends at Cherry Lake, Dad. You won't be as lonely."

"What makes you think I'm lonely?"

Her father slammed a plastic bowl on the table and walked away, grabbing a chair and the refrigerator and everything in his path for support. He made it all the way out the back door. He was sitting backward on the picnic table bench, panting, when Grace joined him in the back yard.

"I know you don't want to move, but you can't manage a two-story house anymore. And Gloria and I were worried about you."

"So stop worrying!" he yelled.

She told herself to remember what a big change this was for him. She sat down next to him on the bench and gently touched the back of his hand. "Dad, I know this all must be hard for you."

He wrenched his hand away and pulled an envelope out of the breast pocket of his shirt. "I'll tell you what's hard for me. You using my address to solicit propaganda."

"What?" Grace asked, her voice pinched. "What are you talking about?"

He thrust the envelope at her face then slammed it down on the picnic table. The words *Stop Crimes Against Children* were stamped in red across the front. The acronym *PAIN* was written in bold letters above a return address in Wisconsin.

On her second day in Buffalo, Grace had driven to the downtown library to use the computer. She'd searched the internet for information about the Catholic Church and the scandals beginning to unfold on the nightly news. The group Priest Abuse Information Network was collecting stories and advocating for victims.

She sent them an email describing what happened to Frankie, including her dad's address and phone number and inquiring what to do. She asked the librarian for the addresses of Holy Mother of God Church and the Los Angeles Police Department.

"Do you have any idea who these people are?"

"Oh, yeah." She nodded. "That's the priest abuse information group. I contacted them because something happened to one of my students."

She had avoided the conversation with her dad. The pleasant exchanges of the past weeks had helped assuage her guilt for leaving, as if the past twenty-five years were merely a detour and they were back together on the same road. She didn't want to disturb the sweet easiness of their new connection by raising any hard questions about his beloved Church. She knew it would be difficult, but she hadn't expected this level of fury.

"If you ever…" He jabbed the envelope with his finger. "If you ever allow left wing slander of this sort in my house again, young lady. I mean *ever*…" The threat hung in the air unfinished. He was breathless, his ears red with rage.

This was the reactionary, mean spirited side of him that Gloria remembered. The side he reserved for her rebellious teenage sister and had rarely shown Grace, the family good girl.

"Dad, I don't think you understand. They're trying to stop the Church, you know, people in authority, from abusing—"

Grace jumped when his fist banged the table. He grabbed the thick envelope and attempted to tear it up with trembling fingers. He threw it on the ground and crushed it against the grass with his foot.

He pulled himself up from the bench and stood to face Grace. A snarling sound arose from his throat. "I said *ever*."

Then he turned and limped into the house, slamming the metal screen door behind him.

The pamphlet was written for members of parishes in which a priest is accused of abuse. Its tone was supportive and sympathetic. Grace read it in bed that night, searching for wisdom about how to respond when she was not a part of any church congregation, about where to begin when the case was fifteen years old, the victim had been killed, and his family knew nothing about the abuse.

The pamphlet advised her to pray. She hadn't prayed in years, and this was probably not the time or reason to start, especially since the pamphlet suggested she pray for the perpetrators as well as their prey. She read the pamphlet with tear-brimmed eyes. Certain phrases stood out.

Pray for the accused as well as the victim. Keep an open mind and remember that abuse is common. You are not powerless. Feelings of anger, betrayal, confusion, hurt, and worry are normal. Your focus should be love for all those involved. Remember that God loves each of His children.

Then she read its final directives:

19) Contact the police or prosecutors. *It is the duty of a citizen to contact law enforcement if they have any information about child abuse by church leaders. It is the responsibility of a citizen to seek justice when people in authority break the law and abuse their power.*

20) Contact the leadership of the church. *It can be emotionally stressful for parishioners to reach out to those in authority, but it is their moral obligation to inform the church leadership as soon as possible of any knowledge or suspicion they have of abuse by priests in their parish. It is the duty of a Christian to protect children from harm.*

What the brochure didn't explain was how to muster the energy to do the right thing. Grace slipped the pamphlet under her pillow and laid down. She considered praying but had no idea what to say or where to begin.

Over the course of her first three weeks back in Buffalo, Grace drove six carloads of boxes to the St. Vincent De Paul Thrift Store. Except for the big pieces of furniture that would be moved to Cherry Lakes or sold in the estate sale, most of the house was cleared out. The room she slept in was barren as a hotel. The kitchen was packed up except for silverware, a couple settings of Corelle Ware plates and cups, and the solitary pot and pan her dad would take with him. The basement was eerily empty; the living room was stripped bare. The only rooms left to clear were her dad's bedroom and the attic.

While her dad was napping on the sofa, Grace made herself a cup of mint tea and shuffled into his bedroom. Rosaries, saints' medals, and framed photos gathered dust on the dresser. His closet bulged with memories: shoeboxes full of curled-up photos the color of tea, scrapbooks whose pages were flaking, a yearbook from Bishop Fallon High School dated 1932. Her mom's yearbook from Detroit's East High, 1942. A locked metal safe box with no key.

She climbed the steps to the stuffy attic. Her mother's shoes were still in boxes. Practically new dresses hung in dry cleaning bags. Plastic bins of her mother's shirts and polyester pants, smelling of mothballs, had been tucked away in the stuffy space. Grace lifted a plastic bag and stroked a beige cashmere sweater. Its softness was as unnerving as the intransigence of her dad's grief. Her mom's stuff had been up here for nearly thirty years collecting dust. It was as if he had meant to go through it all but had never had the strength to venture up.

Grace's old books had been jammed into five boxes and piled in the far corner. Two boxes were heavy with novels and textbooks, easy enough to dump. Two were full of saints and philosophers and words of wisdom—Kahlil Gibran, Tolstoy, Edgar Cayce, *Good News for Modern Man, Something Beautiful for God*. The last box held three years' worth of teenage journals, each written in her youthful, loopy scroll. The heat in the airless attic pressed into Grace as she fingered their dense pages, her back against the wall, and read the first line from 1970:

I fainted at school today. Mom came and picked me up. It was joyous at first, but later things got really hard. Please, God, forgive me for my weaknesses and give me strength to love.

13

September 18, 1970

*G*race heard the nurse calling her mom to tell her she'd fainted. She felt at peace, meditative; the cool cloudiness she felt in her head in art class, before the fall, had transformed itself into a lightheaded high.

The nurse gave her apple juice and asked, "When is the last time you ate, young lady?"

It was a quarter past two, and she hadn't eaten since breakfast. She'd finished her homework in the cafeteria instead of eating lunch.

When her mom came to pick her up, the nurse told her, "I don't think this girl is getting enough food. Adolescence is a time of growth and development, you know. They need lots of milk, meat, fruits and vegetables, and grain."

Grace watched her mom study the Four Basic Food Groups poster taped to the wall as she spoke.

"Yes, thank you. I appreciate everything you've done."

Grace put the Bread album on the turntable and lifted the needle, careful not to scratch her favorite part: "I would give everything I own, give up my life, my heart, my home..."

The path to what was right and true was given simply to Bernadette of Lourdes. She was fourteen—a year younger than Grace—when she was gathering sticks in the woods and stumbled onto a vision of beauty so clear and shining she couldn't ignore it.

She was chosen by God to be the witness to the face of Mary in the rock. Bernadette's sisters mocked her at first, too, but eventually, everyone believed her. It seemed easier back then, in a poor family, living in the countryside, to

*be a glowing channel for the Spirit. Grace wanted to be that receptive too;
she wanted to give everything she owned, but she had no idea how to do it or
where to go.*

*Everything was complicated. She imagined her life as a book, her purpose
in life written on a few key pages. But the pages were stapled together, and
she was wearing boxing gloves.*

*She studied for her Earth Science test until ten o'clock then closed the
book and turned off all the lights. She tiptoed to the closet and fumbled around
in the dark for her meditation box.*

*The box had been moved from the shelf where she always kept it. She
pulled the string to the bare light bulb and blinked. It was on the floor. Her
sister couldn't resist messing with her stuff. Fortunately, nothing was gone.
Her two pencil sketches, a bare tree against a moonlit sky and a rendering of
Jesus on the cross, were both there. The scented candle and smooth black
stones were there.*

A note had been folded and placed beside them. Grace opened it.

You are so weird.

*She yanked the string and darkness closed over the closet again. Light
from the streetlamp outside guided her to the middle of the floor. She unzipped
her jeans and pulled them off. Then she rolled up the rug and sat cross-legged
in her shirt and underpants on the wood floor.*

*She arranged the items in front of her. As she lit a match, she prayed The
Lord's Prayer. She hummed,* Oh, Lamb of God, who takes away the sins of the
world, have mercy on us, *then focused on her breath.* In with peace, out with love.

*The candlelight quivered and twirled. She started to caress her inner
thighs with her fingertips, tracing circles up the velvety flesh, approaching the
place of fluttering pleasure she'd discovered between her legs then stopped.*

*She pinched her thighs hard and clenched her fists until her fingernails dug
little moons into her palms. Breathed* in with patience, out with forgiveness.
Forgiveness. *She needed a bucket load of that.*

*She prayed until her toes tingled and her knees grew hot. As she blew out
the dripping candle, a car whooshed into the driveway. Spinning stripes of
light split the darkness of the room.*

An unfamiliar male voice wafted in through the window, muffled and low. Her mother's voice rose next, high and questioning, then her dad's. She watched it all from above—a police officer holding a flashlight, her parents beside him, and her sister leaning against the car, arms crossed.

Grace lifted the window slowly. She heard the rise and fall of voices, the words marijuana and alcohol and driving. She shut the window, closed the curtain, and snuck into bed. The door slammed. She covered her head with her pillow and secured her hands safely under her head. She lay like that in stuffy silence, waiting for her sister to come upstairs, before drifting away.

When she woke up at five o'clock the next morning, her sister was not in her bed. The covers weren't rumpled from a night of sleep; the box and its contents were where she'd left them the night before. Her mother had left a note on the kitchen table.

We're at the emergency room. Don't worry. Just go to school.
PLEASE EAT. Mom.

Grace sat and waited for some kind of prayer or mantra to come to her, something to calm her trembling hands and relieve her pulsing head. Nothing came. No hymns, no chants, no Bible passages. She began to recite the Lord's Prayer aloud, but every line emerged as a question.

Hallowed be Thy name? Thy kingdom come? Thy will be done?

Her sister's voice clouded her head, and the words sounded mocking and blasphemous. She stood up, scraping the chair across the linoleum to stop the voice. She opened the refrigerator, grabbed a Tupperware container of cold spaghetti, and ate it out of the plastic tub. She covered two slices of bread with butter and jam and ate them in three bites. She poured the fatty broth from a can of chicken noodle soup into a pot, added water, and paced the length of the kitchen while she waited for it to bubble.

The prayers returned. Not mocking but sad and sincere. She was so full of sin, of ordinary stupidity. There was no way she could rise up and out of this world. She couldn't stop the magnetic pull of desire.

As much as she tried, she couldn't imagine herself sporting a nun's stiff habit and sequestering herself away forever. She couldn't imagine being told by some Mother Superior that she couldn't play her records and dance wildly around the room. All the saints in the stories she read seemed fragile and frail. Why did they need to live only on lettuce? Why did they have to make themselves sick and weak to feel close to God? She didn't understand. She was miserable. There was nothing she could do but go to school and wait.

All of her classmates in American History turned their heads to look at her when the voice came over the P.A. "Excuse the interruption. Grace Schreiber, please report to the office immediately."

Grace's mother was stiffly polite when she picked her up.

"Thank you for your help as usual," she told the receptionist in the front office. She signed Grace out on the clipboard and walked ahead of her until they got to the car. Once inside, she laid her head on the steering wheel and closed her eyes. "I don't know what to do. I don't know what we did wrong."

Grace stared at her mother's hands clenched around the wheel, the bony ridges of her knuckles. "What's going on, Mom?" she whispered.

Her mother gasped. Tears spill over her hands. Grace turned to her and pulled herself into a ball, arms around her legs, chin to her knees. Her mother wiped her eyes with the palms of her hands and turned on the ignition. They drove home in silence.

It was as if her mother needed the light of the fluorescent lamp and the smooth Formica tabletop beneath her hands in order to begin. "Gloria is a troubled girl."

"I know that, Mom."

"We're very worried about her."

"Mom, what happened?" Grace took a deep breath, in through her nostrils then out slowly through her mouth. She tried to stop all the images racing through her head. If she could focus her breathing on this moment, recite an emergency prayer—Oh, Lord, release us—she'd be able to resist the temptation to run out of the room and eat the whole bag of peanut butter cookies stashed in her bottom drawer.

"Your sister was brought home by the police last night. There were five kids in the car. They'd been drinking and smoking marijuana." Her mother

pronounced it mary-joo-ana and shook her head. Her eyes sparkled with tears. "They found some in the glove compartment of our car. She took our car! Your father was furious. We went into the basement to talk to her. I wanted to try to work something out. I thought maybe counseling…"

She reached for a tissue and blew her nose, eyes fixed to the shiny tabletop. "This is all so embarrassing."

"What, Mom?" Grace felt restless, angry.

"Your father started yelling. He told her he was ashamed of her. Gloria said she didn't want to live here anymore. She's only a junior! They screamed at each other for a long time. Then your sister hit the wall with her fist so hard she made a hole in the wall. I was afraid she broke her hand. When I said that to your father, he said, 'Good.' Can you imagine? He said, 'Good.'"

Grace's mom started to cry again. Then she wiped her nose. She flattened out a clean tissue and laid all the soggy ones on top. "We had to take her to the hospital in the middle of the night. We waited in the emergency room for hours."

Grace pictured them sitting in the cold hospital waiting room while she slept. Nobody talking, her mother crying, her father staring red-faced at the wall, her sister stubbornly refusing to cry or talk or apologize. All while she was sleeping like an idiot, oblivious.

"Where is she now?"

"We had her admitted to the psychiatric ward after talking to the doctor. He said she had alcohol, marijuana, and pills in her blood. They were worried about her trying to hurt herself. Maybe—" By now her face was blotchy and red. "I'm a bad mother."

"No, you're not, Mom. You're a good mother." Grace's shoulders tightened. Her teeth clamped onto her tongue.

"I'm glad you don't have any problems. I couldn't handle any more."

She reached across the table and folded Grace into her arms, then they parted, looked away, and sat together in silence.

They drove to the hospital and walked down the long corridor that separated the psychiatric wing from the medical floors. The air was damp with the thick smell of overcooked food. Gloria was asleep. She looked slight and harmless in her white polka-dotted gown. Her hair was tousled, and her mouth was open. The sheets were tangled around her legs.

69

"How long will it be?" her mother asked the nurse who came in to take her blood pressure and pulse. "How long do you think it will be till she's normal again?"

Everybody wants to be normal, *Grace thought. Normal is what she wanted to escape with all her being. Normal people don't want to experience the riveting thrill of a pink sunrise because they are too lazy to get out of bed. Normal people don't seek joy. Normal people don't want to feel hungry; they want to stay numb. Her sister wanted to break out, but not for joy. She was angry all the time. Grace didn't understand any of them.*

"There's no way to know in situations like this, now is there?" the nurse replied as she walked out the door.

Her mother looked wrung out. "I need to go home. I'm tired. I've got a terrible headache again, like a knife in my temple. And a stomach ache too."

"I'm not going home," Grace said. "You can go home without me, and I'll stay here tonight."

"You can't stay here, honey."

"Mom, I'll stay here and take care of her." Grace felt good about the motherly tone in her voice.

"You can't sleep in a chair," her mother murmured, worrying the edge of her sleeve. "You'll need dinner."

"I'm fine." Grace's voice was firm and confident.

She watched her mother leave, how her shoulders sank as she crossed the room, how she straightened her back and forced a smile when a nurse passed by.

Grace laid her head back on the cool lounge chair next to the hospital bed and looked at the square grey tiles of the ceiling. She put her feet up on the mattress, rustling the thin covers and pressing her toes against her sister's unbroken hand. She sighed as the cold hospital air blanketed her. Gradually, she drifted off to sleep.

When she opened her eyes, Gloria was sitting up and staring at her. "Hey, Holy Girl, you want to see something?" she asked.

"I guess."

Gloria held out her broken hand with its bandage and splint then pointed to the skin above it. *She peeled off a large piece of tape that covered a swatch of bloody gauze, revealing fresh slice marks on her skin.* Life Sucks *was carved, pink and puffy, into the white skin of her forearm.*

"Ewwhh. That's gross. What's wrong with you?"

"What's wrong with you? You think it's normal to not eat?"

"I don't want to be normal if that's what you are."

"I know you don't. You want to be perfect."

"I'll never be perfect." *Grace wished her sister had even the foggiest glimmer of who she was and what she believed in. Grace had no idea what it was like to want to be bad.*

Grace winced. "Who cuts themselves on purpose? That's disgusting."

"It's not a big deal. It doesn't hurt that much. You might try it if you weren't perfect," *Gloria said.*

Grace stood up to leave. Why did she bother to talk to Gloria? She lived on a different planet. If she wasn't so exhausted, she'd try to pray.

Gloria grabbed her arm. "Don't go. I'm just giving you a hard time. You can think it's gross if you want to. You have my royal permission. Please stay. But don't pray for me, okay?"

Gloria laughed, and Grace's muscles relaxed as she looked at her big sister in the rumpled white sheets and the red smear of the bandage lying on the pillow.

"You are so weird," *Grace said.*

71

14

Grace felt exhausted and riveted at once. In the attic's stifling heat, she'd relived vivid scenes of her family's life in a way she never could have without these journals. She had all but forgotten her sister's screaming bouts with her dad, her mom's embarrassed confusion in response to Gloria's rebelliousness, her own repressive sanctimoniousness. Grace stood up and stretched her cramped legs. She stacked the journals back in their box and lugged it down the stairs.

Maybe her dad would be up for a drive to Castaways, his favorite bar and grill on the lake. She longed to sit on the restaurant's deck facing the lake and feel the cool breeze on her cheeks. She needed a break, but she couldn't wait to lay in bed with the journals and reenter that long-ago world. He agreed, good-natured after a nap, and said he could use a drink.

Thanks to a few Manhattans and strawberry daiquiris and the view from the restaurant deck, they relaxed. They watched as sailboats slid through the silvery water. Gulls screeched at the bits of pretzel a boy tossed in the air. A sexy waitress, eyes ringed in black and gold, brought them appetizers and refills of their drinks.

Her dad took a gulp of his cocktail, then set it down in its puddle on the table. "What do you call a nun who sleepwalks?"

He'd told her this one before, but she feigned ignorance. "I can't imagine. What?"

"A roamin' Catholic." He grinned and stirred the watery drink.

"Good one," she said.

"Did I ever tell you about the nun who asked her class of second graders what they wanted to be when they grew up?"

He had.

"No, tell me."

"One little girl said, 'I want to be a prostitute when I grow up.' The good sister almost fainted. She couldn't believe her ears. '*What* did you say you want to be when you grow up?' The little girl repeated what she said before. 'I want to be a prostitute.' 'Oh, thank heavens," the nun answered. She was *so* relieved. 'I thought you said you wanted to be a *Protestant.*'"

Grace laughed. He had been serious and moody the last few days. It was a very good sign that he was telling jokes again.

"Those nuns could be quite funny. People take them much too seriously. I remember one of the sisters wagging her finger at us after a parent meeting. 'I know why you're all devils,' she told us. This is a true story." Grace had heard this story many times, and each time she saw a child's glee in her dad's eyes. "'I know why you're devils. It's because your mothers are devils. With their red lips and their red fingernails!'" He passed his fingers over his lips and fingernails with theatrical flair. "Now that's funny."

"It's a pretty strong statement," Grace said.

"Don't be so serious. You young people always make more out of that kind of comment than need be. We knew what they meant."

"That all of the mothers were evil because they wore makeup?"

"No, of course not. They were just making a point. Now, you. Tell me about your work. You're a teacher."

His comment threw her off guard. He hadn't asked her anything about herself since the day she'd arrived.

"Well, Dad, you know I quit."

"I guess I did know that. But I don't know why. Weren't you happy at your school? I thought you loved your job."

She used to call him once a month when she lived in San Francisco to tell him the inspiring stories she knew he'd want to hear. He was impressed and proud when he could tell his friends that she taught sixth grade English at the prestigious Warren Academy in Berkeley.

He had expressed a different kind of pride when she announced she was leaving San Francisco and moving to the war zone of South Central LA to teach at Cesar Chavez Community Education Center.

When she'd described her new school to her father over the phone, he had said she was "doing the Lord's work" by "devoting herself to the needy." She didn't tell him that the reason she did such noble work in LA was to escape Jake. She had never told her dad or her sister about Jake in the first place.

Her father scraped his chair back and excused himself to hobble to the restroom. Grace watched him make the precarious trip, holding onto the wall as he walked. She turned to watch the lake darken as the dusk deepened. *So much goes on under the water*, she thought, *hidden beneath the silky surface.*

Her mind drifted back to the journals and the memories she'd left buried in them. She'd forgotten most of the details in her past, and she knew much of her forgetting was deliberate. She knew, too, she would never say anything to her dad about her many secrets. She'd never tell him about her violation of her virginity which he would only see as a sin, a stain at the base of a porcelain toilet bowl, unscrubbable. She'd never tell him he had a grandchild out there somewhere, a girl she didn't raise and would probably never know.

And she couldn't confront her dad about what the Church had done to Frankie; she didn't know how to broach it without infuriating him. He held the Church—its actions and its teachings—in a protective box, cordoned-off holy ground, not to be questioned.

"I loved a lot about my job," she told her dad when he returned. "But some of it was unbelievably hard. I worked way too many hours. And my students were very poor." And the sad truth was she wasn't a good teacher. She tried to be. She wanted to help her students, but the energy required to prepare lessons riveting enough to divert the attention of these neglected kids away from all their other worries proved to be far too much for her.

Her face would flush, standing up there in front of all those kids, and she'd experience pure panic. Chavez was another planet from Warren where she'd had twelve kids in a class, more resources, and very supportive staff. Janeen could do it because she was tough with the kids. She knew what they were going through.

She didn't take their rude comebacks personally. She didn't consider it a personal failure if they could hardly read or if they stared into space when asked to write a paragraph. Janeen, as she explained it to Grace, "interrupted" their negative behaviors and "re-directed" them. But the students had Grace pegged as someone unequipped to wrestle down their demons; they sucker-punched her every day.

The waitress came over, and her dad ordered another Manhattan with two maraschino cherries.

"That's the nutritional part," he said with a wink. "Remember when you were a teenager, and you wanted to work with the poor in that soup kitchen? The Catholic Worker House? You were a very religious young lady. Other youngsters were going to the prom, but you wanted to dole out soup and sandwiches to old men. That was righteous work, what you did back then." He nodded in approval.

"The St. Laurence House of Hospitality," Grace said, hoping she'd written about it in one of her journals. "I do remember it. Vaguely."

As they finished their drinks, they watched the sun rest its head on a pillow of orange clouds before slipping into its bath of black water. The waitress brought the check, and they decided to walk a little way down the pier before returning to the car. It felt good to be out in the breeze, but her old dad's sore hip made it impossible to go far.

They tossed a bit of dinner roll to the seagulls and watched as they descended in a frenzy then rose in a furious flash of wings.

"Look at the intricacy of their design," her father said. "The beak, the feathers, the perfect architecture of flight. How could the creation of these birds have possibly been an accident? How could anyone ever argue it was random?"

A black swan slid gracefully across the surface of the lake, its rapid paddling imperceptible beneath the water.

"There is beauty under the ocean no human eye will ever see. Why else would that be, if not to glorify God?"

Grace studied her dad's eyes as he stared out at the horizon. This was the man whose beliefs had colored her own, for better or for worse. His reverence had infused her with whatever reverie she experienced when she was alone in the natural world. *Rise above your worries, young lady,* he had told her many times. *Remember how small we are in the vastness of God's universe.*

This was the man who held her hand as they walked along the shore when she was a child, extolling the exquisiteness of the seashells, the power of the waves. *Imagine a steel ball the size of the earth. A dove flies by and flicks its wing on the ball once every million years. By the time the ball has worn down to nothing, eternity will have only just begun.*

This was the man who cradled her in his arms when she cried during a thunderstorm, telling her to think of the lightning as a reminder of God's presence.

They stood on the pier in silence in the breeze until darkness closed in and lights flickered on faraway boats.

She drove home slowly, both hands tight on the steering wheel, wide awake in a way she had not been in many months and more than a little drunk.

Grace woke to a pounding headache the next morning. She massaged her throbbing temple and looked around the room where her mother had died after just such a headache.

The clock said 9:18. Without giving it much thought, she picked up the phone by the bed and dialed Gloria's number. Her sister would have already run five miles even though it was two hours earlier there. Grace lay in bed, morning-after queasiness undulating through her.

"Hello, Buffalo soldier," her sister said, her voice cheerful. "How's it going? I wondered when you'd call."

Grace had left her four long informative messages since she arrived, careful to call the house when she knew Gloria was at the café and David was at work. It was time for another update, and she looked forward to bragging about the relaxed time she and her dad had had at Castaways, headache notwithstanding.

"It's going great," Grace said. "Dad and I had a wonderful time last night, wining and dining and chatting. He's in good shape. I'm not feeling too good right now, but I'll be fine. I think I'm going to take it easy today."

Grace started to sit up, but the violent knocking on the door of her brain pushed her back down.

"Um, so…are you getting a lot done?" Gloria's words came out fast and clipped. "Peter, I'll be right there," she said, her hand over the receiver.

"Yeah, getting rid of tons of boxes, going through everything. He'll be ready to move in a couple of weeks. I'm thinking about calling my landlord in Gardena and breaking my lease. And I might start looking for an apartment here this week. Maybe even a little house with a garden. Who knows?" Though she hadn't imagined any particulars until she heard herself utter them aloud, the idea of a new place, a fresh adventure, raised gooseflesh on her arms.

"You're not staying there, are you? I thought this was temporary."

"Me too. I mean...I didn't know. I guess I'd left it open without realizing it, but now..." Grace sighed and rolled over, closed her eyes. "I'm glad to be here. I love the slow pace and the quiet neighborhoods and the waterfront. I needed to get out of the big city. And I think it's good for Dad to have me here whether he knows it or not."

"Grace," Gloria said. "I think you're crazy to stay. There's nothing but bad memories there."

"I'm sleeping in Mom's old room."

"Oh, my God. You are?"

"Yeah. I'm spending time with my old life, looking at old journals and stuff. You're in there."

Gloria let out one long breath. "I don't even want to know." Grace imagined her sister rolling her eyes and shaking her head dismissively. "I'm sorry, but I can't dive into my sordid past right now. David's out of town. I have to make breakfast and take the kids to school. Lydia called in sick, so I have to open. And Mavis has to go to the vet today. I have a lot going on over here. Can I call you later?"

"That's okay. I know you have a lot to do. Just checking in."

"You sure? Well, call me if you need me. Promise?"

"Promise."

Grace covered her head with the blanket then peered out to look at the box of journals she'd set beside the bed. She rose and rifled through them until she found a cloth-covered red one. Inside, as she remembered, were the words she'd written the night her mom had died. The tears came, burning her eyes, clamping her throat, seizing her chest. She closed her eyes to the memory of that day.

February 12, 1970 --- the day my world was destroyed. Mom, how could you leave me? God, oh God, where are you?

15

February 12, 1970

*M*om's door was closed. No dinner was made or served. Dad's voice reverberated throughout the house, perturbed by the girl's bickering, niggling and nervous as a squirrel:

"Turn that record player down now. I told you to cease and desist."

"Make yourselves a sandwich. Make me one too. Your mother's resting."

"This is one of her worst headaches. We'll call the doctor tomorrow if it doesn't go away."

"Sometimes people throw up from pain. It's normal. Don't you worry."

It wasn't normal. Not unless a headache is caused by the end stages of a malignant inoperable cancer. Not unless a headache means waking up dead.

Gloria screamed, slamming the door and running down the ice-slick street in slippers and pajamas. Her father doubled over in the corner of the room, staring at his wife's blank face. Grace shook her mother and yelled at her.

"Stop it, Mom! It's not funny. Stop it!"

Her dad finally pulled her away. He shoved her out into the hall and locked the bedroom door. She ran to the kitchen and called the doctor's number written on a pad by the phone.

A woman's voice answered. "My mother's not waking up," Grace whispered into the receiver. "I don't know what to do. I don't know what to do."

She felt like a tree branch had whipped around in the wind and slapped her hard in the stomach. She couldn't breathe. She laid down on the cold linoleum floor, staring up at the ceiling and its downward pressing. Everything was falling, falling, and she was so scared. So scared. Dead Mother. No.

This terrible inexplicable thing, this couldn't be real. She must be sleeping. What kind of mother goes to bed and dies, doesn't give anybody any kind of warning, doesn't kiss her little girls goodbye? What kind of mother just dies?

A silent inward echoing scream filled her head and then nothing.

Mom, how could you leave me? God, oh God, where are you?

No answer, no mother, no God, no words, nothing.

16

race returned to sleep, the journal and its grief splayed open beside her. When she awoke at three o'clock, her head still throbbed, but the nausea had abated. She felt the same black pit in her stomach that had plagued her so many mornings.

Frankie had known the same emptiness. *It was like something got taken out of me,* he'd written, *like an organ or something.* Maybe someone who experienced this profound a loss can never be whole. She felt a wave of loving empathy for herself and Frankie and Gloria, every day walking through the world pitifully incomplete.

She pulled on a pair of jeans and walked downstairs. Her dad was sitting at the kitchen table, slurping a cup of instant coffee.

"Afternoon," she said, putting the kettle on to boil. "I think I'm going to take another box of stuff to St. Vincent de Paul. I found some of mom's shirts and pants and your old sweaters in the attic yesterday before we left for the restaurant. There was also a box of blankets and sheets. You wanna come?"

"I don't *think* so," he said, staring at the refrigerator door. "I can't be up and down all the time, you know. I'm not young anymore, and if you remember, I fell not too long ago. You run along."

Sympathy for her father welled up inside her. His loss, too, was profound. He'd been alone for twenty-seven years. His wife had been cruelly wrenched from him; all his hopes for a lifetime of living with and loving her mom had been dashed.

"What about dinner? Can I make you something when I get back?" She'd bought two fresh sacks of vegetables a couple of days ago. "I could make a salad or a stir-fry and defrost some chicken."

"Do you think I had somebody make dinner for me when you were living all the way on the west coast in California? Do you think I starved when you weren't living here and the refrigerator wasn't packed with your food?"

"No, Dad, I don't think you starved. I was just trying to be helpful."

"And you giving away all my things and everything that reminds me of your mother? Is that your idea of being helpful? Excuse me."

He stood up slowly, walked over to the freezer, and took out a frozen pot pie. "This is what I'm in the mood for this afternoon, and I am perfectly capable of making it myself."

His fingers struggled with the cardboard box. He opened the oven door and stuck the pie on the top rack. The chair creaked as he sat back down. Grace stood for a moment, watching yellow sunlight gleam through the leaves of the maple tree in the back yard. Her dad pushed his chair out again and turned the knob on the oven to 400 degrees.

Grace gathered the bags she'd set aside the day before and drove once again to St. Vincent de Paul Thrift Store. When she arrived, the clerk told her they had more than they could use but that the St. Laurence House of Hospitality on the Eastside was always asking for donations.

It was easy to find. She sat in the car out front as she studied the place.

St. Laurence had once been a fire station. Its brick façade formed a square arch over a mouth-like metal door. Three large windows on the second floor looked like eyes and a nose. The metal door had since been soldered shut and was painted with a once colorful mural of Jesus on the cross, floating in a cloudless sky, now gray and dingy. His muscular bare arms extended the width of the door, and his head was crowned with bloody thorns. His eyes looked benevolently at the cacophony of faces below, in all shades of skin tone, their eyes looking upward at Him.

St. Laurence had been welcomed by a neighborhood that had seen so much devastation. Riots had followed Martin Luther King's assassination in April 1968. Looting had forced many businesses to leave, and fires had left more than a few charred buildings too damaged to renovate. The Polish and Lithuanian inhabitants, whose stationery stores and shoe repair shops, butcheries and bakeries were once vibrant and vital, began moving to other neighborhoods in town or out to split level houses in the suburbs. When the businesses vanished, the city was deprived of tax revenue, and the government made no effort to revitalize the area. By the time St. Laurence House came along in 1970, the neighborhood was inhabited by folks too poor to move, most living hardscrabble lives cobbled together with under-the-table work, late-night low-wage work, or drug dealing.

Grace surveyed the block. After thirty years, the destitution of Fillmore Street had solidified. Markets were boarded up, ancient For Sale or Lease signs nailed to their front doors. At least half of the Puerto Rican eateries, Caribbean grocery stores, and hair salons with hand-painted signs were closed, and the rest looked like they were in danger of closing. The Tabernacle of the Living Water competed for shabbiness with the Holy Word Church of God in Christ across the street.

Disquiet filled her as she contemplated stepping out of the car and trudging with her stuffed bags up the walk. She remembered the day she'd first walked through its doors—the lightheaded feeling, a kind of swooning—as if she had found something that might help lift her out of the fog of her grief. The people had been so welcoming; the purpose of the place was so basic. For a moment, she felt a pulsing desire to comfort the young girl she was when she first entered this place. She wasn't sure if she was ready to see it again.

Grace struggled to carry two full paper bags and a stuffed plastic garbage bag down the side alley. She followed the sign on which someone had etched an arrow and the words *Donation's This Way* with a ballpoint pen.

A young man with dreadlocks and an older sunburned woman with stringy hair huddled against each other in the alley. Their heads were bent over a stack of creased photographs.

"That's my baby," the woman said to the man. Grace had to step around them to continue. They didn't seem to notice her.

"She's a cutie," the man whispered. "Just like her mama." He puckered up his chapped brown lips and planted them on her pink cheek.

The woman giggled then whimpered. "I miss my baby."

Grace averted her gaze and sidestepped their intimate encounter. She rang the bell with her elbow and waited. A tall, slender man opened the door, took the bags from her arms, and said, "Thank you. God bless you." He turned to go back in.

"Um, can I, uh, ask you something?" Grace stammered to the man's back.

What was she doing here? What did she think this place could offer her anymore, other than a reminder of her own loss and how needy and naïve she'd once been? The transcendence she'd experienced here had since proved elusive.

He turned around. "Yes, ma'am?"

"Um…" Her heart raced. "Do you need workers or volunteers or anything?"

The man smiled, displaying a whole top left side of missing teeth. "Of course," he said. "Come any afternoon between four and five and sign up. We needs people to pick up donations of food, do shifts to cook, clean up after dinner, serve food, mop. You know, that kinda thing."

He put the bags down and reached out a calloused hand to shake hers.

"Name's Alvin. I used to live in the streets, but now I live and work here. Me and Father Luke and Sister Genevieve, we live here and runs the place. I'm in charge of volunteers. We always needs volunteers."

"Well, great," Grace said, offering a hesitant smile. "I used to volunteer here a long time ago."

"Okay, then. God bless."

Now she'd done it. A mixture of curious excitement and trepidation danced in her stomach. She retraced her steps to the car, stepping gingerly around the murmuring couple, and drove to a deli in the more prosperous Elmwood Avenue area. She bought a salad and sat in her car to eat before returning home to her dad.

He was asleep in his clothes, sprawled on top of the blankets on his bed. She turned off the stove and the bright overhead lights and locked the doors before settling herself in her room. It was only six-thirty, but she looked forward to being in bed, encircled by adolescent journals.

Grace had spent most of her adult life locking away unpleasant thoughts. Memories would sneak into her consciousness of their own accord, but she practiced pressing them away until it became a hard-wired habit.

But now she wondered if it might be time to tiptoe back into her past, her story. Ever since she'd lost her mother and her baby, she'd worked hard at not revisiting all those desperate feelings and unmet needs. Ever since she'd renounced her religion. No, that was too strong a word, too deliberate. Since she'd *lost* her religion, since it fell like a gold ring into a lagoon, she had given up hope for ever finding it again.

Now here she was, tentatively entering the murky water. But maybe that was why she was here. She would revisit St. Laurence Hospitality House. She would read all her journals. She could do this. She wanted to do this. She was ready to scour the bottom and see what she could dig up. She stayed up till midnight reading and reeling with memories.

Grace woke up early the next day and continued to clean and pack with her dad. After his afternoon nap, he shuffled into the kitchen and jammed another frozen pot pie in the oven.

It seemed to her like permission. After a long day of working together, he appeared to want to be alone. She told her dad she'd be back in a few hours and left him alone at the kitchen table with his crossword puzzle.

As Grace drove away from the landscaped perfection of the green suburb, she felt relieved. They'd finally packed up everything, and her dad was set to sign the papers since they'd easily sold the place to a young couple with twin toddlers eager to move in. She'd begun to fantasize finding her own apartment and volunteering at St. Laurence.

She drove south through the suburbs and the neighborhoods hugging the Elmwood strip, then meandered toward the west side, once known for its Italian restaurants and bowling halls. She parked the car and put as many quarters in the meter as it would take. She strolled down Niagara Street in the hot sun, sweat dribbling down her back.

She watched her wilted reflection in the windows of White Castle, Big Money's Grocery and Cigarettes, the Bodega Borinqueña, and the Salvation Army Thrift Store.-Her red hair was frizzy and wild in the humid sun. *Puff Ball, Lollipop, Frizz Head, Dandelion*: she remembered all the names Gloria had called her whenever her hair poofed out of control, usually accompanied by a poke or a bruising pinch. Almost every thought of Gloria was tainted by a memory of mild abuse.

She wandered the side streets for over an hour. Cars cluttered the curbs. Toys were overturned in lawns. She spotted a yellow sign on a corner. *4 rent 2 BR 1 Bath $500/mo util incl. 234 Jersey Street.* If she were frugal, she could live for at least six months without working on the thousand she'd saved and the $5,000 her dad generously gave her after the sale of the house and car.

She walked up the sidewalk to the front of a two-story, three-apartment complex. A short walkway led to two entrances. Both doors were painted red.

"Excuse me."

The middle-aged man clipping the bushes that separated the house from the peeling one next door straightened his shoulders and turned around. Grace studied his broad smile, the Grateful Dead t-shirt draping his brawny frame, and the dirty Buffalo Bills cap on his head of sandy brown hair.

"I'm interested in seeing the apartment. Do you know who I should talk to?"

"Sure," he said, setting down the clippers and wiping his hands on his jeans. "This is my building. Let me show you what we've got."

She followed him through the red door labeled Apartment C.

"I just painted it," he said, stroking the white wall in the small, empty living room. "And it's clean. The neighbors are friendly. Really sweet."

He showed her the newly tiled blue bathroom with its footed tub and pink striped shower curtain and the cheerful and compact kitchen. The walls and cabinets were painted yellow.

She felt a small thrill when she saw the spacious bedroom and the smaller room at the back of the house. She could buy a futon for the big room and use the smaller one for an office. It could be a place where she could think, maybe write or even paint. Maybe it would be her yoga room. For a minute, she imagined herself as an artist, working only on what inspired her and only when she wanted—at least until her cash ran out.

"Well," the man said. "What do you think?"

"It's pretty," Grace answered. "It's like a gem."

"I'm Brian," he said, reaching out his hand to grab hers. It was warm and strong. "I live next door. I take good care of this place and my other properties. I'm around most of the time if you need anything." He seemed sure of himself but in a nice way. "You can move in whenever you're ready. I'll help carry your furniture in if you want."

The summer sun painted a square in the middle of the shiny wood floor. Grace breathed in the lemony scent of mopped floors and the faint hint of new paint. Starting fresh in this clean, uncluttered place might be just the remedy for whatever afflicted her.

"I'll take it," she said.

Grace stopped at a payphone on the corner. In what she at once recognized as a masochistic move, she dialed Gloria at the café.

"I've found a house in town. The owner says I can move in immediately."

"You," Gloria responded, "are certifiably nuts."

Grace drove back to St. Laurence House. Alvin answered the door and led her to the chapel.

85

She answered Alvin's questions about her intentions. She had worked at St. Laurence a long time ago and wanted to help out, she said, because she thought they were doing important work. Said she liked helping people and she'd been a teacher.

Most of her emotions went unexpressed: that she felt shy, that she was curious about God and Jesus and the saints and how they figured into the lifeblood of this place, that she wondered if there was any way to re-experience the singular joy she'd found here before it all turned sour.

He showed her around the kitchen and introduced her to the other volunteers. The place was abuzz. The volunteers and community members moved quickly around the oversized kitchen, cutting piles of vegetables and laying out stacks of white bread on trays. Her eyes traveled over the woman stirring white rice in an enormous pot and the man opening can after can of beans.

"Welcome and blessings to Grace!" Alvin shouted, and two dozen eyes looked up and welcomed her. Then Alvin directed her in an authoritative voice to slice a small mountain of carrots.

She snuck glances at the kitchen crew as she chopped. When she was a young woman, the volunteers were youthful and playful and spirited; this group was serious and much older.

She had confessed in her interview that she wasn't Catholic. Alvin said it didn't matter. "We all God's children serving God's children," he said, but she knew she wasn't there for pure intentions. She was an interloper. She felt a little giddy at the prospect of lying in bed later that night, comparing her present impressions with the musings in her teenage journal.

When the food was prepared and the pots set to soak in the sink, the metal trays filled with rice and cooked vegetables and beans and ground meat, and the bowls stuffed with cut up lettuce and wilted cucumber slices, the team of choppers stood in a circle and bent their heads to pray.

"Let's make it official, there, Father," called a short, sweaty man wearing a Peace in the Middle East T-shirt.

"Yeah, Father Luke, come bless this mess!" Alvin yelled over his shoulder.

Father Luke entered the kitchen laughing. He broke into the circle to hold the hands of a grinning short-haired woman and a tired-looking, heavyset man. Grace smiled to herself as she remembered Father Luke. He was the young priest she'd met when she first volunteered here. She was surprised to see him still here after all this time. He was more full-bellied and bearded, and his brown hair had gone white. He was probably sixty by now. She wondered if he remembered her.

Everyone bowed their heads as he began to pray. "Father God, we thank you for this opportunity to give back, to share our joy in you with your people. Thank you for living among us in the lives of the workers and the guests. Mother God, bless our loud friend Alvin and the ever-patient Sister Genevieve. And welcome to our new volunteers, Nina and Grace. Lord Jesus Christ, bless and protect them. And yes, bless this mess."

There was a murmur of "Amens" all around.

Isn't life interesting, Grace thought, and shook her head. That life was interesting was a thought that hadn't occurred to her in a very long time. The workers released their hands and rushed to bring the steaming trays out to the dining hall. As soon as a volunteer opened the door, a haggard collection of folks filed in, some talking loud, some mumbling.

Grace stood for two hours ladling out food to the crowd then worked for another hour scrubbing the kitchen and straightening tables and chairs. She drove home as the sun set over the city, feeling both exhausted and happy.

17

1970 - 1972

During the end of Grace's sophomore year, then throughout the long, lonely, numb slog as a junior and senior, she attended Mass with her dad every Wednesday morning at six and every Sunday morning at nine. She found consolation sitting in the pews at St. Mary's Cathedral. The wooden pews were cold and uncomfortable, but it seemed right, even in this small way, to suffer in a house built to glorify God.

She felt seized by beauty. The sun shone through the stained-glass portraits of the saints in rays of yellow, blue, and green. Votive candles in red glass holders shivered and shimmered. She loved the pungent puffs of musky incense, the otherworldly voices of the choir wafting overhead like birdsong, the comforting repetition of the Creed. Sitting in that pew made her feel part of something bigger than her insignificant teenage self.

She waited through the hymns and the sermon for the Eucharist. She yearned to walk to the front of the church with an open heart and receive the Body of Christ. She was always hungry from fasting. She longed to open her mouth, hands folded in front of her and to receive the tiny white wafer of spiritual sustenance on her tongue. She knew that Jesus' body and blood were proof that she was nothing, but through the sacrifice of the Mass someone as unworthy as she was could be brought into grace.

Lord, I am not worthy to receive you. Only say the Word and I shall be healed.

After she returned to the pew, she nestled her head in her open hands and prayed with words of Thomas a Kempis, whose admonishments she had copied over and over in her sketchpad. Learn to obey, you who are only dust! You earthen clay, learn to be humble and place yourself at everyone's feet! Learn to crush thy passions, and to yield thyself in all subjection.

She and her dad were making their way together, navigating their rickety boat through the turbulent waters of loss. Neither of them steering, just praying they wouldn't capsize as the waves slapped the sides. The shore looked so far away. Her father never mentioned his wife's death, but Grace could hear his muffled sobbing in the middle of the night. It surprised her that she sometimes missed her sister who had raged through her last remaining months of school, skipped her graduation, packed in a huff, and drove off to Denver.

Her dad went to work early every day, leaving her to her morning Bible reading and her regimented breakfasts. She pushed herself through her high school days, eating next to nothing, not allowing herself to think about much besides Jesus and how she needed to behave to glorify him. She volunteered at the tutoring program downtown or at the Association for Retarded Children on Delaware Avenue after school, came home late, and made simple meals her father liked. Macaroni and cheese, spaghetti with sauce from a jar, franks and beans.

After dinner, she would finish her homework at the kitchen table while her dad worked on the papers he'd brought home from his job at American Axle Corp., listened to the Glenn Miller Band on the stereo, or read the National Review.

Some nights they watched William F. Buckley on Firing Line. Grace felt an inarticulate frustration watching Buckley's attempts to pigeonhole Huey Newton or condescend to Michael Harrington, whose ideas about sharing the wealth sounded pretty Christian to her. Her dad felt the exact reverse. He would pound his fist on the armrest when a guest argued with Buckley or slap his knee and say "Yes!" at Buckley's rebuttal.

Occasionally, her dad asked her how school was going and, regardless of what was happening, she always answered, "Fine."

No matter that she always sat with the same boring girls at lunch, the ones everybody called eggheads, who talked about The Young and the Restless and homework and cute boys they'd never talk to. They wore their sweaters buttoned up to their necks, hair pulled back in barrettes, plaid skirts over their bare knees. Grace thought they were insipid—her new favorite word, thanks to Buckley. She wore her curly hair long without barrettes and donned bell-bottomed hip-huggers. She was a little too pretty and not quite smart enough to sit with them, but she certainly wasn't as attractive or as dumb as the popular girls or as loud and out there as the freaks who smoked on the grate behind the cafeteria.

Nobody was into Jesus and The Way that she knew of, and she certainly wasn't going to talk to anybody about it; she couldn't bear to be laughed at for something that important. Nobody else knew or dared to ask what it is like to be motherless.

Instead, she just sat with them, drinking juice, praying that the hunger she felt at this hour would melt away and that she'd make it through lunch, through Chemistry and Chorus, through her hour of afterschool volunteering, without passing out.

She cried herself to sleep almost every night, visited by unbidden memories of her mother kissing her goodnight as she curled under the sheets. Before sleep each night, she recounted her day to her mother. She wrote questions for her mother in her journal, questions about all the things she never got to ask.

She never asked her father these questions. Even if the cutest boy in art class looked at her contour drawing of a woman and teased her that it looked sexy, rubbing his arm against hers as he said it. Even if Geometry class was so dull she fell asleep, and the teacher woke her by slapping a ruler on her desk. No matter if they were learning about the Reformation in AP Euro and she found Martin Luther inspiring.

"Fine" seemed to be an adequate answer, and he never pressed her on it. He routinely said, "Good, good," and shared a joke he'd heard that day.

Their quiet routine was altered when she told him she read in the paper about St. Laurence Hospitality House. She told him she wanted to help. She could take the bus on Tuesdays and Thursdays to the refurbished fire station on Fillmore where the Catholic Church had opened a homeless shelter.

If it worried him that she'd be taking the bus home at nine o'clock in the dark by herself, he didn't say. If he wondered how she spent her time in that grubby old building two nights out of every week during the last two years of high school, on nippy fall evenings, during biting winter storms, in the sparkly green light of spring, he never asked.

18

"Good morning, Father." Grace found Father Luke in the dining room, sweeping the floor after the morning meal. "How are you?"

"Feeling fabulous," he said. "Best day of my life."

She laughed. "Is that right?"

"Better than yesterday but not as marvelous as tomorrow."

She was beginning to get used to the exuberance of the intriguing priest and his effusive friendliness with all the volunteers and guests.

"What do you need me to do today?"

He beamed. "Why don't you do what you do best? Serve coffee and mingle."

After she moved into her Jersey Street apartment, Grace started volunteering regularly at St. Laurence. Some days she assisted Sister Genevieve, the congenial gray-haired nun who busied herself in the women's dorm and the supply room most of the day. Other mornings she helped Alvin unload boxes or organize donations or worked alone scouring toilets and rinsing pots. Occasionally she and Alvin played Crazy Eights with regular residents like Charlie and Mr. Anderson.

She quickly got over her initial shyness and unease. It had been so easy to start working here. She was glad to have such a kind-hearted group to be part of and pleased she had something valuable to do. She felt a bit guilty about that fact that that she could live for a little while, for the first time in her life, without a paying job thanks to her dad's gift. But the thought made her dizzy with happiness at the same time.

Four new overnight guests slumped in chairs in the sitting room. One man snored, three grungy plastic bags in his arms. Another man with creased and sunburned skin pulled crumpled papers out of a grimy backpack, flattened them, then pushed them back in, cursing and mumbling. An older woman looked up at the ceiling and muttered to herself while a skeletal young man with long, tangled black hair played *Let it Be* on the out-of-tune piano. From the looks of it, the guests hanging around today were deeply ensconced in their private worlds.

But Father Luke had asked her to mingle.

"Okay, then," she said and made her way to the folding table, which was cluttered with a coffee maker, sugar, creamer, and stacks of Styrofoam cups. When she was done straightening up, she wandered through the old firehouse, revisiting the rooms that had drawn her in so many years ago.

The dining room, empty now, was tranquil and clean. A huge homemade crucifix had been nailed high on one wall. Under it, a mural depicting St. Francis was faded and in need of retouching. The saint's arm was outstretched, and a bluebird was sitting on his hand. A disproportionately small lion, deer, and lamb were huddled at his feet. A sheet of loose-leaf paper had been taped near the saint's elongated arm, a quote penned across it: *When I give food to the poor, they call me a saint. When I ask why the poor have no food, they call me a communist. — Dom Helder Camera.*

On another wall, in simple silver frames under the painted gold title "Martyrs," hung portraits of six Jesuit priests and their two housekeepers, all killed by deaths squads in El Salvador in 1989. Beside the portraits of the priests was a poster of Archbishop Oscar Romero. Under those hung framed photos of Ita Ford, Maura Clark, Dorothy Kazel, and Jean Donovan, nuns raped and killed on a remote road near San Salvador.

A bookshelf in the corner was stuffed with tattered copies of religious and political books, including Dorothy Day's autobiography *The Long Loneliness, Easy Essays* by Peter Maurin, Martin Buber's *I and Thou*, Gandhi's autobiography, and a stack of old Catholic Worker newspapers. A poster of Martin Luther King, his head heavy on his fist, was fixed above the bookshelf along with the quote: *We must learn to live together as brothers or perish together as fools.* Next to it, Eugene Debs stared down at her, a convict's number around his neck. *While there is a lower class, I am in it. While there is a criminal element, I am of it. While there is a soul in prison, I am not free.*

She studied another fading poster, its tape dried and crumbling, threatening to fall off the wall. It depicted Gustavo Gutierrez, the founder of Liberation Theology, in front of a sea of faces. His words were displayed in a circle around the edge: *Two-thirds of humanity live in poverty so profound it can only be called death. As humans and as Christians, we should express solidarity with the poor and try to change their situation.*

She wandered through the whole house again, following the tinkling of the piano keys back to the sitting room. When Father Luke entered, she was on the sofa, eyes closed and head back, listening to the melodic chords.

"Grace, may I ask you something?" the priest said, looking at her while filling a ceramic mug with hot coffee.

She sat up straight. "Of course."

"You are a writer. Isn't that right?"

She wasn't. But she had wanted to be. How did he know that?

"Well, sort of. A long time ago. But I haven't written anything in quite a while."

"Alvin tells me you're a journalist, and you've taught writing." What she hadn't told Alvin was that she took a few courses but never earned her journalism degree. She'd never published an article. What had she said in her initial interview?

"Well…I've taught poetry and essay writing to kids in middle school. But that doesn't make me a writer. Why do you ask?"

"I need us to get some publicity." He sat down heavily on the other side of the frayed old couch. "I want a story about us in *The Free Press*. You know, the weekly alternative paper? I've already asked them if they'd print it if we write it. It's been a long time since we received media attention. We're in dire straits financially. A story would do us good, bring in donations and cash."

"You could invite a reporter from the *Buffalo News*. I'm sure somebody would be interested in writing a story."

"Ah, but I want you," he said with a wink. "I remember you, by the way."

"You do?" Grace raised her eyebrows. She had decided to pretend she didn't remember him. She preferred to keep her memories, at least at this point, to herself. She was starting fresh after all.

"I remember you because you were the youngest volunteer we've ever had." Luke closed his eyes as if envisioning her at sixteen in her baggy sweaters and khaki pants, her hair long and unruly. "You were very devoted. How wonderful that you've decided to return."

A pot fell in the kitchen with a clang. "Jesus fucking Christ!" Alvin bellowed. "Good Lord! Praise God! I'm sorry! Forgive me!" he yelled even louder.

"It's okay, Alvin," Father Luke called into the kitchen. "Do you need some help?"

"A whole blessed pot of boiling water all over the goddamn floor!" Alvin responded. "But no problem. I got it. Apologies, Father."

"At least it was blessed water!" Father Luke said, looking at Grace, his eyes crinkled in a smile. "I love that Alvin."

"Me too," she said. "I'll do it. I'll definitely write about this place."

Father Luke, she had to admit to herself, intrigued her. She liked his thin white hair tied into a neat ponytail, his white-gray beard, his round glasses and pleasant pink face. She like the openhearted gladness he showed in putting his arms around the guests whose breath and clothes literally reeked. He reminded her of a bear, and the guests were his cubs.

Grace tried to work up the courage to invite Father Luke to meet her at the Java House to interview him about his history here. She wanted to get him away from the house, take him out of his element. She'd watched him in action for a month now, and he seemed *married* to the place. She fantasized a giant hand picking the roof up off the house and lifting him out.

She didn't even know if he was allowed time off or if he had any kind of social life. She knew he thrived on caffeine, and like all good Catholics, he probably drank wine. But she didn't know if he ever left the confines of the Hospitality House to venture out into the world of self-indulgence and pleasure-for-its-own-sake.

She would interview him first. Write a feature about him and his role there. Then write another article about the house and all its characters. The more she imagined it, the more excited she felt. She longed to sit in a quiet place and talk with him. She could taste it on the back of her tongue like too-strong, too-sweet coffee. She'd publish a series. Even if it was in a free alternative paper. She'd become a writer.

Grace went looking for Luke during her shift the next day.

"Do you ever get a night off, Father Luke?"

She would have loved to meet with him alone on a weekend evening. Friday and Saturday nights usually found her feeling sad and restless.

But Saturday night seemed like a strange time to interview a priest, and Friday nights were traditionally Free Bread and Soup Discussion Nights. Grace had attended once, her curiosity getting the better of her. While the weather was still good, community members, volunteers, students, and others would sit on the concrete slab behind the building under a string of Christmas lights, drink herbal tea, eat soup and fresh baked bread, and meet for what Peter Maurin, the Catholic Worker's co-founder, had called "clarification of thought."

They held a simple prayer service in the Father Bissonette Chapel then went outside to debate a topic related to some pressing social issue—the ongoing conflict in Israel and Palestine, the peace process in Northern Ireland, how to respond to the call for Clinton's impeachment, asylum for immigrants, "going green." The topics and times were written in blue on the dry erase board in the community room. A cross laden with a crown of thorns was drawn in red underneath. So Friday was out of the question.

"I have every Thursday night off to do as I please. Within bounds, of course," Father Luke said with a wink. "Why do you ask?"

"I thought maybe we could meet for a cup of coffee. I want to start the article by interviewing you about your work and the history of St. Laurence."

"Sounds illuminating. For you, that is," he said and laughed. "Except for the coffee part. I get plenty of high-octane fuel here thanks to the diesel you brew. I may need to imbibe something less stimulating."

"Such as?"

"Such as they offer at a quaint little tavern I know called Hooligan's. It's walking distance, just a few blocks away. I'll happily enlighten you with the history of the place."

"Great."

"But, before we do that, I have to ask a favor of you."

"Yes?"

"You've never attended Mass with us, have you?"

"No." In fact, she'd avoided it. She'd been invited many times by

Alvin and Genevieve and once or twice by the other volunteers. But never by Father Luke.

"Will you agree to attend Mass with us here this Sunday at ten a.m.? I'd like you to witness it. Then we can have a drink and talk the following Thursday."

She hadn't been to a Catholic Mass since Frankie died, and before that, since she'd lived in Buffalo as a teen. The mere thought of Catholic Mass brought up waves of unwanted feelings. But she knew it made sense that she should attend a Mass at St. Laurence if she was going to write a piece about it.

"It's been a while." She made herself smile. "Okay. Sure."

19

1970 - 1972

race learned to like the smell of the St. Laurence House of Hospitality. It was an earthy mixture of brewed coffee, ammonia, and sweat. Always sweat. The first few times she volunteered, the smell made her queasy. She would hold her breath as long as she could until the air burst out in a rush and she had to inhale through her mouth.

When she became aware of what she was doing, it embarrassed her, and she vowed to stop. She would get used to the pungent smell of people who live for days without bathing or deodorant and wrap themselves in layers of old, musty clothes to stay warm. And after a couple of months at St. Laurence, she noticed that it had finally happened. The smell was no longer offensive but familiar, almost welcoming. She imagined that even though she showered every morning, washed her hair, and wore clean underwear and fresh clothes, she belonged there. She was one of them.

At sixteen, she was the youngest volunteer. The college students who worked there took her in. She was around people who understood what it meant to be a Christian in the world, what it meant to give yourself over to something bigger than self.

They were funny and happy. They sat around on raggedy sofas, singing and playing guitar when they were done cleaning up the kitchen. They sang, "Dear Father, we need, we need, while we wait, while we may," from Godspell, and Suzanne *by Leonard Cohen. The music was sweet and soft, like a blanket of peace.*

"All good gifts around us are sent from Heaven above. So thank the Lord, thank the Lord, for all his love." Somebody would laugh at that this point and stand up and belt out, "I really want to thank you Lo-o-ord!"

Grace was enamored by their baggy pants and holey sweaters, their long hair, the way they debated about anarchism and corporate control and fighting the power, argued about how to live the life and expose the hypocrisy of the system. She never said much, just listened and absorbed their enthusiasm.

She loved Tina, who cooked donated meat for the homeless men because it was free and she didn't believe in wasting anything. But she never ate the stew herself because she was trying to live in harmony with the planet. She respected all God's creatures.

And Marcus, whose blue eyes beamed at her when she chopped onions and carrots. And young Father Luke, the priest who lived there and prayed with them. His laughter was unique, a gasping, a deep inhaling, as if joy entered through his mouth, opened up his broad chest, and settled into his heart.

20

The next day, Grace visited Cherry Lanes for the first time since her father moved in.

The sliding glass doors opened to a neat foyer. Generic landscape paintings in gold frames were hung every few feet on the walls, and artificial flowers had been arranged in bronze vases on the lacquered tables. She breathed slowly as she walked its hallways, cheerful with their maple leaf wallpaper and matching rust-colored carpet. Each of the other residents had a little shelf outside his or her door ornamented with stuffed animals, ceramic birds, baskets of plastic flowers, or dolls wearing crocheted dresses. These expressions of personality were a sweet reminder of the quiet lives behind the walls. This place was her father's fresh start, just like the townhouse was hers.

Now that he was moved in, she was determined to spend quality time with him for an hour or so each day, leaving her free to create her own life during the remaining hours. She was pleased with the arrangement and decided to pay better attention, to ask him about himself, to mine his memories as she rediscovered her own past. His stack of crumbling photo albums seemed like a good place to start.

They laughed as he showed her photos of himself in his Bishop Fallon High School days. His hair was slicked back, thick and glossy, and his eyes were bright. His uniform was cinched high around his waist.

"That was the year the school started its first football team. Here's one of me in my Fallon jersey and leather helmet."

"What position did you play?"

"Second string if you want to be nice to me. Bench warmer if you don't."

"You were a handsome young man." Grace slid closer. "Even if you weren't a star athlete."

"I don't know about that," he said, turning the page to a photo of him and three guys goofing around. Her dad had a clay flower pot on his head. "But we did have our fun."

In the next album, he stroked a faded photo of his young wife. Her knees were bent, her arms jutting out like bird's wings, and she had a baseball bat on her shoulder.

"Your mother was a beautiful lady. Do you know how we met?"

Grace knew, but she never tired of hearing it. In his mind, her mother would never languish miserably with headaches in her insomniac room. She wouldn't perish before her time. When he relived the moment in this photo, her mother was alive and healthy. She was still a first-rate hitter for the Buffalo Beauties, the first women's baseball team in the city, and he was an amateur photographer strolling through Delaware Park on the hunt for an original subject.

"Tell me."

"I'm sure I must have shared the story before."

"Maybe," Grace said. "Go ahead."

"Your mother was a looker. That hair in the sunlight. And her trim figure. I noticed her right away. Not that I was looking, mind you." He winked. "I was scouting out pretty flowers. I promise."

"Uh huh," Grace teased.

"But I came across the girls' baseball team, and I can assure you, I'd never seen anything like it. They were wearing the shortest little skirts! I watched them play for seven innings. By the time the game was over, your mother had hit two home runs. I was besotted. I asked if I could capture her image on film, and she said—I'll never forget this—she said, 'Capture me if you can.' From that moment on, I tried. Believe me, I tried."

Grace hoisted another heavy book onto his lap. "This one has wedding pictures in it," she said.

"Oh, dear." He opened the book and lifted a translucent sheet off the large black and white portrait on the first page. Her mom sat smiling, a fitted white dress exposing her smooth shoulders, hair crimped and styled. She was holding a bouquet of roses and baby's breath. Her father stood behind her in a suit and tie, sporting glasses and a thick swatch of neatly trimmed hair. His hand lay on her shoulder, and his face was lit up.

"The best day of my life," he said. "It still amazes me that she agreed to my proposal."

"What was your wedding like?" Grace asked. "I don't remember hearing any stories about it."

If Grace looked hard enough, she could see a hint of sadness in her mother's face. While her dad grinned directly at the camera, her mother looked slightly away.

"It was simple," he said. "We held it at St. Mary's downtown. Father Meissner officiated. My family came and some of our friends, you know."

Grace knew the outline of her mother's story. She had moved from Detroit to Buffalo in her mid-twenties to play baseball for the city and go to college. She studied part-time and worked as a department manager at Hengerer's downtown but then quit her job and dropped out of college when she decided to marry. But otherwise her mother's past was a blank book, a few sketches scribbled in pencil then erased.

"Do you have pictures of Mom as a child?" Grace asked. "Of her mother or father or life in Detroit?"

"She didn't bring anything with her when we got married. She kind of left her past behind." He coughed, straightened, and wriggled his hips away from hers. Restlessness seemed to shudder through his bones.

"What about Mom's family? What can you tell me about them?" Grace had learned very little about her grandparents. She wasn't even sure if she had aunts and uncles. The wedding album on their laps seemed like a mystical holy book that held impenetrable truths.

"It's a sad story," he said, patting the page and closing the old book. "They had a falling out. They didn't come to the wedding. I never met them." He pulled out a hanky and wiped his nose. "That's enough for one day. Let's go get some lunch. I'm starved."

While he walked to the bathroom to run a wet comb through his puff of hair, Grace gazed through the picture window which overlooked Christ the Redeemer cemetery. A breeze shook the sturdy oaks shading the scattered headstones. The thought of waking up to a view of the graveyard frightened her, but she knew it was because her life felt unfinished. She hadn't accomplished anything worthwhile yet. Maybe by the time she turned eighty-five, she'd finally be able to say she'd *done* something and the thought of her imminent demise wouldn't be so daunting that she'd mind staring down the graves every day.

"Shall we?" her dad asked. She waited in the hallway as he fidgeted with the lock then slowed her pace to walk beside him down the hall and into the elevator.

"Did you hear about the important man who asked the lift operator to take him to the tenth floor?"

The elevator door opened, and Grace leaned against it as her dad shuffled in.

"When the lift reached the tenth floor, the elevator operator said, 'Here you are, my son.' The important man was quite upset. 'Why did you call me son?' he asked. 'I am not your son!'"

Grace turned to look at her father's animated face in anticipation of the punchline.

"'Well,' the elevator operator answered. 'I called you son because I brought you up.'"

Grace laughed. She looped her hand around her dad's elbow and gave it a little squeeze.

They decided to have lunch at the Village Gate Inn. Grace ordered a bowl of tomato soup and an iceberg lettuce salad. Her dad asked for a hamburger and French fries and coffee. With his first bite of the burger, a dollop of ketchup dripped onto his already stained shirt.

"I had a nice morning," he said. "Three of the fellows in the Cherry Lakes coffee klatch went to Bishop Fallon High School. We spent over an hour reminiscing. They call themselves the Rome Club and said I was welcome to become a member."

"How nice. Is it some sort of Catholic organization?"

"It stands for Retired Old Men Eating."

Grace grinned. "Dad, I'm glad you're making friends."

"I know you're probably thinking I told you so." He took another messy bite of burger then wiped his chin. "But one good hour a day isn't enough to change my mind. I still wish I hadn't moved."

Her face fell. "I'm sorry."

"You're always sorry!" he said, his voice getting high. "Don't be sorry! It's my life!"

She cut a chunk of the pale lettuce and dipped it in Italian dressing. "I don't know what to say."

"There's nothing to say. What's done is done. I'll be fine. I have my coffee klatch to look forward to every twenty-three hours." She kept quiet, afraid he would snap at any response she made. "I shouldn't complain. The first thing St. Peter is going to ask you when you get to the Pearly Gates is, 'Did you complain?'"

Grace had taken his oft-repeated wisdom to heart. Whenever she felt a nagging criticism creep into her brain, she'd give herself a mental slap. *Be positive, be grateful, be good.*

"Did you hear the story about the monks who took a vow of silence? They were only allowed to utter one sentence every ten years. After the first decade, one monk said to the abbot, 'This bed is hard.' Ten years later, he said, 'The food is bad.' Another ten years went by, and the monk went to the abbot and said, 'I quit.' The abbot shook his head and said, 'I'm not surprised. You've been complaining ever since you got here.'"

Grace smirked and took a gulp of her coffee. "Very good," she said. "I get the message."

"Did I tell you about when we were kids and used to sing the old hymn *Gladly the Cross I'd Bear?*

"Remind me."

"For the longest time, we thought it was about a cross-eyed bear named Gladly. And we joked about how strange it was that so many of the hymns were about a fellow named Ollie Louyah."

Grace appreciated her father's ability to make her laugh. She wanted to be less intense and worried all the time, but she didn't know how. She'd read an article that morning about a parish in Lansing, Michigan. She had decided when she finished reading it that this was the day to start talking with her dad about what was happening in the Church. She had promised herself never to forget Frankie and what happened to him.

"Dad, there's some disturbing stuff going on in the Church now, right? I read about a priest named Father DeLaw in the paper today. He abused a sixteen-year-old boy twenty years ago. His mother reported it to the bishop. The bishop told her he'd handle it, but he never did! He never did anything! The priest was moved to another city and appointed as the pastor of a different church. He abused two more boys there. This time the bishop is sending him off to live in seclusion. And he was never arrested! Don't you think that's awful?"

Now she'd done it. Would he bang his fist on the table in public?

Her father had been looking down at his burger while she talked. He finished chewing and patted his mouth with a greasy napkin. He leaned in and said in a firm voice, "You know better than to believe everything you read, young lady."

"Dad, I know someone who was abused like this. One of my students."

"Well, you can never be sure in these cases. People make things up for complicated psychological reasons. People lie. Especially people who are out to get the Church. Don't let yourself get too involved in this just because it's the latest obsession of the liberal media. You have to be careful."

He motioned to the waitress. She came over and chatted with them about the various sugar-free dessert offerings they had. Neither father nor daughter spoke as she poured more coffee, cleared the table, and brought their desserts—pie with ice cream for him and rice pudding for Grace. They remained quiet until they finished.

"Did I tell you about the horseshoe tournament next Saturday?" her dad asked. "Why don't you come? All the fellas will be there. It ought to be fun."

"Sure," Grace sighed.

"Wonderful! Oh, and I read a fascinating article today," he remarked while counting out cash to pay the bill. "It seems the Queen is a secret Catholic. Now *that's* interesting."

Two days later, as Grace's dad worked in a ledger on his desk and Grace rested on the sofa, President Bill Clinton's image appeared on the small TV in the living room. Grace opened her eyes to watch the President deliver his speech.

"What I did was inappropriate. In fact, it was wrong," he said. "I misled people, and I deeply regret that."

"Imagine." Grace eyed her dad. He grimaced at the television screen.

"Jeopardizing his position in that way. Taking advantage of his power and authority. Preying on someone so young. And in the Oval Office, of all places. Then covering it up."

"I agree," Grace said. The Monica Lewinsky scandal, and Clinton's testimony before the grand jury, had dominated the news for days. "Abuse of authority, right? Someone who takes advantage of a young person then thinks he's above the law. Right, Dad?"

She swung her feet around and swerved in his direction.

"Though we have to remember," her dad said, his eyes back on his financial records. "It takes two to tango. She's obviously a licentious young lady, a seductress. She has to take her share of the blame."

Grace face felt flushed. His comments triggered a wave of frustration. What had she done to respond to Frankie's abuse? And the little effort she had made—what good did it do?

Her first act after unpacking in her new home had been to write three letters: one to the police department in LA, one to Holy Mother of God Cathedral, and one to the Priest Abuse Information Network. She had asked them to remove her dad's address from their mailing list and use her new Jersey Street address instead. Three weeks later, the LAPD sent a form letter informing her that in light of the date of the charges and the statute of limitations, the Frankie Morales case was impossible to pursue.

She received nothing from the Diocese. No letter. No packet. The President of the United States was being held accountable for sexual misdeeds, but apparently, the Catholic Church didn't have to obey laws forbidding the abuse of children.

"Dad, are you serious?"

"I couldn't be more serious if the house was on fire and I was trying to save your life."

He looked up at the clock. "It's time," he said. He left his desk and ambled over to the sofa. Grace scooted over to make room. "Now let's watch something more edifying, shall we?" He picked the remote up off the coffee table and scrolled through the channels.

He had asked her to stay for the afternoon and watch the World Youth Day ceremonies on TV, so she put her feet on the coffee table and settled in. One after another, groups of young people from Italy, Thailand, Brazil,

Namibia, and Poland came on stage and performed songs and dances of praise to God.

When it was time for Pope John Paul II to speak to the assembled throng, her father's attention was rapt. The pontiff's message was one of hope in the midst of sin, of unity in a world bent on divisiveness, and of the importance of abstinence and moral rectitude in a culture of temptation. Of course, there were no references to the priest abuse scandals or birth control or abortion. His speech was uplifting and vague.

When the program was over, her father's eyes were filled with tears.

"There is hope," he said, his voice catching. "The Holy Father will have an influence on all those children, and they will change the world. There is hope."

"Oh, Dad, please!" Grace pressed the mute button on the remote. "How can you trust them? What about the Church's secret underbelly?"

"And what is that supposed to mean?"

"The Pope hasn't done anything about the priest abuse scandal! And here he is admonishing the world to protect and care for the children! It's hypocritical, Dad!"

"How *dare* you? The Pope has said that molestation is wrong and has done all he could to stop it. And the amount that is reported in the news is exaggerated. It has to be."

"I doubt it! If anything, it's underreported because victims are afraid."

"Victims! The Church is a victim! It's a victim of the liberal press. I've read all about it. They distort and scandalize the Church." A cough gathered like pebbles at the back of his throat. "The secular press uses hate to sell papers. If you don't believe it, read *First Things*. You should read it." He nodded toward a stack of conservative Catholic periodicals piled up next to the TV. "Since I was a child, I have been taught to 'safeguard the faith.' And that's what I intend to do. And that's how we raised you."

"Regardless?" she challenged.

"Yes," he said, his voice raspy. "Regardless of the attempts of the world to lead us astray, we must protect Our Lord's Church. By good reading, by study of the gospels, by avoiding fallacious teachings. Otherwise, we get tossed and turned and confused."

"Dad, we've been told a lot of lies by the Church."

He crossed his arms. "Oh, we have, have we?"

"And besides, forty percent of priests are gay! Probably more. In a church that denounces homosexuality as if it's the plague. How duplicitous is that?"

"Where did you hear that?"

"I read it in the New York Times."

"Well, that explains it." He pointed at her. "That is exactly my point. Beware of the man with one book. You need to do your research!" His bony finger jabbed the air. "From a reputable source, that is."

It was no use, but she persisted. "And who do they think they are, anyway? Men who know nothing about children, who don't have families, who don't believe in sex…telling everybody how to raise their kids? That's about as convoluted as it gets!"

Her father turned away and stared at the wall. She took a deep breath and made an attempt to soften her tone. "Dad, all I'm saying is that there are two Churches. St. Vincent de Paul, soup kitchens, Mother Theresa, Dorothy Day. I love that part. I absolutely adore St. Laurence House and what they do. You remember the priest in charge, Father Luke? He's wonderful. And I like the incense and the beauty of the Mass. I do. Everything they said for World Youth Day was nice, but there's also the crime and cover-up side. You have to admit that."

"I don't have to admit anything." He pulled himself forward as if he was ready to eject himself from the sofa. Spit had gathered at the corners of his mouth. "There is as much or more so-called sexual abuse of children in the Protestant church and in public schools, for Heaven's sake, as there is in Our Lord's Church. I'll bet they left that part out of your article in the New York Crimes."

Grace got up and gathered her things. "I'm glad I came over, Dad. And I'm sorry this topic is so hard."

"I'm happy every time you come over. I wanted you to watch World Youth Day. Now, take a *First Things* with you. Promise me you'll read the other side."

"I will," she lied. "And I'll see you soon." She grabbed an issue from the top of the pile of magazines then leaned over and gave him a hug and a kiss on the forehead. "I love you in spite of yourself."

"I love you in spite of yourself too." He grinned. "And don't forget about the horseshoe tournament."

Grace left the apartment feeling a tumble of emotions. Her father was so childish and obstinate sometimes. How dare he tell her to read more, to "beware the man with one book?" How dare he tell her to ignore all the evidence against the Church and to stuff the truth away from the light of day in order to "safeguard the faith?"

A groan rose in her throat at his stubbornness. Then she remembered the delight in his eyes as he watched the international children's groups singing about love and hope. He did have a good heart. He probably couldn't afford to let himself see all the failings of his cherished Church because if he did, one by one the precepts he lived by would crumble.

Grace had adored her dad when she was a child. She had thought he was the funniest, warmest man to walk the earth. By the time she pulled in her driveway, her head was full of childhood memories. Splashing in the waves on trips to the ocean. Making cakes for him in her Easy Bake oven and serving him milk in a wine glass. Beating him at Monopoly. She treasured the rhyming notes he left in her sandwiches: *To a wonderful student at school. To a great swimmer in the pool. Awake or asleep, I love you a heap, because, dear Grace, you're cool.*

She rested her head back on the car seat and stared out the window at the trees. Her mother was subdued much of the time, working hard to keep the place in order. By contrast, her dad had been playful, telling his wife to "let them have fun" when she tried to get the girls to clean up or quiet down.

She closed her eyes and visualized the cartoon doodles he made of her and her sister; she could hear his voice when he laid in bed with them at night playing word games and telling silly jokes. When she was light enough to wrap her legs around his waist, monkey-like, he would carry her up to her room. He'd sing *You are my sunshine* in a soothing baritone, her head floppy against his strong shoulder, until she fell asleep. From him, she learned what being smitten felt like, a feeling she had sought in lots of wrong places ever since.

Early Saturday morning, Grace settled herself into a lawn chair on the hill of dewy grass facing Cherry Lakes' main building. She watched as the older gentlemen wandered toward the horseshoe field and the ladies busied themselves at the refreshment table. Her dad fidgeted inside his pocket for a Rolaid and popped it in his mouth.

He dabbed the moisture on his forehead with an embroidered hanky. It was the birthday gift she'd made for him when she was nine. *Best dad in the world WJS* was stitched in green and blue. She'd sewn little yellow flowers around his initials. It had taken her days. She'd wanted it to be perfect, and he had been pleased. How kind of him to still use it and remind her subtly of their long life together. She knew this man so well yet hardly at all.

"All right, gentlemen. Let's begin the match!" a disembodied voice boomed over the PA system. "Team One, representing Bishop Fallon."

Her father grinned and pushed his glasses up his nose. He waved at Grace. "Here we go!"

Keeping one hand on a card table for support, he propelled the heavy horseshoe into the morning air. It landed with a thump at least ten feet from the red metal rod poking out of the lawn. Her father's laugh blasted like a bugle's call from his open mouth. He smacked his teammate's back.

"Now, that's the way you play!"

Grace watched as her father walked toward the contestant's sitting area, looking happy. He breathed heavily and waved at her from across the lawn.

21

Sunday morning, before leaving for Mass at the Hospitality House, Grace lay face down on the hardwood floor of her extra room. She pulled herself up into the Sphinx pose, then the Cobra, stretching her tight shoulders and neck. She stared up at the ceiling. Maybe yoga could help her center herself.

She used to enjoy yoga. She had attended a regular class with Jake in San Francisco. But after everything that happened between Jake and their yoga instructor, she had lost all motivation. Now it was time to reclaim it for herself.

She maneuvered her body into plank position then stuck her butt up in the air and pressed herself into Downward Facing Dog. *A perfect nickname for Jake.* She couldn't remember the next step in the Sun Salutation. She knew there was a tadasana in there somewhere but couldn't remember where. She didn't care. It felt good, after so many months of resistance, to stretch and pull her muscles. She inhaled and exhaled slowly, in rhythm.

Jake was the one who taught her to re-experience her body and its life-giving breath. He had convinced her their spiritual connection was rare. He entranced her with stories of Sadhguru, the visionary whose mission began when he had his first encounter with the amorphous divine.

How had she not seen it coming? It amazed her that she had let a man have so much power over her inner life that she was blind to his infidelity. She never questioned why he left for yoga class an hour early. "Deep preparation," he called it. She didn't stop to wonder why he insisted on attending monthly retreats with the lithe Linda.

It annoyed her that she still missed his neck kisses, his muscular hands on her back, the garlic soup they cooked when he was fasting. She even found herself missing the intensity of his late night, naked, pot-filled reveries about the day Sadhguru sat on a rock with his eyes open and became aware that he was no longer in his body but connected to trees, birds, and air, and his spirit was formless and interwoven with all other beings.

It exasperated her that she hadn't stopped thinking about Jake and what he was doing with Linda. She stood in Tree pose for a few seconds, struggling to balance on her left leg without her right leg slipping to the floor. She stood in Warrior pose, one foot facing forward, the other firmly planted, arms strong and outstretched. Then she balled her fingers into a fist and threw a jab and a kick, imagining Jake at the receiving end. From now on, she would use this private little chamber to rally her spiritual and physical forces. From now on, this would be her Warrior Room.

When Grace arrived at St. Laurence, the folding tables were pushed to the outside walls of the dining room and decorated with vases of fresh-cut flowers. Regular residents, street people she'd never seen, staff, and volunteers sat in rows of metal chairs, chatting as they waited for Mass to begin. She found an empty chair in the back near the portraits of the Martyrs on the wall.

The bone-thin, cinnamon-colored young man with the straight black hair who'd played the piano the other day stood in front of the group. "Good morning to everyone. I would like to introduce myself. I am Tall Tree."

The crowd grew still as he began to play a sweet, breathy tune on a flute. When he finished, he stood aside, and a tiny, pale woman limped up to the front, sat down on a plastic chair, and played a rough version of *Day by Day* on a guitar. The listeners tried to sing along but had to stop and restart every time she struggled with a new chord. Father Luke stood up and hugged them both heartily when they were done. He wore an embroidered purple vestment, and his hair wasn't tied back in a ponytail as usual. It was combed out neat and thin and long on his shoulders.

"Dear Father, Mother God, we are so blessed!" he shouted. "Please join me in a song of praise for this glorious day that the Lord has made!"

Grace looked through the window above the crucifix. Glorious was not the word she would have chosen to describe the October sky, thick and sheepskin white. It was the cusp of the cloudy season when day upon day would be overcast and chilly.

111

"The next song is on the first page of your bulletin," he announced.

The crowd sang off-key:

"Praise for the singing

Praise for the morning

Praise for them springing

Fresh from the Word."

Grace might have sung this, one of her favorite hymns, to her baby, a daughter who would be twenty-five this year. She would be the mother of an adult daughter, maybe a grandmother, at this point, if she hadn't given her baby up for adoption. A different path through the woods would have opened into an unknown clearing. The urge to cry caught in her throat.

"Please stand for the prayer." A small woman wearing a huge green army jacket, her head bowed, stood in front and raised her hands.

"Oh, Lord," she said, her voice thin and wispy. "You have given everything in the world a place. No one can change what you have made. Everything that surrounds us was made by you. You are the Creator, the Lord of all."

"Thank you, Miss Lillian." Father Luke smiled at her. "In nomine patris, et filii, et spiritus sanctum." He tapped his forehead, his belly, his left shoulder, and then his right. "May the grace and peace of our Mother and Father God, the love of the Lord Jesus Christ, and the fellowship of the Holy Spirit be with you all."

The crowd murmured in unison, "And also with you."

Miss Lillian spoke again. "Now it's time for the penitentiary rite. It's on page two, um, of that paper you got in your hand."

The confessional prayer was pretty rough. Some of the congregation read along steadily, but most were too loud and off rhythm. "I confess to Almighty God, and to you, my brothers and sisters, that I have sinned through my own fault, in my thoughts and in my words, in what I have done and in what I have failed to do."

Alvin was sitting behind her. He started sniffling. Grace's father had often teared up at this part of the Mass.

Grace didn't know what to do with the concept of sin. She had dispensed with the notion of God's forgiveness long ago. She had come to see the stupid things she'd done over the years—the fornication that led to an unexpected pregnancy, letting go of a baby, her thoughtless comments, inconsiderate acts—as bad things, but weren't they more mistakes than sins? Her selfish actions often embarrassed her. They twisted around inside her for days and haunted her dreams. But were they *sins*?

She'd convinced herself a long time ago that the psychologically healthy thing to do was to learn from her mistakes—if possible—then move on. Not wallow.

But then again.

"Forgive yourself, and the rest will follow," Jake had often said, which at the time had seemed so wise. Once, when she'd mustered the courage to talk with him about something insensitive he'd done, he'd closed his eyes and said in a quiet voice, "The important thing, Grace, is that I have learned to forgive myself." She rolled her eyes at the memory.

"Oh, Lamb of God," a man's baritone sang deep and strong from the back of the room. Hot pinpricks of tears tingled behind Grace's eyes. She swallowed and blinked them back as the crowd echoed the refrain.

"You take away the sins of the world. Have mercy on us."

A man who'd been sitting cross-legged in the front stood up and turned around to the group. A piece of paper rustled in his hand. He held it up and read fast, the words tumbling out. "Father Mother God, your love for us passes all our...surpasses all our hopes and desires. Forgive us for all of our failings. Give us peace in our...peace in our hearts and help us work for peace in the...in the world. Give us courage and strength to fight the demons within us and the challenges without. We ask this through the Lord our Lord and Savior, Jesus Christ, who lives and rains *on us* now and forever."

He sighed. "Was that good?" he asked, fixing his eyes on Father Luke.

"Brilliant!" the priest bellowed. "I knew you could do it." He turned to the group. "Give Mr. Anderson a hand, everybody. Bravo!"

The crowd clapped, and Mr. Anderson smiled, displaying exactly three teeth, one north and two south. He bowed low from the waist and sat down in the front row.

Father Luke walked to the front of the room, spread his arms wide, and shouted, "Let us sing a song of praise and gratitude! Sing Alleluia!"

His loud singing was soon absorbed in a chorus of voices singing a joyful Alleluia. The singing at St. Mary's never sounded anything like this, so primal and earthy. This crowd didn't have much to be thankful for, but they were full of praise nonetheless.

For the first time since the Mass began, Grace started to sing. The stinging behind her eyes returned, her throat tightened, and a tear dripped down her cheek. *Oh, well,* she thought. *Oh, well.*

Grace didn't hear the gospel reading. She stared at the gray hair of the man in front of her and thought of her dad, who had taken her hand as a young child and led her into St. Mary's. He'd instructed her in the ways of holy water, dipping his index finger into the cool water in the pretty porcelain bowl, crouching beside her and making the sign of the cross, then showing her how to do the same.

She looked forward to the moment after Mass when they'd walk up to the rows of candles in front of the statue of the Virgin. She'd pull a long wooden stick out of a hill of sand, light it with the lead candle, and carefully carry the flame to another candle, adding to the shimmering sea of light that made Mary's face radiant. The more the candles glowed, the more it seemed that Mary was pleased, her hands held out and open.

"We are so happy you all are here!" Father Luke called out, this time from the back of the room. He'd slipped unnoticed around to the rear of the dining hall during the Gospel reading, and now his voice slid up her spine like a low rumble of thunder.

Father Luke preached as he ambled down the center aisle. "We are loved! Even when we suffer, even when we are hungry or lonely or living on the street, even when we are cold or sick or afraid, God asks us to remember that He loves us, He knows our deepest hearts, and He knows what we need. Today He has provided us with a community of caring and support. Look around you."

He made a wide gesture with his arms and turned his head to look at everyone.

"You are surrounded by friends and neighbors who love you. Through them, God makes Herself known to us. God's infinite caring makes itself known through the acts of others. We are called to love. Love calls to us. Just love. Not work, not service, not duty, not even charity or sacrifice or any of the things that we sometimes mistakenly think of as love. We are called to the simplest human response possible—to love.

"God loves us simply too. Remember Matthew 10:29: 'You can buy two sparrows for a penny, but not a single one of them falls to the ground without our Lord's consent. And as for you, even the hairs of your head have all been counted. Do not be afraid! You are worth much more than the sparrows!'

"Go into your day today with the confidence that comes from knowing you have a lot of love to receive and much to give, and that you are bolstered in the process of this transcendence by God's unwavering love.

"Please stand now," Father Luke said. "It's time for the profession of faith."

Grace listened to the Apostle's Creed as if for the first time.

"He came down from Heaven, was born of the Virgin Mary, and became man." Grace was tempted to smirk or snicker. She looked around, wondering if she might catch anyone else looking as cynical as she felt. "We believe in the resurrection of the body and life everlasting. Amen."

The resurrection of the body? Grace started to shake her head, then caught herself. What the hell is that? *Born of a Virgin?* Did people still believe that? She felt as if she'd fallen for a trick, letting herself get all weepy and nostalgic. She had allowed her sentimental heart to elbow aside her rational mind. She made a mental note to discuss the virgin business when she met with Father Luke on Thursday. And she wanted to confront him with the cover up of sexual abuse by priests. How would he respond to all the cruelty in his sacred Church? Why the need for the resurrection of the body?

"And now, the most important and joyous aspect of our time together in this holy place. My favorite part! I invite you all to join me as we celebrate the sacrifice made by our Lord and Savior Jesus Christ. Gentlemen and ladies—you know who you are—would you please help prepare us to receive the Body and Blood of Jesus?"

Genevieve entered the community room from the kitchen wearing a purple vestment like Luke's. The servers followed her bearing large trays covered with colorful linens. Each tray was piled high with torn pieces of homemade bread and tiny paper cups filled with grape juice. Father Luke and Sister Genevieve looked like gray-haired twins as they walked up and down the rows passing out the trays so the congregants could take a piece of bread and a cup. Grace didn't partake of the Eucharistic offering. She was here as a journalist, not a Christian, certainly not a Catholic. Yet she found herself again moved by the hushed intensity in the room.

"This wine is your blood, but for the sake of Alvin, Joey, Delia, Mr. Robinson, Jeffrey, Lucille, Maylene and Jeb"—Luke looked at each person as he said his or her name then winked—"we are imbibing metaphorical wine today. We don't want anybody getting drunk on anything but God's love this morning!"

Alvin said, "Amen."

Maylene raised her hands in the air.

Delia shouted, "Thank you, Father! I'm drunk on God's love!"

Father Luke lifted his cup high into the air as if toasting a bridal couple. In his other hand, he lifted a hunk of wheat bread.

"The Lord be with you!" he shouted.

"And also with you," the crowd returned.

Genevieve spoke next, her voice bright, full of emotion. "Lord, thank you for finding us worthy to receive you."

Grace felt the back of her throat close at the rewording of the prayer. How many times had she repeated the traditional refrain, "Lord, I am *not* worthy to receive you"? How many times had her father squeezed his eyes closed, beating his chest with his fist, while he chastised himself?

"Only say the word, and we shall be healed."

Genevieve took the chunk of bread she had been holding and lifted it above her head, raising her eyes to study it. With her left hand, she lifted a paper cup of juice. "This is the blood of the new and everlasting covenant. It will be shed for you and for all women and men so that sins may be forgiven. Do this in memory of me."

Grace watched the congregants as they drank their juice and swallowed their chunks of bread. Then Luke spoke: "Remember, Father, those who have recently died: Leonard Applebaum, Meredith Benson, Crazy John Brown, Pinky, Mr. Matthews, Leticia Baker. Is there anyone else we should remember?"

Alvin rose from his seat. "I want to remember my mother who gave me life and was disappointed by me living on the street and drinking and my lifestyle. Even with her emphysema, she stuck it out long enough to be there for me after I got sober so I could go to her and help her and ask her to forgive me. And she did. I could have went away out of shame, but I didn't. I thank the Lord for that. I still miss her."

His lip quivered, and the crowd murmured, "We love you, Alvin. God bless you, son. Thank you, Lord. Amen."

One by one, twenty or thirty members of the congregation stood up and said names. Grace's mom's face, her eyebrows laced together in a frown, came into Grace's head, but she pressed it away.

"Please all stand and join hands. Let us celebrate together as neighbors and friends in the words our Savior gave us."

There was a great rustling of bodies and hands as everybody reached to touch someone. The grey-haired man turned around and said, "Peace be with you." A black-haired woman sitting next to Grace extended a manicured hand. Grace stretched her arm to connect with a teenager sitting two rows ahead. Soon all their bodies were linked in an awkward spiral, and hands were lifted into the air. As the crowd belted out The Lord's Prayer, Grace watched Father Luke. Tears spilled from his closed eyes down his pink cheeks and into his beard; fat droplets stained his purple robe.

After a pause, Miss Lillian spoke again. "The words to the ending song are at the back of your paper. Sing it with the same tune as *Row, Row, Row Your Boat*, okay? Do everybody know that song?"

The group was almost giddy now. Everybody was giggling or smiling as they sang:

*"Live your life in peace
And justice every day,
Give and share and love and sing
Thank the Lord and pray. "*

"One more time! In a round!" Father Luke called. With big sweeping arm movements, he directed half of the room to sing the first two lines then motioned to the other half to start. A couple of strong voices came in on time; the others joined too early or too late. The round continued a few more times, but each time was sillier and more confusing than the time before until chuckles devolved into raucous laughter. Father Luke seemed to be having a good time.

Grace got up to go as soon as he dismissed them, hoping to slip out the back to avoid the hubbub. She wanted to go to the Java House for a coffee and sit by herself and think. Her heart was thrumming as she walked out, eyes fixed to the floor.

Someone tapped her shoulder, and she turned around. "Thank you for coming! The peace of the Lord be with you, dear Grace!"

Father Luke's voice was boisterous and jovial, and he pulled her into a warm hug. As he stepped back from their embrace, his hands on her shoulders, he looked her in the eye and said, his voice almost intimate, "I'm glad you came."

Grace felt unsteady as she watched him turn to hug each of the people who had formed a line behind him.

Alvin sauntered over, grabbed her hand, and held it. "Whatdya think of our little Mass? Pretty special, huh? It's what hooked me when I stayed here. There is a lot of joy in the place, right? This is a healing place, Miss Schreiber. You did the right thing to come, not worryin' if you's a Catholic or not. The Lord don't care!"

"Thanks, Alvin," she said. She felt in awe of Father Luke and blanketed by tenderness for Alvin, for these struggling folks, for this whole crowd of odd ducks. No matter what she thought about his paradoxical Church, she knew she belonged here with them.

Alvin nodded. Both hands holding hers were warm and firm. "We all need healing, Miss Schreiber. We do."

"Thank you, Alvin," Grace said and shook her head. She stood there awkwardly for a minute as Alvin turned and wandered back into the crowd. Then she slipped out and jogged back to her car.

22

Grace dreamed of the Mass for three consecutive nights. In one dream, Father Luke helped her climb into a rickety canoe. They paddled down a rocky river that flowed into the middle of the dining room. Alvin got in the boat which by then had become a car in an amusement park ride. The three dug their nails into each other as the car climbed up the steep incline and screamed as it raced down the thrilling hill.

In another dream, Father Luke kissed her on the top of her head, placed a piece of bread between her breasts, and ate it off her chest, shouting, "*This* is the body of Christ!"

The last dream was a nightmare. A boa constrictor slithered up and down the legs of a folding chair. Father Luke bent down and grabbed it, letting it circle his arms and wrap itself around his neck. Her father took the snake from Luke and stuffed it into a metal box. She woke up sweating.

Each morning, she wrestled with her memories of the strange Mass. Its sweet inclusiveness moved her. The startling fact that it was officiated by both a man and a woman. Its ability to take in such a raggedy crew, Father Luke's simple sermon, the lack of pretentiousness, the laughter. And the way it sent her tumbling back to the purity of her spiritual longings during those hungry teen years. But she remained annoyed about the particulars of the doctrine.

Why the need to stick to the dogma of the resurrection and the Virgin Mother? Why the need for a priest, however unorthodox, to lead them? Why the dying Jesus hanging there, glorifying suffering? Why all the talk of sin?

And what about Frankie?

The horrific abuse of children continued to unfold in the news. Every week there was a new revelation of a predator priest shuttled from one parish to the next after being accused of sexual molestation or rape. What did Father Luke know about the unraveling saga of cover-ups and scandals? How would

Anne Meisenzahl

he feel if he read Frankie's essays incriminating the sanctimonious Father Santiago who had the nerve to preside over Frankie's funeral Mass?

Before she left for the bar to meet Father Luke, she made the calls. She told the secretary for the Los Angeles Diocese that she needed to report a case of child abuse. The woman took her name and number and said someone would return her call. She called Holy Mother of God Cathedral and asked to speak to Father Santiago. He was out.

"Do you want to leave a message?" his secretary asked.

"I want to talk to him about one of his altar boys," was all she said.

Hooligan's was less upscale than the outdoor cafés on Elmwood Avenue. It was cool and dark inside. The booth they chose smelled of stale beer, and the wooden tabletop was sticky. A young man walked over to their table to take their order.

"Guinness Stout," they said at the same time, then laughed.

"Nice, very nice," Father Luke said, looking around. "It's been a long time since I've been in a pub."

"How old are you, Father?" Grace asked. She guessed he was at least fifty-five, perhaps sixty. He had been at least ten years older than she was when she started volunteering in high school. "Can I call you Luke?"

As the words left her mouth, she heard how they sounded. Familiar, flirtatious. She sat up straighter.

He smiled and lay his palms on the table, then lifted them quickly and motioned for the bartender to bring a wet rag. "You can call me Luke, and I'm not much older than you."

"How old do you think I am?"

"Why, not a day over thirty, of course."

"No, really," she said, serious now.

"Fifty-three. And you?"

"I'm forty-three," she answered. "Father Luke, you remember that I used to volunteer at St. Laurence when I was a teenager. I have some vague memories of meeting you then. It would have been twenty-seven years ago."

"You stood out from the others. You were so selfless and hardworking! You had long red hair back then too."

120

"That was me."

"You seemed shy. Quiet and observant. Very committed."

"My mom had just died. It was a hard time for me and my family."

"Oh, my. I didn't know."

How interesting that he remembered her, that someone held in their brain an image of her from her other life. But the fact also made her uncomfortable. Would he assume she was the same pious Pollyanna she was when she knew him then?

The waiter returned and wiped off the table, and Grace relaxed and leaned in. "I've got a lot of questions," she said, pulling them back to the present. "I hope you don't mind, but there are some things I have a hard time understanding."

"I'm with you there. But first, let me ask you a question. What did you think of our Mass?"

"Well…" Grace slumped in her seat. "It was quite unusual. Pretty moving at times. Not like any other Mass I've been to."

"You liked it? I hoped you would."

"My father would have had a fit if he'd been there. He likes his Masses to be Latin and pre-Vatican II."

"And that we're not."

"That's the part I loved about it. It was genuine. Everybody was connected. People were involved, not just going through the motions."

"Good."

"It was almost theatrical. Everybody had a part."

"That's the thing, isn't it? Each person has a part to play. In this life, every one of us is important, down to the most insignificant, the most downtrodden. Mass is the essence of community."

"Can I be honest with you?"

"Nothing less from here on in, agreed?"

"Okay," she said, sitting up again, a quizzical expression on her face. "I have a lot of mixed feelings about the Mass. Like I said, I loved the sense of community. But it's hard for me to take it all literally, or to imagine that everybody there takes it—you know, the Creed, the miracles—as literal truth."

"You don't need to," he said. "Take it *essentially*. The idea, I believe, is to absorb the truth behind the words. The Bible is the holy book that resonates for me because that's the text I was raised with, but there are others. Thomas Merton studied the Bhagavad-Gita. He was compelled to explore Buddhism, to find the universality in faith. He recognized that there are many paths to God."

The waiter came back to mop up the table and set down a bowl of popcorn. She took another sip of her ale and dug her hand into the bowl.

"The right approach, I think, is to let the essence—the truth—flow through you like water, soothe you like a cool breeze. It's not to dissect these ancient texts like a historian seeking facts or like a scientist collecting data but to enter into them as a seeker longing for wisdom. To swim into them, like a diver transfixed by the ocean's beauty. Perhaps, as a writer, you might think of the words in the Bible as spiritual poetry rather than as literal truth."

Grace knew that if she had been born and raised in India, surrounded by the culture of Hinduism with all its gods and rites, all its spices and colors, she'd have embraced it the same way she'd glommed onto Christianity as a child.

"I guess I'd be questioning any religious text, no matter how I was raised."

"Questioning is good," he said. "But don't let it get in the way of your openness to God's unconditional and uncompromising love and to undeniable, universal truth."

She nodded then reached into her bag for her steno notebook and pen. "Can I start the interview by asking you about yourself and your beliefs?"

He wrapped both hands around the wet mug. "Shoot."

"Tell me about why you became a priest."

He smiled. Why had she started with the most personal question of all? A cool blast of AC raised bumps on her bare arms, and she looked down.

"I hope that's okay to ask."

"Of course. I haven't been asked that question for a long time. I'm so shut in, settled in my routine. Everybody knows me as Father Luke, and nobody thinks of me as anything else." He took a long drink. "No one thinks of me as a man."

Grace felt her neck grow warm. Father Luke swallowed a mouthful of popcorn before continuing.

"My parents were both lawyers. They expected me to become a defense attorney or a civil rights lawyer. When I told them I wanted to join the priesthood and serve the poor in person, I think they thought I was depressed or borderline schizophrenic. So they sent me to a therapist."

"Did you find out if you were crazy?"

"I am indisputably crazy."

Grace thought of Peter Maurin, the French socialist who founded the Catholic Worker movement with Dorothy Day. Before she could say it, Father Luke continued. "Do you know my favorite Peter Maurin quote?"

"'They say I am crazy...'" Grace began.

"Yes! 'They say I am crazy because I refuse to be crazy—'"

"'—the way everybody else is crazy.'"

They both chuckled.

"I love that you know that," Luke said, and touched Grace's hand. "My parents didn't have the faintest idea why I wanted to become a priest and commit myself to the Church. They didn't understand that, in addition to becoming a Christian and believing in salvation, I was also renouncing a lifestyle I thought was perverse, acquisitive, and detached from sincere spiritual connection to others. I was captivated by Dorothy Day's ability to integrate faith, service, and non-violent resistance to war and injustice."

"When you decided to give up a normal life and take a vow of poverty, did they feel you were renouncing *them*?"

"I think so. But I came to see that God requires self-sacrifice of us. That to love others we must give of ourselves. Not just our money or our time, but our lives. We have to give up those things we want most in order to give Him our best. We can't understand the poor if we are not poor. We can't work to eliminate hunger if we don't know what hunger feels like. My parents did good work, but they believed that because of it they were entitled to eat well and spend their hard-earned money to buy expensive things and a nice house that they could throw parties in."

Father Luke clasped his own hands and shook them as if he were about to throw a pair of dice on the table. "Where does it end? Does taking good care of myself mean I should have one TV, or two? One expensive car, or three? It's a never-ending system of self-justification.

"To quote my mother: 'We deserve to have a good time because of all the good work we do!' She actually said that. Lots of boards and foundations and philanthropic stuff. They became very rich."

He shook his head, the look on his face one of pain, as if he were describing not a much-coveted human achievement but a terrible crime.

"Maybe the art is in the interplay between loving other people and loving ourselves," Grace said. "Taking care of others *and* taking care of ourselves." Though she still hadn't figured out how to do either very well.

"Yes, but the love of self generally takes over unless it is held in check. You have to make rules about your behavior, or you can become self-absorbed."

As a teenager, Grace had measured her saintliness by her skinniness, her goodness in God's eyes by how many hours she went without juice. "But self-denial can be obsessive too," she said, her eyebrows raised.

"Renunciation ought to be for love," Luke answered. "Self-sacrifice for love of God, and the love of neighbor."

Luke sat back against the booth and took a handful of popcorn. He lobbed one kernel into his mouth at a time. "You know what the poor live with? They live with constant discomfort. They live with stomach aches from bad food, food from the garbage can, not enough food, or too much coffee because you can get it for free at the grocery store with lots of sugar to stave off the hunger. They live with rotten teeth and sour breath. They live with sore backs from sleeping on concrete or park benches. And there are hardly any decent benches any more. All the new ones have armrests in the middle that make it impossible to lie down."

Grace looked down at her notepad. It was empty. It was hard to take her eyes off Father Luke as he spoke.

"They live with bronchitis and pneumonia and the flu from sleeping in damp sleeping bags in the park. They live with lice. You know, once you get lice you can't get rid of them unless you have a washing machine and medicine. The poor live with shame and embarrassment and anger. It's a wonder that the people I've grown to love over the years are as cheerful as they are, considering how cruelly they're treated on a regular basis."

Grace shifted in her seat. His compassion, his knowledge about others' lives and hearts, his willingness to put himself in their place—this was real. It wasn't an idea or an unfulfilled dream. The AC kicked on again, cooling her flushed face. She pulled on the sleeves of her cotton blouse.

Luke ate another handful of popcorn then leaned forward. "Yesterday we got a new guest, José. He told me that he stood by the side of the road and collected change from passing cars, eventually saving up enough to go to a diner. Sat in the booth ready to order, happy to sit in an air-conditioned restaurant for half an hour and eat a decent meal. But his food was brought to him in a to-go bag.

"Can you imagine the insult? These guys, José and all the rest of them who stay a while and pass through, they live in fear of being beat up by mean kids or being kicked out of the library, the one free public place where you can sit in a soft chair for an hour." Luke shook his head. "They feel rejected everywhere."

"My dad occasionally gives a twenty, or a fifty-dollar bill even, to a person asking for money on the street. I asked him once why he gave such a large amount. I thought he might have made a mistake. He said, 'How do I know that wasn't Our Lord?'"

"Good man, your father. When do I get to meet him?"

Grace ignored the question. "I used to give money to homeless people when I lived in San Francisco, but it never felt like I was doing anything. There were so many of them. I carried dollar bills with me purposely."

When she first moved to the city, she'd been alarmed on a daily basis by the huddled heaps of men in doorways, in parks, sometimes with faces flat against the concrete, close enough to the quick feet of passersby to get kicked in the head.

"That counts. People should do that."

"But after a while, I stopped. The truth is…I'm ashamed to say this. The truth is I stopped noticing them."

With that, they both grew silent. They took sips of their Guinness and looked around at the photos on the walls and the people in the next booth, at anything but each other. Grace worried that Father Luke would find her incapable of simple caring and withdraw his request that she write about St. Laurence. She got up to go the restroom. When she came back, Father Luke was smiling.

125

"What is it?" Grace tilted her head. "What are you smiling about?"

Luke leaned back and folded his hands atop his paunchy belly. "I believe in living in community and living with the poor," he said, "but I'm not into total self-denial. As you can see, I'm no scrawny saint. I think we should reward ourselves for such an enlightening discussion by ordering something to eat. We deserve it." He winked.

Grace ignored him. "I have another question. Are you…are you…"

Luke scooted over on the wooden bench. "This sounds like it may be a good one. I'd better excuse myself and go to the restroom first. I'll be right back."

He touched her on the shoulder as he passed, and she shuddered. The question she planned to ask next was about his vow of chastity and what it meant to him. This one felt particularly personal.

In her teens, she'd dealt with her exploding body and her burgeoning, uncomfortable sexual feelings by reading about monks and nuns who sequestered themselves from the world. Nuns mythically betrothed to Jesus, wearing gold rings and reciting marriage vows to the Son of God, lying prostrate on the floor, renouncing the old life of the flesh. For a short while at least, she understood the appeal of celibacy.

When Luke came back, he sat down and stared at her. "Let the inquisition begin."

She made a note to discuss the Inquisition later. "What I want to ask is, are you happy? With your lifestyle choice, that is?"

"The obedience part or the poverty part or the chastity part?"

"All of them, but I guess right now it's the chastity I wonder about."

"Am I suffering from my celibacy?"

"Well, yes. And why? I guess I want to understand why you feel it's important to separate the life of the body, the body's desires, from your service to God. Why is the repression of sexual feeling necessary? Not to the Church and Papal doctrine, but to you?"

Luke smiled placidly as he looked down into his beer. The amber liquid shimmered in the overhead light. He tipped the glass back and forth, making waves. "You know, Grace, repression is a part of everyone's life. When people get married, they repress their urge to have affairs with other people every day. Fathers have to watch their beautiful little girls turn into women and actively repress any feelings of attraction they might have. Without repression, many more people would steal and cheat and say cruel things to each other. I would venture that most men repress their desire to smack someone on a daily basis."

"I know, but if you repress your desire to abuse or hurt someone, that's a moral act. If you choose not to have normal adult sex, you're only denying yourself." She could handle this touchy topic intellectually, she thought. She liked how clear and thoughtful she sounded.

"Unless by denying yourself, you can turn your attention to things that matter to you even more. It's less denial than sublimation, I think. Channeling loving energy. Transferring, or transforming, sexual energy into a life-changing force."

"Is it a question of time?" Grace asked, looping her curls into a loose braid over one shoulder. "Because having sex doesn't take much time. Especially if two people have been in a relationship for a while."

"Sex may not take time, but love does. To give your heart to another person is a commitment of time and energy and attention. I don't know that I could fully give my heart over to God if I didn't allow myself time to meditate and pray. And I don't think I'd do as good a job attending to the needs of the folks who come into St. Laurence House every day if I had a wife and a family. They would be my first priority."

"I guess that's the question then. What is it about you, about your particular heart, that it wants to devote itself to poor people walking in off the street more than to a family?" She was afraid she was sounding judgmental and harsh. She didn't do very well in the family department herself. Who the hell was she to be asking these questions? "I love what you do. You save lives. I've never met anybody as devoted or altruistic as you. Please don't take this as criticism. I admire you so much! But I don't understand how or why you would choose to give up something as primal and fun as sex." She finished in a huff and blushed.

"Grace, I made a vow to live in accordance with what I perceive to be God's calling for me. It's not right for everybody, but it's right for me." After a pause, he asked, "And what about you?"

"What about me what?"

"Are you married? Do you have kids? Have you been married?"

The Irishmen on the wall above them laughed at the question. Grace glanced up at the greasy poster on the other wall. The Buffalo Bills looked uncomfortably inflated in their shoulder pads, holding their helmets and staring intently over her head. Men surrounded her.

"Um, yes and no," she said. "Not technically."

"Not technically?"

Where to start? And what was this anyway? Confession? What did he think he was doing, turning the tables on her? Interviewing her for an article on lonely, involuntarily celibate single women? Did he expect her to tell him everything? Confide her dismay about the entire enterprise of marriage and not-marriage? And then what? He'd absolve her? Give her an assignment of a hundred *Hail Marys*? Tell her to come back in the morning on her knees, clean of regret, irritation, disappointment?

"You know what? I'm not feeling that great. I better go to the restroom a minute. I'll be back in a bit."

The back door of the pub opened up to a parking lot. Grace walked out back and sat on the steps. She needed a minute to think. Then she'd go back in, order a stronger drink, be polite and aloof and dismissive because she had no intention of telling him her whole life story. She considered the cars lined up in neat rows. She wished she smoked. If she wasn't so responsible, she'd walk out and keep walking.

"I feel better," she said as she slid across the wooden seat. Luke had drunk all of his beer and ordered a new one. Two plates of cheeseburgers and potato chips had been set down on the table while she was gone.

"I was starting to get worried about you. And I got you food. Thought maybe you might be hungry."

"Not to worry," she said. "I didn't get much sleep last night. Probably had too much coffee this morning. It bothered my stomach. I think I'll order a gin and tonic."

"So...have you been married, technically, that is?"

She stroked her hair as she worked up an answer in her head. She had to sound upbeat, not annoyed. "No. I've had a few relationships over the years, but I prefer to be single right now. I like my life. Coming back to Buffalo is a new adventure for me, and it would be too hard if I were married or encumbered. I'm in a good place."

"I guess you're a voluntary celibate right now too?" He grinned.

Very funny, she thought and faked a smile.

"I've wondered about marriage myself, of course. Sometimes I think about how different my life would have been had I chosen to go that route. What I would have gained and what I would have lost."

"Hmmm." Grace pulled out her notepad. *Wondered about marriage,* she wrote.

"My life would have been pretty different if I'd fallen in love and had a family," he said. "But I think love comes from God." He looked at the table for a few seconds then up at Grace. "I think love is the manifestation of God on earth. It's His spirit shining through us. The love of a man for his wife and children, the love of the priest for his flock, a neighbor for another neighbor—that's God. Alive in us, living through us."

"What is God, Luke?" First probing her love life, then preaching. If she spoke slowly, she could keep impatience from rising in her voice. "Isn't it circuitous reasoning to say 'God is love'? It doesn't answer the question of what God is or what love is."

"God is the name we humans give to the endless love that created us and created the beautiful sunset, the cooing baby. It doesn't matter what you call it—Jahweh, Allah, Our Lord, or simply Love. What matters is that you let it come into you and move you. What matters is that you give yourself over to it, whatever path it takes you down."

"What about Father Geoghan, Luke?" Her exasperation was full-blown now; she could no longer contain it. "What about the priests who don't repress their desire for sex and instead unleash it on children?" She pushed her plate away.

Luke sank his teeth into his burger and took his time chewing. "They have strayed from God," he said, looking at her steadily. "They have strayed from love."

23

Luke was on his hands and knees in the corner when Grace walked into the dining room the following Monday. Hair had slipped out of its rubber band and was hanging in thin wisps around his face. His cheeks were red and sweaty when he looked up at her.

"Just doing a little scrubbing," he said as he scooped out a spongeful of suds from a bucket and slathered them on the floor

"I see," she said. "Do you need a hand?" What would she do? Get down on the floor with him, hips bumping while they scrubbed? "You want me to get you a towel or something?"

"Sure, thanks. Grab me a couple of towels so I can wipe this up."

"Okay." As she walked out of the room, she heard him laugh. "Today is a beautiful day, is it not?"

She turned and looked down at his bearlike bulk. "It is. Yes."

"A beautiful day the Lord has made."

Whenever Jake used to pontificate, he would rest his head against the back of Grace's futon, eyes half-closed, the stub of a joint between his index finger and thumb.

To love is to let go. By connecting with nothing, we connect with everything.

She'd nod and murmur agreement. For eighteen months, she had listened intently to every word Jake uttered. She'd swallowed his deliciously slippery wisdom as if it were chocolate ice cream.

"Detachment is the highest form of love," he had said on more than one smoke-filled occasion.

Grace thought of Jake's platitudes as she left the room in search of a towel for Father Luke. Almost every time she entered St. Laurence House and felt herself drawn to its worn carpet and scruffy linoleum floor, its dull yellow walls, she remembered Jake's comments about detachment. Whenever she listened to a new resident's story, watched someone who hadn't eaten for days wolf down a plate of hot food, or played Crazy Eights or Rummy with the guests, she knew she was anything but detached.

She felt a pang in her heart whenever she saw the huddled cluster of hungry people waiting outside the door to be let in for a meal. Where did they go when they weren't here? What she felt for this house and these folks was more like a passionate attachment, like a stomach scraped empty by hunger, a craving. Though for what she remained unsure.

A shriek interrupted Grace's next interview with Luke, mid-afternoon the next day. "Got it! Y'all keep talking," Alvin panted as he rushed past. Maybe the dining room at St. Laurence wasn't the best place to meet.

"Appreciate that," Father Luke called after him. "Let me know how I can help."

A shuffling of feet, a clanking sound, then silence.

"Father Luke, I need to ask you about something before we start in on the history of St. Laurence House. Did you hear about this priest who just died, a Father Lawrence Murphy? He taught at a School for the Deaf in Milwaukee for over twenty years and molested over two hundred boys!"

"No. I haven't been reading the paper lately with so much going on. But the news of these priests—it's almost incomprehensible."

"The church officials and the police did nothing. The students went to the police and the District Attorney when they became adults, but nobody believed them or thought their allegations were credible because everybody loved this guy! He was transferred to another parish where he worked for another twenty years. And—this is the sickest, worst part—he admitted everything! He admitted that he molested the boys *during confession!*"

"Violating the sacrament of penance is an offense under canon law," Luke sighed, his voice small.

"Not enough of an offense to have them do anything."

"Terrible, terrible."

Luke looked at the wall, at the table, at his hands. He covered his face with his hands as if he were praying. Silence rose like a shield between them. Grace felt stuck. The topic had caused him to retreat into himself. She needed to say the right thing to get him talking, not shut him down.

"Tell me about how you came to St. Laurence House," she offered, making a show of taking out her notepad.

"Let me start at the beginning." He shook himself alert, walked over to the coffee pot, and poured a cup for himself and Grace. "But first we need some cookies."

He took his time walking into the kitchen. She heard him humming an old hymn. He piled a plate with ginger snaps and vanilla wafers and set it down in front of her on the table.

"After seminary, I thought the best way to help the poor and rectify injustice was to work in a wealthy parish."

Father Luke described how exhilarated he was to speak directly to parishioners and admonish them to open their hearts. He wanted to unsettle their contented lives in order to, as Peter Maurin had said, "comfort the afflicted and afflict the comfortable."

He reveled at the chance to find those gospel messages that would hit right at the heart of the problems of inequality and injustice. He told her with a laugh how young and naïve he was in 1969. He was only twenty-five years old when he was assigned to Holy Trinity in Amherst. He thought he could shake up the congregation, form a social justice committee, organize a Fast for a World Harvest.

He would excite them into action with a sermon about camels and needles and rich people and heaven, a sermon that would have them emptying their pockets, maybe even their bank accounts. They would be ready to give it all away and "live simply so others could simply live."

He shook his head. "But that's not quite how it worked out."

"Tell me," Grace said. "Tell me how you got from there to here."

"Well, I tried to be a good suburban priest, to be an example, giving hard-hitting radical sermons to the entitled. But it just wasn't my calling."

More and more homeless people had been hanging around upscale downtown Amherst, with its pretty benches, pots of flowers, and fancy brick walkways. Holy Trinity was across the street from a busy street full of expensive shops. After Luke had served there seven months, a drunk man wandered into the church and fell asleep in the back pew.

"I was torn. I remember clearly thinking I should let him sleep it off there, but I also knew the lead pastor wouldn't approve. I worried that I had to impress him in order to have more responsibilities in the church. Father Moynihan was a very powerful man. So I woke the poor guy up and told him he had to go. He balked, tried to argue with me; he was wasted. But I held firm and told him he had to go."

Luke pressed his open palms against the tabletop. Grace wrote some notes and waited.

"He staggered off. He was completely plastered. After he left, I went up to my office. As if it were no big deal to send a desperate person away. How lonely he must have been. How horrific to be told by a priest, the one person he should have been able to trust, that he wasn't welcome here."

Grace put her pen down and studied him as he continued.

"But I was oblivious, caught up in my own self-serving concerns. I started preparing for a sermon when I opened a prayer book to the Prayer of St. Francis. It was one of my favorites: 'Lord, make me an instrument of your peace. Where there is hatred, let me sow love…Where there is despair, hope.' The man was in despair. All he wanted was a place to sleep it off, and I didn't offer him hope. I was worried about what Father Moynihan would think. Silly, selfish pride…"

Luke's voice got lower. "And then, after reading St. Francis' words, I felt compelled to open the Bible. I randomly flipped through it. My eyes fell on Matthew 25:43: 'When I was a stranger, you did not take me in.' While I was reading these words—'Whatsoever you *did not do* to the least of my brothers, you *did not do unto me'*—the secretary walked in to announce that there had been an accident in front of the church. I went out to see what happened and discovered it was my drunken friend. I was devastated."

He paused, inhaling slowly and closing his eyes. Grace had only written a few lines. Looking at the steno pad meant taking her eyes off his beard, his pink skin, the spider webs in the corners of his eyes.

"He walked right out into a busy intersection about a half a block away from Holy Trinity and got hit by a car. He was killed on the spot. To this day, nobody knows I had the chance to save him, and instead I sent him out of the church and into the road." He looked sadly at her notepad.

"You didn't send him into the road."

"It's as if I did." Luke was shaking his head now, concentrating on the

133

table as if the homeless man's image were staring up at him from the plastic tablecloth.

"In hindsight, I believe St. Frances chose that moment to speak to me, to tell me to renounce my obedience to the wealthy parish and take care of those who needed my devotion. Jesus is a drunk, a drug addict, a street person. The message from St. Francis couldn't have been more clear.

"I prayed to St. Frances every night after that. When I learned ten days later that there was a need for a volunteer at St. Laurence House, I knew I was meant to take it. Priests don't typically live in Catholic Worker Houses, but I asked the Diocese for special permission. St. Frances gave me spiritual direction. He answered my prayers."

Grace lay in bed that night and reread the notes she'd scribbled in her pad, many of them framed as questions: *A life changing experience? The intervention of St. Frances? A life governed by prayer? Total commitment to the poor? Jesus as a drunk?*

Luke's words bewildered and intrigued her. He was a real-life embodiment of the imagined saints she'd revered as an infatuated young woman. She had so many questions. His words intertwined with her dreams as she twisted fitfully into sleep.

24

The girl sitting on the back of the sofa in the corner of the community room had plucked her eyebrows out then drawn on thin curved black lines. Her hair was bleached blonde, but a thick swash of light brown down the center of her skull betrayed her true color. Her eyelids were painted a glittery blue, bright in contrast to her ashen skin. Gold spheres the size of hockey pucks hung from her earlobes. Her shirt was tight and low over her breasts.

Father Luke leaned against the wall, arms folded over his big belly, and studied the girl as she perched on top of the sofa. He had just begun to engage her in conversation, inviting her, as he typically did to new residents, to, "Tell me a little bit about yourself."

"I'm not into, you know, telling y'all all a that. You being all up in my business and all, I'm not having that."

"Okay," Luke said, his eyes never leaving her face.

"I'm just sayin' I'm not into diggin' up the past and shit, telling everybody shit they don't need to know 'cause they don't know me. I'm just takin' care of mines and then steppin'. You know what I'm sayin'?"

"I think so," Luke said, his eyebrows raised. "But tell me more because I want to understand."

"I'm *sayin'* I got me a baby to look out for. I gotta get something to eat and a place to sleep. Then I'm stepping *off*."

"A baby?" Luke uncrossed his arms and tipped his head to one side. "Where's the baby?"

"Inside a my stomach is where. I been pukin' for a week."

Grace lingered by the coffee table, eavesdropping as she scrubbed invisible stains. The girl couldn't have been more than seventeen years old. Grace shivered at the memory of her own unsettling nausea during those early, scary months.

Luke's forehead was scrunched into a frown. "That must feel pretty awful."

"I'm awright. I just need some sleep."

"Well, we're glad you're here. After dinner, you can get a good night's sleep."

"Who'd you say you is?" The girl slid down from the top of the shabby sofa and lay flat on her back across the seat cushions, one leg hanging over the armrest.

Father Luke put his hands in his pockets. "I'm Father Luke," he said.

"You ain't one of them peddy... You know, pedo-type priests on the TV, is you?"

"No need to worry. This is a safe place."

"You sure?" The girl smirked. "You real sure?" She kicked her slipper off the hanging leg, revealing bright red toenails.

"Yes, I'm sure. You'll sleep in the women's dorm."

"Jeez. A fuckin' slumber party." She laughed and relaxed back against the couch cushion. "Sorry about my mouth. You know, y'all bein a church and all."

"It's okay, my dear. We've heard and seen it all. You're safe here. Tell me, how old are you?"

"I'm sixteen. And did I tell you I'm preggers? God*damn*."

Grace flinched. *Sixteen.*

"You did. We'll try to help you with your pregnancy. Where are you from? You sound like you have a Southern accent."

"I'm not from nowhere. And don't start getting all in my *bidness*." She pulled herself up, slipped her shoe on, and walked out of the common room. She wandered outside then came back in when dinner was served.

After the residents and guests and volunteers had all filled their plates, a yell interrupted the dining room's din. "Hey!"

The high voice startled Grace from her focus on her coffee and lukewarm stew. "Leave me the fuck *alone,* I told you." She looked up to see the pregnant girl across the room slapping at Charlie, the round-faced, scruffy-looking middle-aged man sitting next to her. "Get your pervert hands *offa* me."

"Whoa, whoa, no violence!" Grace watched as Alvin jumped up from his seat and jabbed a stiff arm between them. "Stop that there right now!"

He stared down at Charlie. "You know there ain't no touching, Charlie! What you doin', man?"

"Nothin', boss. Nothin'. This girl starts talking to me. I tell her she's cute. She gets all up in my face. I swear I didn't do nothin'."

"Both of y'all move or leave. You hear me?"

"I ain't movin'. He's the pervert," the girl whined.

Grace stifled a smile. This girl was tough. She imagined she'd had to fend for herself for a long time. What brought her here, and where could she possibly be going?

"Then you're leavin'." Alvin crossed his arms and glared first at the brown stripe in the middle of the girl's head and then at Charlie.

"Awright. Jeez!" The girl picked up her plate and sat at another table by herself. She glowered as she stuffed a roll into her mouth.

"Charlie, man, let's go."

Charlie's face reminded Grace of a basketball, orangey and stippled from too much exposure to sun and wind. The unhealthy color deepened as it betrayed his shame.

"Sorry, boss. I'm a dumbass. I'm sorry," Charlie whimpered as he stood up. He looked like somebody who'd been told to move a lot in his day.

"I know you are, man. I know," Alvin crooned. He took Charlie by the arm and pulled him down the table to sit next to the unfazed Sister Genevieve.

Grace went into St. Laurence on Monday morning after a weekend off. After finishing her tasks, she asked Luke about the pregnant sixteen-year-old girl. She had fallen asleep after dinner, her head on the table next to her empty plate, until someone tapped her on the shoulder and she shuffled off to her bunk.

"I didn't have a chance to talk to Genevieve, so nobody called to find services for her yet. The next day, right after breakfast, she took off and hasn't come back."

"I wonder how far along she was," Grace said. "I hope she found somewhere to stay."

"I know," Luke said. "We're not the right place for a girl like that. She's too young to be here. She may have worked as a prostitute. She's probably a runaway. And if she is pregnant, that's a whole other story. A girl like that doesn't usually stick around very long."

It occurred to Grace that she, too, had been a runaway of sorts. What would Father Luke think of her if he knew her story?

Grace turned away from the priest and grabbed her jacket from the back of a chair. She could tell he was watching her. What if, when she was eighteen and pregnant, she had stumbled into a Catholic Worker House in San Francisco and had been shepherded by the crew there, welcomed as part of the "family"? How would things have turned out differently for her if she hadn't gone through her pregnancy isolated and afraid?

She shivered at the memory, put on her jacket, and hugged herself. She imagined putting her arms around the girl...or was it her fragile teenage self she pictured?

Grace had obsessed about the girl while she wrestled with the covers the night before and was greeted by thoughts of her when she woke up. She didn't understand everything that the teenager had gone through. *A prostitute, my God.* But she did know what it felt like to be alone.

"I hate to think of her outside all day. And all night. I hope she comes back."

25

Autumn arrived with sudden and alarming beauty. Trees weary of greenness had awakened wearing flaming crowns of red and orange. Cold breezes fanned the blaze. Grace felt seized by a new energy as if a firm but friendly coach tapped her on the shoulder in the morning and insisted she shake off her slovenly ways and run.

She jogged one block and then walked for two, trying to relieve the burning in her chest. She took off after her breathing evened out. Her lungs ached, her left knee felt stiff, and her feet hurt. But she kept at it. Every couple of days, she added another block until she didn't need to stop and walk anymore and was able to focus instead on watching the sleepy city arise.

She explored this town that was both familiar and new. She jogged south of Allentown, across Porter Avenue to Niagara Street, over to the churning gray undulations of the Niagara River, then south to the marina and the vast brown waters of Lake Erie. Some days she drove to join the inveterate runners pounding the forested path around the golf course in Delaware Park. She came to prize her solitary mornings.

She would head out at half past six and return around eight, sweaty and red-faced, her hair tied back in a loose braid. Brian was always working in the yard. Every day he expressed his approval of her efforts and invited her to join him for a cup of tea. Every day she thanked him and begged off by saying she had to shower and get going.

She knew the minute she met Brian that he liked her. He was pleasant enough looking, and he certainly was gracious, but she didn't let herself imagine him as a boyfriend or even a date. Falling into another disastrous affair was the last thing she needed now that she'd finally found a modicum of contentment. She had succumbed to Jake's charms, but now with over a year's perspective, she saw all the ways she'd been deluded.

She didn't want to fall for anybody's tricks again, but she wasn't sure she'd recognize if she was being tricked.

Things were going well now, and she didn't want to jinx it. It was enough to watch Father Luke in the morning as he managed the medley of characters camping out at St. Laurence, visit her dad for lunch, and return to her quiet little jewel of a house in the late afternoon which just happened to be owned by a nice, handsome, hardworking man.

The evening after Mountain Saunders moved into the apartment next to hers, Brian walked her over to where Grace was sitting in a folding chair on the lawn thumbing through a magazine. He set out another lawn chair and introduced them to one another.

"Our new neighbor," he said.

"Nice to meet you, Grace." Grace stood up. Mountain wrapped her arms around her, then stood back to look at her. "You know, I already feel good energy from you."

Her face was plump, pale, and freckled. A gold ring sparkled in her nostril, and gray hair fell over her shoulders and down her back. A braided leash connected her wrist to the neck of an enormous black lab. His soulful eyes searched Grace.

"Nice to meet you too. What a big dog!" Grace reached down to scratch the dog's neck. She looked around for Brian, but he had disappeared back into his apartment.

"Would you like a beer?" she asked Mountain. "Or maybe a glass of wine?"

Mountain plopped herself onto the other folding chair. The dog circled himself down next to her on the lawn, his tail slapping the grass.

"Good boy, Magic. No, thank you, my dear," she said. "It's been many years since I have expanded my consciousness with mind-altering substances." She laughed, gulping in big breaths of air. "My struggle is with food. I eat too much and too often, and it plays havoc with my colon. Do you have any vices?"

"I suppose I do," Grace said.

Mountain leaned back and grinned. "Do tell. I'm all ears."

Grace liked the woman's forthrightness. She silently enumerated her own shortcomings, which she knew all too well but was not at all inclined to share. She drank too much coffee, and she could go a whole day without vegetables. She was worried she drank too much. She wasn't disciplined enough to do even ten minutes a day of yoga. She may have been addicted to sex with Jake.

"I'll get back to you on that," she said. "In the meantime, how about some water or herbal tea? I have grapefruit juice too."

"Water with lemon would be fine if you have it. I just had a bowl of granola and a glass of spinach carrot juice, so that should keep me in vitamins and amino acids for a while."

Grace retreated to her apartment and returned with a tumbler of water and a bowl of apple slices for her new friend, a coffee mug full of red wine for herself.

That night began the tradition of sitting in folding chairs on the modest front yard of the Jersey St. house, chatting, taking in the neighborhood's changes, sharing goodies. Brian would drag out the chairs and provide four cans of Michelob or a bottle of white wine for himself and Grace.

Mountain drank hot peach or ginger tea and offered a variety of snacks: deep fried zucchini flowers stuffed with goat cheese; grilled eggplant, onions, and peppers; skewers of watermelon and plum; blueberry cobbler crusted with granola. Grace brought crackers and wedges of cheese, pear slices, or nuts. For over an hour every evening in the cold waning daylight of October, they feasted and talked.

They watched the neighborhood kids ride their bikes and kick balls around, commented on the on-going angry arguments between the woman and her motorcycle-riding son across the street, and shook their heads at the cars driving too fast. Calvin and Chris from next door would throw a football back and forth in the descending coolness, yelling out insults with each pass or missed catch. Brian introduced the women to Mr. Davidson, who walked by with his Chihuahua at precisely six and always waved.

Mountain said she moved back to Buffalo to care for her mom, who died shortly after that. She described her three boys, Brook, Harmony, and Rain, now grown men, whom she'd raised alone at Sweet Valley Farm in

North Carolina after their father took off to Orlando to help Maharishi Mahesh Yogi start a theme park called Vedaland. It never got off the ground, but he never came back.

Brian told them he had studied philosophy and physics. Grace liked that he could quote Rilke, Rumi, Kerouac, and Gregory Corso verbatim. He sometimes veered the conversation toward Buddhism or Sufism. In addition to owning their townhouse and three other buildings and being a gifted repairman and craftsman, she learned that he loved auto mechanics, archeology, baseball, and the Grateful Dead.

Grace told them bits and pieces about where she had lived and why she returned. She was more content to listen to them than to share. She wasn't ready yet to reveal the muddied depths of her psyche. In the cool night air, under a canopy of dry golden leaves, she felt a quiet longing for connection to these two kind souls.

Grace occasionally spoke to a young man named Sage who hung around St. Laurence. His clothes were disheveled, his curly hair greasy and uncombed. He always seemed occupied, playing chess or cards, telling animated jokes, smearing cream cheese on donated bagels for himself and whoever else was around.

Grace understood that he was a volunteer and not a guest when she saw him bound up to the third floor where Luke and Alvin lived. While she was waiting for Luke to meet her for their next installment, she decided to ask him if she could get his perspective on the place.

He'd been volunteering at St. Laurence for the past three months, he told her, and felt like he had finally found a spiritual home. "I grew up Catholic," he said, his broad, apple-cheeked face shining with sweat. "But I wanted a deeper experience, an immersive spirituality. Let's just say I found the traditional Church lacking. After I graduated from college, I cooked for a Buddhist retreat center in upstate New York. I lived there and meditated and all, but it was a little high end." He laughed.

"People paid thousands of dollars to go there and demanded all-organic locally-grown vegetarian Thai meals. Which was fine. For them. But not for me. So I moved in with the Hare Krishnas. I loved going out to the parks and giving away free food, but I needed something more authentic, more…I don't know…responsive.

"When I read about the Catholic Worker, I knew this was it. So now I'm back in the Church but in an alternative anarcho-personalist sort of way." He laughed again, his curls shaking. "It's pretty exhausting here. There's no time to do any side projects or anything, but I love it."

Teaching at the Cesar Chavez Community Education Center had been exhausting, too, but Grace never felt the kind of camaraderie and community she experienced here. What sustained these people? "Don't you ever get burned out?"

"Sometimes I go to my room to rest, but almost like clockwork, I get interrupted because somebody needs something. How can I say no? It might be Jesus knocking!"

Grace frowned as she wrote down his words.

"I feel like this place, these guys…" He nodded at a group arguing over a game of dominoes. "This is home."

"Thanks. I'll quote you."

Luke walked up and patted Sage on the back. "Good. You've talked to Sage. He's the real thing. Ready to continue the interrogation?"

"I'd like to hear the story of St. Laurence," Grace said as she and Luke set up folding chairs on either side of the table. "I assume he was martyred? Why is he your namesake?" Grace had forgotten most of the stories of the saints she read so devotedly as a teen.

Luke nestled his large frame into the small chair. "This is a wonderful story. St. Laurence is one of my favorite saints. He's the patron saint of cooks, you know. Which is fitting, don't you think, since we serve such fabulous gourmet fare?"

Grace opened her notepad to a clean page. She watched Luke prepare himself to tell the story. He reminded her of her dad, the way he opened his hands toward his audience as if he were on stage about to do stand up.

"It was 257 in the Year of our Lord. It was a time of great persecution of believers by the Romans. Pope Sixtus was sent to his death by the Roman Emperor Valerian. Over the course of the next three days, a local government official ordered Laurence, a deacon of the church, to turn over the church's treasure. Since the Pope was about to be killed, the official wanted to hurry up and get his hands on the church's wealth.

"St. Laurence responded to the orders by wandering the streets and gathering together all the poor people he could find. He brought together beggars, prostitutes, women with babies, the disabled, sinners, and gave all the wealth of the church *to them*. He gave them gold and silver, marble statues, jars made of alabaster. Then he told them to meet him at the government official's headquarters.

"Of course, the official was appalled. 'What is the purpose of gathering this misery before me?' he yelled. 'Where is the treasure of the church?'

"'Here,' Laurence answered. He waved his arms over the crowd. 'Why are you not pleased? These poor people are the treasures of the church!'"

Luke's eyes widened, and he spoke in a low voice. "'Don't make me roast you!' the official shouted. 'Where are the treasures?' But Laurence would not back down, and the official ordered that a giant iron griddle be built to broil the young man to a crisp. They stripped him down to nothing, tied his naked flesh to the grate, and lit a bonfire under him."

The creepy story reminded Grace of the ghost stories her father used to tell them in the car on road trips at night. The car lights would make eerie statues of the trees while her father's resonating voice, disembodied in the dark, painted terrifying images of monsters and ghouls.

"Laurence was remarkably good-natured about his hot ordeal. As they roasted him, he laughed and shouted, 'Turn me! This side is cooked enough!' The soldiers leaped up and turned him, watching his skin blister and bubble until he was fully roasted. 'I am finished cooking,' he said. 'Now you may eat!'"

Grace scrunched her nose and mouth into a look of disgust.

"The story goes that God smiled down on Laurence that day. He saw the sacrifices he had made and said, 'Well done, my son. Well done!'"

Grace shook her head and rolled her eyes. Luke scraped back his chair, stood up, and laid his hand on her shoulder. "I joke, of course, but there is truth at the center of the story. The people who live here in community with us workers are the wealth of the Church. Its center, its heartbeat." He looked down into her eyes. "The people who live here with us are Jesus. Not just the people of Christ but Christ Himself. They remind us every day to love, to be kind, to share everything. Not just the extra we have left over after we've sated ourselves. Everything."

Grace missed the weight of his warm hand when he lifted it and pushed in his chair. "There is someone else I want you to interview," Luke said. He took her by the elbow and led her across the dining room into the chapel.

"Lance." The man sat alone in the darkened space. "This is the person who is writing about us." He turned to Grace. "We call him 'Philosopher.'"

The man looked serious, mournful. A ropy black scar divided his nose in half and extended across one of his mahogany colored cheeks. He wore bulky glasses, their frames fastened at the bridge with Scotch tape.

"Lance just returned yesterday after a visit to his family in the Bronx," Luke explained. He turned to face Lance and gripped the young man's shoulders. "Something you could never have done before without being pulled back into drugs. Am I right, my man?"

"You are indeed correct, Father," Lance replied, his voice somber. Lance turned to stare at Grace. The irises of his eyes were black, the whites yellow, streaked with red. "St. Laurence House provides me with an alternative to the black hole of drugs. It gives me strength. You are writing an article, you say?"

Grace nodded.

"Here's what you should write." Lance pointed at the notepad in her hand. "The beauty of drugs is that you don't have to cultivate relationships. You can live in the delusion that you don't need a blessed soul. But…it's an illusion, a convoluted delusion, a lie.

"We all have an urge to connect. We all have spiritual holes. Drugs attempt to fill those spiritual holes, but they fill them with poison." His eyes narrowed to slits. "Society wastes people. It throws them out like yesterday's crumpled newspaper, like a stinking fish carcass. We don't waste people here." Lance patted Luke's back. "Father understands, like Jesus did, that we all have spiritual and physical longings. St. Laurence fulfills them both."

He closed his eyes and took a deep breath then turned toward the chapel door. "That will have to be all, Father. I'd better rest."

"Thank you," Grace called after him as he exited the chapel. She jotted Lance's quotes on her pad. Luke stood smiling, his hands clasped in front of him.

"There's a lot of wisdom here," she said, "in this odd place."

Luke nodded and walked away, leaving Grace to her thoughts. She felt windswept, as if at the center of a whirling storm.

She took the measure of their lot. Luke was amazing, the affable, unimposing heartbeat of the place, the center of the whole enterprise. Alvin, kind and indefatigable; Genevieve, patient and steadfast. The dedicated Sage and the other volunteers, young and old, who left their comfortable lives to take turns cooking, cleaning, and collecting food.

Lance the Philosopher; Tall Tree, enigmatic and gifted, but timid. The slight and pretty transvestite Daniella, all makeup and sparkly thrift store purses, who sometimes referred to himself as The Artist Formerly Known as Danny. Charlie, the daft and gentle lug; Mr. Anderson, skinny, stuttering, and scared; Malcolm, a gruff leather-skinned alcoholic, regularly reeking of drink, every day swearing it off.

An epileptic woman with cerebral palsy named Happy; Delia who cursed and cried; Maylene, quiet and polite; Lenny X, huge and surly, who rarely spoke, ate three plates of food at dinner, and wrote haiku on napkins and passed them around the table. The tough new girl from who-knows-where, too young to be alone in the world.

Some of them—the residents Alvin referred to as "the family"—had made St. Laurence their home and were always around. Others, sometimes as many as a hundred, stood outside in a clump waiting for free lunch or dinner after a night of awkwardly sleeping in abandoned cars or face down in the grass at the park. Some tumbled in once and never returned.

All of them were weather-beaten and warped, weary and worn down. Grace was seized by the memory of contentment she'd experienced here as a teen. Perhaps she had found a place where finally—again—she could be part of something bigger than her own small concerns. She sighed, a half smile on her face, and made herself a note to look up St. Laurence in *The Lives of the Saints* when she got home.

26

Grace found Sister Genevieve at her desk in the women's section. She had worked beside the nun on a few occasions, but they'd always been in the midst of residents and volunteers. The thought of living a life of service in a Christian community intrigued Grace, but the prospect of growing old there and wearing Genevieve's button-down sweaters, wool skirts, and thick-soled shoes made her shudder.

"Hello, Sister. Am I interrupting you?"

"No, not at all. What can I do for you?" Her eyes were kind and bright.

"May I ask you some questions about St. Laurence for the article I'm writing for *The Free Press*?" Grace was riveted by Luke's rambling tales, but it was hard to pin him down to a simple chronological story.

"Why, yes, of course," Genevieve answered. "Let me finish this journal entry, and I will be happy to oblige. Let's talk in the Bissonette Chapel."

The nun's small wooden desk pressed up against a window like a plant seeking sun. Taped to the wall were two photos: a frowning Mother Teresa cradling the head of a wrinkled bronze baby and Dorothy Day, legs crossed in a chair, staring sternly up at two armed police officers during a migrant farmworkers' strike. A quote written in magic marker hung by the photo of Mother Teresa. *In this life we cannot do great things. We can only do small things with great love.*

Sister Genevieve wrote a few sentences with an ink cartridge pen in a cloth-covered book and blew on the words. She made the sign of the cross, closed the book, and set it next to a white candle. The two women walked together to the chapel. The nun was a tall woman with a full figure, broad shoulders, her hair cut short.

Genevieve is old enough to be my mother, Grace thought, but from what she observed, the older woman was solid, centered, and practical. She had an easy laugh and a calm demeanor; her mother had been anxious and sad. *What a different person I would have become.*

Genevieve fingered the words etched into the bronze nameplate screwed to the chapel door: *Father Joseph Bissonette, Martyr for Justice.* "You need to know first about this man," she told Grace, tapping the word *Martyr.*

"Father Bissonette was a Catholic Worker in the truest spirit of the term." Genevieve put her hands in the pockets of her overlarge brown sweater. "He devoted his life to his parish church which was a dwindling community of very poor people on Grider Street. He was a friend. He was killed eleven years ago, but it still feels like it was yesterday."

Genevieve closed her eyes and paused. Grace wondered if she might be praying. "He was completely devoted. He refused to take a vacation. We talked about it. He would come here often for suppers, and he would be exhausted. He was usually battling a cold. His brother wanted him to go to Florida for a break, but he refused. Said he wouldn't ever take a vacation to a place his congregation couldn't afford to go. His church was a sanctuary for illegal immigrants and refugees from Honduras and El Salvador and Guatemala. He told me he didn't believe in borders."

"Was his murder politically motivated?" Grace asked.

Genevieve traced Father Bisonnette's inset name again. "No, not at all. So tragic. Two teenagers. Kids he knew, troubled kids. They came to the rectory late at night and told him they'd been thrown out of the house. Joe invited them in and made them sandwiches, but then the boys demanded that he give them money. He did. A couple hundred dollars. I guess it wasn't enough. The boys stabbed him to death."

"Oh, my God," Grace said. "How awful."

"When you commit yourself to the poor, as he did, as we do"— Genevieve lifted her finger from the plaque and took in the chapel, the kitchen, the whole ramshackle building—"you commit yourself to exist with them in the tragedies of their lives. You become a part of their suffering."

Grace nodded, though she couldn't imagine pledging herself so totally to others.

"Ten days later, Father Herlihy, an older priest, was killed by the same two young men using a similar tactic. The boys were caught and imprisoned for life." She shook her grey head. "Imagine. For life. Luke and I visit them every year on the anniversary of Joe's death. They are repentant."

As the women headed into the chapel, Happy lumbered over, snuck up behind Genevieve, and slipped her hands over her eyes. Genevieve put her hands over Happy's and laughed.

"Let me guess. Alvin?"

"No, Sister. I ain't no man!" Her voice was rough, her words slurred. "Guess again!"

"Delia?"

"Nope." Grace noticed that her lip was cut. A nasty bruise had spread across her chin. It looked fresh.

"Is it Mary, Mother of Jesus?"

"You better know it's me, Happy!"

"Oh, why didn't you say so?" Genevieve spun around and caught Happy in a tight hug. Then she pulled back, hands on Happy's shoulders, and studied her. "What happened, my dear? Did you fall?"

"Just another seizure. It ain't nothing. I didn't break no teeth this time."

"We have to get you a helmet, don't we?"

"Would you? Would you, Sister? I think I need one."

Happy waved cheerfully at Grace and hobbled away. Grace wondered if she'd ever been part of that kind of love. Clearly, these were two people who found pure delight in each other. Could she ever relax enough to be that intimate with the guests? With anyone for that matter?

Genevieve walked into the chapel and settled herself into a worn wooden pew. Grace sat in the next pew, twisting her neck to face the nun. "Tell me how you all got started."

St. Laurence House, the nun told her, had been started in 1970 by a group of young people calling themselves Catholic anarchists. Christian communists with a small c. They initially squatted in the building while renovating it. They transformed it from an abandoned fire station that the city couldn't afford to refurbish into a shelter for street people, alcoholics, and drug addicts.

"Eventually, Father Luke came on the scene. I think the Buffalo Diocese liked having St. Laurence House around so they could say they were doing God's work. But they basically ignored us and let us alone to do the heavy lifting." Genevieve chuckled.

"And you?" Grace raised her eyebrows and hugged her notebook to her chest. "What brought you here?"

149

"Now for me," Sister Genevieve said, "it all began a long time ago. It started when I learned about Mother Teresa in 1956. I read that she had brought a dying woman to a hospital in Calcutta and was refused entry because the woman couldn't pay, so Mother started her Homes for the Dying Destitute. They scoured the streets to find people dying alone, outdoors, shunned because of leprosy. They gave them a safe and loving place in which to die.

"I'd been raised Catholic. My parents were decent, charitable people, but I'd never heard of anyone taking their faith to that level. I was smitten."

Genevieve's eyes slid over to the crucifix on the wall, and she rubbed the small metal cross hanging from her neck. "I had no plans for my future at that point, but I knew I couldn't see myself as a wife and mother living a bland and ordinary life. I surprised my poor parents by going off to join the Missionaries of Charity."

"That's quite a big decision," Grace said, her eyes wide. Her notepad was in her lap, pen resting in her open hand.

"I began my aspirancy in Rome. I was a novice for a year in the Philippines. Then they transferred me to Calcutta to serve my period of postulancy. Those were life-changing years. After that, I was moved to Tegucigalpa for four years, then to Quito where I worked with orphans for another four years."

It occurred to Grace that Sister Genevieve may not have told her life story to anyone in a long time. Why wasn't she in a convent now? Wasn't that where nuns lived?

"I loved serving the poorest of the poor. I truly did. But my questioning got me in trouble right from the beginning. I didn't tell anyone my doubts except my one dear friend, another young nun. Secretly, it bothered me. Like the 'custody of the senses.'"

"Which means...?"

"Which means we were taught to abstain from hearing, seeing, or touching anything unnecessary when we were out in the world doing errands or traveling from one community to the next. We had to keep our heads covered and our eyes lowered at all times in order to avoid the temptations of the world."

"Oh, my."

"Lord knows, this lovely world of ours is much more tempting if one is *not* allowed to look at it! So…" Genevieve raised her index finger and stared pointedly at Grace. "After eleven years as a Spouse of Jesus Crucified, eleven years of total subservience to the rules of the order, eleven years of believing—because this is what they taught us, drummed into us—that Jesus wanted me to obey, to suffer, to expiate sin with corporal penance—"

Genevieve lowered her voice. "They taught us to whip our thighs with little ropes and wrap spiked chains around our biceps and waist." She pushed her sweater up her arm to reveal a thin, bumpy scar. "They went too far. I tried to be pure for God, but ultimately…" She looked around as if to see if anyone was listening. "Ultimately, I think all that self-punishment was ridiculous. Something in me knew God didn't want us to hurt ourselves! I mean, *rope whips?*"

Sister Genevieve laughed, and though Grace was stunned, she smiled, caught up in Genevieve's sparkle.

"You see, during my last year in Ecuador, they allowed me to go visit my family. After ten years! Of course, I couldn't help but hear about what was going on in the world. Liberation theology was on fire in Latin America. Vatican II and Pope John the Twenty-Third changed everything. He encouraged land redistribution, labor rights, giving excluded people a voice. Instead of accepting that 'the poor will always be with us'"—she paused to make quotes in the air with her fingers—"liberation theology sought to analyze the causes of poverty and come up with solutions.

"Oh my goodness, after eleven years of what I thought was a lifetime commitment, I joined those people who were finding Christ in revolutionary change, living the Gospel message of justice and non-violence." Genevieve stopped and clasped her hands together. "Now this is turning out to be more about me than you asked. Shall we get back to the early years at St. Laurence for your piece?"

"No, this is great. I would love to include your story."

Genevieve's story excited a low rumble of recognition in Grace. Had one or two things gone differently, she could have traveled this path. If she'd been able to exercise self-control, if she hadn't succumbed to the desire for touch, hadn't gotten pregnant, would she, too, have become a nun?

151

"What happened after eleven years? How old were you then?"

A scream pierced the quiet reflectiveness of the chapel. Grace raised her eyebrows in surprise. Genevieve rose and eased herself sideways out of the pew.

"Shall we check on the most recent crisis?" she asked.

Grace followed her into the dining hall where Alvin, Tall Tree, and Maylene were huddled around Daniella, who was on his knees. He was wearing fishnet stockings and a mini skirt, and he was fanning himself with his sequined purse.

"What happened? Are you hurt?" Alvin reached a hand down to pull Daniella off the floor.

"That man!" Daniella brushed himself off and flattened his long hair with the palms of his hands. He pointed at Lenny X, who faced the corner. He was bent over almost double. "That man was trying to attack me! He had his hands in his pants and said he wanted to *show me something special!*"

Grace watched as Alvin marched over to Lenny X and tapped him on the shoulder. "What's goin' on, Len?"

Genevieve also moved in closer. "Lenny, tell us everything that happened. We love you, but certain behaviors cannot be tolerated. You know that."

Lenny turned his bulky frame around slowly, wiggling and twisting. Grace wondered if he was having a seizure or some kind of a breakdown. Had he actually tried to molest Daniella in public? She knew so little about these folks, and it occurred to her for the first time that this could be a dangerous place.

"I can't get him out! He won't come out!" Lenny blurted, sticking his hands in his pants. He dug first at his groin and then around his thigh. The small crowd stood transfixed as a lump migrated down Lenny's leg and a skinny brown ferret poked his head out of Lenny's pant leg, sniffed his ankle, and wriggled back up his leg.

The group laughed as Lenny jumped. "I can't get him! He was safe under my shirt, but then he got away!"

Alvin led Lenny into the bathroom so he could take off his pants, all the while telling him the ferret would have to go.

Maylene put her arm around Daniella and said, "You're awright. It's safe here, baby."

"But the little guy don't got no home," Grace heard Lenny mutter as she and Genevieve returned to the chapel.

"Oh, my, where was I?" Genevieve asked as settled herself back into the same pew.

"You were saying you left the Missionaries of Charity after eleven years." Grace found it hard to stifle a grin as she thought about Lenny's dance with the ferret.

Genevieve, on the other hand, appeared unruffled.

"Yes. I was twenty-nine years old. I had taken my vows: 'wholehearted and free service to the poorest of the poor,' poverty, chastity, and obedience. I could live with everything else, but the promise to be obedient stuck in my craw. And I couldn't ignore the fire smoldering all around us. I couldn't devote myself to the poor without criticizing the system that created the poor in the first place! Mother and the Missionaries didn't like that. They didn't like anybody speaking out, and I got myself in a bit of trouble."

The nun surprised Grace by winking.

"I didn't know if I wanted to renounce my vows completely or try to transfer from the Missionaries of Charity to a different religious order. I got lots of resistance from my superiors, but Mother finally granted my request. When a nun wants to leave, she has to do a year of exclaustration. You live in the world but keep the vows. I grew up in Syracuse. During that release year, I lived at home with my parents and was free to explore. My exploration led me to the Buffalo Nine."

Grace had heard her father mutter about the Buffalo Nine many years ago, calling them draft evaders.

"Can you imagine?" Sister Genevieve continued. "A group of draft resisters protesting an illegal, horrible war, sought sanctuary in a church, the Unitarian Church on Elmwood. A few days later, the FBI, US marshals, and police stormed the church. They were violent. It was unnecessary. They arrested the young people."

Genevieve shook her head and scowled as if it had happened last week. "I joined the small Catholic War Resistance organization that was formed as a result. We all worked to start St. Laurence in 1970, modeling ourselves after The Catholic Worker in the Bowery in New York. I requested a transfer to the Sisters of St. Joseph, who allowed me to live with the poor in the world without being as tied to the order. That was the right way for me." She patted Grace's hand, which clutched the back of the pew. "I needed the freedom to protest what is wrong while living what is right.

"So much was going on. The same year we opened, Father Berrigan was convicted and sentenced to prison for his role protesting the war with the Catonsville Nine. Do you remember that?"

Grace had been fifteen at the time. She shrugged. "Not really."

She did remember her family's reaction, tense and contentious, to the images of the Vietnam War wafting into the living room in black and white every evening before dinner.

27

1969

*T*he table was set, and the casserole was in the oven. Mom had everything ready, so they could eat as soon as the program ended.

Grace sat on the floor, transfixed by aerial photos of white explosions over grey water. The voice of the TV anchor was as serious and heavy as her history book. He explained that unbeknownst to Congress or the American people President Nixon had authorized secret B-52 carpet bombing raids of Cambodia back in March.

Her mother let out a short, loud intake of air. Her father was sitting in his chair, silent and still as stone. They watched the exhilarating images that followed: 200 anti-war activists at Princeton seizing the administration building, wrestling out six deans, locking themselves in, getting roughed up by the police and thrown out.

Her father sprang from his chair, turned off the TV, and huffed out of the room. Her mother stood up without speaking and turned the news back on. She watched intently, her elbows digging pockets into her thighs, until the oven's buzzer went off.

Grace's mind ricocheted back to the group of seniors at school who had put together a "protest club" made up of kids who insisted they should "stand up to power." They wore their hair long and their bell-bottoms low. They huddled over the grate behind the school and smoked during lunch.

They had started posting mimeographed flyers on lockers: Stop the War, Sit In and Fight Back, Give Peace a Chance. None of the flyers mentioned Jesus or God or the Sermon on the Mount. How did they not know that Christ is the one who revealed the way to peace?

Grace was mesmerized by them. She kept track of their moves, but she *wasn't ready to join them. She was still shy about confessing her devotion to the teachings of Jesus. So she watched them from afar as she prayed for peace and for the war to end. When the images of brutalized babies and burnt huts rushed into her brain, she pushed back with love.* Bless the soldiers, bless the babies, bless the draft evaders, bless Nixon.

"I know your father doesn't agree with me," Mom said at dinner after finishing her tuna noodle. She had turned her body a full ninety-degree angle away from Dad and faced Grace. Gloria was sulking in her room. She had refused to eat again after declaring that she couldn't stand mushrooms or peas or crumbled potato chips. "But I think this war has gone on too long. Now, I don't believe in taking over buildings or defacing property or breaking the law. That's not the right way. But too many people are being killed. It's terrible what's going on."

Grace's father got up slowly, carried his plastic water glass to the sink, and dropped it with a clatter. He stormed out into the front yard, slamming the door behind him. The car's engine revved as he sped out of the driveway.

"Mom, why does he do that? Jesus wants us to be peacemakers. He said, 'Blessed are the peacemakers.'" Tears began to burn behind her wide-open eyes.

"I don't know, dear. I don't know."

"How can a Christian love war?" Grace rarely talked with Mom alone. She felt a rush of love for her being brave enough to share her views in spite of her husband's unnerving explosions of fury. "How come he gets so mad when you say you're against the war? Why isn't everybody in the Church working for peace?"

"Honey, I've given up trying to understand. The Catholic Church does a lot of good things. They're against the death penalty, for one thing. Some of them are working against the war. And they do a lot for the poor. But they're not perfect. They can be very strict. They don't let people get divorced, even if their marriage isn't good. And they don't allow Catholics to marry people of other religions, like Jews or Protestants, unless they convert and give up their beliefs. I don't think that's right."

"Mom, why does Dad go to church and you don't? You're the one who believes in peace. I don't get it."

Her mother's absence from Mass had become more frequent. Headaches and insomnia and needing to sleep in late were sometimes the excuse, but lately she stayed home on good days too. Grace missed leaning against her soft arm during the monotonous homilies.

"Oh, honey," her mom said and ran a finger along Grace's chin. "There is so much you don't know and can't understand. But we'll talk about everything at some point. When you're older and know more about the world."

"I am older!" Grace craved more of this unfamiliar intimacy. "I know a lot about the world!"

"To everything there is a season."

Her mother patted her hand and rose from her seat. She scraped Grace's little pile of tuna and her dad's unfinished noodles onto her plate and gathered up the crusty silverware.

"There is a time for everything," she said. "Now it's time to clean up."

28

Sister Genevieve leaned back against the rough pew and tucked a loose strand of grey hair behind her ear. "Father Dan Berrigan, Phillip Berrigan, and seven other activists broke into a draft board in Maryland and pulled out draft files. They brought them into a parking lot in wire garbage bins, poured homemade napalm over them, and set them on fire. Dan said it was better to burn paper than children. Those were the times we were living through."

Grace wrote quickly as she tried to keep up. "You've had quite a life," she said.

This non-descript woman whose days were filled with sweeping floors and cooking oatmeal, praying and writing and interrupting fights, had been part of history. She had protested war and injustice, not just complained and worried. She had done something important with her life and lived out her beliefs. Next to Genevieve's stories, Grace's life experiences were as small and scattered as dandelion fluff.

"And now. Now we are moving in a new direction. Something which has been a long time coming."

"New direction," Grace noted.

"The *truth* is..." Genevieve stopped and looked around the room as if its darkness were a kind of protection from forces not ready to hear her secret. The chapel smelled of perfumed candles and burnt wax. She continued in a whisper. "What I want more than anything else is to become a priest, to co-officiate in the administration of the sacraments. Father Luke is fully on board. This is, of course, a blatant violation of canon law. We are taking great risks. I'll undoubtedly have to leave my order. But I feel I've waited long enough. I don't want to be hush hush any more. I want the public and the hierarchy to know about my equal role in the Mass. And I want you to write about it."

Grace's head spun as she thought about Genevieve's revelation. She found it unsettling, which surprised her since she considered herself a progressive, an open-minded feminist.

The truth is.

During her early years, while Grace was smitten by love for God and the Catholic Church, she had never let herself imagine the priesthood as an option. If she were to have committed herself to the Church, it would have been as a nun, the life of quiet obedience promising spiritual completeness. But being a priest, with all its singularity and otherworldly power—listening to confessions, absolving sins, marrying and baptizing and preaching, blessing wine, transforming it into the Blood of Christ— the thought of it was unnerving, wild, dangerous even, scary.

The next morning, Grace found Alvin behind St. Laurence sweeping leaves into piles. The three huge orange mounds he'd already collected reminded her of the running jumps she and Gloria would take into heaps of dry leaves on the lawn. She took a deep breath, letting the memory of the crunching sound and the musty smell wash over her.

"Hi, Alvin," she said, picking up a rake and joining in. "Can I help?"

"No, thank you. No need."

"But I'd like to. I haven't raked leaves in a long time."

"Oh, right. You're from *California*!" He laughed.

"I'm from here, but I've been gone for years. I missed the fall for sure."

"Fall's pretty, I know, but the bad part is it reminds us winter's comin'."

"True! But I'm kind of looking forward to winter. I haven't seen snow in forever."

Thoughts of winter evoked images of wonderland, snow angels, and sledding. Days off from school, snowball fights, building igloos, and drinking cocoa. She knew it was pure nostalgia. She hadn't lived in Buffalo long enough on this return trip to experience her car getting stuck in the snow or careening off the ice. She didn't remember what it felt like to experience power outages or ice-block toes or raging blizzards.

"Don't you love how pretty it is?" she asked.

"Pretty bitter, pretty icy, pretty horrible. I had me one bad winter living outside, and I ain't *never* gonna forget it or forgive it." He shivered as if it were freezing out even though the temperature was fairly mild for October. "You don't know winter till you have to find a vent behind the bus station and wrap yourself in a plastic bag and three jackets to keep from freezing *to death*. You know St. Laurence saved my life? You know that, right?"

"Alvin, I'm writing an article about St. Laurence for *The Free Press*. Can I interview you? It would be great to have your perspective on the Hospitality House and what it means to you."

"No, Miss Schreiber. I don't want my name in no paper. Just tell everybody it saved me from the demon drink and brought me closer to Jesus. Gave me a place to go every day and a place to get sober until I was in good enough shape to take good care of my moms while she was dyin', and then gave me a chance to give back to my brothers from the streets. That's all."

"How long were you here? Before you got sober, I mean?"

"Off and on, you know. I lost track. Maybe a year, maybe two. Kept coming back though 'cause they take such good care of people. Warm food and dry clothes and a bed and all, and everybody in a sweet mood. It saved my life."

"If you don't mind me asking…why did you start living on the streets?"

"It's one bad thing and then another, you know." Alvin resumed sweeping but kept talking. "I was a truck driver. The big rigs. I had me a good situation. A little money. But I let it go to my head. Gambling and drinking and thinkin' I can live without the Lord. I hit somebody with the truck late one night. Didn't kill 'em, but I hurt 'em. Bad. Scared the hell outta me, and I started drinkin' real heavy. Lost my job, of course. My wife was already sick a me, being a good church lady herself. She told me to go, and I don't blame her. I don't blame her one bit."

"Wow," Grace said. Alvin had impressed her as being sensible, so disciplined and kind. She couldn't imagine him as a gambler or as a drunk, living on a grate. One after another, these interviews with the workers at St. Lawrence left her feeling floored.

A memory of Frankie and his weekly revelations swirled through her mind like the leaves that danced around their feet.

"You have an important story, you know, Alvin."

"Ah, no. It ain't my story that counts. You know what I'm sayin'? It's this place. After I got healed, they gave me a job and peoples to care for and love and to love me back. Sister Genevieve, now, she's a sweetheart. Deep down good, you know. And Father Luke. Ain't no better kind of man anywhere. You can look far and wide. You won't find no one better than that."

Grace set the rake against the wall and sat down on a bench. "Have you lived here a long time?"

"After getting clean, I lived and worked here twenty-one years. It's my true home now, and I give my all. That's all I do, praise Jesus. I give back in gratitude."

Grace paused before continuing. *I give back in gratitude*, she repeated in her head. She would write that on a post-it note and put it on the mirror. "Thank you for sharing your story with me, Alvin. Can I write about it in the article?"

"Why not? But don't say my name. Call me Denzel."

He let out a low rolling laugh, his cheeks round and freckled in the sun. He gripped the handle of the broom and bent down to Grace's eye level.

"Or Frederick. Or Malcolm." He nodded, serious again. "Call me Martin. I'd like that. That's good." He chuckled again and turned his attention back to the leaves. "That's real good."

As October progressed, even the puffy purple ski jacket Grace had found in the supply room wasn't enough to keep her warm when she sat on the lawn with her friends at dusk. But she couldn't bear the idea of moving inside. She loved watching the darkness descend through the silhouettes of the trees.

One afternoon after visiting her dad, she drove to a home supply store and bought a washtub and a stack of split logs. She set it up on the grass and built a fire. When Brian discovered what she had done, he went to the back of the house and retrieved some bricks to support the tub. Mountain was delighted and offered to peel sticks to roast chunks of pineapple while they talked.

They huddled around the fire, crackling and smoky, the leaves of the maple trees rustling overhead. They watched the boys across the street wrestle on their front lawn. Grace wondered if they should intervene before one of them poked the other's eye out.

"Grace, did you ever want kids?" Mountain asked.

Grace stared at the boys as the little one gave his brother a stiff kick to the chest and ran off laughing. "Well, I don't know how to answer that. I'm not sure," she said.

Brian and Mountain both turned to face her. As cold as it was, she sweated under her puffy coat. Her brain felt as if it were stuffed with cotton balls. Maybe the fire's enveloping heat was too much. Likely she'd had too much white wine.

She pushed her chair back. She didn't want to lie to her new friends, but she didn't want to talk about children, her pregnancy, or giving away her baby. At least for now. She wished the boys would come back so she'd have a distraction.

She had thought about kids. Or about one kid. She'd used the image of her daughter, healthy and happy, at one point or another, to ground her. But she could never wrap her mind around the idea of a flesh and blood being needing her that much. And anyway, the opportunity never arose. She had probably blown it. She'd given away a winning lottery ticket; what was the probability of ever winning again? As if she deserved to never get a second chance.

"Maybe at one point I did," she said. "It's kind of confusing."

"It's okay. I'm just curious is all." Mountain's eyes were piercing but gentle. "How about you, Brian? You don't have a kid sequestered away somewhere, do you?"

"Ha! No, no kids. But I always wanted children. It blows me away that it never happened. I'm fifty already and never had a family. For a while, I thought…I don't know where the time went."

Grace watched his large, taut body relax as he lowered himself in the chair, unfolded himself like a carpenter's ruler, and looked up at the darkening sky.

"So you've been in love then?" Mountain asked.

"Deeply. Twice. Married even, for five years. Things just didn't work out like I wanted or expected." He closed his eyes and sighed.

"That's the problem, isn't it?" Mountain mused, grabbing a couple of Oreos from the tray and biting into one. Black crumbles dusted her flowered sweatshirt. "Wanting and expecting—gets us in trouble every time."

"And you, Grace?" Mountain continued her gentle prying. "I'm sure you've been in love."

She hadn't planned to tell them about Jake. She wanted to start fresh, no backstory.

"Well, you know, I…"

The two friends waited as she paused. She didn't even know where to start.

"I was. Not that long ago. In love."

"How long ago?" Brian turned to face her. He rubbed his knees, then massaged the back of his neck. He seemed nervous for her.

"It's been more than a year. I should be over it by now, I guess."

"Breakups are always hard," Mountain said. "You take as long as you need, dear girl."

"I guess I was pretty badly…Oh, that's funny. I meant to say madly…"

Now she was blushing. She fumbled with the paper towel in her lap, crumpling it then folding it.

"I guess I was madly in love. His name was Jake."

Now she'd done it. She'd revealed her vulnerable self, something she'd had no intention of doing. She needed to present this in the right way. "But then I broke it off."

"Why?" Mountain asked, rocking slightly. The firelight made the moment feel intense and a little magical.

"Well…" They were being so kind to her. "I guess *he* did, break up…I mean…by cheating on me with his…with our yoga instructor. They moved into an ashram. A spiritual commune, I guess. Right down the road from my place. I packed up and left town…It was hard."

Brian's forehead crinkled into a frown. "I'm sorry, Grace, but you're lucky to be rid of him. This guy sounds like a first class jerk. Talk about sullying the waters of an ancient and sacred art."

"I, for one, hate this guy. If I could," Mountain said, "I'd lock him into Cobra position and throw away the key to his higher consciousness."

"I'm going to start meditating on some serious back pain for Jake the Yogic Jerk," Brian said. His hand was suddenly on her knee. He held it there for less than a second.

An unexpected wind slapped at them. Grace felt as if the weight of Jake's memory had been gently pushed off her shoulders by their compassion.

"Thank you," she said. "Thank you both for listening." She rubbed her eyes with her gloved hands so the tears wouldn't break free. Then she leaned in closer to the fire and put her hands in her pockets.

"It gets tiring, doesn't it?" Mountain said. "All this longing, hurting, being hurt? Sometimes I just want to be a cup of water. Just give and get, take what comes, give when asked. Empty, full, empty, full. What would that feel like, to not expect or want anything?"

"Hmmm. To be water," Brian said. "'We are born and live inside black water in a well. How could we know what an open field of sunlight is? Don't insist on going where you think you want to go.' That's Rumi."

Grace raised her eyebrows in response to the beautiful, perplexing poem. She wanted a swig of wine more than ever, but by now the jar was empty.

"Nice," Mountain said. "Where you *think* you want to go. Nice." She sat up. "I *think* I want to go get soup. A big ceramic crock of homemade broccoli cheddar soup."

"If you *insist*," Brian said. He stirred the dying embers and covered the washtub with a lid. They folded their chairs and leaned them against the house, gathered up their goods, and marched in a single file up the stairs into Mountain's second story, spicy-smelling kitchen, Magic padding along behind them.

It occurred to Grace how lucky and grateful she was now. She had two new friends and a sweet, lumbering dog living next door. She had Luke and Genevieve and Alvin at St. Laurence. She had her dad back, and she was carving out a life for herself.

Grace had hung two bulletin boards on the wall in her Warrior Room. She tacked her favorite pages of Frankie's essay and the program from the memorial Mass on the first one. The second displayed the dog-eared and underlined sex abuse clippings she regularly collected. There were too many to fit; they overlapped and spilled over the edges of the bulletin board, an inky river of sadness and scandal taped across the wall.

A few pencil sketches of trees and flowers were taped randomly on the other wall. She'd set up an altar on a makeshift table near the window and decorated it with candles, some polished stones, a potted plant, and a framed photo of her mom on a red sofa, two-year-old Gloria snuggling next to her, newborn Grace in her arms.

Grace inhaled, counted to ten, and tried to clear her mind. She stood in Tree pose for a minute, did a cobbled together version of the Sun Salutation, and cradled herself in Child pose. Then she lay on her back and stared at the ceiling. A wellspring of resistance rose within her as she again reflected on Linda Starflower's tranquil space at The Light Within. It had always made Grace feel a little jittery and irritated, not exactly in a state of yogic centered calm in spite of the eucalyptus incense, the tinkling waterfall audiotape, and Linda's soothing miso soup of a voice.

"Take a breath as you allow the distractions to flow through you, not bother you, not interrupt your deep ujjayi breathing," Linda said on the many occasions Grace had tiptoed into class at ten past the hour. She would rush to set up her yoga mat while everyone else sat in full meditative lotus pose.

Sinewy and elastic, graceful and flat-chested, yoga tights glued to her perfect form, Linda emanated ballerina discipline and calm. Next to her, Grace had always felt bumpy, full, and bloated. There was no way to measure up to Linda, who occasionally demonstrated her ability to raise herself on her forearms and bend her torso back until the soles of her feet rested on the top of her head.

Grace finally figured out that Linda began class fifteen minutes before the stated start time. Even when Grace was on time, she was late. And she extended class beyond the end time. Inevitably Grace had an appointment or a lunch date or just grew restless after an hour and a half of strenuous stretching and fire breathing and had to tiptoe out.

All the while, Linda's satiny voice intoned, "Impatience, frustration, jealousy. Whatever emotions you are feeling now. Noise, commotion, irritation. Let it go. Let it all go. Try to let these temporary distractions wash over you like wind across a field, like water flowing over a stone."

Grace rolled her eyes at the memory. Maybe yoga wasn't the route, but since she could remember, she'd longed for some version of transcendence, something to lift her toward love and away from her petty preoccupations. She sat up, wincing at the stiffness in her joints, and studied the impatiens plant she'd stuck in a clay pot and placed next to the frame on the table.

It was rooted in dirt, dug itself deep into the earth in order to survive, but it also craved the sun. Its shiny emerald leaves and orange petals leaned toward the light. Isn't that what she was doing? Even though she was stuck in her needy, earth-bound body, even though her head was abuzz with confusion, wasn't she leaning toward the light?

29

At six o'clock, it was already night outside the window of her dad's apartment. Streetlights punctuated the blackness. Grace was on her back on the sofa. Her dad was sitting at his desk. The ABC News broadcaster reported the gruesome news that a Buffalo obstetrician had been murdered two days before. The story that had been all over the paper and local TV was now national news.

"On October 23rd, Dr. Bernard Slepian was killed when he returned from synagogue after attending a memorial service for his father. James Kopp, a long-time anti-abortion activist, shot him through a window in his home. The ricocheting bullet almost killed his son. The next day, pro-life protesters carrying huge photos of mangled fetuses and posters that read *Stop Shedding the Blood of the Innocent* rallied in front of the clinic where he had worked."

"Terrible shame," her father said, looking up from his papers. "Just awful. But you could easily argue that the abortion doctor got what he deserved."

"Dad, how can you say that?" Grace bolted upright and swung around to face him. "He was murdered."

"Grace, eleven million babies have been murdered."

"*What?*"

"The National Right to Life Committee sends me the numbers. Over eleven million babies have been killed so far. This may be the Lord's way of punishing this doctor. Of course, I don't know that, but it does make you wonder."

Grace let out a gasp.

"If you were in Germany during World War II, would you have protested if Hitler had been killed?"

"Dad, I don't—"

"No, you wouldn't have, because you would have been glad the world was rid of his evil. After this terrible incident with the abortion doctor, I would love to be in the presence of the Holy Mother," he said. Grace held her breath as she looked at her dad.

"We, as a society, have an obligation to make amends with the Holy Mother. I have to go to the Cemetery of the Innocents at St. Ignatius in Lackawanna."

"Dad, I—"

"They do a special devotional Novena to Our Lady on Wednesdays. I'd like you to drive me. You'll need a veil." His eyes were red-rimmed and pleading. "Please. This is very important to me."

Saint Ignatius was dark and somber. The special Mass in Veneration of Mary had already begun when they arrived.

The prayer was led by a woman. She knelt in the first pew, a lacy black veil covering her hair. Her shoulders curled around a heavy, leather-bound book. Her back to them, she intoned: "Mother most chaste, Mother inviolate, Mother undefiled, Virgin most prudent."

Grace knelt, not sure what to do with her hands.

"Virgin most venerable."

"Pray for us" rose from the throats of the other kneeling penitents after every invocation. Her father joined in, hitting his chest with his fist each time he murmured the response, his voice soft, begging.

"Mirror of justice."

"Mystical rose."

"Tower of ivory."

"House of gold."

"Gate of heaven."

"Morning star."

"Queen of patriarchs."

"Queen of virgins."

Grace understood how the simplicity and the meditative repetition gave solace. The poetry impressed her. If she didn't think about the meaning of the words, the droning, prayerful chanting calmed her. After ten minutes of listening, Grace shifted her weight. A twinge of pain shot from her left knee to her hip. How did people kneel for hours at a time? How could people not question the irrationality of what they were repeating? *Mother inviolate?*

Grace's dad slipped a rosary out of his shirt pocket. He stroked each plastic bead as he mumbled the Hail Mary. Grace longed to find spiritual meaning; she always had. But she refused, in the process, to sacrifice her questioning mind. Accepting the tenets of the Catholic Church seemed to her like some kind of Faustian bargain. You get to feel loved, have peace of mind, etc., but only if you hand over your brain. Like a plate of food offered to a starving person in exchange for an organ or an ear. She felt herself pushed and pulled again, here at this bizarrely sweet little Mass, into the salty ocean of feeling, back to the shore of her logical mind, rocking, out to sea and back again.

The tiny white crosses at the Cemetery of the Innocents next door looked like a veteran's memorial for dolls. Thirty rows of twenty-five handmade crosses were placed in neat lines on the great leaf-covered lawn. A wooden sign at the entrance read *Shrine to the Unborn, In Memory of the Holy Innocents Lost to Abortion Placed under the Protection of Our Blessed Mother*. An image of Mary holding the baby Jesus was painted underneath the words. Hand-lettered placards leaned against the surrounding fence: *4,000 Abortions Daily; Abortion Kills Children; Adoption: The Loving Option; Let Your Baby Live.*

Grace's father made the sign of the cross. "It's all so sad," he said.

Grace stared at the vast lawn, stunned. There had been protesters at the clinic where she went to get prenatal care in Berkeley so many years ago. Men, women, and children had held signs with photos of bloody aborted fetuses; photos of embryos in watery sacs above the words *God loved you before you were born;* photos of healthy babies that read *My heart was beating at eighteen days.*

Some of the protesters screamed, "Don't kill your baby!" and pushed signs in the faces of the women and girls as they walked into the building. *Never to Live, Never to Laugh; Abortion Hurts Women; Baby Killers Should Be Brought to Justice; Don't Kill the Holy Innocents.*

The clinic was one of the first to offer legal abortions after Roe vs. Wade was passed, and everyone who got services there had to v ''-

through a jeering crowd. The memory chilled her. She did the right thing by carrying her baby to term and giving it up for adoption, didn't she? Those people had made her feel shame nonetheless. She'd gone through the pain of labor, succumbed to the numbing of Demerol, and signed the relinquishment papers, "out of wedlock" circled in red like a curse on the forms. She'd dripped blood for a week, wore plastic-backed pads under her bra to catch the unrelenting milk, and dipped into a dense depression.

How would it have felt for the women in her same shoes who couldn't do what she did? Women who felt they had to have an abortion and were harassed on their way in to do the deed? She'd seen some of them crying in the waiting room—young girls, older women, most of them alone.

"We must pray to the Blessed Mother to forgive us for not protecting all these innocent children," her father said, pulling his tangled rosary from his pocket. "It is the Church's responsibility to protect the children."

Grace wanted to scream. For the first time since she read Frankie's essay and learned of his violation by a priest, she didn't feel sad or helpless or overwhelmed or confused. Instead, she was overcome by a burning, roiling rage. It was all about sex. What was it about the Church that attracted and cultivated and perpetuated sexual violence? How could her dad justify it?

How could he not see the Church's hypocrisy regarding sexuality of all stripes and its refusal to recognize or respect all the gay people in their ranks? How could he accept that the Church didn't tolerate any sexuality outside of traditional marriage? Didn't he recognize the terrible, twisted way sex would express itself in these profoundly immature men, forced to be repressed and celibate?

The Catholic Church's aversion to sexuality was so great that—in Grace's view—it actually *contributed* to untoward sexual behavior toward innocent young people. It *led to* unwanted pregnancy and therefore to abortion due to its medieval prohibitions against birth control.

Grace stared at her father and ground her teeth together. She gripped the fence until he finished his prayers.

They drove home from the cemetery in silence.

When Grace arrived at her dad's apartment the next day, the living room was cluttered with videotapes and books. An unwashed cup rested atop a heap of Catholic magazines in the middle of the coffee table. Grace pushed a pile of newspapers off the end of the sofa and sat down.

Her dad sat at his desk and shook his head. "Grace, I need to ask you something."

"Yes?"

"Why are you no longer a Catholic? Did Gloria do this to you?"

"Dad, what are you talking about?"

"Did she infect you?"

"Did she *what*?"

"I've always wondered if Gloria convinced you to leave the Church. You were such a devout young lady. It was an inspiration. But after you left for California, you changed. She had drifted so far from the Church. She must have poisoned you."

"No, Dad, not at all. She didn't try to convince me of anything."

"Or was it living out there in California with all the hippies and homosexuals and the drugs? I shouldn't have allowed you to go there."

"Dad! No!"

"Then what did I do wrong?" His voice was small and pleading. He picked up a pencil and rolled it between his palms.

"Nothing." She knew there was no way he would ever understand her calamitous journey away from the confines of the Church. He'd be horrified if she told him everything that had happened to her since she left home. He didn't even let her ask him any questions about the Catholic Church's awful misdeeds.

"I must have done something wrong. Or it was your mother, with her lack of interest in the faith. I should have done more to overcome her doubts, her apathy."

"Dad..." Grace could see his eyes reddening.

"What did I do to instill such doubt in my family?" His voice grew hushed as if he was no longer talking to her but to a foreboding and ethereal presence. "Where did I go wrong?"

For a moment, Grace wished that she could go back, that she could have held more firmly to the faith that had once centered and grounded her. She'd feel less confused, and they wouldn't have to have all these awkward and unhappy conversations. He'd be pleased with her, he'd continue to admire her, and they'd both feel content for a change.

Grace had caught herself thinking of the pregnant girl during the Veneration of Mary and at the abortion cemetery, emboldened by the groundswell of anger she'd felt.

"The virgin birth," Grace said to Luke the next day. The two were alone in the community room after dinner. "This may be a naïve question. But do you truly believe in it?"

He surprised her by laughing. "Of course. Of course yes and of course no. It's not scientifically possible, but it's spiritually possible. It's metaphorically beautiful. I've never seen a miracle, but it doesn't mean there couldn't be one. It doesn't make sense, and yet it does."

She let out the breath she had been holding. She didn't know what she had expected him to say. Something treasonous and shocking?

"But, why a virgin?" she asked. "What is virginity a metaphor for? Why does the absence of sex make Mary's womb a holier place than any other woman's?"

Like say, mine? she thought. *Or that girl's?*

"Because God's love is holier than the love of a mere man."

"Can't a baby born of an ordinary woman still be holy? Aren't all babies holy, Father?"

In light of this topic, it was hard for her to think of him as anything but a priest. Why did Catholics teach that followers should cringe at lust, the source of the life force? How would her life have been different if she hadn't been taught that sexual desire was a sin, a burden to be carried around like a basketful of stones? Or if somebody had taught her about birth control, for God's sake? Why didn't her mother even mention birth control?

Father's Luke expression softened. "Yes, Grace, I believe all babies are holy."

"Father, I have to tell you I find some of this stuff *very* strange. 'The Veneration of Mary.'" She made air quotes with her fingers. "Wow. I mean, I know you believe in women's equality." She hadn't yet talked with him about Genevieve's request that Grace write about the nun's role in the Mass.

"Grace, don't you see?" Luke's chest rose as he inhaled; his shoulders sank as let out a sigh. "I believe in women's equality, fully and deeply. *And* I believe in the Virgin birth! I believe in the purity of love and God's love for humans. And please call me Luke."

"Maybe I'm being too frank," she said, pressing her clasped hands between her knees.

Luke looked at her steadily. "I appreciate that you are being straightforward. Do you know how rare it is for me to talk candidly this way? I love what I do. I love St. Laurence House." His voice dropped to a whisper. "But sometimes it does get a bit lonely."

A little butterfly of discomfort batted its wings inside her. Houses of Hospitality were not supposed to be forlorn places, and lonesome, single, middle-aged women were not supposed to have this kind of conversation with priests.

"When I first encountered Dorothy Day, it was through her autobiography, *The Long Loneliness.* Learning about the Catholic Worker Movement…I'm not sure how to say this." He balled his hand into a fist and tapped his chest. "It was something like what I imagine it feels like to fall in love."

Tall Tree tiptoed into the room and sat on the piano bench facing them. "May I beg your indulgence that I might play?" he asked.

"Thanks for asking, Tree," Luke said. "Okay with you, Grace?"

Grace nodded. She had grown to love Tall Tree and his flowery nineteenth-century diction. She looked forward to the lush melodies he teased from the piano every day.

"Will you play something from Godspell?" she asked. "Do you know that song 'Save the People?' Or 'All Good Gifts?' I used to love all those songs. And 'We Beseech Thee.'"

"With the deepest pleasure and gratitude, I shall endeavor to play for you." He bowed, turning to face the piano. He played the opening chords from 'All Good Gifts' delicately, liltingly, as if in accompaniment.

"Dorothy Day and Peter Maurin," Luke continued. "Now, there was a pair. They were celibate, of course, but intimate."

Grace stared at him for a second. She reached inside her bag for her notepad and a pen. She felt heat rise in her cheeks as she transcribed the line.

"They called what they were doing 'love in action.' I lived at the Catholic Worker House on the Lower East Side once for a month. Nothing theoretical, nothing ephemeral about it. It's an amazing, busy, down and dirty, very spiritual place."

"Love in action," Grace said. "It's from *The Brothers Karamazov*. I remember the quote. 'Love in action is a harsh and dreadful thing compared to that in dreams.'"

Father Luke slumped into the sofa as he listened to Tall Tree play. Grace pressed her elbows into her thighs, rested her head in her hands, and sighed. They'd said enough for now. After an energetic rendition of 'We Beseech Thee,' she bundled herself into her jacket and said goodnight.

Part Three

Do not be afraid of men, then.
Whatever is covered up will be uncovered,
and every secret will be made known.
What I am telling you in the dark
you must repeat in broad daylight,
and what you have heard in private
you must tell from the housetops.
—Matthew 10:26

30

Grace gasped at the sight of the girl, pink and pasty, on the couch in the community room. Black eyeliner formed raccoon-like rings around her eyes. The girl stared ahead blankly as Grace sat next to her on the sagging couch.

"Hey," Grace said. "Welcome back."

"Who're you? You live here?"

"Nope," Grace answered. "Just help out."

"Ain't you noble and good then."

Grace laughed. "Hardly."

The girl winced. "I feel sick."

"Where have you been since you were here last time?"

It had been over a month since the girl had come to St. Laurence and then disappeared. Her pregnant belly was showing under her tight, fraying red sweater.

"You people ask a lot of fuckin' questions." The girl pushed herself up, then sank back down. "I'm about to puke."

Grace sprang from the couch and jogged to the kitchen, almost bumping into Alvin. *Sorry. Emergency*, she mouthed. She pulled a large bucket from the broom closet and ran back. She held it out for the girl, who grabbed it and retched, coughing up some yellow liquid.

She wrinkled her nose and laid her head back when she was done. "Yuck."

Grace studied her as she relaxed against the sofa cushion, her eyes closed. She pressed a tissue into the palm of her hand. Why wasn't this child getting medical attention? What should, or could, Grace do to help her? She was seized by a rush of relief—gratitude even—that this wayward creature was back.

"What's your name?"

"Crystal."

"Crystal, have you been to a doctor?"

"Naw. I'm awright."

"Where have you been living?"

The dishes were washed, and the floors mopped. Grace had nothing better to do than sit there. Maybe because of that, and maybe because Crystal could barely move off the sofa, she let down a bit of the guard that had protected her on her last visit to the shelter.

"Just around," she said. "Here and there, you know."

"Are you done with this bucket?" Grace asked.

She took it to the bathroom and rinsed it out. Then she brought it back and set it on the floor by Crystal's feet. She was laying down now, her arm over her face.

"Can you stay here for a while this time while we find you a doctor and help you figure out what to do about this baby?" Grace asked. Her voice was unnaturally high. She was aware that it sounded a little like begging.

"'Kay. I'll stay."

"Good. Give us a couple days before you take off into the cold. Promise?"

"Yeah, yeah, I promise. I need that pail." She threw up again, wiped her mouth on her sleeve, closed her eyes, and fell fast asleep.

Grace emptied the bucket again and walked through the kitchen. Alvin and Lance were unloading bags of bread on the counter.

"Hey!" she said when she saw them. She returned to the community room to place the bucket at the girl's feet and make another pot of coffee.

Father Luke walked into the room and greeted Grace as he did now every afternoon. "She's back," Grace said, pointing her thumb at the girl. "And throwing up."

"She got here after two this morning," the priest told Grace between gulps of coffee.

"She looks terrible," Grace whispered. "She seems too frail to be out in this weather." November's skies were lamb's wool grey, threatening to explode with snow. "I told her to promise to stay till we could find her a doctor and a permanent place. She seemed to open up to me a little."

"Good," Father Luke said. "Wonderful." He smiled as he stirred sugar into his second cup. "Maybe you're her guardian angel."

He turned to go but turned his head around to look at Grace. "Thank you for making the coffee strong, by the way. We need to be wide awake around here."

When Crystal woke up thirty minutes later, she bolted upright and scratched her greasy, uncombed head. "Fuck!" she groaned. "Pail!"

"At your feet, my queen," Grace said. The girl leaned over to pick up the bucket but missed. She took one look at her vomit-stained shirt and started to cry.

Grace put her hand on the girl's skunk stripe. "Come on, sweetheart. Let's get you cleaned up."

"Gross," Crystal said. "So fuckin' gross."

"True." Grace held the girl's arm and led her up the stairs to the women's dorm. Grace had contemplated spending the night here a couple of times. Alvin had asked her if she wanted to take a shift once a week, but she'd declined.

Ten sets of bunk beds crowded the women's room. The residents' smelly stuff was piled everywhere. Women of all ages and sorts lay around in various states of disarray. Nobody ever got a solid night's slumber, and Grace had enough trouble sleeping all by herself.

"Let's get you into the shower."

Crystal wasn't wearing anything under the soiled sweater and the dirty sweatpants. No t-shirt, bra, or underwear. Despite her full breasts and the bulge below her belly button, she was bony. A purplish-blue bruise the size of an ostrich egg was splattered over her ribs on her left side.

While Crystal was in the shower, Grace rinsed out the pukey sweater and threw it and the dirty pants into the bin in the laundry room. She grabbed a clean long sleeved t-shirt and pajama pants from the storeroom. When she returned, Crystal was sitting on a plastic chair in the shower room, her scrubbed, rosy body wrapped in a fluffy white towel. Her hair was rolled up in a turban.

"God, I feel better."

"Good," Grace said. "Let's get you to bed. I'll bring you some crackers. Okay?"

Crystal nodded. "Yeah."

"Tomorrow I'm going to make calls so we can get you seen by a doctor. Deal?" Grace shivered as the question left her lips. Nobody had brought her crackers or asked her how she was feeling when she was pregnant. She'd had to seek out a clinic in a new city all by herself.

"Okay," Crystal said.

"But first, you have to tell me about the bruise." Grace touched her lightly on her bare shoulder.

"I don't *have to* do nothin'." Crystal jerked her shoulder away, a wounded, defensive bird. "You people *kill* me."

Brian knocked on her door at six o'clock in the middle of a downpour.

"Can I get shelter from the storm?" he asked. He was holding two bottles of Corona. His Bills cap protected his head, but his shoulders and pant legs were soaked.

With the descent of winter, Grace had changed her routine. She had dinner with her dad a couple of evenings a week. It was too gray and chilly to sit outside and eat, so the neighbors met at Mountain's every Monday for cornbread and vegetable stew, then went on about their solitary winter lives. Hanging out with Brian alone was not part of the new routine. But here he was, a wet dog in her doorway.

She hesitated. She didn't want him to think she was interested in him, but it would be rude to say no.

"You're sopped," she said, sizing him up and giggling. "Don't you own an umbrella?"

"I guess I thought I could make it without getting drenched."

"Come on in."

He stepped inside, thanking her. He took his jacket off and hung it on the doorknob, kicked off his shoes, peeled off his soaked socks, and rolled up his pants.

They talked for over an hour, chugging the cold beer, facing each other on the sofa. He described the renovations he'd recently finished on his other townhouse and told her about its new tenant, a college kid. He asked her about her father. She told him about the Cemetery of the Innocents and the Veneration of Mary.

"I still feel drawn to the Hospitality House. The simplicity of the lifestyle they live, it's calming. I'm trying to help a new resident, this pregnant teenager from somewhere down south, find a place to live."

She grew animated as she mimicked Crystal and related how much she worried her. She recounted the story Luke told her about St. Laurence burning at the stake, requesting that he be broiled to a crisp.

Brian chuckled. "That's about as bizarre as it gets," he said. "The Catholic Church has all the elements of a cult."

"Hmm," she murmured and raised her eyebrows.

"It's been so normalized that we don't see it. If a new religious group came along, and the leaders said they had supernatural powers, performed alchemy, told their followers they had to worship someone who was murdered, they'd be so far out of the mainstream that we'd warn our children about them. If a new religious sect forced people to obey their rules or they'd kick them out, if they told their followers they had the power to ban them to Hell, we'd recognize them as a cult."

"Hmmm." He'd summed up all her questions and reservations in a few sentences, though she reserved the right to feel a bit protective of Genevieve, Alvin, and Luke. If theirs was a cult, it was a pretty generous one. "I guess you weren't raised religious?"

"Not really," he said. "We enjoyed the secular version of the holidays, but that's about all."

"I'm kind of jealous," she said. "I think religion did a number on me. I'm still sorting it all out. Whether it was good for me or not. The good, the bad, and the ugly. Do you consider yourself an atheist?"

"No," Brian said. "Even that's too dogmatic for me! If anything, I'm an anti-dogmatist." He stretched out his legs, planted his bare heels on her coffee table, and sunk deeper into her sofa. He slung his arm across the back. His hand almost reached her shoulder. He was such a large man. "I'm sort of a nothing-ist, I guess...which is not quite the same as a nihilist. Maybe I'm an anti-ism-ist. If for no other reason than because it's fun to say."

"Are you saying no belief system defines you? Do you have a set of beliefs?" She didn't give him a chance to respond. "I feel like I have so many conflicting values. I'm drawn to goodness, to simple kindness, which is located right at the heart of Christianity, but I'm repelled by some of the Church's teachings. They're so antiquated and illogical."

Brian nodded. "I have a lot of beliefs," he said. "I don't know about a *set*. I think we're all in this boat together, trying to figure out the trip. Most of us are lost and confused. It seems the least we can do is be kind to one another."

Grace propped her head on her hand as she studied him, his green eyes moist with emotion.

"I think we have to be open and reflective, receptive to ideas, and willing to question everything. I believe in not-knowing. I embrace it even. Do you know the book *Zen and the Art of Motorcycle Maintenance*? It changed my life."

"How?"

"I've read it many times. 'The place to improve the world is first in one's own heart and head and hands, and then work outward from there.' That may be my favorite quote. Pirsig—Robert Pirsig, the author—gave me the courage to leave graduate school and take up carpentry. I think I became wiser and more centered for it."

Grace regretted not settling into a career or going to graduate school. Her years in San Francisco after college were a jumble of incomplete pursuits. Her life reminded her of a messy artist's loft full of half-finished paintings, none of which ever got hung on the wall. She'd repeatedly find herself growing impatient or getting distracted. She'd had no guidance, no mom to counsel her. She'd never asked her dad or her sister for advice for fear of appearing less than together.

"I only have a Bachelor's. I never figured out what I wanted to study." She sighed.

"School is one way to learn," Brian said. "But it's not enough. Pirsig would say that we have to engage both our hearts and our brains. That so-called rationality and intuitive thinking can co-exist. That wisdom can come from not-thinking, by existing in a state of centeredness. Not everything can be explained with reason."

"It's funny," Grace responded. "Both religion and science attempt to explain everything."

Brian nodded. "I think we can live with a kind of optimistic agnosticism, a hopeful uncertainty. It's hard for most people to live without certainty. It's hard to be unafraid in the face of the great questions."

"I guess I'm beginning to feel..." Grace hesitated. She hadn't been able to articulate her views about religion or Catholicism since having re-immersed herself. When she was with Luke, she'd taken to listening to and questioning *his* beliefs without expressing her own.

"I guess I'm beginning to feel like we can take the best of whatever religions or philosophies we're drawn to," she continued.

Brian watched her. His eyes were patient as she worked out what she wanted to say.

"Like we don't have to take on the whole package but can embrace the parts that resonate for us. Like God, for example. It's ironic, but in a way, religion presents God in limited terms. It wants to confine ideas of God to one teacher, one book, one set of principles. But it seems much bigger and more complex than that. More mysterious and confusing! Maybe instead of continually convincing ourselves we've found the answer, we should be busy seeking out the answers. *If* they're even possible to find!"

Grace inhaled, and in the pause, noticed that their knees were touching. She wiggled ever-so-slightly away. "I don't know if I believe in God, but maybe it doesn't matter as long as we're always seeking, trying to figure out how to be good people, how to experience wonder."

Brian considered her words, his head cocked to one side. He shifted forward, and his damp knee grazed hers again. "I agree. Here's a quote for your Father Luke. Pirsig wrote: 'When one person suffers from a delusion, it is called insanity. When many people suffer from a delusion, it is called a religion.'"

Grace straightened her legs. "That's a good one."

Thunder rumbled. They both looked outside at the night. The wind rattled the windows, and wet leaves slapped against the panes and stuck.

Brian turned toward her, his eyes crinkling into a smile. "I guess if I have to *be* something," he said, "I'm a live-in-the-present-moment-be-compassionate-small-b-buddhist. You know, just trying to 'Be Here Now.' With you." He laughed. "Or the more succinct version of that ancient Buddhist wisdom: 'Beer Now.'" He winked then reached out to Grace's arm resting on the sofa and caressed the back of her hand with his thumb.

At his touch, a small shock of electricity sparked through her. *Damn,* she thought. She retrieved her hand and shoved it under her thigh, a snail into its shell. Grace turned again to look at the sky. The bony fingers of the trees seemed to be pointed at her. *Watch out, girlie.*

She got up slowly and walked into the kitchen to crack open two more bottles of Corona, slice some limes, and pour tortilla chips in a bowl. She wished she could relax and let him be nice to her. She wanted to be able to spend time with him, drinking and prattling on about religion and whatever else skittered across their minds, no touching allowed. But he'd crossed the line.

She brought in the beer and the chips, looked at the clock, and kept up the patter until precisely seven-thirty.

"Time to visit my dad," she lied, gathering her keys and purse. She'd just drive to the lake and back. The rain had ceased its pouring, but a gray foreboding lingered.

"Do you want to get dinner afterward?" Brian asked.

"Oh, no. Thank you, though! I never know how long I'm going to be gone. It was great hanging out with you tonight." She locked the door and walked out with him into the musty drizzle. He stood and waved as she drove away.

31

Grace set a newspaper article in front of Luke after they'd settled into their booth at Hooligan's. "I think this is your pastor from your old church."

$ 1.5 Million Lawsuit Alleges Priest Abuse and Cover-up
The Buffalo News
November 13, 1998

An Amherst man claims in a State Supreme Court lawsuit that, as a teenager in the early 1970s, he was repeatedly molested by Rev. Joseph Steele, Assistant Pastor at Holy Trinity Parish in Amherst, New York.

David Ostrepski, 40, claims in his $1.5 million lawsuit that he and his parents went to then Pastor Leonard Moynihan of Holy Trinity to report the molestation, who in turn accused them of fabricating the accusations and warned they could be excommunicated for lying about a priest.

"I tried to forget it, tried to bury it in my psyche," Ostrepski said in an interview with the Buffalo News on Tuesday, "but I never could. After my parents were threatened, I never followed through. I never had the courage."

Ostrepski's lawyer, Ralph Holmes, argues that while the statute of limitations has passed, courts may make exceptions in cases where a claimant is threatened. "We can't underestimate the extent to which the threat of excommunication is frightening to Catholics," Holmes said.

"I finally decided I needed to tell the truth," Ostrepski said. "I was forced to have sex with a grown man when I was fourteen-years-old on nine occasions. I've told it. I'm not intimidated by them anymore. And I'll never let a child of mine set foot in a Catholic Church."

"Oh, no," Father Luke said when he had finished reading. "I feel like this is all my fault."

"I didn't mean that," Grace said.

"Maybe I never should have rattled Father Moynihan. If I hadn't left, this Father Steele never would have come on the scene. He was the one who replaced me."

Grace watched Luke as he mumbled almost to himself, staring at the shiny gloss of the table. "I should have known something like this would happen. I should have tried harder, or at least stayed in touch with that parish. I had good relationships with some of those children in Religious Education; I should have tried to protect them…" His voice trailed off. He pushed his beer aside.

"Didn't you leave because you felt bad that the drunk man was hit by a car after you sent him away?"

"Yes, but all the while Father Moynihan was working to get rid of me. He was incensed by everything I did."

"I thought you said you were compelled, by a vision, sort of, of St. Francis telling you to come to St. Laurence." Grace leaned down to catch his eyes.

"Yes, but it coincided with my mandatory transfer. The diocese, the Bishop, sent me to St. Laurence. But I'd prefer that not be made public if you don't mind."

Grace took a slow breath. Why had Luke felt he needed to lie to her, albeit by omission? To make up a story about St. Francis? Why wasn't he angry that they had the right to transfer him at whim?

She lowered her voice, crafting the anger she'd carried since her day at the Cemetery of the Innocents into a gentle question. "Why do you feel you need to be part of the Church knowing everything you do about the hierarchy and what they are capable of?"

"Ah, dear Grace." Luke recovered himself. "Because the hierarchy is not the Church." He shook his head and shifted his bulk against the back of the booth. "The Bishop is not the Church. These abusive priests are not the Church. Let me tell you a story."

Grace slid over to the wall and rested her head against it. She was becoming used to his ministerial assumption that he had a right to command the conversation. But he was a good storyteller. His voice was like honey at the bottom of a cup of hot tea, soothing her tired head.

"I went to Oaxaca for a year in 1968 as part of the base ecclesiastic community. This was before I went to Holy Trinity. Before I left the country, in December, I had the privilege of being part of Las Posadas. It's a celebration in honor of the nine months the Virgin carried Jesus. It lasts nine days. I wasn't there as a priest. I was just a member of the group; it was one of the most spiritual experiences I have ever had, and it wasn't led by a bishop or a priest. It was all lay people, full of love and hope.

"For nine days, the people in the community reenacted the birth story. My hosts Manuel and Luisa invited me to join them; we waited outside their house until dusk. It was a beautiful night. Everything glowed. Lots of neighbors came over," Luke said, "and then we all walked about half a mile to another neighbor's house, down a narrow dark street and then on a dirt path up a hill. Two of the adults carried statues of Mary and Joseph."

Grace felt her impatience dissipate as she imagined the group walking up a hillside in the breeze under a black sky sprinkled with sugary stars.

"A little child dressed as an angel led the crowd. Everybody carried candles." Luke stopped and rubbed his eyes with his fingertips. "They sing a song back and forth. The crowd sings, and the people inside the house respond as if they are the innkeepers who don't have room for the Holy Family. They refuse to let us in. They sing, 'This is not an inn. Get on with you! I can't open the door! You might be a rogue!' And the crowd sings back that in fact, this is the Mother of God, the Queen of Heaven.

"Back and forth. 'No, let me sleep. We won't open the door.' Finally, the folks inside understood that we were with the Holy Family and they sang back." Luke cleared his throat and sang, "Entren Santos peregrinos, peregrinos, reciban este rincón, no de esta pobre morada, sino de mi corazón."

Grace looked around at the other patrons to see if anyone was staring.

"Beautiful. What does 'Peregrinos' mean?"

"Pilgrims. Enter holy pilgrims," Luke said. "And then they took us in and served us ponche, a stewed fruit punch, hot coffee, bunuelos, and tamales. Every night for nine days in a different home—each very simple and clean—and in each a feast." He shook his head. "And piñatas shaped like stars! The children were thrilled with all the candies that spilled out on the floor. In most of the homes, it was a dirt floor."

He lifted his hands in the air the way he did when he held up the Host then set them in his lap. "This experience revealed to me in a powerful way that ours is a living church. A church that doesn't need me, or any priest, or the *Bishop,* to witness the miracle of Christ or to participate in the essence of faith."

That was a sermon, she thought. He had successfully skirted around his own self-reflection and circumvented the topic of priests who rape children. She sat in silence and revisited her memories of the Spanish Mass at Holy Mother of God, Frankie's essays, Victoria's phone call, the depraved Santiago. Luke hadn't answered her question. He'd taken the stage, pontificated, swept her concerns, like itchy sand, under the rug— and she was furious. She could handle the abstraction of the Virgin birth, but not the perversion of trust and faith, not the cover-up of criminal actions, not the lies.

"Luke. Father Luke, *please.*" Grace's voice was low and breathy. She struggled not to yell. "Something has to be done. Children are being victimized by the people who are supposed to be protecting them. It's completely twisted."

Grace registered the look on Luke's face as one of alarm. She'd finally allowed herself to express genuine emotions with him.

"Yes, yes, yes," he said. He slid to the edge of the booth, looking steadily into her eyes. "You're absolutely right. Forgive my digression. The story about Pastor Moynihan has me very upset. It is all horribly wrong. I must go. I need to pray about this. I trust you will forgive me for leaving so soon."

Grace found Luke in the corner of the dining room the next day. He was writing on a legal pad. She set a pile of papers next to the pad, intentionally not saying hello. On top was a clipping from the New York Times about a Florida bishop who admitted to molesting five boys in three different parishes. Under it was Frankie's confession.

"I had a student in LA named Frankie. I need you to read what he wrote about your church."

Luke skimmed the article, shook his head, then opened the file folder and read Frankie's final essay without interruption. She watched the expression on his face change from curiosity to dismay. He looked up when he was finished.

"Quite a tragic story," he said. "But you helped him. You gave him a voice."

"I didn't help him. He died."

"What do you mean? What happened?"

"I don't know. I keep imagining the worst. That he was shot, his past life in the gang caught up with him, or he was in a terrible accident. Victoria, his wife, said she was keeping it a secret for some reason. He was out of prison. He had a new baby. He was trying so hard to make it right. You can tell from his writing what a good guy he is…was…"

Father Luke inhaled. His broad chest rose, and he let his breath out slowly. He pinched the bridge of his nose and closed his eyes. Grace could tell he was trying to keep himself from crying even though he'd let the tears flow during that joyful Mass.

"Such a waste of a young life. The funeral must have been so sad."

"It was. I went." Grace had been standing all the while he read. Now she positioned herself in a chair across the table.

"The family must have been glad you came."

"I didn't talk to them."

"Why? He was your student, wasn't he? And he shared all of this with you? Don't you think they would want to know you after all of your influence on him?"

"No, he just needed a place to write about his life."

"Don't underestimate what you did for him. You may have helped save his soul before he died."

Oh, please, she thought.

"Maybe. Maybe the opposite. Maybe me making him write about it tortured him, and he couldn't stand it. He didn't come back to class after he wrote that."

"And thanks to you, he may have felt God was hearing him. He may not have felt quite as alienated from his faith after expressing his anger and sadness about his experiences."

"I don't know about that. But it was pretty hard to go to a Catholic Mass for his funeral and see all those people mourning his loss, not knowing what the church had done to him. And Father Santiago officiated the Mass."

Father Luke bent toward her. "The Father Santiago in the essays?"

"I assume so."

"Oh, no. That's bad." Luke tapped the tabletop with his index finger.

"I know. It's horrible. Why is he still there?" Grace's voice sounded high and shaky. "Who knows what his history is? Frankie never told anybody. I've been meaning to follow up somehow, but I don't know what to do."

"We need to do some research." Father Luke reached his hands back to rub his neck, looking up at the ceiling. "I've been praying about this since we spoke last evening. These violators have to be stopped. It's precisely because of what they have done that causes good people like you to become disenchanted with the living church. I'll see what I can find out. See if we can't get to the bottom of this."

The next afternoon, Tall Tree found Grace standing by the coffee pot. He wanted to be a part of the article that she was writing. He explained that he'd been a promising young cellist at the Eastman School of Music in Rochester before his breakdown. Now at St. Laurence, he told her, he composed a concerto every evening in his head on his twin bed in the men's dorm.

Father Luke came by and touched her arm. "I have something for you," he said. "In my office. When you're done." She politely begged off from Tall Tree's tale by asking if he'd play a rendition of his latest composition when she got back.

A disorderly pile of file folders and books overtook what little surface there was on Luke's small white desk. He smiled when he saw her and opened a drawer.

"It's cash," he said, handing her an envelope. "For you to go to LA. And I've got all the information we need to set up a meeting with the Cardinal so you can show him Frankie's essays."

"What? Where did you get it?"

"My mother sends me money to visit her. I can never get away, so the money just sits there. It's enough for a flight and a motel. Think of it as a gift from my mother to you. An opportunity for you to challenge the Church to do the right thing."

"I'm not sure what *I* can do."

"You can show these essays to the diocese and demand a response. I'll help you by setting up the appointments. Make it official."

"Well…thank you."

This gift, if that's what it was, felt exciting and burdensome at once. It would mean leaving her life and going back there, but it would also mean doing something big, something meaningful, about Frankie. For Frankie.

"I'm not looking forward to it, but I'll do it."

"And then, of course, you'll write about it."

"I could. I should."

"Wonderful. I knew you'd do it."

The next day, Grace found Genevieve in the storage room, picking through a huge mound of donated clothes. After a morning of scrubbing toilets, Grace had made fifty peanut butter and jelly sandwiches in anticipation of the lunch crowd, refilled three coffee pots, and swept the kitchen floor.

"How are you doing this morning?" she asked the nun, who was slumped over a pile of worn clothing. "Can I help?"

Sister Genevieve straightened and nodded. "That would be appreciated, dear. Let's divide these into men's winter coats, shirts, and pants. The same piles for women. And we'll make a discard pile of holey or soiled clothes. Why people think the poor want to walk around in rags, I'll never understand."

Grace held a silky blue blouse against her own frame. "What do you think?" she asked Sister Genevieve.

The older woman tilted her head. "Quite stylish. Take it."

Grace started a small pile for herself. She found a large maroon velvet jacket in perfect condition; it was embroidered with birds and flowers. She held it up to Sister Genevieve. "I think this is you," she said.

"Oh, my, it is quite beautiful." Genevieve tried it on. Her face glowed pink against the jacket's warm colors. "Shall I?"

"Of course," Grace said. "It's gorgeous! Think of it as a gift you're giving yourself."

"Now that's something I haven't done in quite a while," Genevieve said, buttoning the cloth buttons and stroking the smooth fabric. She fingered the bluebird on her chest.

"Can I ask you something?" Grace's whispered. "About Father Luke?"

Genevieve put down the sweater she was folding and turned to face her. "You may."

"What do you think of him. As a man, I mean?" Grace's neck flushed the color of the velvet jacket. "As a person, rather?"

She had no idea those words were going to tumble out of her mouth. Her perspective about the priest had shifted. He was so different from Jake. His large presence projected strength, character, and deep warmth. Thanks to Luke's confidence in her, his honesty, his willingness to help her confront the Church, she started thinking about him as an interesting man. And she knew that to him she wasn't just one of the flock. She knew he cared for her.

Sister Genevieve looked as if she were stifling a smile but otherwise continued unfazed. "I've known him since the beginning, it seems. We're a team. He's dedicated. Hard-working. Funny. The guests love him. He's a very good man."

"He is, isn't he?" Grace asked. Her eyes narrowed, and she fiddled with her hair. "He seems to be a good man."

Grace's anger at Father Luke faded. She liked Luke. She didn't want to be irritated with him. She appreciated that he'd come around to doing the right thing and felt emboldened by his decision to finance her trip back to LA, incendiary essays in hand.

She had used a portion of the money her dad had given her after his move to purchase a new computer. That night, she began working on the article. After three months of volunteering at St. Laurence and too many evenings interviewing Father Luke, she was ready to put into words the rare combination of community and compassion she'd found within its walls.

She stayed up until four o'clock in the morning composing and revising until she had a complete 2,000-word draft. She brought the paper copy and a floppy disk to St. Laurence that afternoon.

"Wonderful!" Luke proclaimed. "This calls for a snack!"

As he read the article, Grace walked to the kitchen to gather up a couple of slices of leftover apple pie and pour them both a mug of coffee. Luke was bent over the draft, his index finger underlining each sentence as he read it, when she came back in. He didn't look up until he was done.

"Excellent! Very well written. You captured everything. Our start in the seventies. The story of Saint Laurence. You have Genevieve and her history. She's terrific, isn't she? A true soul. I like that you quoted Lance and Tall Tree. And Sage. He's a gem. Your description of the Mass was poetic. And I love that Alvin is Martin. He's a remarkable man, and you portrayed that well."

Luke was buoyant, obviously pleased with all her hard work. As she continued to stand over him, he looked up and caught her eyes. I like that you described me as a jovial, white-haired priest who has dedicated his life to serving the poor. White hair is a fact of life. What can you do? Thank you. This will bring us donations. I know it will."

He told her he would hand deliver it to *The Free Press* the next day and invite a photographer to come and take pictures of the place as soon as possible so they could print it next week.

"Are you sure?" she said. "It's just a draft."

"It's wonderful," he said. "Perfect. You're a talented writer."

"Thanks. I mean, wow! I'm glad." She hadn't been sure if it was good; she had thought it might need more work. She was dog-tired and exhilarated. She sat down across from him and took a swig from her cup then started in on her pie.

32

inter invaded like an enemy nation, ravaging its victims' ordinary lives. Grace woke at dawn every day after the snow began to fall to find her nose tingling with cold, her toes tiny slabs of ice. She pulled a sweater over her long johns and slid slippers over her socked feet before tiptoeing into the kitchen.

While water boiled for tea, she wrestled on her cold coat and stiff boots. She tramped to the car in the dim light and chilly air, carrying her keys, a shovel, and a scraper. She turned on the car so it'd be warm by the time she had to leave, dug out the tires, and brushed off the fluffy new snow. Then she turned to the task of scraping off the crystal images of mountains and moonscapes that were painted anew on the windshield every night.

Sometimes a neighbor's car was stuck, and a group would materialize to help. Brian would be there first on the scene with chains and sand and shovels. She loved being part of the effort: the wheels spinning, everybody pushing in one motion against the back bumper, a revved engine and then *whoosh*, out of the rut, over the hump, a wet spray of heavy snow, a collective *uh* and then *alright* and the car sailing off, freed to leave. All of them sweating and pleased to be part of something useful, something requiring kindness and strength.

With the advent of snow, Grace had decided to work both morning and afternoon at St. Laurence, only taking a break for lunch with her dad. Heading out into the cold, she said a silent prayer of thanks. To whom? To God? To the universe? To the splendor of the snow? It didn't matter. She was grateful for being here, in winter, in Buffalo, of all possible places.

There was a surprising amount of work involved in getting ready to go out in the world in winter, but after a new snowfall, the world was a glistening miracle. Each tedious step required to keep herself from freezing was worth it to see branches thick with ice shimmer in the new light of morning and the stark blazing whiteness of snow covering over every flaw. Every dawn a dazzling new day.

Father Luke was already in the booth when Grace arrived. They had agreed to continue to meet on Thursdays even though the article was done. "I enjoy our discussions," Luke had said, "and it's good for me to get out."

"Um, sure. Of course," Grace had stammered, surprised but not surprised.

Father Luke's nose was red, and his teeth chattered as he recovered from his windy walk. She needed to remember to offer to pick him up at the Hospitality House and drive him back next time.

This is silly, she thought, *me meeting him here as if we're sneaking around.*

He didn't say hello or bother with any banter. He just started talking.

"When are you going to LA? What did you decide?" He didn't give her a chance to answer. "It feels urgent now that we've hatched this plan."

She liked that he said *we*. They were in this together. But she wanted to wait and go to LA with his mother's money after the holidays. As selfish as it sounded, she didn't want to leave the snow.

"I think I'd like to wait till January," she said. "My dad and all."

Luke's eyes were red-rimmed as he stared at her, his cheeks flush from his walk in the wind. "I understand. It's important to be with family for Christmas. You'll go after. So..." He seemed hesitant, searching for what to say. "The article was a success. We've had quite a few calls. Lots of donations. And *The Free Press* has agreed to print a follow up next month."

"Genevieve asked me to write about her offering the Mass."

"Oh, she did? I'm surprised. I thought we had agreed to..." His eyebrows knitted together as his voice trailed off, uncertain.

"She said you had talked about it. That you were on board."

"Yes. Of course, I am. Just the timing. I...."

"What will happen if we do write an article? You've been doing this for a while, but what if it goes public? Genevieve seemed excited."

"She should be. This is important. And big." Luke sighed and took a long gulp of beer. "I've been in contact with the Quixote Center in Maryland. The consequences are great."

He explained that Father William Callahan had formed the Quixote Center in 1976 in order to protest the US support for the Contras. He'd raised thousands of dollars in humanitarian aid for Nicaragua before getting himself in a great deal of institutional trouble with the diocese there.

"Since they started, they've ministered to gay Catholics and handed out condoms to people on the street. They promote the use of birth control. They're especially outspoken about the equal participation of women in the sacraments." He shook his head. "Of all things, that's what made the authorities crack down on them. They turned a blind eye to their opposition to Contra aid but got all hot under the collar about women participating in the consecration and celebration of the Eucharist."

Luke scanned the bar to see if a new basket of popcorn had emerged. The bartender knew by now to bring their beer to the table when they arrived, and he kept a full basket of popcorn on the counter for them to retrieve whenever their basket was empty. Grace slid out of the booth to grab it.

"And we're also meeting with Jim Callan in Rochester. He's had a woman at the altar since 1988! Since then, he's been performing homosexual marriage and inviting non-Catholics to Communion. Of course, the new church they started is not recognized by the diocese. But I admire his bravery. Thank you," he said, digging his hand into the salty mound. "It takes great courage to do what he did. But we're ready to join them. Gen and I have been strategizing for a while."

"What happened to Father Callahan and Father Callan?" Grace asked, eyes wide. "What will happen to you and Genevieve? What will the establishment do?"

"I can tell you our esteemed Bishop Head probably won't tolerate it. He's on record for calling the ordination of women a grave transgression. And Callahan...well, he was expelled from the Society of Jesus in 1991 and forbidden to act as a priest. And Jim suspects he's about to be suspended any minute."

"They suspend people from the priesthood for advocating that women become priests, but they do nothing about pedophiles sexually abusing children? How backward is that?"

"Backward and immoral," Luke agreed. "And the impact can be catastrophic. Everything that's normal for them, everything that they've come to love and depend on—financially, socially, where they live, the work they do—can be pulled out from under them like a rug."

"My God, that's terrible," Grace said. She was struck by the assumptions—and the acceptance—of power within the strange, insular culture of the Catholic Church.

"Jim was transferred to a tiny parish in Elmira by the Rochester Bishop, Matthew Clark, last August. But he's so committed and solid. He's been clear that he won't stomach the hypocrisy. He and his associate pastor, Mary Ramerman—she's not ordained yet, but she plans to be—they're going to start a new church."

Grace twisted her hair into a loose bun behind her neck. She had reread her previous published article several times, and for the first time in a long time had felt truly proud of herself. And she felt inspired by these brave people to write something bold. "If you want me to write about Genevieve's participation in the Mass, I will. I would love to write whatever you need."

"Good," he said, but he was frowning. He wasn't his usual jocular self. Purple circles sank like half-moons under his tired eyes. "Grace, can I tell you something? I'm…I don't know…struggling a bit here. Maybe having a crisis of faith, as pat as that sounds. I am dedicated to the vision of the true church and still committed to change. I'm willing to do whatever we have to do to stay true to the words and the life of Christ. But—I know this sounds strange—I think I've worn a groove in my life."

Grace's eyes scanned the pub. The place was almost empty. They were the only ones crazy enough to come out on such a treacherous night. "Oh?"

"I feel like it's going to take a lot of energy to move into this new phase. Meeting with Jim and William has forced me to face the consequences of what we're about to do. It's shaken me a bit. I haven't talked to anyone but you about this. Not even Genevieve; she's so clear in her convictions. Sometimes I don't know if I can do it."

"Do what?" Grace tilted her head to the side. Luke regularly celebrated the Mass with Genevieve; they hadn't hidden the fact. Nothing was going to change except they'd be publicly letting the diocese know. Why was it so important to him that he be a Catholic priest? Wouldn't he find it liberating, like Callahan and Callan, to start something new? Didn't he want to do what he knew was right without all the authoritarian constraints?

"I'm being pulled into two. The spiritual me who loves God and wants to do what is right and good, wants to challenge the forces poised against us and devote himself to what is right. The part of me that loves God's people. *All* of God's people."

He extended one palm as if in supplication then opened the other one. "But then there's the other part. The man who is lonely and weak."

Grace felt a wave of panic at his words. She tugged on the scarf around her neck, exposing her throat, and draped the scarf like a shawl over her shoulders. She looked down at her mug. How is it that it was empty already? What could she possibly say to someone whose life had been so driven by clear purpose? Someone who had never wavered but who now was experiencing doubt?

"I don't think I'm the best one to talk to about this, Father Luke. I didn't last too long as a good Catholic."

"I know. But I appreciate your kindness and your listening ear. For whatever reason, I'm feeling racked with horrible doubt. Not about our mission or about St. Laurence, and not about Gen or women in the priesthood. None of that. I'm doubting *my* mission, *my* purpose…whether I have the stamina for this new effort." His voice grew smaller and smaller until she could barely hear him. "This could be a huge change for me, and, in the context of this corruption, of all the scandals, the cover-ups…"

Grace leaned forward, her eyes narrowing.

A new patron walked into the bar, and a stab of icy air braced them. Grace hugged herself.

Father Luke stood up and grabbed his jacket off the hook above the booth. "I'm sorry to be abrupt, but I've got to get going. We're having twenty-eight new guests in for dinner today, all of whom need to stay, so we're setting up mattresses and sleeping bags on the floor in the dining room. That means a ruckus and not much sleep for anybody."

Grace nodded and stood. They wrapped and zipped and heaved on all their stuff before making their way toward the door.

"Alvin and I are walking the grates all day tomorrow and bringing in whoever else we can so nobody dies this winter. Don't forget that we're having our fifteenth annual Homeless Person's Memorial Mass next Friday," Luke said as they stepped out into the raw wind. "I won't be able to meet with you next Thursday. I need the night to prepare. I think you'll want to come. You can write about the Mass in your next story."

"Okay." Grace stumbled over the word, her lips already stiff with cold.

"Oh," he said, looking at her as he yanked on his gloves. "Please disregard everything I said about my doubts. It's freezing! And I feel like I haven't slept in days. I'm completely overwhelmed. I know I shouldn't complain, though. I'm sure this is a temporary feeling. It'll pass."

He grabbed both her arms with his gloved hands then turned away, his shoulders raised against the wind, and trudged through the crunchy snow. She decided against going after him and asking if he wanted a ride.

33

race let herself into her father's apartment, finally having persuaded him to get her a copy of the key. Her dad sat at the table, back bent, shoulders hunched. An old-fashioned adding machine, a stack of file folders, crumpled receipts, and a box of pencils cluttered the table. He leaned into the ledger book, entering figures into columns in his careful hand.

A Chopin piece blared from the kitchen radio. She turned it down then walked over to him, pressed her cheek against the top of his head, and gave him a brief one-armed hug.

He flinched in alarm. "Oh, hello, honey. I didn't hear you come in."

"You look busy," she said.

"Well," he cleared his throat. "I've calculated. I can afford to be alive for exactly three years and three months."

"Oh, no!" She laughed.

"Unless the rates go up," he said. "Then it's two years and four months."

"Dad…" Grace turned away from him and fingered the books in the bookcase. "I want you around for longer than three years! Even if all your money runs out, we'll figure something out."

Grace had no idea what she would do if his savings were depleted. Bring him to live with her? Send him to the "county home," as he called it, for "indigent old people"? She could hardly imagine next week much less three years from now.

"The important thing…" he said, straightening his papers then rising creakily from the chair. "The important thing is that I don't spend your inheritance on doctors and respirators and nursemaids. Here's a check for you." He handed her an envelope. Her name was penciled across the front in shaky handwriting. "I'm sending your sister one too. Hers is a little more. For the kids' college."

She opened the envelope. It was a check for another $5,000.

"Dad, are you sure? Don't you want to save this in case you need it?"

"Oh, no. That's what money's for. I'm a lucky old man to have had a wonderful wife and two fine girls."

Holding her father's generous gift, Grace felt a confused queasiness in her gut. She was thrilled she could continue to volunteer and not have to look for work for another few months. She could buy herself a fridge full of food every week, a new pair of boots, some pretty winter sweaters. But at the same time, she felt dizzyingly guilty in the knowledge of the despair that brought people to St. Laurence every day without a dime to their names. People who couldn't afford rent, a dentist or a doctor, a meal or a pair of shoes. People who didn't have a parent with a bank account to rescue them when times got tough. She thought of Crystal, who had nothing and nobody.

"Dad, that's really nice of you. I don't know what to say."

"How about you thank me by coming over on Friday night to watch Mother Angelica? She and her orphan choir are having their annual Children's Christmas Mass."

"Friday isn't good," she said. "It turns out St. Laurence is having a Homeless Person's Memorial Mass. I have to go. Father Luke wants me to write about it for my second article."

"Alright, then, we'll catch it another time," he said. "Let's go downstairs and get some lunch."

The dining room tended to put her dad in a good mood. He raised his arm in a wave when he entered and saw familiar faces. Father McNab and two gray-haired women invited him to join them for lunch.

"This is my daughter Grace," he said as they settled in.

Everyone nodded and said hello and proceeded to order lunch.

"I love the holidays. Don't you, ladies? Father?" Her dad turned toward the aging priest, who was bent over his chicken cutlet.

"Yes, indeed. Lovely time of year. Everybody's spirits are high," Father McNab said.

"Have I told you the one about Saint Peter welcoming three new people into Heaven on Christmas Eve?" He winked at Grace.

"Do tell." Father McNab sat up straighter and watched as her dad set down his coffee cup, put his napkin in his lap, and cleared his throat.

"This is going to be good," one of the women said, elbowing the other. "He's quite a card."

"Well, Saint Peter told them that first they had to show something in their possession that reminded them of the holy season, something that symbolized Christmas. The first man looked in all his pockets and pulled out a lighter. 'This symbolizes a candle,' he said. Saint Peter let him pass.

"The second man fumbled in his pockets, pulled out keys, and jingled them. 'These represent bells,' he said.

"'You may enter the Pearly Gates, my son,' Saint Peter told him."

Grace looked down at her plate. She cut her broccoli and lifted a bite to her mouth. Everyone else had stopped eating in anticipation

"Now the third man searched frantically through his pockets, knowing he had to come up with something festive or he'd be sent down below. So…" Her father paused again for effect. He took a sip of his coffee and covered his mouth over a cough. "Finally, he pulled out a pair of women's panties." One of the women giggled.

"'And just what do those symbolize?' Saint Peter said.

"'Oh, these,' the man answered. 'These are Carol's.'"

When they returned to the room, Grace was happy to see that her dad's mood was still upbeat after the light-hearted exchange at lunch. She prepared to say goodbye and gave him a brief hug when she remembered the valuable check folded in her pocket. "Thanks again for the gift," she said. "It's a lot. It's going to be very helpful."

"You're welcome. I'm feeling grateful today." Maybe he too was thinking about the profound inequity that enabled them to enjoy an abundance of good food, warmth, and cash while so many others struggled to get through the day. "You know what? I think I'd like to go to that Memorial Homeless Mass. Get out of here and do something different for a change. I can watch Mother Angelica another time."

"Are you sure?" Grace asked.

"I am. Pick me up Friday after supper."

The meeting area behind St. Laurence House glittered with strings of white Christmas lights. The snow had been shoveled and salted, leaving the concrete dry and safe. Poinsettias and candles had been set out on tables along the wrought iron fence. A statue of the Virgin, sprigs of holly at her feet, stood in the corner of the lot. Alvin, Genevieve, and three of the residents handed out programs and cups of hot cider to people as they straggled in. Grace held her dad's arm with a gloved hand, looking around for Luke.

"Is the Mass going to be outside?" White puffs floated in the air as he spoke.

"I don't know. I hope not." Grace frowned. "It's pretty cold."

They waited awkwardly as a small semi-circle of volunteers, residents, and street people formed, all of them mittened and wrapped in scarves and hats.

"I'm not sure I'm up for this," her dad said.

His pale skin looked whiter than usual. Streaks of pink marked his cheeks like war paint. His lips were tinted blue. Grace wondered if she had made a mistake bringing him out here in the frigid night. She probably should have discouraged it, but she was aware that she might, after all these years, have something she needed to prove.

She wasn't sure what. That she was still connected to Catholicism, albeit of the radical sort? That she was still a good girl? That she wasn't just a lost person living on her dad's money while she figured out how to get her life together? That she was a journalist? Whatever it was, it was selfish. The old man didn't need to be paraded around in temperatures below freezing just to make her feel better about herself.

When a pair of cold hands suddenly covered her eyes, her body jerked. "Guess who?" the raspy voice behind her asked.

Grace grinned. "Happy? Is that you?"

Maybe this was a sign that she was one of them.

"You guessed!" Happy shrieked.

Grace turned around and pulled her into a brief hug. A snug helmet covered her curls, the strap tight around her chin. "You surprised me!" she exclaimed. "Happy, this is my dad."

Her dad nodded and frowned. "How do you do?" he asked.

"Hi," Happy said shyly, then limped away. Grace watched as she snuck up behind another unsuspecting volunteer and slid her hands over his eyes.

The singing started. Tall Tree sang, "Christ has died. Christ is risen. Christ will come again." The group responded, "He is our saving Lord. He is joy for all ages."

Grace wondered what it would mean to believe in a savior now as a worldly, experienced adult. Would it make her feel safer? Less befuddled? Less self-concerned? She remembered the guilt she'd felt when her dad offered her a fat check. Wasn't it good that she was using the money to support her work at St. Laurence? Wasn't she giving back to the community? If she believed in the Lord, would it make it easier or harder to know what was right?

Father Luke walked onto the parking lot carrying a large white candle. Its flame flickered and fluttered in the breeze. He joined the circle, holding the candle aloft.

"Father and Mother God, we thank you for bringing us all together on this brutal winter evening for the awesome and sad privilege of honoring those members of our family who have died this year. Some of them died alone in the hospital of preventable illnesses. Seven of them died in the street, victims of hypothermia and poverty, victims of a society too full of its own greedy aspirations to care. All of their deaths were tragic.

"We are grateful to have known and loved Meredith Benson, Mr. Stinky Matthews, Leticia Baker, Charles Walker, Frederick Douglass Jones, Susan Parson, Crazy John Brown, Pinky, Willie Waters…"

Grace counted the names on the program as he recited them from memory. Fifteen people who had died alone without family or friends or doctor's care or shelter.

"Let us light our candles and remember our friends with a moment of silence before we proceed inside," Genevieve said in a deep, resonating voice. She lifted her small white candle to Luke's in a gesture that seemed to Grace to be almost intimate then turned to Alvin and lit his. The flame passed around the circle, illuminating each of the faces with a soft orange glow. Everyone looked flushed and beautiful in the light.

"Seven people died outside?" her father whispered as the candlelight flashed between them. His hands were shaky, and she was worried he might drip wax on his gloves. "It's hard to imagine, isn't it?"

Inside, Genevieve read a gospel verse and gave a brief homily. She shared in the consecration of the Body and Blood. Sage, Alvin, Luke, Genevieve, and three other volunteers served the bread and grape juice Eucharist by walking up and down the rows of people sitting on folding chairs. Everybody shook hands and mumbled, "Peace be with you."

"Go in peace." Genevieve's voice aroused Grace's dad from a nap.

"Time to go, Dad," Grace said, her arm under his elbow as he rose from his folding chair. "Are you tired?"

"Oh, my goodness, yes. I haven't been out at night in the cold in years, it seems."

"What did you think of the service?'

"Very nice," he said, pulling on his gloves. "Although it *was* a bit unorthodox for my taste."

"Shall I introduce you to Father Luke?" she asked.

"Well, I suppose. If we can make it snappy. I'm going to need to get back."

"Sure," she said. She walked up to Luke, who was folding the red cloth that had covered the makeshift altar.

"I'd be honored," he said when she asked him to come over for a quick hello. "Any family member of Grace's is a friend of mine." He looked at her for about three seconds too long.

"That was quite a Mass, Father." Her dad shook Luke's hand with what Grace knew was an intentionally tight grip. "I'm not sure if it was kosher, but I guess that's what makes it interesting."

"We try to be interesting, Mr. Schreiber."

"Call me William. And thank you, Father Luke. Thank you for your important work. What you do with Our Lord's poorest is very moving indeed."

Grace was startled by the tears that she saw forming in his eyes. What would he do and say if he knew what Genevieve and Luke intended to make public? If he discovered that she was part of it, was going to help them unveil it? The prospect titillated her.

Luke beamed and reached for his hand again. "Please join us any time. Every Sunday at ten we have an equally interesting, un-kosher Mass. And it promises to get more so with time."

34

1962

Gloria wrapped her mother's red shawl around her shoulders then draped a shiny piece of gold fabric over that. With her arms spread wide, she looked bird-like, regal. "Come, my child. Kneel before me and pray.

A lace doily threatened to slip loose from Grace's fluffy hair.

"Wait," she said. "I'm not ready."

"Hurry up, my child. The Body and Blood of the Lord Jesus Christ can't wait all day."

Grace skipped to the bathroom, pinned on the lace, then skipped back. She folded her hands into prayer position and knelt before Father Gloria.

"The body of Christ," Gloria said, holding a dusty gray licorice-flavored Necco wafer aloft.

"Amen," Grace answered. She closed her eyes and stuck out her tongue. Instead of a Necco wafer, Gloria placed a cotton ball on Grace's protruding tongue.

Grace coughed as she picked the sticky fibers off her tongue. "That's not fair! You promised! I want to do it for real."

"I'm the priest. I get to do it how I want." Gloria popped the candy into her mouth and chewed with her mouth open.

"You do not. You have to use a candy. It's not funny. Why do you always get to be the priest?" Grace whined. She wanted to run to her dad and tell him Gloria wasn't doing it right, but he didn't allow the game. He said it wasn't a role girls could play and that the Eucharist shouldn't be taken lightly. Her mother would just hug her, laugh, and return to cleaning.

"I'm older, that's why, stupid. I always get to be the priest. I'll do it for real this time. Honest."

Gloria was nine, and Grace was seven. Grace knew there was no point in challenging the authority of her big sister. Gloria would punch her if she ever told their secret.

Grace stomped out of the room, but turned around and walked back in slowly, her hands again folded in front of her chest. "Say it right and then put one on my tongue."

"Okay, okay."

Gloria took a white cinnamon-flavored orb out of the roll of wafers and held it in the air. It looked the most like the Host, which made Grace happy, though she preferred the spicy purple and the chocolate brown.

"The Body of Christ," Gloria said, her voice low and solemn.

Grace knelt, closed her eyes, and arched her neck. "Amen," she said and uncurled her pink, wet tongue. This time instead of a wafer, Gloria placed a quarter on the center of Grace's tongue. Its cold metallic sting gagged her when she closed her mouth. She spat it out onto the floor.

"You are so mean! Someday I'm going to be the priest and not let you have communion! I hate you!"

She pinched Gloria and received a quick kick to the shin in retaliation. She crumpled to the ground in tears. She wanted the sugary dry wafer to melt in her mouth, her heart open in prayer, more than she could say. She felt lonely and miserable, and there was nobody she could tell.

35

Grace hadn't seen Crystal since she'd scoured the city to find her a place to stay. She'd managed to get her a spot at the Salvation Army Women's Shelter on Allen Street downtown. Even though the harried woman who registered her at the front desk assured her they'd take care of everything—get her to a doctor for prenatal visits, make sure she saw a counselor—Grace didn't quite believe it.

The place was drab and institutional compared to St. Laurence, and the room Crystal was assigned to was pretty dismal. Crystal hadn't seemed quite as tough when she'd dropped her off. She figured that Crystal didn't want her to get more involved. She hadn't looked at Grace or thanked her when she got out of the car.

But it was almost Christmas. Maybe she could bring her a present, put a bow on it, use it as an excuse to check on her. One morning in mid-December, she drove to the mall then over to the Women's Shelter. She asked the same receptionist if Crystal was still there.

The woman rolled her eyes and said, "Oh, that she is."

"Can I go up and see her?"

"Go on," she said. "Room 403."

Two names had been scrawled on a piece of paper taped to the wall. *Crystal Mason. Mandy Tremain.* Grace knocked on the door. When there was no response, she knocked again.

She heard Crystal's voice inside the room, sleepy and irritated. "What the hell? Who is it?"

Then another voice, more shrill. "Who the fuck?"

"It's me, Grace, from St. Laurence. Crystal, can I come in? I have a Christmas present for you."

Grace heard rustling and banging, and then the door opened. Crystal's hair, dyed a stark black, was tousled and unwashed. She sported a huge, ratty grey sweatshirt and no pants. Her smile was shy. "Hey. Hi. You have a present for me?"

"Yup. Hi. Can I come in?" Crystal moved aside as Grace entered the unkempt, stuffy little room.

A large grey-haired woman sat on one of the beds. "Hey. Don't. What? I'm trying to sleep."

She put her hands over her ears and stared at Grace and Crystal, then lay down, curled herself into a ball, and pulled the covers over her head.

"Crystal, why don't you get dressed, and I'll take you out for breakfast? What do you say?"

"Okay." Crystal's lip was bent in a sneer, but her eyes sparkled. "I'm sick of this place. And that lady's crazy."

"What's my present?" Crystal asked as soon as they settled into the booth. Grace handed her the package, and she ripped off the red paper and silver bows. She stroked the thick navy blue scarf, matching mittens, and three pairs of wildly colored and weirdly patterned knee socks. Crystal flipped through the copy of *Your Baby's First Year*, her eyes wide at the images of newborns sleeping and suckling.

"Why'd you do this?" she asked, holding all the items to her chest.

"I don't know. You seem like you need somebody to help your raggedy self out a little bit."

Crystal's eyes narrowed. "Why do you care? Don't you have no kids?"

Grace paused and motioned to the waitress. She asked if they could please have coffee soon. Then she took her time unzipping her jacket and loosening her scarf.

"No, I don't have kids."

"So, I'm like your stand-in kid or something?"

"No!" Grace laughed. Maybe she should tell this girl she, too, had had the chance to nurture somebody once and blew it. Maybe she should lecture her about not caring what people think. Though Grace could stand to learn more from that lesson than Crystal. Or maybe she should come clean about her own story for a change. At some point, perhaps, but not today. "I just thought you might need help, being pregnant and alone and all."

Crystal stared at Grace. Grace thought sure she was going to say something sarcastic and defensive. Instead, she sensed a loosening of the younger girl's tight muscles.

"Well, okay, then. Cool. Thanks for the nice presents."

The first night Brian asked her to go for a walk after a blizzard, Grace was relieved. She had pulled back after their last talk, and the memory of it sat like hardened lard in her stomach. She hoped he didn't think she was rude. Walking in the winter whiteness seemed a benign way to project friendliness, protected by layers of winter gear.

They trekked through the thick snow, exclaiming over the cars covered by a pure white blanket as if tucked in for the night. Grace delighted in the frosted tree branches glistening in the light of street lamps. Fat flakes flittered onto their open palms. Their footsteps forged deep impressions as they tramped across pristine lawns and up and down neighboring streets. Grace's heart beat fast from exertion, and her nose, fingertips, and toes prickled with cold.

As they rounded the corner to their street, Brian bent over and scooped up a handful of new snow. He lobbed it at Grace's chest before she could duck. He darted away from her retaliatory snowball and crouched down again to slap together a new snowball. It hit her right between the shoulder blades. The game lasted all the way down the block.

Grace was panting by the time they returned to their front lawn. "That was fun. I needed this. I'm kind of overwhelmed right now. Thanks for taking me out of my intense life."

"Maybe your life is too intense." Brian's teeth chattered; his nose was crimson in the glow of the streetlight.

"I feel pulled in a lot of directions. My dad needs me. And St. Laurence is packed with new people coming in from the cold. And that pregnant girl. Remember I told you about her? For some reason, I feel responsible for her."

"Taking a break now and then would be good for everybody."

"But—"

"We could go bowling. Or I could show you the American Falls.

They're gorgeous in winter. I could take you ice skating." Brian flashed a big grin. "I think a game of Scrabble at the Polish Community Center followed by a steaming hot plate of pierogies would do you good."

"I don't know," Grace said and laughed. "I think I'm a little too busy."

"Nobody is too busy for pierogies."

"Except me," she insisted. She fumbled for her key before she slid back inside her house. "*I am* too busy for pierogies. Good night."

Grace couldn't help it. Winter transfixed her. No matter how important the mission, she was glad she had decided not to leave yet for the heat and harsh light of LA. She made reservations for a flight out on January 3rd, time enough to enjoy a winter Christmas for the first time in twenty-five years.

Her mom had always insisted on a modest Christmas without a lot of fuss about gifts. They'd had a manger on the buffet and a small silver tree on a table but not much else. Over the years she'd received practical gifts—pajamas, socks, a sweater or skirt, occasionally a doll.

When neighbors decorated their porches and bushes with strings of multi-colored lights and tucked cutout Santas and reindeer into the snow, their mother had called it gauche or ostentatious or gaudy. Unnecessary. Silly. Grace wondered if her mom had even liked Christmas. The nativity scene seemed to be the only thing she enjoyed about the whole season.

Grace set Mary and Joseph and the baby Jesus in the center of the kitchen table, a small yellow candle before them. Despite her mother's impatience with the holiday, Grace found herself delighting in its quaint little customs: the familiar melodies tinkling in her ears, the Christmas cookie parties at Cherry Lakes, the fake tree somebody had donated to St. Laurence laden with glass balls and lights.

She breathed in the fresh-cut pine smell of Mountain's tree, festooned with pinecones, strings of cranberries, and popcorn. Maybe she'd get her dad a tree and decorate it with him in his apartment. She could buy cards, or better yet, set up an art table in the Warrior Room and paint cards herself. She could mail them to everybody she ever knew, tell them about her new life as a volunteer with the poor and the newspaper article she'd written for them. It had turned out to be a pretty good year after all.

36

Grace labored over the second article, chronicling the huge numbers of people seeking refuge from the cold, the attendant need for more donations, the warmth of the memorial Mass, and Genevieve's defiantly instrumental role in it. She quoted both Luke and Genevieve, citing their passion for women's equality and describing the joy Genevieve emanated when she celebrated the Mass.

Luke read the draft silently, nodded, and said it was just fine. He seemed more somber than last time. Genevieve almost giggled when she read it, acknowledging that it was going to stir up serious trouble.

"I'm about to lose it all," she said. "Good thing they don't burn women at the stake for heresy anymore."

When it was published, Grace collected ten copies of *The Free Press* from Starbucks and brought them home. She was eager to give one to Brian, who she knew would be knocking on her door later that evening to invite her to walk in the newly fallen snow.

Though bundled up and booted, he insisted on sitting down and reading the article before they left. She brought them both a beer and scarfed down an entire bowl of nuts while she waited.

"What do you think?" she asked when he looked up.

"Grace, I'm impressed. You nailed it. Good word choice, good organization, excellent quotes, great intro." He read the first sentence aloud: "'A church that rejects and punishes women who seek equality but embraces, protects, and defends men who abuse children is a church in deep moral crisis. St. Laurence House of Hospitality is working to shift the balance.' Nice."

Grace couldn't stop herself from blushing. "You don't think it was too forceful? Too radical?"

"Oh, no. It was very controlled. In my opinion, you can't be too aggressive about this stuff. So what if a woman serves communion? These people—these men addicted to their own authoritarian superiority—they need to be brought down a notch or three."

"I'm worried the diocese might react—"

He tossed the paper down on the couch. "Of course they'll react. They can't stand being held accountable for committing and concealing crimes. That's what these child abuse scandals are. They're not moral failings. They're not 'sins' they can forgive inside their insular fortresses. The Church is part of contemporary society. It's not a medieval fiefdom anymore, and it's guilty of major crimes."

"—and that Saint Laurence House, Sister Genevieve, and Father Luke might all get in trouble," Grace continued, her voice wavering.

"It seems like they want to get in trouble. That's exactly what they mean to do." Brian took off his cap. "I like this Genevieve character. She's got chutzpah. But this Father Luke. I mean…who still calls himself that? He wants to be a rebel but also wants to be part of the patriarchy. Comes across as a pretty arrogant guy."

"What?" Grace loosened her scarf. She had been looking forward to walking in the cold darkness while he praised her writing, but now she was sweating and feeling cautious. "How can you say that? He's amazing. One of the more self-sacrificing people I've ever met. The most, actually."

"Seems like Father Look-at-me could have toned down his own role a bit then and let Sister take the lead. He wants to support women's liberation but still wants to be in charge. Classic," Brian scoffed.

Grace winced. "I wrote it," she said. "I'm the one who decided what to emphasize. I tried to highlight both of them, tried to tell both of their stories. I'm surprised you see him as arrogant. I think he's brave. He's got a lot at stake."

"Okay." Brian held up his hands. "I hear you. Nothing personal." He unzipped his parka and set his beer on the coffee table. "The writing's good. I'm just not sure how much I like this Padre Lucas. Though I can see you're enamored."

Maybe Brian was right, Grace thought. Maybe Luke was arrogant, wanting to advertise their good works. And maybe she couldn't write objectively about something—someone—as important to her as Luke was.

"As enamored as *I* am," he said, "of *you*." Brian leaned in and kissed her. Her head was pressed back into the crook of his arm, his other hand like fever on her cheek.

Oh, my God, she thought, *it's been too long since I've been kissed.* She let him press into her, lips slightly open, dry and soft. *And I like him,* she thought. *He's sweet. He's sincere. Maybe I could love him.*

As quickly as the unwelcome thought formed of its own accord at the base of her animal brain, her nerves reacted. The hand that had unconsciously found its way to his chest lurched backward. Her elbow knocked over the nearly-full bottle of beer on the end table, catapulting it in a golden cascade onto the floor. The bottle lay in a puddle of beer, looking like an abandoned boat adrift on a foamy, toxic river.

"I'm so sorry," she said, pulling herself away and rushing to the kitchen for a rag. "What a jerk."

"Don't be sorry," Brian said. He took off his jacket, plopped it on the couch, and sat down facing her as she wiped up the sticky mess. He watched her silently for a few moments, then placed his hand on hers. She kept scrubbing, still wearing her jacket, scarf, and boots. "Grace, listen. I'm glad you moved in here. I like you a lot."

"Me too...you...I do." She thought about Luke and her growing affection for him, and about Jake and how he'd rattled her. "But I don't think we should do this."

She didn't know how to tell him she was trouble. She liked him but didn't trust herself to let go and love somebody. She enjoyed it when they sat around talking about whatever was on their minds. She liked how direct and honest he was. He was brilliant, he could fix anything, and he was always there when needed. Not to mention he was nice looking in a scraggly, comfortable way. But getting involved with him, she was certain, would end in disaster.

"Why? Why not?" He combed her hair out of her eyes with his fingers, then sat back and rested his hands in his lap.

"I think I'm too self-centered. I may be too selfish for love."

"What are you talking about?"

"I don't know. I just don't think I'm ready." They were both sitting cross-legged on the floor now. Brian faced her, his knee pressed against hers. Grace studied the Ansel Adams tree she'd framed and stuck on the wall.

"I mean, you're great." She was already bored with herself and the tired clichés that gushed from her mouth like a waterfall of beer. "You are. But I'm...I'm not...I guess you better go."

Now she was Meg Ryan, a ditzy, disheveled blonde. They were acting in a moronic romantic comedy. Except this one wouldn't end well.

He unfolded himself from the floor and walked out without saying a word.

The end.

After Brian left, Grace took off all her winter wear and walked into the Warrior Room. The living room reeked of beer. She taped sheets of newsprint together and hung them on the wall. Then she lit the candle, dragged a full-length mirror from her bedroom and leaned it against the wall, and closed the curtains. Even though she shivered—from cold, from the memory of Brian's unsettling kiss, from regret—she slowly stripped and looked at herself in the golden glow of the flame: slender feet and ankles, strong calves, long freckled legs, a triangle of hair below a small swell of a belly. She had a slim waist, round firm breasts, strong, smooth shoulders, a wild tangle of long red hair. It wasn't impossible to imagine that someone might find her beautiful.

She reached for a charcoal pencil and drew a tentative thin line on the newsprint, a contour. She grew bolder with each stroke, using her thumb to shade the curve of her neck, the half circles under her breasts, the bones of her pelvis. The shadows trembled in the flickering light.

Why had it been hard for her to find mutual love? Why had she been so easily misled into believing Jake was sincere? How was it that she hadn't seen through his games? Was it the burden of loss she carried, like a yoke, on her shoulders? Was her mother's vanishing such a profound betrayal she sought out men destined to disappoint her because there was some pathetic comfort in replaying the old script?

Whatever it was, she wasn't ready to face any more disillusionment. She wasn't ready for Brian, no matter how attractive she found him. Maybe Luke had the right idea. The idea of a life without a lover—something she'd entertained as a saint-smitten teen but never considered since—could free her from the confusion of trying to find love. Maybe the only way to clarity was through celibacy, through clean, uncluttered self-denial.

Luke had talked early on about the merits of renunciation. She remembered the discussion as enlightening, distant, and cool. She felt calmer as she replayed it in her head.

Grace worked trance-like for over an hour, examining her likeness in the mirror. She used her thumb, her palm, her fingers, to rub the charcoal onto the paper. She drew the shadows of her muscles, the outlines of her bones, until she felt as if the drawing looked back at her, looked through her, until she stood, spent and bewitched, before the chalky gray image of her naked self.

The call came at four o'clock in the morning. In her dream, Brian was pouring beer on her hair.

"He was stroking your hair with beer," the voice seemed to say.

"Excuse me?" she said, still half-asleep.

"I said your father has had a stroke at Beery Lakes."

"What?" Grace sat up, her heart hammering her ribs.

"He had a stroke at his senior home. At Cheery Lakes. He's been admitted to Buffalo Memorial. We'll need to have you come in as soon as possible."

"Oh, no."

"He's in the intensive care unit."

"Is he okay? I mean, how is he?"

"He's had a terrible shock to his system. The emergency bracelet alerted security at the desk at Cheery Lakes. They called the ambulance."

Grace thought of her dream and felt herself flush with embarrassment.

"Is he going to—?"

The attendant cut her off. "If you'll come down now, the doctor on duty will be able to answer all your questions."

"Okay. Yes. Thank you." She dressed in a fog then rushed to the hospital through a flimsy curtain of snow.

Her dad lay still in the metal bed, naked except for a loose blue gown tied in a bow at his hip and thick white socks on his feet. A sheet and tan blanket were scrunched around his knees. He was fast asleep, his mouth open and dry. A white line of spittle marked the crease of his stubbly chin. His body, like a baby's, curled into itself. She pulled his blanket up, set a chair next to the bed, and waited for him to wake up.

A doctor rapped on the door frame before entering the room. He shook her hand and introduced himself, then brusquely described what had happened to her dad as he read from a plastic chart.

"From our initial assessment," he told her, "Mr. Schreiber appears to have suffered from hemiplegia. With it, we'll probably encounter aphasia and apraxia, and possibly dysphagia. Undoubtedly some shoulder subluxation. We'll know for sure in the next few days."

Which Grace understood to mean, after insisting that the hurried doctor explain, that her dad had had a stroke on the left side of the brain which caused paralysis on the right, leaving his whole right side immobilized, his mouth sagging, and his right eye unable to close.

"His speech will be slow and slurred, he might have difficulty finding words, and he might have trouble swallowing," the doctor said while Grace stared at him. Her mind felt cloudy; she struggled to take it all in.

Unless he had an unexpected recovery after months of physical therapy, he wouldn't be able to return to Cherry Lakes. It was possible, the doctor told her. Possible but unlikely. The prognosis didn't look good. Most probably he would be stuck in a wheelchair and couldn't care for himself anymore.

"He'll need to transition to Immaculate Heart of Mary nursing home," the doctor said, his voice finally betraying a hint of compassion. "I'm afraid at his age there's no amount of rehabilitation that will enable him to go back to living on his own."

Grace watched her dad's chest rise and fall as he slept then nodded off herself. They were both awakened by a nurse who matter-of-factly checked his pulse and the heart monitor and positioned him upright in the bed.

"Your daughter is here to see you." Her voice had a sing-song lilt. She put a pillow on his lap and positioned his useless slug of a right hand in the center.

"I don't know why thish hash hap-pened to me," her father mumbled after the nurse left. A thick tear dripped from his droopy, half-closed right eye. "I don't know why the-the Good Lord hash pun-ished me like thish."

A wave of sadness pinched the back of Grace's throat when she entered the warmth of Cherry Lakes. After spending three days at the hospital with her dad, she missed the welcoming feel of the place, the sense she'd always had there that he was okay.

A cone-shaped silver Christmas tree shimmered in the foyer. Poinsettias in gold foil pots had been set on every table. Christmas tunes laced the air. Her dad would never again shuffle to the door of his apartment to greet her. In his quiet hallway, doors were decorated with wreaths or bells or plastic holly. Little dolls wearing red and green knitted gowns sat on the shelves outside the rooms. Why hadn't she thought to decorate her dad's door?

The task of packing up his room again fell to her. She started in the kitchen, emptying out the cupboards and filling boxes of canned soups and meat and Sweet 'n' Low to take to St. Laurence. She cleared the fridge of jelly jars, open bags of hard bread, and half ham sandwiches in Styrofoam containers. She ransacked the freezer and found stuck-together frozen dinners, three icy half-eaten donuts, two Ziploc bags of frosted grapes, and a Manhattan in a plastic cup, a cherry suspended in it like a buoy in the middle of a frigid pond. She dragged the bags down the hallway to the residents' garbage room, gathered all the newspapers for recycling, and stripped the bed of sheets and the closet of clothes to give away.

Everything he hadn't been able to part with when he left his home had been stuffed in the apartment's bedroom closet. *National Geographics* and *Time* magazines tied with string. File folders of college essays and newspaper clippings. Photo albums with crackling black paper pages they'd just begun to review together. A cardboard box of his photographs of wildflowers and trains. A handmade wooden cigar box stuffed full of religious relics and rosaries, foreign coins and multi-colored bills, and keys. Skeleton keys, house keys, tiny keys to tiny locks. She had no idea what they could all belong to. A metal box in the back of the closet. Grace wondered what could be hidden in there. She tried every key from the cigar box but none fit.

She sat on the floor surrounded by all the stuff she'd have to carry down to the car. She sobbed into her hands. Why, of all times, did this have to happen now? Just when she was starting to like her sweet, unfettered routine.

"I love you as big as the world," her mother sometimes told her when she was little, tucking her covers in. Worthless now. *No mother's big love, no lover, no support from her distant sister, nobody. Only a miserable dad who needs a lot of help.* Her chest heaved, and for a few minutes, she gave herself over to self-pity. When would she get to have a regular life? When would it be her turn to find happiness?

Forget that, she thought as she sniffed and wiped her face on her sleeve. Life was a joke, and she was being mocked; the universe was chuckling.

37

Grace called her sister in an annoyed voice and told her about their dad's stroke then sent her a card, apologizing for being irritable on the phone. He spent five days in the hospital before he was moved to Immaculate Heart of Mary nursing home. She barely left his side for a week. She spent hours holding his hand in front of his loud TV, pushed him in his wheelchair to the café, and wheeled him to physical therapy. She listened as he mumbled and complained and went home each night crying.

Christmas arrived with little fanfare. Brian came by early Christmas morning, stood in her doorway, and asked how her father was doing. He listened while she described the nursing home, its smells of overcooked vegetables, ripe diapers, and ammonia.

Her voice broke when she told him how her dad looked, so small and frail. He reached out to touch her hair then pulled back his hand. She thanked him for coming by and told him she had to go. She spent the day reading aloud to her dad from the newspaper and playing over and over again at his insistence his audio tape of Elvis' mournful *Precious Lord*.

She wrote cards to a couple of San Francisco friends she hadn't spoken to in months and a breezy letter to Janeen. She sent a check to Peter and Jenna without a note.

She left the hospital around seven and swung by the Salvation Army home to pick up Crystal. She took her out for a pancake dinner and gave her a jacket and a pair of polka-dotted flannel pajamas, which thrilled her.

Mountain was waiting for her to come home. She brought over a fresh-baked pie and sat down to chat. Grace thanked her for her kindness, then begged off, pleading exhaustion.

Grace worked at St. Laurence all day on the day after Christmas. After the dinner shift, she ventured out into the subzero air and drove to Immaculate Heart, arriving five minutes after visiting hours ended. She snuck into her dad's room. The building was quiet and full of shadows. All the residents were in their rooms; TV screens flickered ghostlike above their beds. The doors to the rooms were wide open, the occupants unmoving as corpses under white sheets.

Thinking her dad might be asleep, she tiptoed into his room. An aide named Moneeka had finished rinsing his teeth in the bathroom sink and handed them to him so he could jiggle them back onto his gums. She sang a spirited, "Hello, Mrs. Schreiber," when Grace walked in. "Late night visit, I see!"

"Thank you, Monica," he said.

"You're welcome, Mr. William, sir. Now enjoy your dear daughter. Good to see you again, sweetie."

"Mosht of the maidshervants are-are awful, but she'sh pretty good," her dad whispered after Moneeka was out the door.

"Dad, her name is Moneeka, not Monica."

"What kind of name ish that? Is it African? It-it soundsh French. It's shtrange."

"It's not strange. It's her name! And she's not called a maidservant. She's a CNA, a nurse's assistant."

"Oh, my. I'm old, you know. You can't teach an old man new namesh."

Her dad pulled himself up and turned his face away from the TV and toward her. She reached for the remote to turn the volume down, bent over, and kissed his forehead.

"How lovely you-you've come. You're jusht in time."

"For?" Grace was glad to be in from the cold and looked forward to holding his hand.

"Talking with Patrick Jacobsh," he answered. "One of my favorite showsh."

"Okay," she said, pulling a comfortable chair beside the bed and stifling a groan. She had managed to avoid watching the right-wing talk show with him in the past but not tonight.

She worked to suppress her impatience as she listened to Jacobs interview Ryan Reed, author of the latest apocalyptic novel "End Times." The book told the gripping story of a plague that vanquished the earth, leaving only devout Christians untouched so they could form verdant utopian communities of healing and love. The bravest among them were chosen to wander the world and convert the Muslims and Hindus and Jews and heathens and sinners otherwise doomed to live in colonies of anguishing depravity and misery and discomfort until they gave themselves over to Christ. Hell on earth. One hand clung to his; the other tapped the arm of the chair. Her eyes kept flying to the clock on the wall.

During the commercials, she pressed the mute button and attempted to talk with him about anything other than the show. "How did things go today, Dad?"

"Hell on earth," he answered.

Her father's new life was awful. The aides at Immaculate Heart of Mary nursing home were swamped. Though they smiled, eyes kind and tired, when they finally responded to the call bell attached to the side of the hospital bed, they always rushed off as soon as their duties were complete.

He was one of the few residents who could speak intelligibly and who was aware of his miserable surroundings. He complained daily that he didn't have anyone to talk to and that he missed his friends at Cherry Lakes. His shoulder ached. He was stuck like a prisoner in his chair. He couldn't stand that when he ate, drool dribbled down his chin. And the hallways of the nursing home were bleak compared to his cheerful apartment building. The other residents, all sallow cheeks and swollen ankles, either talked to themselves, fell asleep in the dining room, carried baby dolls, or were lined up in their wheelchairs, staring blankly at the elevator door.

"How was speech therapy?" His speech seemed better to her than it did when he arrived.

"Awful. Their politenesh is falsh. They call me honey. They don't lishten to me when I tell them I don't want-want to do their ri-dic-uloush exshershises."

A breath separated each drawn out word; each s came out as a muffled ssshhh as if he were reminding her to hush. His eyes closed. "They inshult me with their con-condeschending attitude. I do not belong here."

"I know." How could she tell him she was planning to fly to LA in a couple of days to confront the establishment about Frankie's molestation and rape? He counted on her companionship to take his mind off his deteriorated state. Grace's eyes filled with hot tears, but she blinked them back. "I hate to tell you this, but I—"

"Well, goodnight, my dear," he interrupted, then puckered up and kissed the air. "I am shud-denly over-whelmed by fatigue."

He was asleep before she could gather her things to go.

When Grace got back home, she dialed the number she'd written on Frankie's file folder many months ago. The phone rang a long time before a gravel-voiced older man answered the phone. Victoria no longer lived there, he told her in Spanish. "Quien llama?" he asked.

"Um, Grace Schreiber. Frankie's teacher. La maestra de Frankie."

"Francisco no aqui. He die. What you want, por favor?"

"Maybe I could talk to Victoria? Está ella en la casa, por favor?"

"Momento."

Another person came to the phone. This time the voice was very young. "Who you want to talk to?" the boy asked.

"I wonder if I could speak to Victoria. Morales, I think? I want to talk to her about something important."

"Who's this?"

"My name is Grace Schreiber. I was Frankie's teacher. I knew him before he died."

"I don't know if she gonna want to talk to you," the boy said.

"Maybe you could just ask her? Would that be alright?"

The boy yelled in Spanish for Vickie, then got back on the line. "Okay," he said. "But she don't like to talk about it."

When Victoria got on, Grace spoke quickly. She didn't want to lose her nerve. She knew that if she heard herself speak, she'd feel embarrassed and ridiculous.

"I don't know if you remember me, but I was Frankie's writing teacher. You know, his GED teacher. You called me to tell me about the memorial Mass and, well, I did come, but I didn't get a chance to talk to you. I wanted to tell you about something important about what Frankie, um…" How should she say it? *Should* she say it? Wouldn't it deepen Victoria's anguish to know

223

what had happened to Frankie before he turned his life around?

"I know who you are."

"Well, I…Frankie wrote about his life in my class. I have the essays, and I thought you might like to have them. The essays are sad. They're about things that happened to him when he was little that he said he never told you."

"Yeah, okay. I want 'em."

"I'm coming out there on January 3rd. I could bring them over."

"You don't live here no more?"

"No, I live in Buffalo. I'm in New York right now taking care of my dad, but I'm coming back."

"You're flying back to give me the essays? You could mail 'em."

"I know, but I want to bring copies to the Cardinal too."

"What Cardinal? Why?"

"I think Frankie was abused by Father Santiago and another priest." Grace's heart was banging. Before she could take a breath, she heard a click on the other end. Now she had blown it. She dialed the number again, resolved to talk even faster.

"What do you want?" Victoria shouted when she picked up. "Why you doing this?"

"Please, I'm so sorry. I know I'm not doing this right. But I'm coming out to LA to tell Cardinal Mahony what the priests from the Cathedral did to Frankie, and I wanted to show you the essays and see if you want to come with me." Maybe Victoria went to Mass at Holy Mother of God, and they would pay attention to her.

"I gotta go."

"Please just think about it."

"I said I gotta go." Victoria hung up again, but this time the click was softer as if the telephone receiver itself was sad.

"Do you want to meet me?" Grace asked Victoria again from the airport payphone. "I have multiple copies of his writing. We could meet somewhere and talk."

She hadn't wanted to pressure Victoria over the phone, but there she was, in the hectic airport waiting area, begging her to listen. She could drive to

Victoria's house and see Marisol. Maybe Victoria would give her a picture of Frankie.

"Look," Victoria sounded tired. "Why you doing this?"

"Victoria, I think the priest who said the memorial Mass abused Frankie. If he still works there, the church leaders need to know. I have a friend who is a priest. He arranged for me to meet with Cardinal Mahony and tell him what Father Santiago did to Frankie so they will remove him before he hurts anyone else."

Grace heard a deep throated gasp. "Father Santiago? Holy Mother of God Santiago?"

"Yeah," Grace said, her voice a rush of air.

"Oh, my God. My God. No, my God. Miss Schreiber, I didn't want to tell you how Frankie died. I didn't tell hardly anybody."

"Did he got shot?"

"Frankie didn't get shot," Victoria said.

"What happened?"

"Frankie told me what happened to him when he was little, but he didn't tell me who did it to him." Grace could hear tears at the back of her voice. "He said he wished he didn't start thinking about it and writing about it, that it was killing him. He said he couldn't take it no more. He couldn't live with it. But I told him I love you and we could make it, and then I went to work that day. And when I got back, he was lying on the floor. He wasn't hardly breathing because he overdosed on smack. The ambulance came and took him, but he died in the hospital in the morning. I sat with him all night. Even though he didn't get high no more, he did it one more time because I think he couldn't live with the shame."

"Oh my God," Grace murmured.

"I lied for him. I covered up for him. Only the cops and the funeral people know. He wouldn't a wanted anybody to know what he did. He was so ashamed. I don't want to read nothing."

Again, the soft click of the phone. Grace was left standing alone, stunned, the dial tone beeping in her hand.

Grace stumbled through the air-conditioned airport, through the motions of renting the car, navigating choking midday traffic, and checking in at the hotel, all the while oblivious to the hot LA sun.

38

Grace drove to the Cardinal's office in the morning and sat in the parking lot. She read Frankie's essays again. She brought along photocopies of everything to leave with the Cardinal. The truth about his death rocked her like the aftershock of an earthquake. He had poured out his fury and grief in writing to Grace. Why to her? Was she culpable in some small way for his death? For making him dig too deep into something that he had been able to repress enough to finally make a good life for himself? She felt eerily responsible for this whole terrible mess.

"I have a two o'clock appointment with Cardinal Mahony," she told the woman sitting behind the desk in the diocese receiving area.

"Your name?"

"Grace Schreiber. Father Luke Boland made the appointment for me."

"Yes. His secretary will be right with you," the woman answered, motioning toward a rose-colored velvet sofa. A heavily shellacked crucifix had been hung on the wall behind it. The wooden Jesus stared down at her as she took a seat.

Grace waited for an hour. She leafed through the magazines fanned out on the coffee table—*National Catholic Register, First Things, The Catholic Voice*. Twenty minutes later, Reverend Joseph Randolph came out to greet her.

He introduced himself with a handshake, his expression friendly. "What can I do for you?" he asked, standing in the middle of the waiting room.

"I was hoping I could talk with the Cardinal about an important matter."

"He sends his apologies. He is very busy today and asked that I handle his appointment. How can I help you?" Father Randolph clasped his hands together.

"Do you think it would be possible to meet in an office?" Grace asked, rising. She looked at the woman who was watching them with interest.

"Of course. Follow me."

Father Randolph led her into an elaborately furnished room, sat down behind a huge oak desk, and motioned to her to sit in the upholstered chair facing him. He nodded.

"Well, I…"

Father Randolph smiled and looked at his watch. Grace took a deep breath and recited the introduction she'd practiced.

"I'm a writer for St. Laurence House in Buffalo, New York. Father Luke Boland suggested I meet with the Cardinal."

"Um hm."

"I wanted you and the Cardinal to know that I think you have a priest in the diocese. He's working, er, serving at Holy Mother of God Parish…"

"Yes?"

"I think he…I should say I know…I know he has abused one of his parishioners. I have an essay here that the parishioner wrote a few months ago about what happened. His name is Frankie Morales. Frankie was killed. He killed himself actually. There was a Mass for him, and Father Santiago, the one who abused him, was the one who said the Mass."

"I appreciate your coming by, Miss Schreiber." He looked at her steadily, his eyes sincere. "We are aware of Father Santiago and know that he has had some psychological issues, but we have been assured that these are well in the past and are not enough to interfere with his priestly duties." Father Randolph pressed his palms on the desk as if he were preparing to spring.

"No, but…I don't think you understand," Grace said. "Frankie was raped by this man. He had a very rough life. He lost his mother and lived with his grandmother, who had a hard time taking care of him. He trusted this priest because he was all alone. Frankie got in trouble and went to prison, but he turned his life around. Please read the essays. I brought you a copy." She placed the file folder on the desk and slid it over to him.

"I'm sure that won't be necessary. I can assure you if there was an issue at all the matter has been taken care of." He patted the folder. "Thank you for bringing it to our attention, however, and for your compassionate involvement with this young parishioner."

"But Mister…Father…" Grace stammered. "He was thirteen years old. He was raped. Behind the altar. Sixteen years later, it still haunted him. He overdosed and died. Don't you see?" Her face burned. Why couldn't she get the words out? Why couldn't she make him understand?

"Miss Schreiber," the man said, his voice steady and slow. "I do understand. Young people—impressionable, troubled young teens in particular—often misinterpret the affection of those in authority as sexual involvement." He slowed his speech as if to tutor her in a difficult concept. "Especially those who have no father figure in their lives and who are hungry for attention. This is a not uncommon occurrence. In fact, we're hearing more and more that some of these stories have been twisted in the news.

"Now if you will excuse me, I have another appointment. But I appreciate your making the time to look out for one of our youth." He stood up and walked to her chair. He reached for her hand and shook it. "God bless you," he said. Then he turned and walked out of the office, leaving her sitting in front of his desk, the essays still untouched.

The woman behind the desk in the reception area was on the phone. Grace stood in front of her and waited. "Excuse me," she said after the woman hung up. "May I ask you something?"

"Yes?" the woman put her hand back on the receiver as she eyed Grace.

"Is there somebody else I could talk to? You see, I came to talk to the Cardinal about a man who was abused by a priest as a boy. But I just spoke with Father Randolph, and he totally dismissed everything I told him. I don't know if he didn't believe me or if he didn't think it was important."

Grace felt desperate. She was finally here face to face with people who should want to know about what happened to Frankie, authorities who should care.

"Can I please make another meeting with the Cardinal tomorrow? Please? This is *really important*."

"Father Randolph is the Secretary to the Cardinal," the woman answered, her voice low.

"I know. But can't I talk to Cardinal Mahony himself? I mean, who would you suggest I talk to?"

"There isn't anyone to talk to," the woman said, averting her eyes and picking up the receiver. "Now if you'll excuse me."

Grace drove straight to Holy Mother of God Cathedral. What had Father Randolph meant when he said, "We are aware of Father Santiago and know that he has had some psychological issues in the past"?

She had left the essays with her address and phone number written on the folder at the Cardinal's office. She held on to a tiny glimmer of hope that he would read them and change his mind about the importance of this matter. But in the meantime, she'd surely find somebody at the church who would listen to her. Somebody not so far up the totem pole. Somebody who knew the priest and would be shocked enough to do something.

Grace walked into the dark cathedral before looking for the office. She inhaled the stale residue of incense and candles and felt chill bumps rise on her skin. She slid into the same pew she'd sat in during Frankie's Mass, lay her head back, and scrutinized the intricately painted ceiling. Gilded robed saints flanked a blonde and beautiful Jesus. He was floating in a cloud in a pale blue sky, his arms outstretched. Over their shoulders hovered naked angel babies with feathery white wings.

How could something so horrible have happened in such a serene and beautiful place?

She walked back out into the sunlight and around the landscaped lawn until she found a door marked *Office*. She walked inside and found the receptionist, this time a more pleasant looking woman, sitting behind a desk.

"May I help you?" the woman asked.

"Yes. Thank you. My name is Grace Schreiber. I was wondering if I might make an appointment with the pastor?"

"Father Santiago is not in now, but I can make an appointment with him next week. What is it in reference to?"

"Oh, is Father Santiago the pastor?" Grace's heart was pounding.

The woman seemed kind if patronizing. "Yes, he's the pastor of Holy Mother of God Cathedral."

"Is there anybody else I could talk to?"

"Father Laymon will be in later this afternoon. Tell me your name again, please?"

"Grace Schreiber. May I meet with him?"

"He is not available today, but I can set up a brief meeting with him tomorrow from four to four-fifteen."

"Thank you," Grace said. "That would be wonderful. It's an emergency."

The next morning, Grace drove back to the Cardinal's headquarters and gave the receptionist a second file folder containing the essays as well as a sealed envelope marked *Cardinal Mahony—Urgent Matter*. She didn't trust Father Randolph to give it to him. If he read the essays, he'd be appalled.

"I'll make sure he gets it," the receptionist said, unsmiling.

Grace arrived at Holy Mother of God thirty minutes early. After an hour and a half of not speaking or looking in her direction, at precisely five o'clock, the receptionist started to pack up her desk and pull her purse over her shoulder.

"Father Laymon wasn't able to make it today," she told Grace. "I'm sorry."

Grace sprung out of her seat. "Are you sure? We had an appointment." She held out the copies of the essays she'd prepared to show the priest himself. The receptionist kept both hands on her purse. Could she have been tipped off? Did the Cardinal's office warn her that she was coming? What could possibly justify their refusal to talk to her?

"Will you give him these? Will you tell him I waited over an hour? Can I make an appointment for tomorrow morning?"

"I don't think that's possible," the woman said, shaking her head.

"I can do it any time in the next two days," Grace pleaded. "I have a flight out on Thursday."

"He's very busy." The woman's voice was high and exasperated. "Why don't you call me tomorrow morning?"

"I will. You see, I have information about Santiago that I think Father Laymon would want to know."

The receptionist stood up straighter and gripped her purse strap so hard that it dug an indentation into her shoulder. "Father Santiago is a good man," she said. "I've worked here for twenty-eight years, and I'm planning to retire in three. I know him and Father Laymon quite well. They both do a lot of good. He officiated my son's marriage six years ago. I couldn't be happier working here."

"Did you know Frankie Morales? He was an altar boy in 1983."

"There have been many altar boys over the years. I certainly can't remember all of their names."

"Do you know what Father Santiago did to him? Maybe to others?"

"I don't know about anything Father Santiago did, and I don't like the direction this conversation is going in."

"Mrs…" Grace looked at the nameplate on the desk, "Mrs. McCollough, will you read the essay that Frankie wrote about what happened to him? I'll call you in the morning about it. Please?"

Grace held out the file folder.

"I'm sorry, but it's five o'clock, and I'm going to need to lock up. Goodbye, and God be with you."

Grace set the folder on the corner of the desk and stomped out.

The next morning, Grace returned to Holy Mother of God ready to sit all day if necessary. She'd made more copies of the essays to give to whomever the receptionist arranged for her to meet. Grace imagined the woman staying up late reading them the night before, resolving to do the right thing. *Please God, have her lead me to the right person*, she prayed. *Someone who will care.*

Mrs. McCullough sighed when Grace walked in. "Mrs. Schreiber," she said before Grace had a chance to address her. The essays were no longer balanced on the corner of the desk. "I know you're upset about this. But I can assure you there is no one to talk to. The matter you are concerned about has been dealt with. You need to take my word for it that the matter has been handled appropriately and through the proper channels. Please understand."

"Are you saying they already knew about this?"

"Let me just say that Father Santiago was treated for depression many years ago and has been doing a fine job as pastor ever since."

"Depression? What do you mean, depression?"

"The life of the priest isn't easy. Hearing confessions. Offering the Eucharist daily. Ministering to the needs of the parish. He runs an elementary school, for heaven's sake!"

"This is where Frankie went to school! It's where he learned to pray. This church is the place his grandmother trusted to look out for him after she couldn't take care of him anymore. She thought becoming an altar boy would help him stay on the right path!" Grace pleaded with the receptionist, this woman who had children of her own. How could she not feel sympathy for this little boy?

"One can only imagine how difficult it must be," Mrs. McCullough continued. "He's always in demand."

"When was he treated?'

"Many years ago. He left for a short time and came back greatly relieved, calmer, healed. Thanks to a monastic community called the Servants of the Lamb, he was cured of depression and has been doing a wonderful job for us ever since." As Grace moved closer, Mrs. McCullough pulled back.

"*What*?" Grace muttered.

The woman straightened, looked Grace in the eye, and whispered, "I am absolutely certain no one will be able to see you about this matter. I am sorry."

"Where is this place?" Grace asked.

"I'm not sure. I do know the Servants of the Lamb community is somewhere in either Arizona or New Mexico. I think it's in Jimenez or Juarez. Maybe Cortez. I know the town has a Spanish name."

The receptionist looked away, unburdened herself of the purse and lunch bag she'd been clutching, and hung her sweater on the back of her chair. She sat down and straightened the pen holder and stapler on the desk, refusing to meet Grace's gaze.

"Mrs. Schreiber, honestly. This all happened a very long time ago. God forgives."

39

The Servants of the Lamb Monastery was located at the end of a long dirt road in a canyon near Juarez, Arizona. Given everybody's reluctance to talk to her, Grace decided to drive across the desert to ask to see their records of the priests who'd been treated for depression. She'd felt compelled, once again, as if an invisible hand was pulling her toward this place.

She had called them to make an appointment, pretending to be a reporter for a Buffalo Catholic newspaper. She stopped at the AAA office and asked them to search for the location and make her a Triptik. Then she bought a coffee and took off. She could make it there by afternoon.

The monastery was nothing but a collection of small white buildings clustered together inside the canyon. The craggy rocks of the surrounding mountains embraced the austere buildings. A ten-foot-tall wooden cross seemed to grow out of the ground in the center of the dusty courtyard. Behind the cross sat a small chapel. The words *Blessed Mother of Priests Shrine* were painted in red and gold on its stucco facade. The rough simplicity of the canyon community was surprising and pleasing to Grace, especially after her non-meetings in the two ornate church offices.

She followed a gravel path to a white adobe building that had a blue cross painted on its outside wall. Clusters of fragile yellow flowers had been planted along the row of smooth rocks which lined the pathway.

Grace knocked on the door.

"Come in!" a voice boomed from inside the adobe building. It was followed by a cough.

She opened the door to find an airy open space, a simple metal desk, a few chairs, and a wood floor dusted with fine desert sand. A white-haired man in a blue cotton shirt and wrinkled gray pants leaned on a cane as he stood up from a chair.

"Hello! What an unexpected surprise!" He laughed at the sight of her. "Do come in, my dear. Do come in."

"Hi, my name is Grace Schreiber," Grace said. The man was at least as old as her dad, if not older. "I made an appointment…"

He looked expectant, his eyebrows raised.

"This is an enchanting place," Grace said.

"Thank you! We do love it here."

His warmth was infectious. "Have you lived here a long time?" she asked.

"Oh, my, yes. A very long time!" His laugh washed over her like cool water tumbling over canyon rocks. "When I came here, I was a young man. Little has changed," he said, "except for the fact that I am no longer a young man! I'm ninety years old!"

"Is this a retreat center? Is it a monastery?"

"We're all just a bunch of old coot monks now," he said. "Too infirm to do anybody much good any more. But in our day, we provided some necessary services. Of course, that was before things changed. We still pray for our brother priests in need."

Frankie was abused in 1983, Grace thought. Father Santiago must have come here after that, after his diagnosis of "depression." Would this old monk have known him? What went on in this place?

"Shall I give you a tour?"

Grace nodded and followed the monk, bent over and leaning on his carved wooden cane, as he maneuvered his way through the door and out into the sunlight. "Another day in paradise," he said, breathing in the mountain air. "I love the breezes. It's my favorite thing about this place. Without them, it can get pretty darn hot."

They walked together toward the chapel, and the monk motioned to her to open the door. Inside of the small space, rows of wooden pews faced an altar covered with a pale blue cloth. They'd placed white candles in silver candlesticks on the altar, their wicks lit and flickering, along with freshy cut white flowers and an ornate golden holder framing a white disk.

Behind the altar was a giant mosaic of Mary, bejeweled in a gown of dazzling blue tiles, cradling the baby Jesus. Halos of sparkling gold tiles encircled both their heads. Grace gasped. Its artful detail glittered in sharp contrast to the rough whitewashed walls.

"Our Holy Mother," the old monk said, genuflecting slightly and making the sign of the cross.

"Gorgeous," Grace said. She walked closer to the altar. "What is this?" she asked, pointing to the round gold frame on a thin stem, encircled by little pointed rays of gold, a luminous white Eucharistic wafer in the middle.

"This is a monstrance," the man said, crossing himself again and bending his shaky knees. "Unfortunately, there are no longer enough of us to practice Perpetual Adoration, in which there is an ever-present prayerful vigil of souls adoring the Holy Host. Instead, we must be content to engulf the Blessed Sacrament with light twenty-four hours a day. When the patients were here in our heyday, this was a pious and holy place, attendees here at all hours, always in the state of grace."

As Grace followed him outside, he said, "We did have a small fire here in the chapel a number of years ago after the transition. Only us older fellas were left. Brother John tripped and fell while lighting the candle, which burned one wall of the chapel and a storage room next door. He needed hip surgery after it all, but otherwise, nobody was hurt. That was quite a day."

The tour took them to the next building, another low stucco structure painted with a red cross. "The infirmary," he said somberly. "One of our brothers passed into Our Lord's hands last week. We're dropping like flies."

Grace's eyes widened. They continued down the stony path past twelve small white cabins, each with yellow, white, and pink mountain flowers planted in the sandy dirt on either side of its blue door.

"These are our quarters," he told her and pointed to a larger building. "And this is our refectory. The nuns cook all our dinners."

"You have nuns here?" Grace asked.

"If you drove up Jemez Road, you may have seen their sister house. They live down the road but make dinner for us every day. We prepare our own breakfast and lunch. They're cloistered but for the few who bring us meals. They pray for the souls of the priests, for our sanctification. That is their vocation. They're the Handmaids of the Precious Lamb. Right down the road," he said, motioning beyond the acacia and lemon trees toward the road to the highway.

"Father—"

"Please. Brother Francis."

"Brother Francis, are depressed and troubled priests…I mean, priests who have committed sex abuse…you know, are child molester priests sent to the Servants of the Lamb when they are having problems?"

The old man stopped and turned to face Grace. His fingers circled her wrist for a second, then released her. "The Servants of the Lamb has been around for a long time. Since 1942. We're a pastoral community of healing. Reverend Leonard Maston founded the community fifty-six years ago to serve priests suffering from addiction to alcohol and troubles of the spirit. Some of the men who benefited from our pastoral interventions struggled with their vow of celibacy; some had succumbed to the temptations of drugs and alcohol; some simply needed a structured retreat environment to strengthen their souls before returning to parish life.

"All the men who came to be with us suffered from sickness of the spirit and required prayerful intercession. And a simple life." He looked out past the buildings at the craggy hills of the canyon. "We don't do pastoral healing anymore. Our programs ended eight years ago, and I can honestly say I don't miss all the hubbub. Now our priest brothers' therapeutic needs are served in Minnesota. May I ask what is your interest in our community? We haven't had a visitor for many months."

"Well, I—I'm doing an article for a Buffalo, New York paper. Father Luke Boland from St. Laurence House is sponsoring my research. I was just in Los Angeles trying to inform the Cardinal about the priest abuse that went on in Holy Mother of God Cathedral about fourteen or fifteen years ago. I learned about your place when I was there. They said Father Santiago might have been sent here. Actually, an office worker told me. The Cardinal's people and the people in Santiago's parish didn't seem interested in speaking with me. They told me it was probably a matter of misinterpretation. But I'm sure that isn't true."

The lighthearted glimmer left the aging monk's eyes. His eyebrows knitted together in pain. "When a man is ordained as a priest, you understand, he becomes an envoy of Christ. He is changed ontologically and is made into a different brand of human being. He obtains a supernatural sacramentality."

"But—"

"There is great honor inherent in carrying the Host to the flock, in being selected as an emissary of God. But with that privilege comes a great weight, despair even. I have seen so much sorrow here that I am glad in my twilight years that our therapeutic services are no more, and we can finish our days in rest and relaxation and prayer. It is much more pleasant to tend to flowers than to men in distress."

Grace felt unsteady at the obfuscation. The old man reminded her of her dad, though his manner was gentler.

"Now, my dear, would you like to join us for supper?"

It was late afternoon, and she hadn't had lunch. She had driven five hours without stopping, then walked and talked with this delightful and stupefying gentleman for an hour. It hadn't occurred to her until now that she was starving.

"That would be great," she said. "Thank you. But first…" They were the only people here, standing in the middle of the courtyard in front of the looming cross under the piercing light of the sun, but she whispered her question. "Is there any way to find out if Father Santiago was here and what happened afterward? Why was he allowed to go back to Holy Mother of God if he raped a boy?"

"Oh, my, so strident! So impassioned!" Brother Francis raised his voice, which precipitated a cough. "Of course, we can't share any confidential information with you about our patients, though they were an interesting bunch!" He put his hand on her upper arm this time and gripped it as if trying to steady himself.

"Forgive my lack of forthrightness. You understand we must abide by the code of omerta. But trust in the Lord that whoever crossed over our threshold benefitted from His healing mercy. And from the all too wholesome meals prepared by the Sisters!" He laughed then coughed again, his face damp and pink.

"Now I need to rest before supper. Any day now, I could be personally escorted by the angels into heaven!" He looked down at his watch. "You are more than welcome to continue to wander for the next three-quarters of an hour, and then meet us as our guest in the refectory at five o'clock sharp. It is certainly rare to have a visitor!" he said, his eyes twinkling in the sunlight.

237

Grace walked around while she waited. She felt shy when she saw the seven elderly monks in the dining hall relaxed into polite conversation as they all ate. When their plates were empty, she gathered up her courage to confront them.

"May I ask you something? I'm a teacher. I had a student who wrote about his life in my class. He had been to prison, got his life together, got married, and had a baby. But when he started to write about his life, he dug up some awful stuff about being thirteen and being abused by a priest. Father Santiago from Los Angeles raped him. Repeatedly. I feel guilty, almost responsible even, because he couldn't face what he had unearthed and he—"

Pinpricks of heat stabbed at her eyeballs. "I have to find out more so I can get the church to take responsibility. Was Santiago here?"

"Oh, no, can't discuss it, I'm afraid. Confidential," one of the monks said as he rose to clear his plate.

"Did you treat sexual predators here?" She looked directly at Brother Frances, then sought out the eyes of the others.

"It's been nice to have you! Isn't it a pleasure to see such interest among the young?" A second man stood up. He smiled as he scraped back his chair.

"We've sworn to not talk about that," another murmured as he collected his plate and silverware.

She turned to the four men left at the table. Each shook his head and looked away.

"Unfortunately, we can't utter a word."

"Delightful to have you visit. Sorry we can't tell you much. Come again!"

"Bless you, dear girl!"

She found herself abandoned in the dining hall, her lone dirty plate and crumpled napkin before her on the table.

Except for the huge American flag fluttering outside, the Juarez Public Library was small and unpretentious. She didn't know what, if anything, she'd be able to find out here.

"Excuse me. I'm researching a place called The Servants of the Lamb. It's a monastery that used to serve priests with depression, alcoholism, and other problems. Do you know anything about it?"

The woman at the information desk frowned, creases forming on her forehead. "I do know about it, and we have some articles that might interest you. There was something of a local scandal involving that place ten years ago. I'll be back shortly."

Grace grabbed a few books off the reference shelf then sat at a table and pulled a notepad and pen out of her purse. The librarian sat down next to her and handed her a stuffed green file folder marked Servants of the Lamb. "You are welcome to browse through this. Most of the articles are from the *Juarez Daily Record*, but we also have clippings from the *Los Angeles Times*, the *Chicago Tribune*, and the *St. Petersburg Times*. I hope it helps."

"Thanks. I appreciate this a lot." A blanket of cold wrapped itself around her bare shoulders, dark pink from her hour in the sun with Brother Frances. It was the air conditioning, of course, but it was also fear co-mingled with anticipation. Maybe she would finally get answers instead of evasion.

Fire Damages Archives of Servants of the Lamb Treatment Facility
Juarez Daily Record
December 20, 1990

Firefighters responded to a call yesterday from a neighbor of the Servants of the Lamb treatment center, located fifteen miles outside of Juarez in the Carino Canyon. A chapel was partially destroyed, and a small storage building housing file cabinets full of records was burned to the ground in a blaze that lasted seventy-five minutes before firefighters were able to extinguish it safely. No one was hurt. The cause of the fire is still under investigation.

"We're all stunned," said Brother Paul Diamond, one of twelve priests and monks who currently live at the facility. "Who would have thought that a candle being carried to the chapel could have done so much damage?"

The Servants of the Lamb has been in operation as a facility for the treatment of troubled priests since 1942. From 1942 until recently, over six hundred and ninety priests have been treated by the clergy and lay professionals at the center.

A lawsuit in January of this year claimed that the center treated pedophile

Anne Meisenzahl

priests and released them to parishes to serve children. The treatment center agreed to pay $4.3 million in damages to seventeen people who claim that Father Anthony Partridge of Des Moines, Iowa molested them as teenagers.

"I can't believe a psychiatric facility would say he was okay to be around kids and the parish would just take him back," said Joseph Berlinger, one of the claimants in the lawsuit. "How could the center tell the diocese he was cured? That's just wrong. It ruined a lot of lives. My abuse went on for six years."

According to unnamed sources, the facility continues to solicit donations to pay off the $4.3 million settlement. "The payment itself is not an admission of guilt," said Father David Maldonado, Director of the center, who is retiring next month. "We continue to stand by our healing work."

Grace came up for air after two hours in the library, dizzy from reading the file jammed with articles about the Servants of the Lamb, including damning evidence of a cover-up. She felt blanketed by sadness. She had found the place so charming.

240

40

Grace snuggled into the plush chair and pulled her red shawl around her shoulders. She'd asked Luke to meet her here at the swank bar at the new Hilton two days after she got back.

"It was a total waste. All your money, all your mother's money, all that time away from my dad who just had a stroke, all that effort to go back to LA to confront the leadership, the hierarchy, the ones who should care the *most*—and I get nothing."

"Okay," Luke said, nursing a gin and tonic and scooping huge dollops of spinach artichoke dip onto French bread. "Start from the beginning. Did you meet with the Cardinal?"

"They never planned to meet with me."

"Did you give them a copy of the essays?"

"Nobody would see me. And yes, I gave them multiple copies. I met with the Cardinal's secretary, Father Randolph, who dismissed me out of hand. I went to Holy Mother of God Cathedral and tried to meet with Father Santiago himself, but he was out of commission. I didn't even get to meet his surrogate priest. I did find out from the secretary that Father Santiago had been sent away a number of years ago to the Servants of the Lamb, which is like a therapeutic holding ground for wayward priests. I drove there, and again nobody would tell me anything. The secrecy is shocking. I assumed they'd take action right away, or at least give me the time of day."

Her idealism had been smashed like the candlesticks that had fallen to the floor when the aged priest tripped, sending the pretty flowers sailing, engulfing the chapel cloth and all the evidence of abuse in black smoke and flames.

On the flight back, she'd thought about Luke and how she would talk with him about her renewed disappointment with his Church. He would tell her they needed to fight the Church's immorality while holding true to the principles of Christian love. It might just be possible, she recognized with a shiver as she flew above the cottony clouds in the cramped air between California and New York, that he could help her navigate the gap. She could continue to question but at the same time give herself over to the best parts of religion—love and the spirit of kindness. She might have met someone who could help her become her best self. Except that he was a priest.

The restaurant at the Hilton was toasty and glowed with low lights. Luke questioned her gently, pressing her for details about her talk with Victoria, the reaction of everyone at the Cardinal's office, the meeting with Brother Frances and the seven other diminished men who were determined to carry their secrets with them to their graves. It was easy to talk to Luke because she knew he cared about Frankie, about doing the right thing, about *her*.

As his eyes looked into hers, her anger morphed into bemusement in the face of her own naïveté and ignorance. A mellow peace enveloped her. Her fourth glass of Scotch and soda warmed the back of her eyes and throat.

"It's all incredibly fascinating, isn't it?" She leaned forward and giggled. "If we just take one tiny teeny step outside of ourselves, go outside of our bodily prisons and watch ourselves and this whole amazing...*God*, it's freaking *amazing,* isn't it?"

"It is amazing," Luke said and raised his eyebrows. "But what are you referring to specifically?"

She was wasted, and she didn't care. Headaches be damned. "It's like we're rolling...riding...What's the word? Bumping along the road of this awesome life and we don't have the faintest clue *why*. It's absolutely stunning, don't you think? That we could be *so* clueless? Doesn't that ever just *floor* you?"

She was holding her head up now with both hands. If she moved one of them, there was a good chance her forehead would slam into the glass tabletop.

"Everybody's got a theory. A wild guess. But nobody knows. I wish all the Hindus and the pagans and the Buddha-pists and the therapists..."

She chuckled. "And the damn Christians are the *worst*. They have rites and rituals and sacred rules for doing every little thing like they don't trust us peons to figure it out ourselves. We have to obey, adore…Perpetual Adoration! What the hell *is* that?

"They should all admit that they're just *guessing* and they don't have any idea! We're all like a bunch of babies staring out at the world, clueless, fucking *clueless*."

Luke let her babble on.

"What I'm saying is, who the hell knows what happens after people do horrible things? They're just *forgiven*? Can they be forgiven for doing *such bad things*? Maybe there is a Hell, you know? How else would it make sense that people get away with the disgusting stuff they do to other people, to *children*, and then just *die?* If we don't punish them on earth, if we let them *get away* with it, how is that right? And the people who know about the criminals—the child abusers, the rapists—and cover it up. That might be worse!"

She paused to swallow a mouthful of dip, then waved to the waiter. "One more, last one," she snickered, holding up her glass. "Who has the faintest clue why people do evil acts and if there's any divine retribution?"

Luke listened, his head close to hers, surprisingly silent and attentive. She knew she was droning on obnoxiously, but she couldn't stop. The candle sputtered beneath their chins; their foreheads nearly touched.

"We just make stuff up, big, giant ideas about why the hell we're here, and how we're supposed to act, because we need something to hang our heart on." She laughed. "Now that's funny. I meant something to hang our *hat* on. But if you tell me you know the truth about why we live on this planet, and you think it's the truth with a capital T and not some idea you cooked up because you don't know, well, then, I know you *don't really* know, you know what I'm saying? Then that's where you lose me. You're either a big fat liar—oh my God, not *you!*"

She released her head and slapped him on his forearm, then slid her hand down and grabbed his. Now it felt like he was staring *into* her.

"Not you. You're not a liar. You are great, and you are totally telling the truth every Goddamn *day* by the way you live. Gen and Al too. They freak me out how they give their whole lives to be good people, not selfish.

Anne Meisenzahl

What *is* that? That whole Mass thing you guys do with all the singing and crying and bread and everybody together and everything—that is *amazing.* You are *great.*" She kept her hand in his, then, finally trusting her head to support itself, picked up her new glass and took a long swallow.

"It's strange, you know, that people call you Father. You are not their fathers. You are not *my* father, right? I am *glad* you are not my father. You know what I'm trying to say? You are *so* kissably great."

She blinked hard and stroked his fingers before releasing his hand and pulling herself up straight.

"Oh, my God. I am being such an asinine. Such an ass. I am *so sorry.* I gotta figure out how to get myself home."

"I'll drive. Don't worry. I'll take you home," he said, his voice like a beam from a lighthouse, leading her back to soberness and safety. "And then I'll drive myself back to St. Laurence with your car. Can you take the bus back to the House tomorrow? Or should I come to pick you up?"

"Yes, good, wonderful. The amazing bus," she said.

On the ride home, Grace rested her cheek against the window, her eyes closed to the streetlights. *You've ruined it,* she thought. The sweet chaste connection you had with this strange, kind man is over because you've gone and shown him who you are. An embarrassing, cynical mess.

She managed to direct him back to the house but almost tripped on the icy sidewalk. He put his arm through hers and guided her up the walk. She fumbled with her keys, and he followed her into the house. Brian's light was on next door.

"Nice place," he told her, taking in her quiet home.

"Look," she said. She sat on the recliner without taking off her coat or boots and loosened her scarf. "That was some display. You're nice."

"Not to worry. It was very entertaining." He unwrapped the damp scarf from her shoulders and wrapped it around his own neck. "It was charming. You are quite beautiful, Grace."

She closed her eyes. A wave of nausea threatened to overtake her. "I think I better get my charming self to bed," she said, sinking deeper into the chair.

"Tomorrow, then," he told her, keeping the scarf. "I'll see you at St. Laurence tomorrow."

41

For the next few days, Grace managed to pretend nothing had happened. As if she hadn't had a disastrous visit to the Cardinal, as if she hadn't gotten plastered and humiliated herself, as if she didn't all but admit she had a crush on a priest. She found a thousand little ways to keep herself occupied at St. Laurence to avoid contact with Luke.

But the following Tuesday, he asked if he could come over to her place instead of meeting at the House or going to Hooligan's. He said he had a couple of things he needed to discuss with her about the Frankie situation, some ideas for how to proceed with the "case."

When Grace opened the door to him at exactly eight o'clock that night, Luke stared at her without speaking, and when she invited him to sit, he sank into the chair that faced the sofa. His eyelids were heavy.

"Um...how are you?"

"I must admit I'm tired," he said. He told her about his difficulty sleeping, how for the past three nights he'd been awakened by crises: a broken pipe in the men's dorm, a fight between two guests, a woman screaming at her boyfriend from the street.

"But I'm not here to complain. How are you?"

"Fine," she said. She remained standing. It was strange to see him in her home; it was hard for her to relax. She started to tell him about her latest conversation with her dad when he interrupted her.

"I think you need to go to the police and file a lawsuit."

"I wrote to them. The police already told me the case was too old."

"This has to be brought to the attention of the civil authorities if the Church is harboring an abusive priest." Luke pulled an article from the *Rochester Times-Union* out of his jacket pocket.

The article described a civil lawsuit against a priest in Rochester seeking $15 million. It accused Rev. Richard Caseman of sexually abusing three brothers, then ages six, nine, and fourteen, in October and November 1987 in the priest's rectory of Our Lady of the Precious Blood Church.

Grace read the article silently, still standing, as Luke slouched in the chair and watched. Caseman, the associate pastor, was accused of kissing, fondling, and exposing himself to the two younger brothers and forcing the oldest to sodomize him. It was sickening; it made her stomach churn. This priest had been sent to another treatment facility in Culpepper, Missouri and released a year later to work with children.

The article reported that in ten civil trials related to sexual molestation by clergy and cover-up by Church authorities, awards to plaintiffs averaged about $1 million. In one case, two twins who accused the diocese of Monterrey, California of abuse won $20 million. In another case, the diocese in Detroit agreed to pay $18.4 million to eight former altar boys. It was all they could afford to pay even though the jury had awarded $110 million.

"Wow," Grace said. "There's a lot of money in this."

"They cover it up intentionally long enough so the statute of limitations will pass because of the cost of this litigation. If this continues, some of these dioceses are going to go broke."

Grace sat down on the sofa. "A lawsuit is a big deal, and getting the police involved...I'm not sure I'm the one to do all this."

The trip had depleted what little was left of her resources and left her even more disenchanted with the institutional Church. It made her attraction to the Hospitality House and its simple mandate more magnetic. And her dad needed her. "Besides, I wouldn't have any idea where to start."

"My parents may have contacts."

Grace raised her eyebrows. "How old are your parents?"

"Mom's seventy-eight. Dad's eighty. But they're pretty active. Retired but still fighting the good fight."

"I'm not related to Frankie, and we don't have any evidence except the essays."

"But you have Victoria. And there may be others. The hierarchy is wrong. They need to be stopped."

He looked diminished. Up until this moment, Grace had regarded Luke as somehow more advanced than an ordinary man. She held him up and revered him as a mentor. A saint. But tonight, slumped in a comfortable chair away from his domain, he was just a man. He closed his eyes as if he might be falling asleep, then stood up and stretched his arms above his head.

"Excuse me, Grace. Where is your bathroom?"

She pointed. The door was ajar, and the nightlight shone into the dark hallway. He walked to the bathroom and shut the door. When he returned, he knelt on the floor in front of her.

Was he praying? Was he going to invite her to pray? He stroked her hair off her face and then held her face in his hands, persuading her with his gentle, rough hands to lean toward him. He moved in to kiss her tenderly.

"I don't know what this is, Grace. You and me. I don't know what I'm doing. What I do know is that I can't stand to not be near you, and I haven't touched anyone or been touched in a very long time."

"I know," she muttered as she studied him. She knew she was having an impact on him; she knew she was attracted to him, but she hadn't let herself imagine *this*. What was she doing?

He stood up and bent down to kiss her first on her forehead, then her ear, then the white exposed part of her neck. He left without saying a word.

Luke knocked on her door the next night. She gasped when she saw his polar bear presence, red knitted cap pulled over his ears, the St. Laurence van parked on the street. It was Friday. He had skipped Free Bread and Soup Discussion. And Brian was on the couch.

"Hey. Well, hi." Grace felt girlish, shy.

"Grace. I—I didn't mean to—" He was actually stammering, this confident pontificator. "I can—"

"No. Hi, Luke. Father Luke. This is my neighbor Brian." She had already been startled once that evening when Brian invited himself in to talk about her trip.

She turned away from staring at her priest and faced her friend. Brian uncurled himself from the sofa, extended a long, muscular arm, and nodded. "Hey, man. Good to meet you. I was just leaving."

Luke shook his hand and nodded back.

"Um, you don't—" Grace began.

"I'm in the middle of re-grouting my bathtub. Friday night's ideal for repair and restoration. No distractions. See you around, Grace." He winked at her, turned to the silent priest, and said, "Mon Pere." He tipped an invisible hat then ducked and slunk out into the cold air.

Grace closed her eyes to the awkwardness. She shut the door with a soft click. "This is a surprise," she said. "You want to come in the kitchen?"

They sat at the kitchen table. The night outside the window was black and blustery. She offered him a beer. "Do you have wine?" he asked, looking at her mouth.

"Of course." She stood up and pulled out a bottle of Merlot. She uncorked it as he watched, poured out two glasses, and set them on the table. "I'll make us some sandwiches."

"Good. I'm famished."

Neither of them talked as she spread hummus on the bread and sliced tomato and cheese. She arranged the two sandwiches on one plate and sat down across from him.

He raised his glass. "To fighting the hierarchy. To journalism. To law."

"Yes," she answered, clinking his glass and taking a slow sip. They ate without talking, eyeing everything but each other.

"This sandwich was delicious," Luke said, brushing crumbs off his shirt. "Grace, can I ask you a question?"

"Of course."

"First, are you lovers with that Brian? Engaged in relations, I mean?"

He sounded so stilted, so unaccustomed to such talk, it filled her with tenderness. She pressed away a smile. "No, no, no. Just friends."

He took in a gulp of air and exhaled.

"Here is the question I came to ask."

She waited while he looked out at the night, collecting himself. He took three more deep breaths before turning back to her. "Do you believe in divine providence? Do you believe two lives can be brought together by God, by a spirit of love, divinely, to serve a larger purpose?"

"I don't know," she said, looking down at the tablecloth.

"I do," he said, pressing his warm fingertips to her cheek. "I think God has brought me to you."

Her heart was whirring like a small motor. "What do you mean?"

He put his hand on hers. "Talking with you in this way over the past few months, seeing your passion for getting at the truth, getting closer to you spiritually, intellectually, getting to know you—and letting you get to know me—something has been changing in me. It's as if I'm bursting inside. I didn't expect this. I truly didn't. Grace, I want to kiss you more at this moment than I have ever wanted any earthly thing."

"Oh, Luke. Oh, no." She stood up, her chair making a screeching noise on the floor. She paced in a circle around the living room. "This is all my fault."

"No. No. Don't you see? I think you were sent to me. I think our connection to one another is divinely inspired. There is not a worldly, base reason for our meeting, but a holy one. My dear."

He stood up and walked over to where Grace had slumped into a chair. "May I kiss you?"

The plaintive look in his eyes drew her in. She lifted her face up to meet his and pressed her lips against his for a second before pulling back.

"I don't think this is a good idea," she whispered. "Aren't you worried about where this could lead? And I'm not...I..."

She started to say she didn't know if she was ready, but her heart and her head were a jumble. What if this was her last true opportunity for happiness? What if what she was doing was wrong? Immoral even? What if she didn't allow herself to feel this, whatever it was?

"Aren't you afraid?"

"I am. I am," he said, standing and reaching for her hands. She raised herself into his arms.

"Me too," she said, falling into his embrace.

"Can we go into your room?" he asked her, his breath hot in her ear.

"Oh my God, I don't know," she whispered. She started to take a step back, but his arms tightened around her.

"Please," he begged.

Her heart throbbed in her throat, and she shivered. Leading a man into her bed had never felt this titillating and dangerous. Her bed was unmade; she tossed the covers aside and sat down. He knelt on the floor in front of her and placed his hands on the backs of her calves. "I don't know what I'm doing. I'm—"

She placed her hands on the top of his head, caressed his temples and ears, and kissed his forehead. "Me either."

"Grace, I'm sorry." He stood up abruptly, shaking his head. "I can't. I need to go." He shuffled into the living room, grabbed his coat, and walked out the door. Grace sat on her bed, her mouth open.

42

Luke returned the next night, leaving the van parked out front. "I'm still afraid," he told her, pulling her close and cupping her head as it rested on his chest. "I don't know what to do. But I think I should trust my heart. Grace, until I met you, I didn't know how desperately lonely I'd become."

They embraced and kissed by the open door. Grace closed it without saying a word, then took his hand and led him into the bedroom. As she lay prone on the bed, he undressed her slowly, kissing her neck, her smooth shoulders, the valley between her breasts. He caressed her neck, her nipples, her mouth, her belly, her soft hips.

He stood up and took off his own clothes, laying each item over the arm of the chair in the corner. She watched him move toward her. Her heart hammering, she put her hand on the curly white hairs on his chest and pressed him away.

"Luke," she said. "Just in case, I need to put in my diaphragm." She didn't look at his expression as she shimmied away and slunk into the bathroom.

When she returned, he was on his back, the sheet pulled up to his neck. She crawled in next to him, and he turned to her, laying the full length of his body on top of hers. He approached her with a shyness and tenderness that made her feel protective. He came quickly, crying thick, silent tears, and held her for a long time.

"I'm sorry," he said. "I thought that might happen."

"I don't care," she said, his face in her hands. She hadn't had sex in over a year. Until tonight when she gave herself over to it, gave herself back to herself.

In the stillness of their togetherness, she thought about religion, that intricately woven mystical scarf which had wrapped itself around her naked neck during the cold winter of her youth. How it eventually unraveled when the sun came out, fiber by fiber, until it disappeared. And how, despite all her previous disappointments, with this religious man at her side, she might finally learn to live in the body with all its beauties and its needs, the animal body that craves other animal bodies in order to survive.

Grace sat up and walked into the bathroom. She filled the tub with hot water and bubbles. Then she pulled him out of bed, across the hall, and into the bath. They folded their limbs into the small space. Grace soaped his fuzzy chest. Without speaking, they caressed the length of each other's bodies and dried each other with fluffy towels.

They lay back in bed and rubbed almond oil with warm palms into the slope of each other's backs. Luke turned so that Grace could rest her head on his shoulder.

"You know that adultery is a sin, Grace? I believe it is. I believe it's a violation of a holy vow."

"Okay?" she asked, lifting her head up onto her hand.

"When a man becomes a priest, he takes the vow of celibate chastity. You give yourself totally to God, to Christ, to souls. With all your mind, heart, and will. According to Church teachings, a priest breaking his vow of celibacy is a sin. I have a friend from seminary who left the priesthood to get married. He had to give up his calling; he was never allowed to administer the sacraments." Luke closed his eyes and sighed, then opened them and stared at her. "That's the most important thing I do."

Grace sat up and hugged her naked chest. Now she felt exposed. "Luke, how can you believe that it's a sin? Celibacy is a choice. But to break it—the vow, I mean—can't be a sin. Sex between adults, consenting adults who care for each other..." She looked away. "That's not a sin."

"I entered seminary school when I was twenty-three years old. I struggled. I didn't know at the time if I was capable of making the sacrifice."

Grace watched him breathe. He lay on his back now, hands behind his head.

"I didn't know if I could do it. But I did do it. I made a vow. At the time, I believed that vow was as sacred as a marriage vow."

"What do you think now?" Grace said.

"I don't know." He sat up. They were two naked birds. He kissed her mouth, her eyes, her forehead. He held her against his warm chest. "I don't know. I don't know. I don't know."

Grace got up and walked into the bathroom. She shut the door, brushed her teeth, and peed. She watched herself in the mirror as she brushed her tousled hair. When she returned, Luke was sitting on the edge of the bed, a slip of weathered yellow paper in his hands. Grace sat beside him. "What's this?"

"I read this every night before I go to sleep to reflect on the Lord. It's a ritual I've developed. It's kind of a habit." He showed her. In neat print, he'd written all the names of Jesus: *Wonderful Counselor, King of Kings, Savior, Prince of Peace, Redeemer, Messiah, Son of God, Son of Man, Servant of Humanity, Good Shepherd, Holy One, Blessed One, Jesu, the Way, the Truth, the Life, Most High, Humble Servant.*

Grace took the paper from him and kissed his cheek. There was more on the other side: *Our Lady, Blessed Mary Ever Virgin, Blessed Mother, Mother of God, Cause of our Joy, Queen of the World, Mirror of Justice, Health of the Sick, Comforter of the Afflicted, Queen of Peace.*

She nudged away the flush of fear that began to rise inside her. How little she knew about this mysterious and alluring man. She folded the paper and put it on the chair. They made love again, taking their time, then finally nestled under the blanket, facing each other, their eyelids heavy.

"My sweet Grace," Luke whispered. "My dear." He stroked her cheek with the palm of his hand. "In many ways like the Blessed Mother."

In all her years, no one had ever called her "my sweet Grace." And certainly, in spite of her ancient longing for purity, no one had ever compared her to the Virgin Mary. Exhaustion as thick and soothing as a feather comforter covered them both. They fell asleep, curled into each other like frightened newborn sparrows under a mother's wing.

A thin slice of morning light woke Grace from a foggy dream. She gasped aloud when she remembered falling asleep in Luke's arms, one of her legs between his. She faced the window, lying still so as not to wake him, and felt her body softening at the memory. How would their day play out?

They'd have coffee and eggs. He'd go back to St. Laurence. She'd call Alvin and tell him she wasn't feeling well, give herself and Luke time to figure out their next moves. They'd meet later at her place to scheme about their terrible, delicious secret, then make love again.

Of course, Luke would have to leave the priesthood. She knew he sometimes questioned his commitment to the Church. But she also knew how much he loved his work and would want to continue what he considered his mission to St. Laurence House. Maybe he could carry on as a lay director. She could become more involved as his partner. They'd rock the boat and get married. They'd be a team. It had been so long since she'd been in love. She turned her naked body over to snuggle up against him.

His side of the bed was made up, the blanket and sheet pulled up over the pillow. She listened for water running or the toilet flushing. He must be in the kitchen, reading or making coffee. She pulled on a robe and padded into the kitchen, her stomach fluttering.

She saw that he'd placed twigs from the pine tree in the yard in a glass and set it on the table. Under the glass was a sheet of paper on which he'd drawn a large heart and written a note in bold letters with a felt tip pen.

I am amazed and in awe at the blessing that is you. Yours, Luke.

She traced the heart with her finger. She shuffled through the kitchen, brewing coffee and frying herself an egg. She called Alvin to let him know she wouldn't be coming in today. Then she took her coffee to bed and fell back into the satiny folds of the sheets she'd shared with Luke.

Grace arrived home from visiting her dad at seven o'clock. Luke knocked on the door at eight, and before Grace could welcome him in and shut the door, he placed his hand behind her head and brought her mouth to his. His chilly whiskers startled her lips, and his tongue found hers. Wisps of snow blew into the living room. The van was parked in the street.

His hands smoothed her hair, massaged her neck. Sought her warm skin under her shirt, discovered her breasts. His thumbs raised her nipples.

Grace moaned. "Luke," she said, her fingers on his full lips. "Should we talk?"

"Grace, I can't breathe." He held her close. "Please. Let's not talk. Let's please go to your bed."

43

Grace tried to keep herself from grinning the next day as she wheeled her dad down the hallway, helped him drink his warm soup, and watched a daytime show. She showed up at St. Laurence after dinner. The volunteers would be wiping down counters and putting leftovers away. She smiled at her ridiculous fantasy of Luke greeting her at the door and kissing her in front of the guests still lingering in the dining room. She let herself imagine them clapping, joyful at the sight of their priest finally allowing himself some normal human sexual love.

But of course, he didn't greet her. Her rational mind knew he wouldn't. Everything had changed and would have to be dealt with stealthily and wisely for a while. No one looked up when she walked through the kitchen, past the library, and into Luke's office. Luke wasn't there.

She walked back into the hallway and down to the chapel. Tall Tree was kneeling in front of the statue of St. Jude, reciting the rosary with his eyes closed. She slid into a pew and looked up at the ceiling. It was yellowed in spots, in need of paint and repair. She wasn't sure where Luke was or where to go, so she just sat.

Five minutes later, a priest walked into the chapel. His black and white starched collar was such a contrast to Luke's open-necked white bolero shirts. His skin was a dark espresso, his hair black and shaved close. His face was smooth and serious, his frame petite and muscular; he looked the antithesis of Luke.

He walked up and asked if her name was Grace Schreiber.

She nodded.

"How do you do?" he asked, holding out his small hand. She shook it, staring at his face. She'd never seen him, or any priest besides Luke, at St. Laurence before.

"Would you please come with me?" he said.

Back in Luke's office, the priest sat behind the desk and motioned for her to sit on a folding chair. Luke's books and papers were stacked in messy piles on the desk and the floor.

"My name is Father Adeyemi. I shall be advising St. Laurence and offering Mass for the foreseeable future. Father Luke said that you would probably be by because he has been giving you spiritual counsel, and he asked me to give you this letter."

Father Adeyemi's African accent was soothing and melodic. Grace sat motionless, trying to understand what was happening. Father Adeyemi held the letter out across the desk, his arm straight. Grace stared at it for a few seconds before taking it. The words *Conscience Matter* were written across the front of the sealed envelope.

"Thank you," she said and stood up to leave. She left without saying hello to anyone and drove straight home.

She poured wine into a juice glass, turned the jazz station up loud on the radio, and sat down at the kitchen table to read Luke's letter.

My dear, dear Grace—

These past months talking with you have meant the world to me. You are a brilliant and appealing and fascinating woman. Because of knowing you, I am a better man.

In a moment of doubt, I allowed myself to be swept up in your charms, not to mention your arms. I allowed myself to question the very principles of the faith I've devoted myself to since I was twenty-five years old. In you, in the light of the luminous moon, I believed for a moment that I had found another path to God. In the bright light of day, however, I do not believe that God's intention is for me to live a secret life of deceit, nor is it to renounce my vocation or my single-minded devotion to His way.

I will be cloistered at the Abbey of the Blessed Virgin for at least a month. After a time of prayer, work, and meditation, God will make it clear what is in store for me and my work at St. Laurence House. I ask that you please not contact me there.

Your questioning mind and your gift for insightful debate are an inspiration to me. I wish you courage as you pursue your steadfast mission of seeking justice for the mistreated and abused.

Your loveliness is a gift of God, and I am blessed to have known you.
Sincerely,
Father Luke

On another sheet of paper, he'd typed a quote by St. Frances de Sales and sketched a cross around it in pencil. *Our hearts should each day seek a resting-place on Calvary or near our Lord, in order to retire there to rest from worldly cares and to find strength against temptation.*

She reread the letter ten times before she allowed herself to cry.

How could she have been so stupid? How could she have not considered what these acts of love—lust, sin?—would do to him? A man who had been celibate for almost thirty years, who had devoted his life to a set of beliefs that still defined him. How could she have thought that she, an ordinary, mortal, non-virginal woman could, with her normal naked body and human mind, trump the Church's doctrine and make him renounce his divine calling? Who did she think she was?

But, she thought with a sudden surge of anger, *who did he think he was?* How cruel to set her up and allow her to fantasize that she could actually be loved, that someone could want her? How mean of him to seduce her, tease her, betray her. He had compared her to the *Blessed Mother.* They were both a couple of selfish fools.

She rose to go to the bathroom and scrub her face. With the light from the hallway, she studied her image in the mirror. She saw a nearly middle-aged woman with auburn hair flecked with the random strand of gray, long and thick with curls, falling to the middle of her back. Creases circled her green eyes, red-veined from crying. She struck a match and lit a candle; the flame danced, and she saw beauty, a golden glow to her skin, a warmth in her sad eyes, full lips.

Beauty and goodness intertwined.

She turned on the overhead fluorescent light, and in its harsh brightness, she saw her dark side, the part of herself she couldn't trust, the not-beauty. Not ugliness, exactly, but selfishness. It was there in her splotchy red skin, the dark circles under her eyes. Which light was true?

Two sides of me, she thought. *Two honest lights, two truths. Beauty and not-beauty at once, living inside the same skin.*

Genevieve was wearing an oversized brown parka, its grey fur-lined hood tight around her head, when Grace found her shoveling snow out back the next day.

"Oh, dear girl, dear girl!" the nun said when she saw Grace, her eyes pink from sleeplessness and sobbing. She stretched out her puffy arms and pulled Grace into an embrace. "I suppose I should have seen this coming."

"Sister Genevieve, I think I've done something terrible. I mean, why would Father Luke leave? This is his home. His place. Why would he leave? Is this my fault?"

Genevieve wordlessly scraped the snow off the rest of the path then leaned the shovel against the wall. "Let's go get us some tea," she said and led Grace inside.

Genevieve took off the parka to reveal the embroidered maroon jacket underneath. She stroked its velvety arms and smiled.

"I'll be right back," she said as she walked into the kitchen.

Grace walked toward the chapel. The door was open, and she saw Father Adeyemi inside. He was standing above Alvin, his hands on her friend's shoulders, praying solemnly. Two women were sitting in the common room, and three volunteers swept the dining room, preparing it for lunch. Grace stood still, energy whirling around her. She felt oddly timid and alien in this place that had made her feel so at home.

Genevieve returned with a tray laden with a metal teapot and two mugs. "Let's go to my quarters," she said.

"Does everyone know?" Grace asked, sitting beside the nun's small desk, teacup in her hands. She looked at the wall. Mother Theresa's expression, eyes focused on the spindly newborn in her arms, comforted her.

"Luke confided in me," Genevieve answered. "We have been friends and co-conspirators for a long time. I have known about the slow unraveling of his heart for these past months. At some point, it was bound to come undone." Genevieve patted Grace's knee, her eyes kind. "You are a powerful force. A lovely young woman with a big heart. You did him in."

"I don't know," Grace said. "All these feelings are swimming around in me. I think—I thought—maybe I was falling in love with him. And I feel like maybe I screwed up, leading him on, not taking his *vocation* seriously."

Grace sighed and closed her eyes, which stung. The tears that had erupted in her every hour since she'd read the letter threatened to return.

"Nothing to blame yourself for. You followed your heart, and he followed his. Now he has to figure out how to handle it. The vocation was his, not yours. He's a big boy."

"Is he gone for good?"

"He's at the Abbey. His life is about to take a different shape."

"I won't see him at all?"

"He thinks it's best if you don't. He's very upset."

Grace cried then, rivers of despair forcing her lungs to emit short, hard sobs. She cradled her wet face in her cupped hands until Genevieve scooted her chair up to embrace her. The older woman let her cry in her arms for a few minutes. Then the nun pulled her away and held her by the shoulders.

She looked Grace in her eyes, stern and motherly. "You need to know something. This, my dear girl, is not just about you. When you were on your trip, we were informed that Father Luke was to be silenced. He received a letter from the Buffalo Diocese telling him he could no longer participate in the Mass as long as I...as long as a woman..." Genevieve shook her head. "But even that I think they might have tolerated because he's been co-officiating with me all along and not keeping it a secret."

Grace studied the nun's intertwined fingers. "It was his financial support for your research on molestation that got him in trouble."

"What?" Grace asked. She wiped her eyes with the backs of her hands. "What do you mean?"

"When you went to LA to meet in person with the Cardinal, they investigated and learned that Luke had given you the money, sent you on his behalf, set up the trip to the Servants of the Lamb..."

"He didn't set up the visit to Servants of the Lamb. I did that."

"You used his name."

"Who is they? And how did they know all this?"

"The Cardinal. Mahony. He's powerful. They all are. They're very adept at communicating with one another. It all came back to the Buffalo Diocese. The Bishop sent Luke a letter."

Grace felt as if she'd been slapped. Luke knew, before they met at the Hilton, before they made love, that he had been exiled. Sent away. That his time at St. Laurence was over. He'd never uttered a word to her about the Bishop's letter.

"If he stayed here and continued to serve Mass with me, he'd be stripped of his rights to perform the sacraments. We knew that would happen if he went public about our Mass in your article. They'd let him carry out his work here at St. Laurence otherwise. But championing your muckraking…"

She paused when she saw Grace's shocked expression.

"Sponsoring your trip to research their cover-ups of molestation, apparently, is impermissible. He was muzzled. Expelled."

Grace pressed a hand against her temple to stave off the headache that threatened to erupt. "How can they do that?"

"Did you know that the Church silenced Brother Thomas?"

Grace shook her head.

"In 1963, Brother Thomas Merton was told by Rome that he had to abstain from all writing against nuclear war. They forbad him to publish a book that was ready to go to press. They censored him and all his pacifist writings."

Grace sighed. "Luke can't come back?"

"Not as a priest. If he disobeys their command that he enter the monastery, he'll be excommunicated."

Grace thought of the brazen way the Los Angeles church had allowed Father Santiago to continue to serve Mass, run a school, and associate with altar boys even after they clearly knew what he'd done and sent him off for "psychiatric treatment." Instead of turning Santiago into the police, they protected him. But Luke…all he'd done was try to protect children, and they'd banished him. It was all so twisted.

"And you?" Grace studied the nun's animated face and the smile lines around her eyes. "What about you? Wasn't what you did…what's the word? Illegal? Forbidden?"

"Absolutely. Not acceptable at all. They're still trying to figure out what to do with me." Sister Genevieve laughed.

"And what about St. Laurence?" Grace asked, her voice a whimper. "What's going to happen now?"

As much as Grace felt she was a part of the Hospitality House, she knew now it had a secret life of its own. People were moved around like chess pieces, and she was just an observer.

"Doesn't St. Laurence get donations from some of the churches in the diocese?"

"Nobody knows yet what's going to happen. I trust things will work out the way God intends them to." Sister Genevieve straightened, rising from the chair. "In the meantime, you'd better get yourself cleaned up. You have research to do, a lawsuit to pursue, an article to write, and a teenage girl to look after. Not to mention a great many hungry people to serve."

44

Grace was afraid she might be damaged for life. Because she lost her mom so young, in such an unformed state, something was wrong with her. She was sure of it. Over and over again, she had let herself dive headfirst into doomed relationships, oblivious to the rocks beneath the surface. How is it she had so little ability to steer herself clear of men who could only harm her?

She'd had affairs with unavailable men and stayed too long with Drew, who didn't love her. Jake had been too young, too impetuous, and had shown signs of interest in Linda early on. She had just been too blind to notice. Luke was a priest who loved his vocation and never would have left the Church for her. Was she so insecure about love after having been abandoned by her mom that she couldn't allow herself to be vulnerable? Was the pattern woven so into her psyche that she wouldn't be able to recover this time?

She continued to move mechanically about her wintery days. Nobody at St. Laurence spoke about Father Luke's palpable absence. She wondered if they'd also been ordered to take a vow of silence. Nobody seemed to notice that Father Adeyemi's presence, his kind but stern demeanor, changed the color of the place from the yellow light of humor and bustle to a more somber pale gray. Thanks to regular visits by the strange new priest, St. Laurence was more organized, quieter, and clean.

She found herself gravitating to Genevieve now that Luke was gone. "How is he doing?" Grace asked under her breath in the donation room.

"Fine," the nun answered. "Got a letter last week. He's baking a lot of bread, attending Mass daily, and hopefully learning to sing better."

"Doesn't he miss it here?"

Doesn't he miss me? Grace pleaded inside her head.

"He does."

"And how are you?" Grace asked the nun. "I know Father Luke was your good friend. Did you expect everything to turn out this way?"

"The diocese has warned us that if I continue to perform the sacraments, they will withdraw all financial support. And Father Adeyemi is absolutely not on board. They've put him here to watch me. I'm biding my time until I am guided by the Spirit as to how to proceed."

"What do you think might happen?"

"I have an idea. I know of a ramshackle old farmhouse on ten acres in Lockport. If I'm no longer welcome here, I have a few Sisters interested in plotting with me to finance another community. We want to call it New Hope for Women Community Farm. It'll be a safe haven for abused and addicted women. I envision some kind of fundraising enterprise, like a cookie baking business, and lots of singing. Maybe we'll perform that new dance exercise, Zumba. And a woman-run Mass every day."

"Wow. That's wonderful." Grace paused as she folded a stack of men's polo shirts, not unlike the donations that had brought her to St. Laurence in the first place.

"But, Sister," she asked, "is it ever hard for you to not be married? Did you ever question your vows like Luke? Ever want to be in love?" Regret slapped her after the words tripped out. "Never mind. It's none of my business."

A chuckle tumbled from Genevieve's throat. "I can see how you turned Luke upside down. You have a way of getting people to look inside themselves. I don't know if you even know you're doing it." Genevieve turned her attention to hanging up men's jackets.

"I'm sorry," Grace said.

"I had a friend. A dear friend. A Sister in Tegucigalpa. I haven't spoken to her or written to her in over twenty years. She helped me see God in a wholly new way."

Genevieve stopped fussing over the clothes and stood still. She stared at her tall frame in the full-length mirror and patted her cropped gray hair. "I don't know what it would be like to see her or speak to her again. We learned about love together. Alma is her name."

"I bet she'd like to hear from you."

"We're both old women now."

Anne Meisenzahl

"It doesn't matter," Grace said. "I bet she misses you."

Genevieve shooed her away. "Run along now," she said. "You've given me enough to think about."

"Tell me how the visit to the doctor went yesterday," Grace said, taking a bite of egg and watching Crystal pour syrup over her French toast. "Maybe I could go with you next time."

Crystal was seven months pregnant. Her eyebrows were growing back in, prickly stubs above her pretty jade green eyes. Her natural brown roots had grown out, too, leaving only the bottom half of her long locks stark black. She combed her hair out straight and shimmering, and she didn't bother with makeup anymore. Grace thought that made her look younger, more naïve. Her belly was round and solid and low.

"I thought of a name for the pumpkin," Crystal said. She pointed down at the globe in her lap.

"You did?"

"I wanna name him Jesse." She slumped into the booth and spread her legs wide."

"Why Jesse?"

"Cause he gonna be an outlaw. Like Jesse James."

"Oh, is that right?" Grace raised her eyebrows and stifled a smile.

"And like that man and his son tryin' to be President."

"You want your baby to be named for an outlaw and a civil rights activist?"

"And for Jesus too."

"Is that right?"

"'Cause even though he gonna be bad sometimes, he gonna be good too. You know? Like Jesus was good and loved everybody. Because he gonna be half white and half black, half wild and half righteous. A little bit bad and a lot good. That's what I think."

"That's what I think, too, Crystal," Grace said. "Kind of like you! And me!" *A little bit bad and a lot good.* She would write that down and tape it on her mirror when she got home.

"These pancakes is so good! I freakin' love this shit!" Crystal laughed. "Oops. Man, this is hard."

264

"What is?" Grace asked.

Crystal put the syrup down and looked at Grace, her eyes serious. "I'm tryin' not to curse no more."

"Oh?"

"I gotta teach him right," she said, pointing to her raised marble of a belly button. "Not like nobody taught me. Didn't nobody teach me nothing right."

"Crystal, where did you grow up? Did you live with a mom or dad?"

"I grew up in Georgia. That's a long ways from here. But I had to get out 'cause my mom was crazy." She drew a circle in the air around her ear with a sticky finger. "She didn't love me, she told me herself. She left me by myself all the time when I was too little to be alone. No food in the house. Nothin'. She got me back after the foster lady beat me and the foster man messed with me. She told the caseworker people she was born again in the Pentacostalist Church, but she wasn't no mother. She lied to them, and they believed her. But she didn't love me. She didn't love that cuckoo church. She loved *crack*. That shit was her *life*."

Crystal laughed again, making Grace jump.

"See what I'm sayin'? Not cursin' is fuckin' *hard*."

"Wow, sweetheart. That's unbelievable. Did you run away?"

"Nope," Crystal said. "Just walked slow. Got a bag together, and just walked and walked and walked."

"And how did you end up here?"

Crystal shrugged and stuffed a sticky forkful of French toast into her mouth. "I don't know, but I'm glad I did," she said.

The doctor rubbed on the gooey gel and swirled the ultrasound gadget over Crystal's swollen belly. Grace sat close in a chair next to the examination table. Together they watched the fuzzy grey image on the screen.

"He's real, ain't he? Is he perfect?"

"Looks perfect to me," the doctor said. "And how about you? Anything you want to tell me about this?" She pointed to the bruise laying fat and yellowish as an egg yolk against her ribs.

"That's nothing. It was a accident is all. Nobody beat me."

"Are we sure about that? Have we seen the baby's father lately?" the doctor asked.

Grace turned to Crystal. The girl was cheerful and bright today, not defensive like when Grace first broached the question back when the bruise was eggplant purple and fresh.

"Nah. Honest. Samuel's gone," Crystal said. "I went to find him in Watertown. He's squatting there. He don't want no part of little Jesse. But he ain't mean or nothing. Just scared and stupid and selfish. And he's a druggie. I don't want none of that for my baby."

"When was this?" Grace asked.

"I went back like a month ago to the nasty old squat where I met him in the summer. I dunno why. I wanted to see him. It's like a burned-out old building with nothing inside. I hitched with Maybelle. It was cool to squat there in summer. It's free, and nobody cares if you're there. But it's dumb in winter. They's about to freeze in there, Magpie and Danny and Samuel. They had built a big fire trying to keep warm. Stupid Magpie was pulling wood from the ceiling and the walls to try and burn, and a big piece of wood fell on me."

"Oh, my gosh, Crystal. That's so dangerous! You could have been hurt. And the baby!" Grace cringed. If Crystal had left to live at the squat or if, God forbid, anything had happened to her, Grace would have been devastated. She was coming to count on the good feeling that came from helping out this child, the way being in her presence and puzzling out her needs washed away her other concerns. She was invested in meeting this baby.

"I know, but I'm good now. I had to check the squat out, you know? Check out if Samuel was a for true dad or a loser. But I'm good. I'm cool. I'm back." She winked at Grace, giving her a look that made her appear older than her almost seventeen years. "I know you need me."

"Brian, can I ask you something?" Both Mountain and Brian looked up from their bowls of chili at the same time. It had been three weeks since she'd met with her friends. She missed their time together.

"What is it?" Brian was always pleasant to her, but it was clear he was keeping his distance. He had tried to keep things light after she rebuffed his kiss, but after Luke's surprising interruption, he had never been back for an evening visit. The only times she saw him were when they were hanging out with Mountain.

"How would you feel if…" She stopped and noticed them staring intently at her. "Did I tell you about this girl I met at St. Laurence?"

"You sure did," Mountain said. "It's quite the story. Sixteen and pregnant and a runaway. Makes you just want to love her up."

Brian chewed his chili and didn't say a word.

"Well, she's due in about a month and a half. I've been checking on her a lot. She's all alone."

"I couldn't have done it without support. I was nineteen with Harmony, twenty-two with Brook. And I thought *I* was a baby. And I had a fine group of mothers to commiserate with. The Sharing Place, we called it. The kids could run free while the women took turns taking care of them. When my so-called husband left after Rain was born, I got even more help."

The conversation stalled. Mountain finished her hot mint tea. Brian dunked cornbread into his chili and took a swig of beer. Magic let out a low moan after licking the last of his food from his silver bowl then rested his head between his paws.

"Come here, Magic," Grace said, snapping her fingers in the direction of the dog. "You are such a good boy."

There was comfort in the presence of the old dog's shiny black fur, his soulful black eyes. He pulled himself to his feet, tapped across the floor, and laid his head in her lap so she could stroke the bone of his long nose.

"How would I feel if what?" Brian asked.

"How would you feel if I…" Grace had practiced asking the question for the past week, ever since going to the clinic with Crystal and seeing the ultrasound pictures projected on the screen. "I thought I might want to ask her and the baby to stay here with me in my extra room. She's due in six weeks. It would just be until she can get it together."

Grace had fixated on the idea since she saw the fuzzy image of the fetus scrunched into a ball sucking his tiny fingers. She fantasized the three of them living with Crystal and the baby. They would have regular dinners where everyone contributed. Mountain would advise her and help them care for the infant. Brian would be there, supportive but at a comfortable distance, impressed with her ability to maintain calm equilibrium in the storm.

"Are you keeping it all in balance, dear girl?" Mountain said as if intuiting her thoughts. "Are you remembering to keep yourself in the center of your own canoe? You may think you're helping people by putting all your weight in their corner, but the truth is, if you don't stay centered, you'll fall in. You'll sink your boat, and you won't help anybody."

"I think so," Grace said, though she wasn't at all sure she knew how to balance her canoe. She set a piece of bread on the floor for Magic then stood up and poured herself a glass of wine.

"Grace, listen." Brian's voice was gentler than it had been in a long time, the kind voice that warmed her when they first met outside the townhouse back in July. "Of course they can live here. You don't have to ask."

"Are you scared?" Grace leaned across the table and placed her hand on Crystal's. It was sticky with syrup. She had to start feeding this girl something more nutritious.

Crystal withdrew her arm and twirled a lock of hair with her finger. "What do you mean?"

"You know what I mean. Having a baby is big. It's a lot to go through." Grace's own sensory memories raced through her brain: the metallic room, the nurses and their masks, the unbearable tightening and throbbing in her pelvis, the pungent smell of placental fluid, the blood, the screaming, the wet baby whisked away. She felt as if waves were pounding against the sides of a small, lonely boat.

"I ain't scared," Crystal answered, now twisting two strands with two fingers. "It's no biggee."

"Well, we'll see about that. Can I feel your belly?"

Grace slid out of the booth and moved over to the other side to sit next to Crystal, who nodded and closed her eyes. Grace passed her hand over the hard knob of her navel then rested it atop the round globe, hoping she'd feel a kick. But the little frog must have been asleep. Her hand hovered over Crystal's belly.

"Crystal, I've been thinking…I think you should move in with me."

"What?" Crystal scooched away and folded her arms over her stomach.

"When we went to the clinic and saw the ultrasound, I thought the baby was beautiful! Why don't you let me help you take care of him?"

"Why?" She raised her nubby eyebrows as she waited for an answer.

"To help you." Grace knew Crystal had a counselor at the Salvation Army who was trying to find her a place, a home for pregnant girls, a foster home, a group home, something. But the woman was overloaded with cases and as of yet hadn't come up with anything. The due date was around the corner.

"I found out what I have to do to become your guardian. There's lots of site visits and paperwork. But I think it would be great."

"Cool. You got a house or a apartment?"

"A townhouse. With nice neighbors, good friends. They want to meet you."

"Oh, man. A house. With like, a TV and shit? And a kitchen and all that? Could I have my own room?"

Grace laughed. "Yup. With the baby, of course. You want to do it?"

"Oh, yeah. I gotta get outta the Army place. It stinks there."

"Okay, cool. Great. We'll get a crib and a bed for you and all the stuff we need."

Grace had no idea what she was getting into, but that was her mode these days. Since she had moved here, she was more willing than ever to dive into muddy water, the bottom murky and treacherous, not worrying whether she would scrape her nose on broken glass, crack her skull on a rock, or get bit by a water snake. But what else was she supposed to do with her life but let it lead her into the black water?

45

From the seclusion of the monastery, Father Luke composed another letter to Grace. He sent it to her through Sister Genevieve.

My dear Grace,

I have been thinking and praying about you often.

I am indeed sorry for portraying myself as someone ready to relinquish his vows and lead the secular life. You are a dear and sincere woman, and through you, over the course of a few lovely days, I experienced a different path to God. Thank you.

I hope you can find it in your heart to forgive me. I may, in fact, have used you to help me understand the new direction toward which I have been called by Christ—away from daily service and toward spiritual solitude.

I am sequestering myself away for as long as it takes for me to do penance. I am working with Genevieve to transition St. Laurence House out of my care.

Grace finally understood. She was disappointed in herself as much if not more than she was angry at Luke for breaking her heart. She had allowed herself once again to get sucked into an ideal vision of a man. She had admired Luke, but she never actually understood him, and he never sought to truly understand her. As much as he had tried to support her in getting justice for Frankie, he wasn't willing to go public. He was wedded to the Church, however flawed, and he still needed to pretend that the choice to enter the monastery was his alone.

Every day I garden and bake and chant and pray.

I understand now that I have been called to the monastic life.

May the blessings of Our Lord and Savior Jesus Christ give you strength and courage for your journey.

Brother Luke

A week later, Genevieve told Grace she had something else for her from Luke. She led Grace into her room and handed her another envelope full of money. A type-written list of instructions was folded alongside the bills.

1.   *Go to the office of David Halpern of Halpern, Spriggs, Mason, Hartwich and Associates at 6788 Monterey Boulevard, Suite 14F. (My mother contacted him, and he knows you are coming.)*
2.   *Get Victoria to go with you.*
3.   *Write an article. You're a good writer. You have a calling.*

His last risky venture, in spite of having been censured. No mention of love, no hearts, no apologies, no quotes or prayerful pleading. No signature even. Just a list of commands and a thousand dollars cash.

Saying goodbye to her dad was hard this time. He depended on her daily visits. Though she knew she could trust the aides to take good care of him, to be efficient and kind, the fact is that they were overwhelmed and rarely checked on him. He lay alone in his bed for hours at a time or sat immobile in his chair in the hallway until someone had the wherewithal to ask him if he wanted to move.

"Didn't you just go to California to visit your friends?" he asked after she announced she had tickets and needed to fly out again. "What am I going to do without you? How am I going to get to Mass?" Since his stroke, she'd taken him every Sunday to the Mass in the nursing home's chapel. She would only miss one Sunday, but it was the highlight of his week.

"I've arranged for a volunteer to take you."

"But I want you. I'm glad you've started going to church. It means a lot to me. Just like the old days, remember? And it means a lot to Our Lord."

She tried to call Victoria one more time. But this time she waited until she had left the airport, settled into the hotel, and could walk to a park and sit outdoors to call. She'd bought herself a mobile phone so that she could be reached at any time. When no one answered, she left a message.

"Hey, Victoria. It's me, Grace. Schreiber. Frankie's teacher. This is my new number." She recited her cell phone number, slowly, twice. "I'm in LA again. Will you meet me so we can talk? I know about a lawyer who can help us. Help you, I mean. Please call me." She took a deep breath and hung up the phone.

Thirty seconds later, the phone rang.

"What kinda lawyer?"

"I don't know. Let's go meet with him and bring the essays and see what he can tell us. A lot of people are suing the Church for money when there's been abuse."

"I don't want money for Frankie's life."

"I know. But the Church should pay. The Catholic Church has covered this up, and who knows what else has been going on? We need to stop them from doing this to another child. Why don't we just talk to the lawyer and see what they have to say?"

"I gotta work."

"When are you off?"

"I work tonight. Tomorrow I'm done at three. But I gotta get Marisol at school."

"She can come. Why don't I pick you up, and we'll go together? I'll make an appointment."

Victoria's place in Compton was tidy in spite of the paint peeling on the window sills and the worn wooden steps leading up to a dusty porch. Purple pansies poked out of a plastic flower pot. Victoria stood on the porch wearing shorts and a tight t-shirt, Marisol in her arms. The little girl waved as Grace got out of the rental car.

"Hi, sweetie!" Grace said, raising her arm to wave back. She feigned calm, though she felt out of place and nervous. The child's face was a shiny amber gem. Her black hair had been pulled back into tight ponytails. She held her arms out to Grace.

"Can I hold her?" Grace asked, smiling at Victoria. "She's precious."

"Okay, sure." Victoria frowned. "Then can we go?"

Grace took the little girl who must have been close to two and bounced her on her hip. "How are you, sweetheart? How old are you?"

"I'm gonna bring pictures of Frankie to show them. I gotta get them in the house. Get down now, baby. Let the lady alone."

Grace set Marisol down, and she took off running into the house after her mother. She toddled through the thick air of the dark living room and into a bedroom as Grace followed her lead.

"This is my Frankie room. It's like, you know, my memorial room," Victoria said. The dense air of the house, heavy with hope and loss, pressed against Grace's chest.

The diminutive woman climbed up on the bed against the wall and carefully ripped off a photo of Frankie grinning at the camera. He was sitting on the front steps of this house, making a muscle. She chose another of him laughing and holding a crying Marisol. Then another, tired and happy, looking into his new baby's eyes.

"I want them to know he loved his baby and he was a good papa," she said, pulling off four more photos.

The wall was covered with snapshots and penciled notes, letters, and poems illustrated with hearts and stars and flowers. *I LOVE VICTORIA AND MARISOL* and *THANK YOU BABY* were inscribed in fancy block letters across the tops of the drawings. Grace recognized the neat, labored handwriting she'd been studying for months and felt like she wanted to cry.

Marisol wrapped her arms around Victoria's legs as she climbed off the bed and grabbed for a picture with her little hands. "Papi," Marisol said. "Papi, hold you!"

"She don't know he gone for good. She loved her papi," Victoria said, setting the pile on the bed and picking up Marisol. "Okay, baby. Okay, mija. Okay. Mami hold you."

"Oh, I'm sorry. This must be so hard for you and Marisol. I don't know what to say. Frankie was great."

Stop talking, she thought. *Breathe, let yourself be in this holy place with this woman, this adorable baby, this sad wall. Just shut up for once.*

"Whoa. It's true what they say about lawyers." Victoria combed her mass of black hair out of her eyes with her fingers and pulled at her shorts as they made their way into the parking garage below the stately building on Monterey Boulevard. "Damn." She turned around and patted Marisol on the knee. "Here we are, baby."

The law office was polished, sparsely decorated, and cool. An enormous vase filled with fragrant flowers adorned the information desk. "We have an appointment," Grace said. "With David Halpern at 4:15. Grace Schreiber and Victoria Morales."

The two women and Marisol were ushered into David Halpern's office right away. The lawyer waited while they settled into velvety chairs. "Would you like water or coffee? Soda?" the receptionist asked.

"No, nothin," Victoria responded.

"Water, please." Grace's throat was parched.

"Here you go, sweetie." The young woman gave Marisol a cookie.

"Say thank you, baby," Victoria urged. Marisol took a nibble of the cookie then buried her head in her mother's neck.

Victoria looked at the tall, balding man sitting behind the enormous desk in front of them. Before he could stand and introduce himself, Victoria spoke. "We got the name of a priest who did unmentionable things to my Frankie, and we want you to help us. Here's his pictures. He was a good papa and a good husband to me. We was married on December 26, a couple of months before he died. And then, when he was in Miss Schreiber's class, he wrote about his childhood and the priest and what he did, and it brought up in him the shame."

She put the pile of photos on Halpern's desk, then looked away. Her voice shook. "Mrs. Schreiber, will you hold her? I gotta go blow my nose."

Victoria gave Marisol a peck on the top of the head and handed her off to Grace. She stood up and walked out without another word. The baby sat stunned on Grace's lap. When her mother didn't immediately return, she started to wail.

Grace rocked her knees up and down and put her arms around Marisol. The lawyer waited, his hands crossed on the desk. Victoria returned, her nose pink, eyes swollen and red. She pulled the sobbing Marisol onto her lap and snuggled her against her chest.

"What I'm tryin' to tell you is that all the pedophile priests and bishops and cardinals—Father Santiago and Cardinal Mahony and all of them— helped kill Frankie who was tryin' so hard to get straight, who was a very,

very, very good man. They are supposed to be the holy church, and what they did to him was so bad that it made Frankie shoot up to get relief from the pain. And now they're doing it to some other kid. You got to stop them. You understand? You *got* to."

Halpern nodded, stood up, and shook both of their hands. He wore a fine suit and a silk tie. As moneyed and glamorous as this place appeared, he seemed easy going and kind. He settled into his chair again.

"I do understand. Tell me what you have, and I'll tell you what I think we can do."

Victoria talked for fifteen minutes. She cried again, openly this time. Grace felt her own eyes fill with tears and her chin tremble as Victoria described how she and Frankie had planned to get good jobs. She was studying culinary arts; he wanted to be a mechanic. They were going to get out of Compton, have two more kids—another girl and a boy—and were going to take a honeymoon next year when they could get the cash together.

"He didn't want to get married at Holy Mother of God, but I put pressure on him, you know? And he said okay. He gave in for me and my family. When he told me why, after he wrote about it for school, I said I was sorry for making him do that. I pushed it, and I hate myself for that. But I didn't know."

Grace nodded, wanting to reassure the young woman, and even more, herself. If she hadn't pushed him to write, she thought, none of this would have happened.

"He came home one night after school all mad and sad, and I asked him what was up. He told me. He cried. I told him, 'I love you. We can get through this. Stay strong.' I told him it wasn't his fault, and he said, 'I know,' but I think he thought he did something wrong, like he kind of made it happen without meaning to."

Marisol stared up at her mother then nestled under her chin.

"He told me he couldn't take it. But then I had to go to work. When I got home, he...he...he was lying on the floor. He had overdosed on junk. His lips were blue. He was hardly breathing. I called 911. They rushed to the hospital. I stayed up with him all night, but they couldn't help him. He died the next day.

"He didn't do drugs no more. Honest. But he felt so bad he couldn't take it. He needed to escape. I know he didn't want to kill himself. It…it was an accident. He would of never done that to me and Marisol. He loved her so much. He always said that we saved his life."

Grace got up and asked the receptionist for a tissue. She brought back a handful for herself and Victoria. By now, tears were drawing mascara lines on her face. Victoria was sobbing as she spoke, and the baby started to whimper.

"He didn't want to hurt nobody," Victoria said between gasps. "So he hurt himself. Sometimes I don't know if I can make it myself, you know? But I got to," she said as she pulled Marisol close and stroked her hair, "for the baby."

Grace wiped her face and blew her nose. "Santiago stayed at a treatment center called Servants of the Lamb a long time ago. Even though I don't think there's any evidence left." She told the lawyer and Victoria about her visit to the facility in Juarez and what she had learned from the clippings in the fat green file. She handed Halpern photocopies of five articles describing how the evidence had been destroyed.

Halpern took the snapshots and Frankie's essays and asked Victoria to fill out a form. He promised to begin researching their claims against Santiago right away. They were in the process of contesting the statute of limitations in priest abuse cases. Minnesota and New Jersey had successfully overruled the church's statute of limitations arguments there.

"You are not the first. I want you to know that," Halpern said. "There are currently fifty-two other plaintiffs signed on to a civil suit against the Los Angeles Archdiocese. And our Father Santiago already has another complainant."

"Oh, no." Grace closed her eyes.

"Now, this could take a while. The Catholic Church is wielding its substantial power to keep its records secret. The Archdiocese of Los Angeles has hired some high-priced law firms to aid them in their attempts to deny the allegations and stall the proceedings." He clasped his hands together.

"But we are making headway. In a jury trial against a priest named Houghton in Stockton two months ago, three brothers won a $7 million settlement when it came out that our esteemed Cardinal Mahony—he was bishop of Stockton at the time—knew the priest was a serial pedophile and a danger to children but shipped him off to 'psychiatric treatment,' just like your Servants of the Lamb that treated Santiago."

He pointed his index finger at Grace. "They claimed he was cured. Sent him to another parish, where he abused again. Of course, Mahony asserts that he knew nothing about the allegations against Houghton. Another abuse case against Mahony is in the works as well. In this case, under federal racketeering laws. They're trying get them under Rico, accusing the church of being a corrupt institution. It's a clever angle."

Halpern paused and straightened. He rested his fingers against his lips as if he were praying, looked first at Victoria, then at Grace. He smiled at Marisol, who was now contentedly twirling the earring dangling from her mother's ear.

"We can assure you that, with the scandal and the public outcry, with the willingness of brave people such as yourself to go to court…" His eyes were kind as he nodded at Victoria. "I can assure you we will get results. But it won't be easy. This," he said, his head bobbing, fingertips pressed together, "promises to be very, very big."

Part Four

The truth will set you free, but first it will break your heart.
—Flannery O'Connor

46

The call from the nurse came at a quarter past eight that night. Her father had taken a turn for the worse. He had developed pneumonia, so they had to put him on a ventilator.

"We transported him from the nursing home to the hospital a few hours ago," the nurse said. "It would be best if you come soon. He's not…He's not looking good."

Grace dressed and checked out in a blur. She drove to the airport, returned her rental, waited seven hours until she could arrange an alternate flight, and went directly to the hospital.

She finally arrived in his room, exhausted and scared. Her dad lay pale and vulnerable in the hospital bed. His mouth was open, and tubes were hanging out of his nose and attached to his arm.

A young doctor walked into the room. "He's in stable condition for now," he said, "but there's no certainty he's going to pull through. His pulse is low. I'm afraid he might not make it through the week."

The waiting room was cold. Grace rubbed her hands up and down her arms. Overhead lights buzzed. Numb, impatient, needing desperately to sleep, Grace paced as she called Gloria.

"Gloria, Dad is failing. The doctors are saying he may only have a few days."

"Okay." There was hesitation in her sister's voice.

"I just wanted you to know."

"Grace, can I ask you something? Do you want me to come?" It was the first time Grace heard an admission of uncertainty, an ambivalent wavering, in Gloria's voice.

"What do *you* want to do, Gloria?"

"I don't know. Do you think Dad cares one way or the other?"

"What are you talking about? Of course he cares. He always talks about you."

In fact, before she left on her trip, he had asked Grace to tell him how Peter and Jenna were doing. He had only met them on three occasions, and he wasn't sure they would remember him. A month ago, he'd asked her to find his will so he could reread it and make sure there was enough for the kids.

"If you're going to visit, now's the time."

Grace's heart sank at the words. For the first time, she understood the reality of the situation. She'd only had a few good months with him, such a short amount of time to restore what had been lost in the years in between. And now time was a rug being swiped out from under her feet, and she was falling.

From the minute Grace picked up Gloria from the airport, she felt awkward. Gloria's straight reddish-brown hair was stylishly highlighted and neatly cut. She was every bit as put together as the last time Grace had seen her: eyes made up, lips glossed, nails pale pink and perfect. As she watched her sister approach baggage claim, Grace tied back her wayward hair and zipped her jacket to hide her wrinkled shirt.

"How was your flight?" Grace smiled.

"Fine."

"Want to go to my house or the hospital first?"

"I made a reservation at a hotel downtown," Gloria said. "To treat myself. No offense. And let's go to the hospital first to get it over with. Then we can get me checked in. Is there an expensive restaurant we can go to after I get a shower and a nap?"

This visit was going to prove to be even harder than Grace had imagined. She had dreaded it, but pressed for it, knowing it was the right thing to do.

Gloria didn't relax until they drove into the hospital parking lot and began to trudge their way through the salted heaps of gray snow. "Wow, this is a trip. Back in the Buff. It's been ten years, you know? And the last visit was horrible. The kids were young. They hated it. Dad's a pretty pathetic grandfather."

"The last time you saw Dad was ten years ago?"

"He came to visit us a couple of years after that. So, it's been what, eight? Yeah, eight." She looked at Grace. "When he came out to us, it started out fine. He liked the café. He drank coffee and chatted to the customers. For a few hours, I felt like I had a normal dad. But when we got home he hardly related to the kids. He just wanted to drink martinis and sit around. He seemed bored. I had the feeling he couldn't wait to get back home."

"Do you guys talk on the phone a lot?"

"Some. David reminds me to call him every couple of weeks. He wants to be sure we're written into the will."

Grace stopped focusing on the puddles and stood still. "*What*?"

"I'm kidding. I'm kidding. Lighten up, Saint Grace."

Grace ducked into the room and found their dad bent in sleep, thin sheets tangled around his bony legs. "Gloria, let me go down to the coffee shop and get us something. That way, you can be here when Dad wakes up."

"That's okay. I'll go," Gloria said without looking in the room.

"No," Grace insisted. "You stay."

"I don't know if he's going to want to see me. I don't even know if I want to see him, to be honest." She sighed. "But I'm here, I guess." She gingerly pushed open the door and tiptoed into the room.

When Grace returned, Gloria was holding her dad's fingers in her hand as she watched him sleep. The tube in his nose made his breathing sound watery and raspy.

"Hey." Gloria let go of his hand as she turned to face Grace. "It's funny, isn't it?"

"What?"

"In my mind, he's big. I always imagine him as towering over me. But he's not a big man. He never was. He looks so weak and thin now. It's kind of shocking. I mean, it's like..." She bit her lip. "And the house is gone and everything."

Grace and Gloria sat that way for an hour, watching their father breathe. Grace filled Gloria in on what she had learned about her dad's condition, how his heart needed continual monitoring, and his lungs were full of fluid, so he required a ventilator. A nurse came in to check his vital signs without speaking then left.

"Let's get dinner," Gloria said. "Preferably Asian."

"Okay," Grace said. "I wish he woke up."

"This is enough for me today. I'll come back tomorrow. Before I get on the plane."

They finally talked. Two glasses into their second carafe of red wine, plates empty of Indonesian coconut curry, Grace decided she could unclamp some of the heavy armor she'd been carrying around. She told Gloria everything—about St. Laurence House, Crystal and her pregnancy, Brian, Mountain, the trips back to LA, and the slightly sinister encounters with the hierarchy of the church. Everything except Jake and Luke. She simply ignored the question of love and let Gloria think she was lonely and single all these years. Even drunk, she knew enough to avoid that topic.

"I see you've got a lot going on in your new city."

"And you?" After her monologue, it was only right she ask about her sister's life.

"Grace, I'm fine. My life is where I want it to be. It's difficult coming back."

"Gloria, what? What is so hard about visiting? Has it really been eight years since you've seen Dad? I mean…" Her voice dropped to a whisper. "He's *dying*."

"Grace…you don't know what happened, do you?"

"When?"

"Before I skipped town, never to return."

What could have been worse, Grace thought, than their mother dying in the middle of the night in the middle of a frigid winter?

"Besides mom dying? No."

"Didn't you wonder why Dad and I had an all-out screaming match before I left?"

"Honestly, no." Grace poured her fourth glass of wine with care. It wasn't unusual for her dad and sister to scream at each other. After her mom died, the air in the house was as tight as a stretched rubber band. Grace left the room to pray whenever the rubber band appeared ready to snap.

"I never forgave him for the things he said to me. I'm sorry; I know you believe everybody should be forgiven."

"No, I don't. You don't know me, Gloria." Grace shook her head. "What happened?"

"Dad hated me, and part of the reason was because I would never be a good girl like you. I hate to say this, but by being so pure and perfect, you made my life miserable."

"You're blaming me for being good?"

"Yes! You were irritatingly good! You always did good things. It was *so* annoying. He always praised you, but when I was normal, he hardly noticed me. He only paid attention to me when I was bad or when you went off to do your save-the-world volunteering."

There was a long pause, nothing left to do with their hands or mouths, plates clean and glasses drained. "Go on," Grace said.

"Before she croaked, Mom and I were just starting to talk about stuff, about life. She cried a lot, but she also listened because she was worried about me. When she died, I missed her so bad I could hardly stand it."

Grace studied her pretty, intense sister. Sadness pooled inside her. How was it that she and Gloria hardly ever talked about their mother?

"I got pregnant about a month after she died. I was terrified and I...I had an abortion."

Grace's eyes widened. "Gloria, you were pregnant? You had an abortion?"

"See, I knew you'd judge me."

"I'm not judging you at all. How come you never told me?"

Two days after their mom died, Gloria had packed all her stuff up from their shared room and moved into her mother's room, insisting she needed to get away from Grace and "be alone" with her memories of Mom.

"I thought you'd hate me. You were so pious and self-righteous. I don't think you know what you were like back then." She spoke in a whisper as she stared at Grace. "I lost a lot of blood and stayed home from school. When you asked what was wrong with me, I told you I had the flu."

Grace realized her mouth was open, and she was leaning so far into the table that her chest almost touched her plate. She sat up and rubbed her eyes. "So it was awful?"

"I was scared to death. I'm lucky to be alive. The guy gave me some money but not much. I worked overtime until I could make enough. It cost like $300. I went alone to a house in the city that a girl at school told me about. A man and a woman both answered the door. They took the cash from me before I even walked in. They told me to take off everything except my shirt and to lie on a bed with a white sheet."

Gloria looked down at her plate as she talked, her elbows on the table, chin on her fists. "They gave me some drug to make me pass out. I can't imagine my daughter going through such a thing. When I think now about how risky that was…When I woke up my vagina was stuffed with gauze. They gave me a bunch of pads and told me I would have cramps for a while. And, of course, it wasn't legal."

"Gloria, how awful." Her sister's story was as depressing as her own. And more dangerous. Between them, they'd spawned two babies they would ever know. "What did you tell Dad?"

"When Dad asked me what was wrong with me, I told him. Telling him was the stupidest mistake I've ever made in my life."

"What did he say?"

"He said I was evil. I would burn in hell. I was a murderer. The Lord would punish me. And on and on and on for days. It felt like forever. Sometimes he screamed it. Other times he said it real low and pitiful like he was sorry for me. He never said anything around you, because he said he didn't want to 'taint' you. And for it to happen right after mom died. What he did was really mean. That's when I started hating him, and I vowed never to talk to him unless I needed money or something. I made myself finish school so I could leave and start fresh."

"Oh, my God, Gloria. I'm so sorry."

"Sorry for me or sorry because you think you did something wrong?" Gloria said, her voice tight.

Grace pulled herself together. She felt both aloof from her body and stuck in her pulsing head. "I don't know. I'm just…I'm blown away. Both, I guess. I can't believe I was so oblivious."

Gloria's shoulders relaxed. "We were both a mess. We'd just lost our mom. That's huge."

"Are you okay with it now?" Grace asked.

Perhaps she was also asking herself that question. Was she okay with her decision to hand her child over to a stranger? Was she okay with the fact that there was absolutely nothing that could be done about her own choice, made in a state of such profound ignorance, loneliness, and grief?

"Sometimes, I regret it. Sometimes, I wonder what it would have been like to keep it. But mostly, I don't. I was young and stupid. I would have been an awful mom."

Grace shook her head. She understood.

"You know the worst part?" Gloria asked. "Dad never apologized."

"That's bad." Grace knew her dad wouldn't have forgiven her either; she had left to escape his fury. And she knew she should share her story with her sister who'd just been so honest with her. Maybe tomorrow, she thought, when she wasn't so exhausted and worried and drunk.

"That's really bad. Thank you for telling me. And I'm sorry."

"Don't be," Gloria said. "You're as innocent as a lamb in this."

Grace sighed. She felt about as fragile.

"Listen, I was a troubled kid. Losing Mom was the worst thing that has ever happened to me, and then Dad essentially doomed me to hell. But otherwise, I turned out okay. It took a while, but I turned out okay." Gloria raised her empty glass and laughed. "And I take back what I said about it being dumb to come back to Buffalo. I wouldn't choose this life"—she shrugged her shoulders and made a shuddering sound in her throat—"and God knows why you did, but it seems right for you after all."

"Well, thanks."

"Cozying up to all your new Catholic buddies and reconnecting with your Operation-Rescue-Right-to-Life papal-worshipping father—that's nice."

"Gloria!" Grace's mouth dropped open. "Are you mad at me? I said what he did was terrible."

"Grace, I'm just razzing you. You've got to lighten up. I decided to forgive him for being a royal ignoramus. I don't have time to obsess about his stupidity. Really, I'm over it. I wanted you to know what happened, but I also want to move on and say a proper goodbye to him before he dies. So, yeah. Enough."

Gloria motioned to the waitress to bring them the check. "Back to your new life. Have you fallen for anybody yet now that you're a Maid of the Mist boat ride away from the Honeymoon Capital of the World?"

"No, no one," Grace lied. She'd tell her everything someday, but not until she was ready.

Their dad slept in the thin morning light for two hours while the sisters flipped through magazines. Finally, he stirred.

He turned on his side to face his daughters sitting watch by the bed. "Well, look who'sh here," he said, his voice ragged and rough. "Aren't I lucky?"

"Hi, Dad." Gloria reached out to pat his hand. Her fingers got intertwined with the tube running from his forearm to the intravenous feeding bag. "How are you feeling?"

"Much better," he said. "Now that I'm—sheeing you. I get to shee Grasche—every day." He had been taken off the ventilator, which Grace took as a good sign. His breath came out in short puffs. "Which I love." He reached his good hand across the metal guardrail on the bed and patted Grace, who had scooted her chair up close. "But thish—is a shpecial treat."

"Dad—" Gloria began.

"Girlsh, a man hash a—lot of time to think when he'sh lying on—his deathbed," he interrupted. His words were firm, though measured. "I'm ready for—for Our Lord to take me. I've had a good—life. And I mish—your mother and plan to ashk her to remarry—me in Heaven."

"Dad, you're not—" Grace felt her throat constrict. She stopped herself from telling him he wasn't about to die.

"And I mished—out on—your livesh too. I should have come to Shan—Franschishco and Colorado more."

An aide came in to bring him a cup of ice chips. She cranked the bed so he could sit up, straightened his blanket, and set his crumpled wrist on a fluffy pillow.

"As I was shaying…" He pressed himself up higher with his good arm. "I mish my mother. She wash—a good woman. Ash good—ash the day is long. Not a shelfish bone in her—body."

Grace and Gloria turned to toward each other, eyebrows raised.

"And she never—complained."

A cough interrupted his words.

"I washn't a—I know it—a very good father. I may—may have a—few yearsh in purgatory ahead of me before I—before I get to see your mother'sh lovely—fasche again." He studied both of his daughters with watery eyes. "But I'm being maudlin. Too much—talk of afterlife. I'm here and—and you're here, and that'sh what—mattersh. I'm very—pleased you came—truly."

He reached out again to pat each of their hands gripping the metal rail and closed his eyes. Within a minute, he was asleep.

Three nights after Gloria's visit, after hours of Grace sitting vigil next to her sleeping dad, he coughed and started awake. Grace panicked and moved to comfort him. She tilted the bed up.

"Gracshe, your mother ish here. Your mother hash—your mother and I have—shomething to tell you." His voice was thick and hoarse, barely above a whisper.

"What, Dad?" she said, shaken. "What do you mean, you and Mom?"

"We've been meaning to—to let you know—" He straightened a bit, then slumped and scrunched his eyes shut as if studying something underneath his lids. "I don't know what thish—ish. If it'sh a dream."

"Let me know what?" Grace's attention was focused on his mouth, his strange words.

"About the shacrifische she made. You're —old enough—you're old enough now to know."

"I know, Dad." Grace felt an urgency to soothe his agitated state. What was he experiencing behind his eyes, in his dream space, in this near-to-death place?

"She gave up sho much—"

"I know she started college late and then quit school to raise a family." She stroked his hand, which was so smooth and cool. "I know she wished she'd gone back to college. She gave up a lot."

"You know? She told me—you didn't know." The words tumbled out of his droopy mouth more comprehensible than they had been in days. "She is a brave and beautiful woman. Your mother shacrifisched everything for me. Everything. Even her own family. I didn't desherve her, and I don't know if she'll want me when I arrive." His face contorted as he covered his weeping eyes with his good hand.

"Oh, Dad."

"She tellsh me to tell you to chooshe the path that'sh right for you." Now his voice was quivering. "Don't do anything jusht becaushe people tell you to. Maybe it'sh a dream, but it'sh her voice. I don't know what it ish, but her voische ish sho real."

Grace scooted in her chair and lay her head on her dad's shoulder. As if by getting closer, she could see her mother's face who was somehow communicating with him behind his eyes.

"You're a good girl, Grasche," he said. "Make sure you keep getting good gradesh, pray every day, and be kind. Your mother and I are proud of you. Don't you change."

47

Grace slept for an hour in a chair in the hospital room, dreams rumbling inside her slumped head. Her mother handing her a gardenia from the window of a speeding train. Her father gasping in agony, a metal box covering his face as he struggled to breathe.

She was startled awake by a sharp, insistent beeping. She sat up and rubbed her eyes. A nurse studied the heart monitor, wrote on a clipboard, caressed Grace's father's forehead, then patted Grace's hand. "I'm sorry, Miss Schreiber. Your father has passed."

Grace gulped and held her breath. She reached over to lay her hands on his forearm, his bony shoulder, his bald head. *Not yet, not yet, not yet*, she chanted inside her head. *I'm not ready. We were still talking.*

And then out loud, "No, it can't be true. Oh, no."

And then the sinking. She had missed the surrendering of his spirit. How could she have been sleeping? How was she so selfish as to miss the passage from the precious pulsing of his heart to stillness, to silence? Shouldn't she have been holding his hand, listening to his murmurings, alert and alive to him in those early hours beside his bed? Shouldn't she have been present instead of sleeping like an idiot?

She sat for an hour with his motionless body. Her own breath seemed like a miracle, streaming out of her nose and mouth in a steady, regular rhythm. She couldn't bear to leave his side, so she just sat there, unable to feel or pray or cry. She stared at his open mouth, his papery dry body, his eyes unmoving under thin, closed lids. Where was his spirit? Where was her beloved, loving, bewildering, difficult, dear, dear, dear dad?

She sat while the nurses came and did all the things they had to do, sat while orderlies came and took his body away, then sat in the empty room for another hour and wept. Then finally, numb to the cold, she left, dragging a suitcase filled with his things.

Back at her place, she called Gloria and Mountain and told them both she needed to be alone. She didn't leave her house for two days. All she did was cry and sleep. When she woke to go to the bathroom or heat up soup, she would walk around comatose for a few minutes then lay back down. Her head swam with her dad's words, the way he seemed to have been speaking to her mother from the world of dreams.

She dragged herself to the memorial Mass that Immaculate Heart held at the chapel and sat stiffly through it. His name was mentioned twice in the otherwise rote recital of the practiced prayers. She rested her head in her hands on the pew in front of her and tried to pray or meditate or think good thoughts about her dad, but nothing came. As droning voices recited the Creed, she felt nothing. Her heart was a boarded-up house.

For the first time since she'd arrived, she questioned why she had come to this city of her childhood pain. How could she remain if her father was no longer here?

She stood by herself at the cemetery, watching as his pine casket was lowered into the gaping brown mouth of the earth. Then she sat on the ground next to her mother's marker in the place where her dad's granite block would be placed.

She'd forgotten to grab a jacket. She hugged herself against the chill. So many hard things had happened to her, and she felt awash in self-pity: her father's sudden death; her mother's tragic demise at too young an age; the whisking away of her own newborn into somebody else's hands; the loss of Jake and Luke.

Black clouds threatened rain, but she stayed, listening to the wind whistle, watching the trees shake and bend as if in some macabre dance. She knew she wasn't alone in her grief. Hard things happened to everybody. She thought of the suffering her poor mom had endured every day, of Alvin's layered losses, of Gloria, afraid and alone. Crystal and Frankie, so uncared for, unprotected, left to survive like pups in the woods. All the people at St. Laurence who had been wounded and stung by the upside-down unfairness of things.

She felt overcome by affection for her wretched self, for all of them, in awe of the relentless interplay between the comings and the goings, the pity and the gift, the bottomless well of sadness and the occasional, unexpected reservoir of clear joy.

Fat drops of sleet slapped her as she walked quickly back to the car, back to her home.

"Do you have regrets?" Mountain asked after Grace returned from the graveyard. She brought over a huge garland of pine branches and holly tied together in a satiny red ribbon and set a pot of lentil soup on Grace's stove.

"Oh, I don't know," Grace said, sitting down at her kitchen table. "I guess I don't."

"That's good," Mountain said, plucking biscuits from a basket and arranging them on a plate. "Regrets are useless. I think regrets are like a clogged drain. They get in the way of life's flowing water. It's hard, sweetie. But we need to live here, now, today."

"I'm trying," Grace sighed.

"Have you checked in with Brian?" Mountain asked. "He was sympathetic when he heard your dad had died. but he didn't know if you wanted to talk to him."

"Should I?" She felt limp and fragile, almost bruised.

"I think it's a good idea," Mountain said. "He cares for you quite a bit, you know." She set down a bowl of steaming soup and the plate of buttered biscuits in front of Grace, then pulled her into a sideways hug. "I feel for you, dear girl."

Grace found Brian working on his car's engine the next day. His nose and cheeks and ears were rosy from the cold.

"Hello," she said.

"Hey," he answered, not looking up.

"How are you doing, Brian?" Grace felt shy, not sure what to do with his coolness. Maybe this was a mistake.

Brian stood up and looked at her. "I'm fine," he said. He squinted a little and stared into her eyes as if about to ask her a question. "Grace, Mountain told me about your dad."

"Thanks. Yeah. I didn't expect it to hit me so hard."

He nodded.

"Well, maybe we can talk sometime," she said, looking away. "Hang out, all of us again. It's been a while. I haven't seen you since my trip, since my dad."

"You know what, Grace. I don't think so." He resumed his exploration of the engine.

"What do you mean? I'm just trying to be friendly is all."

"Grace, let me be honest with you." He straightened, fixed his eyes on hers. "I like you a lot. I'm attracted to you. You sent me a message loud and clear, and I'm stuck here living next door to you and having to deal with your very clear message. I got it, okay? I'm not interested in playing games." He turned back to the engine and pulled the dipstick out of the oil shaft, wiped it off with a cloth, stuck it in again, and checked it.

"I know you're in love with the priest. I know you're seeing him. Instead of being honest with me, you tell me you're 'too selfish for love.' I think you've been really indirect and childish." He paused, unhooking the strut from the hood. "I'm sorry about your dad. But I'm pretty angry at you right now. I think I'm done here."

The hood made a gentle tapping sound as he closed it, metal on metal. She stood stupefied as he turned and walked into his house.

48

Grace pried all her father's photos from their corners and laid them as neatly as possible, curled and torn and mangled, in a big, flowered box. She fingered the items in his wooden cigar box: Mass cards, laminated pictures of the Pope, a half-evaporated plastic medicine bottle of Holy Water, the foreign coins and keys.

She studied the metal safe box without a key. The thought of the box's contents made her hopeful, one more thing that might connect her to her dad. Maybe her mother's ring was in it. Something to remember both of them by. Maybe more photos. Maybe nothing special—stamps or useless coins.

She bent its lock with a screwdriver and mauled it until it snapped open, its metal mouth an angry maw. Inside, she found a faded manila envelope. A dusty string encircled its paper clasp. It contained a stack of envelopes tied together with a ribbon. Grace fanned through them.

Each was addressed to Renata Mehlman, 6720 Pine Hollow Road, Detroit, Michigan. And in red, underneath her mother's name and address in the corner, the words *Return to Sender*. Grace couldn't imagine what the letters might mean. She walked into the kitchen and grabbed a steak knife to slice open the thin gray envelopes, making in each one a bloodless incision.

July 17, 1952

Muter, dear Muter,

Please do not abandon me in my time of need. I am certain I must to marry this man, but I also need you to be there for me as I make my way down the aisle, and as I raise a family. Don't you see? I do not have a choice in whom I love! Please, I beg you to rethink your decision.

Your daughter, always, Roberta

July 22, 1952

Mami, dear Mami,

   My heart is hurting as I realize how strongly you hold to your conviction to never see me or speak to me again. If only I could have one afternoon with you to explain how worried I was I would never meet someone, and how much relief I feel knowing now I can finally settle down and have a family. But how wonderful it would be for me and my children to have you in our lives! Mami, I'm in such pain at the thought that you and Tate would deny your love to your only child. Isn't your heart breaking, too?

   Your daughter, always, Roberta

July 23, 1952

Muter,

   If only I could make you understand why I made the decision to marry William despite your disapproval. Mother, I'm thirty! I'm not sure if I love him, but I was so worried I wouldn't meet someone if I continued on my independent way. I am willing to take the chance that I will fall in love as we get to know one another better. Did you love Tate when you got married?

   William's parents are also opposed to our marriage. When they learned that I am not of the faith, they refused to agree to it. But William stood firm and said we did not need their permission or their blessing, though we would like it. I don't know how much I look forward to having them as in-laws, especially because they have not been particularly welcoming. This is all very sad and disappointing and not at all as I had imagined.

August 3, 1952

Dear Muter,

   I have to convert. It is not my choice. William's church will not marry us unless I undergo a series of trainings and accept the Catholic faith. I feel so betrayed and yes, angry, right now. Since you are returning my letters, I guess I am writing them for my own release. So I will say this: all this rejection and all this compromise is enough to make me want to scream.

August 5, 1952

   I have to meet with the parish priest, read the Catechism, participate in

295

Rite of Christian Initiation Classes, be baptized, take communion, and become confirmed, all before I can be married. And the truth is I didn't believe much I was taught in Hebrew school, and I don't believe much of what these new doctrines have to teach me either. Forcing me to swallow these ideas whole, to convert just to get married! What kind of God makes you feel isolated from your own faith, the one that comes through your mother's milk, circles through your blood, beats in your heart? What kind of God makes you relinquish your mother's love in order to give yourself over to a man of a different faith? What kind of God believes that your marriage is not a "sacrament" if you don't give up everything?

September 15, 1952

So, a wedding was had, and of all the dates a woman should feel happy in her own skin, loved and embraced by God and her family, I felt bereft. You and Tate should have been there, and I should not have to have lied to get married and have a family. Here is a photo of me in my wedding dress in a church so you can see what Roberta the Unwilling Christian looks like. Life is funny, isn't it?

November 29, 1952

We've just celebrated Thanksgiving with William's mother, father, sisters, and their husbands. Everybody friendly enough, if reserved and too proper for my taste. Dry turkey, bland salt potatoes, corn, squash, pumpkin pie. I miss your brisket. And I am pregnant with a little Catholic baby. I beg you to change your mind and be a grandmother to this child.

Revelations are like rain. Before the downpour, the sky is dark and foreboding, ominous and threatening, like anger.

For most of Grace's conscious life, her mother's depression had left Grace lonely. Her death had left her bereaved and confused, hanging on to a handful of random clues with no solution, like a mystery novel with the last chapter ripped out. Since she was a child, Grace had understood unconsciously that there was nothing she could do but wander meekly under the black clouds of unknowing, worrying and waiting.

Now she sat, stunned, the pile of envelopes in her lap. A cloud burst, a rush of relief, the sky breaking, cold water pounding, after all those years of clenched holding. After all those years, she had something. She had her mother's letters. The clouds lifted, steam rose off concrete; suddenly the world was brighter, greener, glistening.

"Gloria," Grace said, her voice hushed. She held the phone between her shoulder and ear as she arranged the letters on the kitchen table. "Give me an uninterrupted hour. Go to a room where you can be alone. I have something shocking to read to you."

"It's so sad," Gloria said after hearing it all. "But it helps explain things."

"I know." Grace put the phone on speaker, set it down, and put her head in her hands. "Her depression. Her lack of interest in church. Maybe the insomnia even."

"Another example."

"Of?"

"Of your father being a control freak," Gloria scoffed. "I mean, making the woman forsake her religion so they could get married in the Catholic Church. Forcing her to give up her own family in order to marry into the monarchy of King William the First. It's appalling!"

"But her parents, too, right? Her mother renounced her. It doesn't look like she ever wrote back. We never had grandparents."

"Pathetic. I hate what all these smug, pious, supposedly superior people do. Compete over who's got the best religion. The one and only true faith. It's all a bunch of hooey."

"It is kind of stunning how a proscribed world view can excuse almost anything."

It seemed now to Grace that her entire project since she'd returned to Buffalo had been to understand the Catholic faith and the role it had played in shaping her sense of herself, her values, her longing, her guilt, her desire.

"But there are some good things about religion, right? There are people trying to do good things under the mantel of faith, right?" Grace asked weakly.

"Sounds like somebody's trying to convince herself," Gloria said and laughed. "Some of the coolest, kindest activists I know are atheists. Religion has nothing to do with being good or caring about people."

"I know that."

"It's amazing. Now I know I'm Jewish, it kind of changes everything. It gives me insight into Mom and what she went through. What if she had raised us Jewish?"

"Being Catholic is such a big part of who I am," Grace sighed. "It's mind-blowing to think I would have been something else, had a different world view, if Mom had been able to be herself. If she had taught us her religious beliefs or taken us to synagogue. Or introduced us to our grandparents, for God's sake."

Instead, the church they were raised in squelched and denied her mom's heritage. The Catholic Church condescended and controlled and indoctrinated people of other faiths. Or worse, killed them. They killed Jews like her mom and her whole maternal lineage during the Inquisition, allied with fascists during World War II. Where was her mom's family from? How had they been harmed by anti-Semitism in all its sordid forms?

The mystery of their ancestry was more complicated than they could ever have imagined. But somehow, the new knowledge offered an odd form of deliverance. Knowing about her parents' lie meant that for Grace nothing was fixed, pre-determined. Maybe having a new identity meant she didn't have to have any identity. Maybe she was finally free to be nothing, uncategorized, un-assigned.

Gloria expelled a puff of air and chuckled. "You've got to admit it's funny."

"What's funny?" Grace asked.

"Two nice Jewish girls named Gloria Faith and Grace Marie. Do you remember one time she played the dreidel game with us?"

"Oh, yes," Grace said. "I do remember."

49

December, 1963

*M*om took the manger out of the box marked Creche. *Each of the miniature ceramic animals and the three wise kings was wrapped in yellow cotton. Mary and Joseph were swathed in festive red and green striped cloth, and the baby Jesus, no bigger than her thumb, was swaddled in a navy blue flannel dotted with stars.*

Grace loved to unwrap each figure and arrange the scene on the top of the buffet. Mom had set out a plate of store-bought sugar cookies, and Burl Ives sang cheerfully from the stereo.

"How beautiful!" she said, hugging Grace. "I just thought of something. I'll be right back." She bounced upstairs and returned from the attic with a small wooden box. She set it on the dining room table.

"Look, girls. I have a secret game I want to show you."

Inside the box were three tops, each carefully carved with squiggles and odd shapes on their sides. She picked one up and stroked it. "This is a dreidel. Let me show you how to play."

She spun the top and watched it careen across the smooth surface before petering out and collapsing on its side. "Oh, wait. We need pennies or peanuts or something."

"I have pennies!" Gloria shouted. She ran upstairs, returned with a piggy bank, and dumped its contents on the table.

"It's good to learn about what the Jews play at Christmas time. This is shin," Roberta said, pointing to the carved Hebrew letter. "It means share. And this is gimmel. Take all. Think of 'Gimme!'"

Grace couldn't remember her mom being this relaxed and happy.

Have a Holly Jolly Christmas *played while the girls twirled their tops and shrieked at their wins and losses.*

Dad's car pulled into the driveway, interrupting their fun.

"Oh, darn it," Mom said.

"Daddy can play!" Grace pulled her coins in close.

"No, honey. Daddy doesn't like this game. Besides, it's our special secret game!"

"Oh, Roberta." William shook his head as he entered the room. He looked gloomily upon the scene: two little girls squatting in their chairs, pennies in piles all over the table, cookie crumbs sprinkled next to half-drunk cups of milk, Ives bellowing, "Don we now our gay apparel, fa la la la la la la la la."

He patted his wife on the top of her down-turned head and picked up the wooden box. "Let's put this away now, girls."

From that day forward, whenever their dad was away, Gloria or Grace begged their mom to pull out the fancy dreidels and play the game that Jews play at Christmas. They had no idea what that meant. But they longed to make the tops coil and loop like dizzy dancers, collect their spoils, and play with their smiling mom.

"No, pumpkin. Not today," she always answered. "Let's just enjoy our own holiday, shall we?"

50

"I'm going away for a month." Mountain's back was to Grace as she stirred a pot of soup. "It's my youngest, Rain. He needs his mama."

Grace stopped chopping tomatoes and set down the knife. She'd hoped, indeed planned, for Mountain to be there after Crystal's baby was born. She had come to depend on her friend's solidity and nurturing presence.

"I'm sorry, kiddo. I wanted to help."

"No, I understand," Grace said, her voice high. She swallowed a swig of tea to keep the lump of emotion in her throat from turning into tears. "You have to go. It's important."

Mountain had told her about Rain, his struggles with drink and cocaine, his efforts to be a good dad to his two-year-old son since the baby's mom had disappeared. How could she be so egocentric as to want Mountain to be there for her when she had heart-rending battles of her own? Mountain wasn't her mother. She had no rights to her.

"I actually need *your* help," Mountain said. "With Magic." The old dog had been sick lately. He slept most of the day. Grace thought that he seemed sad if dogs could be sad. "Will you keep him while I'm gone?"

Grace reached down to stroke Magic's silky fur. "Um…" was all she could utter before Mountain interrupted.

"Brian's allergic, and the old boy's not well enough to go to a kennel. And he loves you, Grace."

"Well, I—"

"I know it's not a good time," Mountain said and laughed. "But let's be honest. When is it ever?"

Grace proceeded through the preparations for baby Jesse's birth. She finished jumping through the county's considerable guardianship hoops and shopped for all the necessary stuff. She told Alvin she could only come into St. Laurence once a week from now on.

Brian moved a bed, a crib, and a dresser into the Warrior Room. Grace helped Crystal arrange two garbage bags worth of possessions into the drawers. Her new roommate, at eight months pregnant, slept a lot, left dishes scattered around the house, and mostly cocooned herself under a quilt in front of the little TV they'd found at the Salvation Army Thrift Store. She spent hours drawing squiggles with markers in the sketch pad Grace bought her or fiddling with an Etch-a-Sketch.

Once or twice, she opened the GED workbooks Grace found for her, but she never got far before crying out in frustration and throwing them at the wall. Her emotions seemed to cycle between miserable, grouchy, and freaked out.

Grace steadied her rustled nerves by walking through the park with Magic. She loved to watch geese V-ing across the sky and velvety new buds unfolding. She navigated muddy puddles underfoot, delighted in the breeze tickling her cheeks. She stood still and listened to distant invisible birds whenever Magic stiffened to sniff.

Don't worry, Grace repeated to herself mantra-like, focusing on her breath. *You're about to have a baby in your life.* Mountain and Genevieve talked about cultivating gratitude. Brian reflected on the power of being present. Whatever it was called, she was beginning to understand that she could let go of her nagging anxieties by paying attention, by immersing herself in the immediate magnificent world.

And then, finally, ten days before the due date, a slow drip of amniotic fluid preceded a gushing waterfall. Crystal stuffed her underpants with pads until Grace could call the doctor, wrangle Crystal and herself into the car, and speed toward the waiting hospital room.

Grace did her part. She talked in a low register and counted the seconds between contractions. Crystal lifted her bulbous self up off the table, paced, lay on her side on the floor, closed her eyes against the waves of pain. She couldn't stay still for more than a few minutes. A perky young nurse monitored the fetal heartbeat. When she saw it rise to 180 beats a minute, she muttered the word *distress* and signaled for an intern to hook Crystal up to an IV bag to keep her from being dehydrated.

Crystal shuffled to the bathroom, Grace and the metal rod of the IV bag in tow. In between waves, more fluid, brown as tea, dripped between her legs.

Grace gasped. "Oh, no!" she squealed. "Don't move!"

She catapulted into the hallway and yelled for the nurse, who zipped toward them and helped a groaning Crystal onto the bed.

"It's meconium," the nurse said as she prepared to wheel Crystal through the curtains and out the door. "If you want to come"—she turned back now to Grace—"you'll need scrubs."

Grace took one look at Crystal's panicked face as she was wheeled past. She rushed to the nurses' station. "I need scrubs," she said, dazed.

The delivery room was like the inside of a steel machine. Its gleaming coldness reeled Grace back to 1973, and in an instant, it was she who was lying on the hard, white platform. It was she whose womb was tightening, muscles and sinews contracting. The IV drip, the fetal monitor, the emergency baby table—they were all the same.

"I can't do it!" Crystal screamed, first on the bed, then on all fours on the floor, then up and circling, then back on the table. "I can't do it. I don't want to. It hurts so fucking bad! Miss Grace." She reached over to Grace, who'd glued herself to a plastic bedside chair. "Hold my hand!"

Her hand was hot and swollen. Grace took a deep breath. She recognized that her job was to be a rock at the center of Crystal's swirling whirlpool of pain. "Hey, sweetie, you can do this. It's going to be all over soon, and we'll have a baby. How cool is that?"

The nurse checked the fetal monitor. The baby's heartbeat had slowed. "It's time to push," she said, her voice measured and reassuring, a clear bell.

Crystal pushed, all of her adolescent anger channeled into the intensity of the moment. She yanked her hand from Grace's to press against the table then pushed against her spread eagle thighs. When another wave of pain hit her, she gripped Grace's hand again.

"You're doing great," the nurse smiled. "Relax now."

A doctor walked in. "She's doing fine," the nurse said, turning to face the tall green-coated man. A mask was looped around his neck. He moved in closer to look between her legs and patted her foot.

"I'm fuckin' *not* doing fuckin' fine," Crystal growled, her face sweat-

303

streaked and contorted. Her heels jabbed into the nurse's palms as if about to leap away. "I can't do it. I can't fuckin' do it!"

"You're doing it," Grace said, words and breath colliding. Her arm ached from Crystal's vice grip. For forty-five minutes, the girl squeezed and shrieked and whimpered until a fuzzy black-haired head poked out of the throbbing red crack between her legs.

"Now stop," the nurse said firmly. For the first time, she sounded worried. "I have to suction his lungs."

She reached behind the head of the mysterious miniature being, stuck halfway between the wet sanctuary of the womb and the dryness of the world, and gently wrestled a tube into his mouth. She aspirated russet-tinted gunk and withdrew the tube.

"Now push again," she said, and Crystal heaved. The baby emerged the color of toasted almonds, lacquered with blood and earthy smelling goo. His shoulders appeared, then his arms and his belly, attached to Crystal's inner world by a ropey grey cord. His squishy wrinkled ball of a penis, his long skinny legs, his feet, tiny and kicking. He was perfect.

His cord was clamped and cut, and he was whisked away to the table. Grace wiped Crystal's forehead. She wanted to kiss the girl's pink cheek but leaped up instead and watched in a trance as the nurses attended to the infant under warm yellow lamps. They suctioned, washed, dried, and swaddled him.

"Where's my baby? I want my Jesse baby!" Crystal screeched as another nurse massaged her deflated belly.

"Push again, sweetheart," she said. "We've got to get the sac out."

It fell out, a gloppy brown balloon striated with green and blue veins followed by a gushing of watery blood. Then the baby came back, dry and wrapped in a thin blue blanket. He looked like a weary, wrinkly old man, eyes closed and puffy from the journey. The nurse set him down on Crystal's full globe of a breast. He nuzzled, found the brown nipple, and latched on. Grace watched mesmerized as he began to drink, and tears spilled down her cheeks.

Caring for baby Jesse and his irritable, sore, immature mother was the hardest thing Grace had done since she returned to Buffalo. Harder than seeing her dad in his crippled, needy state. Harder than losing him or missing

Luke. Harder than the two days on the cot in the hospital, waiting for the x-rays the doctor convinced them were essential. Harder than learning how to pump glucose and antibiotics into the port in baby Jesse's miniature hand.

Harder than hanging on while the non-stop barrage of worker bees buzzed in and out of the too bright, too loud room, emptying the garbage can, changing the sheets, fixing the sink, bringing limp globs of food.

Grace and Crystal were introduced to the awkwardly-named but well-intentioned volunteer support group MAMA—Mothers Assisting Mothers who are Adolescents. The volunteers helped them fill out the birth certificate and newspaper announcement paperwork, taught them about breastfeeding, then sent them home to the beginning of their adventure in a state of primal, wrung-out, bone-deep exhaustion.

For the first week after the baby's birth, she and Crystal dragged through days and suffered through long nights of piercing screams. Grace ached for a mother to swoop in and relieve them, guide them. She worried about that miserable mediport taped to the baby's miniature hand. She offered to wake up every night—if she slept at all—to take two vials from the fridge and hold his vulnerable body close as she attached the bottle to the port. She was so relieved when the antibiotic regimen was finally over and he was declared fine.

During the second week, Grace found herself on at least two occasions wanting to swat Crystal for sleeping through baby Jesse's cries. For one brief, horrible moment, Grace fantasized shaking the wailing baby. She was sleep-famished and angry, and she knew as little about how to care for the six-pound infant as his adolescent mother did.

Three times that torturous second week, Crystal screamed that her titties hurt and she couldn't do it. She took off for hours and left Grace alone and helpless.

She stayed up late, rocking him to sleep, and then woke up when he started screeching to warm a bottle. She found herself crying when he reached up with his worm-like fingers and grabbed her nose, or when he sucked on her knuckle, or when he fell for a half-hour into the bliss of sleep, his small chest rasping, rising, falling.

Brian knocked on the door at ten o'clock one night when all the lights were on. Crystal was curled into a ball on the floor in her room, pillow over her head; Grace was pacing, a screaming Jesse in her arms.

"It's me. You doing okay?" Brian's voice was low and deep on the other side of the door.

A hamper of dirty diapers festered in the corner. Crusted milk bottles tumbled over the counter into the sink, already piled with sticky egg-painted plates. She hadn't made her bed in a week.

Grace rocked the baby in one arm and opened the door with the other. She looked wide-eyed and panicky at Brian, not speaking, just shushing and rocking the baby. The screeching escalated. She had no idea what she looked like; she hadn't checked a mirror or brushed her hair in days.

"What can I do to help?" Brian asked. His hand reached out to stroke Jesse's head, but the baby lurched and convulsed, inconsolable.

Grace let out a low growl and gritted her teeth. "Nothing. I don't know." She felt as if she was shouting through a tunnel though she was whispering. Tears spilled down her cheeks. "I don't know. I'm doing something wrong."

She rocked and shook and cried as Brian stood motionless.

"Thanks, though," she managed. Then, both arms around Jesse, she pressed the door shut with her hip.

The baby continued to cry for another hour before Crystal finally emerged from her room. She pulled Jesse out of Grace's aching arms.

"Let me try," she said. Crystal walked fast in circles around the room that had become their cave. Jesse's wailing reached a crescendo. "I can't stand it!" Crystal grumbled.

Grace put her arms around her two squealing charges. "Okay," she said, trying to keep her voice even. "We'll get through this. Did you feed him?"

"Yeah!" Crystal yelled, her puffy eyes scrunched tight. "I feed him all the time!"

She handed Jesse over again, stormed into her room, and slammed the door. The scream she emitted behind the wall was ear piercing.

"I think we should call those people," Grace said to Crystal one night over pizza. For three weeks, they'd done all they could think of to soothe

the red-faced bundle of flesh that was Jesse, but he mostly refused to comply. He only slept for an hour or two at a time before demanding to be rocked or fed.

Crystal yanked off a hunk of crust and stuffed it in her mouth, then said, her words muffled, "What people?"

"The people in the teen mother program. You know, from the hospital. They said since I was your guardian, you didn't need them to check on you, but we do need them. We don't know what we're doing." Jesse was asleep in her sore arms. She shifted him on her shoulder so that she could pick up a piece of pizza.

"Okay," Crystal said.

"Good," Grace sighed, relieved.

"I'm going to bed." Crystal stood got up and dragged herself across the kitchen, leaving two half-eaten slices in the pizza box. The half-opened box looked like an alligator's jaws, jeering at Grace, flecks of pepperoni in its teeth.

The volunteer from MAMA showed up at their doorstep two days later.

"April?" Grace asked.

"Where's the little pumpkin?" the woman cooed as she walked into the living room. She plucked Jesse out of Grace's arms, one hand behind his head and one cradling his bottom. "Are you the one who's been giving these two ladies the runaround? One munchkin beating up two big ladies?"

Jesse's lips quivered and his face contorted into plaintive whimpering.

April laughed. "Oh, hush now. You just hush," she whispered, but his crying only grew louder and turned into a full-throated howl. "I know this isn't fun for you, so we're going to get you to sleep. I'll need a nice soft blanket." She smiled at Grace.

Grace called Crystal into the room and introduced her to April then grabbed a blanket from the crib.

"There, there," April clucked, laying the kicking baby in the middle of the blanket she'd opened on the sofa. "Now watch this," she said, tucking first one side of the blanket then the other tightly around Jesse's body. She folded up the bottom until his head was all that poked out, a tiny worm in a cocoon.

She grabbed him and stood up. Her arms were plump pillows. She held him against her chest and rocked him, murmuring in his ear. Grace stood passively staring at them as Jesse drifted into a deep sleep.

"Don't be afraid to hold him tightly," she said. "He needs help to feel secure and safe. He wants to sleep. Believe me!"

Holding him against her shoulder, she sank onto the sofa. "One of my first times fostering, I cared for a baby whose mother had left him in a box on a chair in a hospital waiting room. He was a preemie, an adorable boy with curly reddish hair. They found a home for him with an infertile couple. They never found the mom." Grace was enthralled as April moved Jesse onto her lap and laid her hand on his snoozing head.

"Once, I fostered a baby girl whose mother left her alone in a crib for a whole day. No food, dirty diaper, not even a blanket. Can you imagine? While the mother went out and got high. Another time, a father slammed his baby's head against the wall. Those two were my hardest."

"Who could do that?" Grace asked. "What makes somebody do those things to a baby?" The answer was obvious. Thanks to the frustration and helplessness she'd experienced trying to care for Jesse, she understood how desperate someone might become. April's visit was an answer to her inarticulate prayer.

April ignored the question. "They were the ones that taught me how to cope with a screaming baby. They literally cried for days when I first got them till they fell asleep from pure exhaustion. And me too!" She stroked Jesse's moist curls and looked down at his placid face. "I love volunteering with MAMA," she said. "And I love fostering, for *this*.

"The first few months of taking care of the babies I thought I was going crazy. For real. I wanted to give up a gazillion times. But my husband—he wasn't into it at first, he did it for me—he told me, 'You're crazy to quit. You're so good at this! These babies need you.' And now we have our own little man. We got him at six months, malnourished, failure-to-thrive.

"If it wasn't for my saint husband and my mom and my neighbor Sherry…And Ebony, my case manager, who called five times a day to check on me and set me up with Foster Support…I'm not sure I would've taken as good care of LeDarius. Of course, I want to think I would've, but

I don't know. He's a healthy energizer bunny now, though! We adopted him four months ago! He turns three in a couple of weeks."

A whimper escaped from Grace's throat. Losing her dad, followed by the screaming, the worry, the restless nights, and now listening to April's tragic stories—all of it ground her down to a smooth stone. Tears came up and over, washing the stone like rain.

"I had a baby once," she said as she sniffled.

April and Crystal moved their bodies closer, placing her bent-over body in the protective cup of their attention.

"I had a baby when I was eighteen. I've never told anybody. I couldn't. My father, the guy, my friends...nobody ever knew. I was so ashamed."

And there, in that soft bowl-like space made by the bodies of listening women, that physical container strong enough to hold such grief, Grace's secret was finally freed. "I guess I'm just worn out from everything, so overwhelmed by having Jesse in my life. And you, too, Crystal. I never thought I'd tell anybody."

"What happened? Where *is* he?" Crystal's eyes were wide with excitement. Both her hands were on Grace's leg, her knee pressed against Grace's arm.

"It's a she, and I gave her up for adoption. As soon as I found out I was pregnant, I moved. I just got on a bus and told my dad I wanted to go to school in California. I wanted to get as far away as I could."

"Why were you so ashamed?"

Grace turned to face her. "I was this girl who was never supposed to have sex. I was expected to be as good as the Virgin Mary, not desiring anything, trying so hard to be good, to not feel anything. And then it all broke. My father would have been mortified if his good girl disappointed him like that."

"What about your mom?" April asked. "Don't you think you should've told her? She probably would've helped you raise her if she knew."

"My mom would have been embarrassed. She would have driven me to California herself. But she wasn't around. She died when I was sixteen. And my sister had moved out. I never told her either."

"Oh, you poor thing," April murmured, putting a hand on Grace's other knee while holding sleeping Jesse with one arm. "That's a lot to go through by yourself."

"It was, but I didn't think of it that way at the time. I just felt like I had done this terrible thing, and I had to go fix it so nobody would ever know."

"You were pregnant all by yourself in a new city?"

Grace nodded. "I was sick for about four months, but I had to work to pay rent. I was just kind of numb. And, oh my God, I was so lonely. I didn't want to get to know anybody so nobody would ask me any questions. The landlady tried to find out who I was and why I was pregnant alone, but I never told her anything."

"I could never give up my baby." Crystal moved next to April and stroked Jesse's head. His nose crinkled, and he wiggled. She bounced up and sat back down next to Grace.

"Oh, sweetie." April's gaze was maternal as she eyed Crystal. "It's a hard choice. She did what she thought was right at the time. And the baby probably got adopted into a nice home."

Grace closed her eyes. "It's such a relief to finally say it."

"You poor thing," April said again. "You poor, poor thing."

April taught Crystal how to help Jesse latch on better to nurse longer, instructed them in how to use a bottle with a more natural-tip nipple, and explained how to hold the baby against the chest under a thin blanket and rock him with a steady motion. She suggested a sling, "so you can hold the baby close and still keep your arms free to do what you gotta do," and long drives in the car.

"They like moving," she said. "It's like the waves of the womb. And noise. Vacuums, fans, any whirring noise. It calms them. If it's gas, you can lay him on your legs and rub his back." April plopped him onto her legs to demonstrate. "And don't be afraid to use a binky!"

She pulled a pacifier out of a baggy in her purse and tickled Jesse's lip with it. He immediately took to sucking. "And a Papa Bear, if there's a man around. Sometimes those big manly chests really do the job." She laughed. "I'm guessing we don't have a daddy in the picture?"

Both Crystal and Grace shook their heads.

"Isn't there family? Sisters, brothers, cousins who can help you?" April asked, looking around the room as if a family member might walk in.

"No family," Grace said. "My dad recently died."

"Oh, honey!" April's eyes widened, and she shook her head. "What about friends? You both look like you need a break every now and then so you can sleep."

"My friend Mountain's away for three more weeks. Perfect timing, huh? We're watching her dog." Grace snapped her fingers. Magic unfolded his creaky bones and tapped over to her, nestling into a ball at her feet. Magic lay in the corner most of the day, occasionally throwing up on the floor. He didn't always manage to make it outside in time.

"He's sick." Grace sighed. "And Brian, well…we're having, I don't know, like a fight."

"That big man? You fightin' with him?" Crystal held out her arms and April transferred the sleeping Jesse to her. Brian had smiled kindly at Crystal when he met her and helped them move in all the furniture for her and the baby, but had otherwise kept out of sight.

"Kind of," Grace said. "More like not talking right now."

"He don't need to talk to be a Papa Bear," Crystal said. "Just stand there and hold the baby while we sleep. That's all he gotta do."

"True," Grace said. "He could do that. I could ask him to help."

51

Brian melted like a statue made of butter. His powerful frame and wary demeanor softened when he saw Grace approach holding Jesse. He stood up from planting tulip bulbs, took off his garden gloves, crooked his elbow, and burrowed Jesse into his arms. He looked down at Jesse's button nose and closed eyes, his long black eyelashes and puff of black hair, and murmured the round edges of a lullaby. The whole while he listened to Grace, he stared at Jesse and hummed.

"So, um, listen, Brian," Grace stammered. "I just want you to know I've been a jerk. I said some stupid things, and I'm sorry. I really am. And I'm not—"

She started to say she wasn't in love with Luke, but she didn't know. She didn't know much about love, didn't even know if she could learn.

"I'm not seeing anybody. I mean, you've been super nice, and I wanted to introduce you to the baby. I know you hear him crying. Crys and I have been totally exhausted, and I knew you were mad at me, and I didn't know if you ever wanted to talk to me again."

"Me too," Brian said. "I said stupid things too." He gave Jesse a peck on his damp forehead.

"And after my dad died, I really wanted to talk to you."

"Oh, Grace." Brian rocked Jesse and stared into Grace's eyes. "I know how much you cared for him and how devoted you were."

Grace looked down. "It's been a pretty hard time."

"Sweetie," he said, extending his empty arm to take her in. In a rush of feeling, she was pressed against his chest, tucked into the cavern of his armpit. She looked up at his chin, a rough growth of grayish-brown stubble along the jaw, and saw the picture of them as if framed for some future mantel. Sleeping baby in the crook of one arm, grieving woman nestled in on the other side, her face flat against the muscles of his chest, the old dog limp and moaning at their feet.

"I'm here," he said. For the first time since the beer cascade, he fingered her hair. "If you need me."

"Are we okay then? Can we be friends again?" So much had changed since the day they first sat in folding chairs on the front lawn. "I miss you, and Mountain, too, and our good talks."

"Grace, please. I don't want to just be friends with you." He continued rocking Jesse but released her. "I'll babysit this cutie pie, though. Don't worry."

"That's great. Thank you."

"Grace," he said, lifting her chin with his finger, "all I have to offer you is me. I'm just a person, just a man. I'm not an ideal or an idea or a saint or a guru. But I'm here."

It was the first Sunday morning of an exuberant April. Crocuses thrust their noses through stubborn clumps of snow. Mountain was back to see Magic one last time because, according to the vet, the cancer had ravaged him, and it was time to let him go. Rain had asked her to move back to Tennessee to be with him and his son.

"Come with me to the vet," Mountain asked Grace the day after she returned. "I would like some of your good energy with me as I lift Magic up."

Mountain had already carried Magic into the truck and laid him on a blanket in the back seat. When Grace climbed in, she looked back at Magic, so weak and thin, and her heart broke. His sleek black face tilted up and he looked at Grace with soulful wet black eyes.

Grace petted his feverish head and murmured, "That's a good boy."

Magic shuddered and closed his eyes.

When they arrived, Dr. Lenore was waiting. She greeted them both with a hug then helped Magic out of the seat. He limped next to them as they walked out to the yard behind Best Friends Animal Hospital. Spring's new grass glistened in the morning sun, and birds twittered above. Grace sat with her back against the chain link fence that separated the hospital from the Wendy's parking lot.

Mountain sat down, letting her huge violet skirt swirl around her. She pulled Magic to her. "Lie down, sweet boy," she said. Her eyes were red from crying earlier, and now they welled with tears again. "Come lie with mama."

Magic bent his hind legs first, then his front, and rested his head in the soft valley of Mountain's lap.

Dr. Lenore had brought out a folding chair, a bed sheet, and a doctor's kit. She lifted Magic's haunches and carefully eased the sheet underneath him. She pulled out a hypodermic needle and a couple of vials of clear liquid.

"I'm going to inject him with a barbiturate first—it's like a sleeping pill—to make him groggy. I'll follow that up with a high dose of pentobarbital to put him down. It won't hurt him a bit." She looked at Grace and then at Mountain. "Is there anything you want to say or do before I start?"

Mountain lifted her eyes up to the sky. Thin wisps of white clouds streaked across the blue. "I am grateful for your love, my dear friend. I bless your spirit as it moves from this earthly place into its next place of rest. A place where there is no cancer. No pain. Just squirrels and birds and other dogs to play with. May Mother Earth embrace you, then let you go. I let you go." She sighed and laid both hands on Magic's head. "Grace, did you want to tell Magic anything?"

Grace looked at Mountain. "I looked up the word euthanasia. It comes from the Greek word meaning 'good death.' I like that."

She turned her eyes to the resting dog and watched his chest move up and down with deep, even breaths. She put her thumb on the arch of bone between Magic's eyes and stroked his head. His fur was hot and silky. She thought of her dad's cool, pale, rigid body, the crumpled pillow beneath his head, the plastic and metal, the glaring fluorescent lights and noise of his last days.

"I love you, Magic. You're a wonderful dog."

Dr. Lenore poked a needle into Magic's haunch, then pressed in medicine from a tiny vial. Magic's eyes closed, and his breathing slackened. The vet pulled the bottle off the needle and replaced it with a different vial then used the plunger to squeeze the contents into the sleepy dog. "Here we go, Magic. Here we go."

The dog's breath stopped. The three women sat wordless as a breeze rustled the branches of the trees, lifting up the wrens and sending them off in a flutter of chirping.

For most of her young adult life, Grace felt protected and warmed by the light of religious belief. It made her feel connected to something bigger, helped her make sense of the enigma of her mother's sorrows. But then it betrayed her, made her feel worthless, guilty, and unloved. She struggled for years to make a life for herself without her childhood faith. But now, face to face with death and loss, she was beginning to understand that she could experience joy, empathy, and compassion for herself and for others, without a prerecorded script, without a prescriptive Savior, without a need for anybody else's particular version of truth.

Something was murmuring within her. Something had changed. She could see now that next door to her sadness about her dad's death was a room full of relief. She felt release from his disappointment in her, from his belief she was not quite good enough. And she could see now that she'd never let herself ever really experience love. For so many years she coveted her freedom, her singularity, while simultaneously yearning for the perfect person to save her from her aloneness.

Both desires, she could see now, were rooted in fear. They sprang from avoidance of the real, messy, complicated compromise of connected love.

On the wet lawn, sitting beside her mourning friend and her handsome, lifeless dog, she knew now that love was hovering. Like the game she played with Gloria when they were little. Grace would lay flat in the bed, her eyes closed, while Gloria raised her hand and lowered it over her face until it got so close Grace could feel its presence hanging there, thick and dark. You were supposed to guess when it was near, floating just above your face but not quite touching you. You had to sense its weight. If you didn't feel it, if you didn't say *now* right before it touched your nose, you would lose the game.

Dr. Lenore's assistants helped her fold Magic into the sheet to ready him for cremation. Mountain and Grace both leaned down one last time to pet the dog's warm fur. They left him there, nose close to the grass, and walked toward the empty truck.

52

Grace and Brian strolled alongside the rail above the American Falls. It was only fair that she should walk with him on one of his favorite trails after everything he'd done over the past weeks—regularly holding and feeding Jesse while Grace and Crystal did laundry or straightened up or ran errands. He'd wash dishes while they were all sleeping and sometimes leave a pot of chili on the stove for when they woke up.

"Let's take a walk," Brian said one afternoon as they stood at the sink together, hips nearly touching. "I'd like us to get to know each other better."

The sky was cerulean blue, the horizon pinkish-white with mist. The rush of white water falling over the edge made her gasp as she gripped the rail. The din of cascading water was deafening. "Wow. Amazing," was all she could muster.

"Seventy-five thousand gallons a second!" he yelled above the thunderous whoosh of water.

"Cool!"

As they walked further along the trail, the waterfall's roar subsided. They could finally talk. "Tell me about yourself," Brian said. "I know the basics. Your twenty-five years in California. But what else—who else—happened besides Jake the Jerk?"

"I do want to tell you, but…" She turned to face him and saw that his eyebrows were knitted together, a mixture of interest and concern on his face. She knew he cared for her; she knew he was good. She looked down at their feet walking in sync on the sidewalk. "But I'm shy," she said. "I don't know. Kind of embarrassed, I guess."

They walked to the end of the path, then stopped to breathe in the moist air.

"You don't have to be embarrassed," Brian said. "You can trust me."

That's my problem, Grace thought. She trusted the wrong people, and they dumped her. She had trusted Drew, Jake, and Luke, even though she knew in some damp cave inside her psyche that she shouldn't have trusted any of them. Brian liked her, and she'd known him for a year now. She'd seen him in action, so she knew he was a decent person. But what about as a *man?* How were you supposed to know?

The waterfall hypnotized her. Her dad had taken them all to the kitschy, touristy Horseshoe Falls in Canada many times in her youth but never once to the American side. Brian slid closer and whispered into her ear, his breath warm on her neck, "Grace, I really like you. Are you willing to give it a try? To let me get to know you, and you get to know me? Not to rush, to take it slow, but to see if…" She turned to face him. "I don't know how else to say this," he said, "but I think I could fall in love with you."

Oh no battled with *oh yes* in her mind, the way it did the night on the couch when she bounded away from his touch and toppled over a bottle of beer. Fascination and longing wrestled with terror.

"Brian, I—"

What if she took the risk, jumped off this cliff, him holding her hand on the way down? What was the chance that they would survive, plunge into deep, clear water, and swim away together? What if he let go, and she landed on the rocks, left torn up and alone again at the bottom? She didn't know if she was brave enough to jump in one more time. She stood there, feeling stiff and stymied by her own confusion.

"You don't have to say anything, Grace, but I want you to know how I feel. I'd really like for you to think about it. Take your time but think about giving me a chance."

"Okay," she murmured. Her heart raced as she imagined kissing him, his hands around her waist, her hands in his hair. She hugged herself and inched away. She would need to take some time. She would need to wait before she let herself be sucked into the current. "Let's head back," she said.

They strolled along the railing and stopped to let the image of the booming falls fill them one last time. They let the mist dust their eyelashes, frost their hair and dampen their skin before walking to the car. They didn't talk until she turned the key to start the engine.

"Pierogies?" Brian asked.

"I'm starving," she said.

I think I could fall in love with you. His words whistled like wind inside her ears. She stuffed the sound into a small corner of her mind. *Not now,* she told herself. *Revisit later.*

"You have been threatening to take me out for pierogies since that first winter walk, so I guess it's time."

"I guess it is."

They got the combination platter at Kowalski's on Fillmore, one of the only authentic Polish restaurants left. Small plump dough pillows, some stuffed with potatoes and cheese, others with sauerkraut and mushrooms, and her favorite, sweet cheese, swam in a pool of liquid butter and caramelized onions. It came with a side of golabki, ground beef, rice, and tomato sauce wrapped in an envelope of cabbage. How had she lived here her whole childhood and never indulged in these?

Brian regaled her with the history of the Polish East Side. To escape religious persecution and find economic opportunities, he told her, thousands of Poles arrived at Ellis Island in the late 1800s and early 1900s, then traveled by train to Western New York. By the turn of the century, almost twenty percent of the city's population was Polish.

"But like in so many Northeastern cities," he said, "the 60's and 70's brought white flight, and the majority of the residents fled to Cheektowaga. They could justify their escape because of the de-industrialization of the city, just like what was going on in other Rust Belt cities. The American Ship Building Company employed a lot of workers, and it was shut down in 1962.

"The city's economy started to deteriorate. Then Republic Steel closed in 1982, and Bethlehem Steel in Lackawanna closed in 1983. Now the old Polish Eastside is mostly black folks trying to make a living. And when the whites left, the city abandoned the area. They left it destitute and under-resourced. There are hardly any jobs."

"And lots of homelessness and hopelessness," Grace said. "There's real desperation."

St. Laurence House had planted itself right in the middle of what had once been the thriving Polish neighborhood and was now a decrepit and neglected urban prairie full of vacant houses and boarded up storefronts.

"It's a shame how little I know about the city's history," she said. "All I really know about the East Side is that my dad would drive here once a month when I was a kid to go to Saint Stanislaus for Latin Mass."

"Saint Stanislaus Bishop & Martyr Parish is the oldest Polish parish in New York State," Brian offered, wiping his buttery lips.

"How do you know all these factoids?" she asked.

"It's just how my brilliant brain works." He winked, making her blush. "I collect them. They come to me, and they don't leave. It's not a choice."

Grace studied him, this cocky, cute man who insisted on trying to impress her. His sandy brown hair had begun to sport strands of grey; today, it was sticking up straight from being ruffled by the wind at the falls.

"Now there's a rich cultural mix in this neighborhood. Jamey's Vegetarian Soul Food is on the corner of Fillmore and Sienkiewicz. That place is awesome. There's a new Black-owned business with New Orleans cuisine called The Big Easy. And I really need to show you the Broadway Market. It's cool; it's got an international feel. You have to see Bartkowicz's Bakery. They have kołaczki, chruściki, Polish donuts. Wiśniewski Seafood and Meats has the best kiełbasa and klopsiki meatballs. Willie's Ribs and Wings is super spicy. Coconut's Jamaican Delights has great meat patties. Czerwonka's Famous Horseradish, Babunia's Pierogies, Sweet Marie's Gelato Delights…You have to let me take you there."

"Oh, I do?" She grinned. "I have to?"

"Yup, it's in the rental agreement. Fine print."

The waiter brought them coffee, and he transitioned the talk away from Buffalo's decline to tales of his own failed love affairs. He grew up in Cleveland. When, at nineteen years old, his first love, Susan, broke up with him, he took to the road. He traveled for three years—camping, hiking, working to make enough to squeak by for two to three months at a time in cities and on farms across the country.

Finally, at twenty-two, he enrolled at the University at Cornell in Ithaca and settled into an intentional alternative Buddhist community. He fell in love with Lana, a student of Zen and a sculptor.

"She didn't want to have kids, and she fell for someone else," he said when Grace asked him what happened.

He dropped out of college after that and started honing his carpentry skills.

"Since that time, I've only been in love once, with Jennifer. She was my sweetie. We were married for five years. She was in a bad car accident and died in the hospital a week later. We were just starting to try to get pregnant."

"Oh, no," Grace said. "You never told me that!"

"There's a lot we haven't old each other. True?"

"True," she said. She had told him next to nothing about herself. "I'm so sorry. That's horrible."

"I guess my heart is still broken in a way. After all these years…" He shook his head and looked down into his milky coffee.

Grace reached across the table and stroked his arm. He turned his hand over, and she placed her hand in his. "I've been missing my old dad lately," she offered. "And thinking a lot about my mom."

"You know the first law of thermodynamics, right?" He squeezed her hand, then pulled his hand away.

"I think so."

"When Jennifer died, it helped me to remember that energy is neither created nor destroyed. I think the person that we are, the physical person that we each are, that Jennifer was, that your dad was, doesn't really die. It's transformed. It changes but doesn't die. Every vibration, every thermal unit, continues to pulsate in the universe, just in another form. It never disappears. And all the photons that ever touched your dad's skin were transformed by him and impacted whatever he touched. As he transforms into the next phase, he'll continue to be present in this world, in your life.

"It's the same idea in the spiritual realm. Buddhism teaches that each person is a tapestry of thoughts, perceptions, and emotions that interact with the body. Our ephemeral and physical selves are constantly interacting with each other in a dynamic and energetic way. So, in death, that mental and spiritual vitality, that life-force, it doesn't disappear. It finds a new home for itself in a new body. This individual energy—what Christians might call a soul—doesn't fade."

Brian took a long drink of water. Grace looked around at the others in the restaurant, chatting, laughing, scraping their plates, then returned her gaze to Brian.

"They linger, your dad and mom. And Jennifer." His eyes were watery, his eyelids heavy. "The people we've loved. I find that comforting."

"Me too," Grace said. "Me too."

Dusk settled over the city on the ride home from Kowalski's. Crystal and Jesse were passed out on the sofa. They both stirred when Grace and Brian opened the door and walked in. Soft light from the window illuminated the two sleepers. Brian took Grace by the hand and led her back outside.

"Let's stretch. My back's hurting a little. Come on over to my house so we don't wake them."

Brian lay his long body on the rug in his sparsely furnished living room, held his arms over his head and reached, then patted the floor beside him. "Time to stretch your weary bones."

Grace remained standing. She lifted her leg into Tree position, extended her arms over her head, and groaned. Brian studied her from the floor. "What's hurting?" he asked.

"My shoulder's sore. From baby holding, I think."

"Come down to my level, girl."

She lay down next to him on her stomach and curled into Child pose. She turned over onto her back, lay her head and its mop of curls in the crook of his arm, and let him massage her shoulder. She sucked in a breath as he gently pulled her arm across his chest.

Well, here she was. It was the first time she'd let him touch her after so many months of living next door, so many months of knowing that he wanted her. She thought of Jennifer, how capable he'd been of loving someone faithfully and fully, how that true love had been stolen from him. She let her body relax, closed her eyes, and told herself not to panic.

"That feels really good," she sighed.

"See, yoga isn't supposed to make you mean." His lips were close enough to her forehead to kiss her, but he continued talking and working on her aching arm. "Like it did to Jake the Snake and—what was her name? Loco Starbuck? Lulu Moonshine?"

Grace giggled. "Linda Starflower."

"It's supposed to make you nicer. Or at least a little less mean."

"I have to admit I hated yoga for a while, thanks to those two unenlightened unspiritual practitioners of the healing arts."

"Let's start over," he whispered into her hair.

Under the covers, the bedroom black but for a flickering yellow candle, they took their clothes off and tenderly, tentatively touched while she talked.

This is different, Grace thought as she scanned his face, the wrinkles around his eyes, his hairless chest. For the first time in her life, she knew for sure that the man in the bed really liked her and wanted to be with her.

She told him everything. About losing her mom and how church had offered her a measure of peace. About finding solace at St. Laurence so many years ago. About succumbing to the demanding boy behind the school, the pregnancy, the lies, the fleeing, the adoption. About Drew, about her many short-term and disappointing lovers, about the loneliness in-between. About the mangled metal box and its secrets, revealing her heritage and her mother's desperation, upending all her assumptions about her childhood. All the while he listened, his index finger tracing soft lines on her face, her shoulders, her breasts, her belly.

"Maybe this time I can hang in long enough with you to see if I might fall in love with you," she confessed.

"I would like that," he said. "Just so you know, I'm already on the path." He kissed her forehead and her cheek. "But I'm willing to wait for you to join me. We can take our time and explore together. Think of it as an adventure."

He stroked her hair from her face with both hands and kissed her. She felt her heart quicken and her body awaken. In her bareness, she felt lovely, lovable, loving. She felt safe, not scared. She stroked the length of him, his arms, the muscles of his chest, the sinews of his legs. She lowered the fullness of her nakedness on top of him and lay together with him for a long minute in a warm embrace.

They made love. They made noise. They laughed and joked and moaned and sighed. They slept curled into each other like puppies until the baby's insistent cry penetrated the apartment wall and yanked them both out of their dreams.

53

"So, listen."

"Hey, Gloria. Nice surprise."

Grace had been calling Gloria on a regular basis for the first five months of Jesse's life, unable to control her urge to report on one or another milestone. Grace sat on the floor, Jesse lying on her legs. His bare feet pushed against the flesh of her stomach. She held the phone to her ear with one hand and tickled the baby's belly with the other. She and Crystal and Brian had formed a tag team, and every minute of the day the baby was against somebody's skin.

"He's too cute today, like a little wriggling worm. You should see him kick these hotdog legs."

"Grace, listen. I'm trying out a new name."

Grace bent her knees, brought her face to Jesse's, and spoke to Gloria in a high-pitched sing-song baby voice. "What did you say?"

"Ever since you read me Mom's letters, I've been thinking about how she was raised, how she would have raised us if Dad hadn't bullied her into turning Catholic. How different our lives would have been. I started thinking I should check out the synagogue, learn more about it. I've been going to services for the last couple of months. Just sitting in the back, listening."

"You've been doing this for months and never told me?" In her excitement about her new life and her desire to reconnect, she hadn't let Gloria get a word in. "I'm surprised. You're so cynical about religion all the time."

"I know, but I wanted to find out more about Mom's heritage. I wondered if knowing more about it might help me feel closer to her. It's like I have a way now to connect with her and give her the chance to not have to give up everything. I know it sounds crazy. Sometimes I imagine myself at thirteen or fourteen, sitting there next to her, as normal as can be. It's like, through me, we can change our history."

Grace murmured, a low humming sound. "Awww." The image of Mom alive and thriving, Gloria leaning against her as they listened to a rabbi lead a service, filled her with a poignant longing.

"It's been pretty special. A couple of the older ladies talked to me one day when I stayed after for coffee hour. I told them about the letters and what mom went through."

"Yeah?"

"When the ladies heard the story, they hugged me. I told them I'd been raised Catholic. They said it didn't matter. That according to the faith, I was a full-fledged, dyed-in-the-wool Jew. And they told me the closest thing to the name Gloria in Hebrew is Odelia. Apparently, it means praise. Like a glory-be-to-God kind of thing."

"Wow, Gloria. That's something else."

"I know. I'm not sure yet how much I believe the religious parts. I'm going to take a class led by the rabbi for people wanting to convert. But don't worry. I won't turn Hasidic and wear a wig. I couldn't bear to cover up my gorgeous hair." Grace laughed. "I know a lot of religious dogma is a load of hooey."

"On both sides, right? Mom's Jewish family was awful to her too. They cut her off for marrying a Catholic. They broke her heart."

"I know. It's totally tragic."

"Do you want to convert?"

"I'm not deciding anything yet. I'm doing research! But I love the community feeling I have when I'm there. It's like I can imagine an extended family now. And the temple I'm going to is reform. They're very liberal, really involved in social justice issues. They're not so strict. You know it's Rosh Hashanah now, right? It's almost Yom Kippur?"

"Yeah. I kind of knew, but I haven't been paying much attention to anything except baby and Crystal and writing. And Brian." Grace liked how the summary of her life sounded, encapsulated in four simple words.

"Well, it is. It's the time of atonement. Grace, listen to the prayer that I learned: 'You remember all the forgotten things. You open the Book of Memories, and it speaks for itself, for each person's hand has signed it.' Doesn't that just say it all?"

"Wow. I'm glad for you. But I'm kind of shocked that you're doing this."

"It's big. But it's all come together in a way that really makes sense for me. And my kids have been pretty okay with it. They're curious, I guess. It's their story, too, in a way. David's been supportive."

"So—" Grace unfolded herself from the floor. She hoisted the baby on her hip, set the phone on the counter, and put it on speaker while she got out the makings for a bottle.

"I'm taking a cooking class. I've learned how to make rugelach with apricots. And honey cake and challah. We serve it at the café. The ladies at the synagogue have sort of adopted me since they heard our story. It's nice to have older women in my life, honestly."

"Gloria, I'm glad for you." Grace understood. Both Mountain and Genevieve had played the part of surrogate mother for her.

"So since it's Rosh Hashanah, I'm atoning. I apologize."

"For what?" Grace held Jesse against her chest and stroked his curls. She'd have to set him down to measure out the powder and add the water, though she hated to release him. "Hang on, okay?"

She plopped him in his seat and belted him in, all the while whispering and cooing. "Just a minute, little one. I just need a minute." She quickly made the formula, then unbelted him and whisked baby, bottle, and phone over to the sofa.

"Go on," she told her sister.

"I said I'm sorry. I mean, for everything. For whatever I did or didn't do. For being stubborn, mostly."

"Thanks. Um…me too."

This was a new Gloria, less edgy, less sarcastic and cynical. Grace sank back into the couch, watching Jesse's eyes sink into half-moons. Her sister had been open with her. Now it was her turn. "Gloria, I haven't told you everything either."

"Odelia."

"Odelia. Remember how I felt all this pressure to be good, to be the perfect daughter, so Mom wouldn't be depressed or get a headache, so Dad wouldn't feel lonely or bad? And all the Church taught me about sex and sexuality…"

"Yeah?"

"Well." Grace paused. "I left Buffalo for San Francisco because I got pregnant. I gave away the baby after I moved there. Gave the baby up for adoption. She'd be twenty-five years old this year."

"You're kidding."

"I'm not kidding."

"You're *kidding*," Gloria hissed. "Why didn't you ever tell me?"

"I don't know. The same reason you didn't tell me about you getting pregnant. I guess we never learned to trust each other. Maybe I didn't want to let go of the image you and dad had of me as the good girl who never did anything wrong. I never told anybody until a few months ago."

"Wow, you're blowing me away here."

Jesse pushed the bottle out of his tiny mouth with his tongue and settled to sleep in Grace's arms.

"Grace, I hate to tell you this, but I have to go to the café. I want to hear more, though. Next time, you'll tell me. Everything. I mean it. Could I call you later tonight? Or tomorrow early? This is the year of truth, I guess."

"Right?"

"Right! We'll keep talking." Gloria's voice was subdued, sincere.

"Good. I'd like that."

"Oh! And in keeping with my new-found identity, I'm supposed to wish you Shanah Tovah! It means a year of apples dipped in honey. To all you guys. To your new, you know, family."

"Well, great. You too." Graced paused. "Did you say Ophelia? Like the crazy woman in Hamlet who was grieving for her dead dad? Are you sure Ophelia is Hebrew?"

Gloria chuckled. "No! *Odelia.* 'Glorify God's name.' I'm getting used to it! It's like I'm honoring Mom, giving her a chance to communicate honestly about herself, her past, for the first time. I feel kind of like we're together again. Finally."

"Gloria, Odelia, that's cool. It makes me happy to hear that."

"Grace, we grew up with a lie. Mom suffered because of a lie. That's a horrible foundation for raising a family. We kept huge secrets from each other all these years. We have to start telling each other the truth, okay? What have we got to lose?"

54

The route to the monastery was dotted with red barns, neatly painted two-story clapboard houses, and picturesque white churches sprouting American flags. The farms in mid-May were already brimming with corn, lettuce, cabbage, and melons. The Abbey of the Blessed Virgin was nestled into a hill outside the tiny town of Mayville, a few miles south of the Lilydale Spiritualist Community. Grace would have liked to have the whole day to explore the area, walk the hills, maybe even get a psychic reading at Lilydale just for fun. But she hadn't ever been away from the baby for more than a few hours, and she knew Crystal would need her soon.

The abbey had been planted atop the hill. It was skirted by a green carpet of grass. Purple chicory, Queen Anne's lace, and Black-eyed Susans sparkled along the dirt road that wound up the hill to the round stone building. From the parking lot, a brick walkway led past a porcelain statue of the Virgin, lovingly eyeing the baby Jesus in her arms. Pink and red roses enveloped the pair. Weeping willow trees encircled the building, and long rows of vegetables stretched out behind it.

Grace entered the dark corridor that led to the chapel and caressed the rough stone wall. A printed poster reminded visitors to *Please Observe Silence Past this Point, We Are a Contemplative Community*. In her youth, she'd imagined herself as a nun, but she knew now she could never have chosen such a simple life. She'd miss the colorful confusion and unpredictability of things. She'd miss sex. She was beginning to feel comfortable with Brian, excited even, about the future in store for them. But she had woken up to a dream of Luke with his hands on her back, his whiskers against her cheek, and felt compelled to see him, if only from a distance.

The parishioners quieted their rustling as the first monks entered. They wore long beige cassocks, hands folded at their chests, heads bowed. Large wooden crucifixes hung around their necks. Two old, grey men shuffled in gripping clunky walkers. One man in a wheelchair was pushed by a younger monk. Luke came in near the end.

Grace hardly recognized him. His long hair had been clipped close to his skull, and his beard was gone. He saw her. She imagined his eyes watering as he stared at her, but he was too far away to see for sure. For the rest of the Mass, he either kept his eyes closed or looked down at his prayer book.

Grace sat patiently through the sweet choral singing of the monks, the long, dry recitations of the Creed, the Gospel reading, and the sermon. She ruminated about Luke, trying to imagine his bland and tranquil new life. She understood the call to religion. She had known it in her bones. But the lifestyle still unsettled her.

Grace felt a headache start to pound inside her skull. She fidgeted on the hard pew as she eyed the others in the chapel. They looked prayerful, at home here. Believers have to compartmentalize, she reasoned. She had done it when she was young and naïve. In order to be at peace with the Church and its teachings, they had to deny the cruel realities of what the leadership perpetuated and its blatant and flagrant cover-up of predators' crimes against children.

Why were churchgoers not protesting in the streets? Just yesterday, she'd read an article in the *Buffalo News* about a priest who admitted to forcing sexual contact on "probably dozens" of teenage boys in the 1960s. The diocese sent him away for "treatment" but continued to allow him to perform his priestly duties.

Last week she called Victoria to check in as she did at least once a month since their visit to the lawyer. No news yet. She remembered Frankie's open face, his dark eyes. Her dear Frankie, so betrayed by a church that was supposed to protect him, so disgraced by its violence against him. And then the bureaucracy's cruel denial of how much they had hurt him and all the others.

She was angry at their lies. She ground her teeth together. A fat tear fell onto her blouse. She had been drawn to Luke because he hated the lies, too, in his way. He protested with his daily life, doing what he believed Jesus taught people to do—to love, to look out for each other. But even after the Church expelled him and forced him to be silent, he couldn't disentangle himself.

Grace waited as the congregants shuffled up to the monks dispensing communion. The smell of incense was sweet. She watched believers open their mouths to let the monks place wafers on their tongues.

She lingered for another hour after Mass, thumbing through Thomas Merton's *Asian Journal* and the *Rule of St. Benedict* in the spiritual bookshop and inhaling the aroma of raisin nut bread and rum cake in the bakery store. She wandered out back through the rows of tomatoes, peas, lettuce, and basil. The day was sunny, and a gentle breeze fluttered through her hair. She walked along the meditation path. Honeysuckle and lilacs were planted on either side of the trail. Dragonflies and butterflies flitted around the flowers; milkweed fluff floated in the air. Despite all her internal wrangling, she appreciated the serenity of the abbey.

She hadn't caught Luke's eyes again, bumped into him in the bakery, or come upon him wandering through the garden. She knew she might never see him again. But that was alright. She was going to be okay.

On the long ride home, she realized that if she wasn't careful her anger at the strictures and duplicities of the Catholic Church would steamroll over the essence of the faith that had inspired her to be compassionate and open-hearted.

She wouldn't allow her frustrations with its limitations to steal from her the joy she'd found in feeling connected to others, or rob her of the awe she felt at the breathtaking mystery of the unfolding universe, or separate her from God, whatever that meant. She resolved to meditate and pray in whatever way was right for her, to pay attention, to feel reverence and wonder. By the end of the ride, she felt cleansed, finished with it all, happy to be going home.

The table was wiped clean, but otherwise, the kitchen was in shambles. Two frying pans were coated with the dregs of pancakes and eggs, coffee grinds dusted the counter, and baby bottles and dirty dishes made a massive mountain in the sink.

"Hey!" Grace yelled. "Anybody home?"

She walked through the rooms to find Crystal in her bed with Jesse, collapsed in a slumbering heap. She had left Brian sleeping in her room when she drove away at eight o'clock that morning. The bed was empty.

She walked outside and rapped her knuckles on the locked door of Brian's apartment. There was no response. She knocked again. "Brian?"

"Grace." He opened the door and wrapped his arms around hers, pulling her close. "Where have you been? Crystal and I were so worried."

"I…I just had to leave. I needed to get away for a bit, that's all. I left you a note."

"Just so you know, Grace, you did not leave a note. And you left your phone at home. Crystal and I had no idea where you were. You've been gone for hours. I was concerned."

"I thought I left you a note."

"You didn't."

"I'm sorry. I meant to."

"I was afraid that…that you left."

"Left? Like moved out? Without telling you? Of course not."

The thought had crossed her mind. She didn't know if or when she'd be able to surrender her defenses to somebody like him—wholly available and ready for connection. Daily, if only for a minute, she pressed away her fears by imagining herself packing a suitcase and moving out. But every day, she also gathered her resources and tried her best to relax, to see how this new relationship might unfold.

"Of course not," she repeated.

"So where did you go?"

She looked down at the carpet. "I just felt like I had to take a break. Go for a drive. I'm tired from watching the baby and all…"

"A five-hour drive?"

"I drove to the monastery. It's over an hour away. In Mayville."

"The monastery?

"Where Luke is. Father Luke, Brother Luke is…It's beautiful and peaceful there."

Brian stepped back. The muscles of his arms were rigid, and his jaw was clenched tight. "Okay, whoa. Now I'm mad."

"Just to get away," Grace said, her voice quavering. "I meant to leave a note."

"You needed to get away? I wake up to an empty bed, a screaming baby, and a surly teenager because you had to get away…to check on your…your old lover?"

"No, I—"

"And you didn't think to check in with me? We've been sleeping together for a week, talking about being open with each other, taking chances…and now you say you need to *take a break* to meet up with your priest lover? I am so angry right now I can't talk." He shook his head. "I have to go."

He brushed against her as he stomped into the kitchen and yanked his keys off the hook. He jerked open the front door, leaving the screen door flapping, and tramped to his car. Through the opening in the drapes, Grace watched, numb, as he drove away.

He returned two hours later. Crystal and Jesse were asleep. Grace had gone back to her apartment and scrubbed the entire kitchen, thoughts twisting and hissing inside her head. She was sitting in a corner of the sofa, thumbing through the morning paper, when he walked in. She startled when he sat beside her and put a hand on her knee.

"Gracie," he said, staring into her eyes. "I'm sorry I drove off. I don't want to do that."

"I don't know why you were so upset. I didn't mean to hurt you or scare you. You stormed out before we could talk about it. I wish you wouldn't just drive away."

Her dad used to yell, refuse to talk, and screech out of the driveway when he was upset. She'd seen her mom's face clouded by powerlessness in the face of his fury.

"Never again. I promise. I want us to learn to talk to each other when we're angry."

Grace inched away from his hand on her knee and his insistent stare.

"Grace, here's my question. Are you in? Are you with me? Or is this just a convenience? Am I just another lover in a long list?"

She shook her head.

"Are you still in love with him? Am I an idiot? Was I duped into thinking you wanted me for something more than a babysitter?" Grace looked at their feet. His right foot rested against her left. He waited, unmoving, for her to respond. "If you are still longing for your priest, if you are just in this because you need somebody to take you out of this hole you dropped yourself into, let me know *now*. I don't want to do this halfway."

"I wish I had written a note," Grace said. "And I should have talked to you about it first." She gulped and lifted her eyes from the floor, turned to face him. She felt a sweat break out on the back of her neck. "I was raised in a family that didn't know how to talk. My parents lived a lie. I've never been in a committed and honest relationship. Ever. The whole idea…well, it scares me."

"I know," he said. "And I'm scared that you're not going to stay with it long enough to see that we can learn to trust each other, that we can heal from all the hurt we've been through. Take care of each other. I shouldn't have stormed off."

"I think I will sometimes need to be by myself in order to think about everything." She closed her eyes to the memory of the long drive home and the confidence and clarity it had brought her. "But that doesn't mean I don't want to work on getting close to you. My falling for Luke was just another escape from intimacy. I know that now. I want the real thing, relationship-wise. Even though I have a lot of old patterns and defenses to work through…doing this here with you, it's what I want."

"There's no way for us to get closer if we don't commit to being honest with each other and communicating as best we can."

Grace laid her head against his shoulder and looked up into his down-turned eyes. Her voice was timid, tremulous. "You are not just a convenience. You're not just a babysitter. There's nobody else. I'm in this."

She looked down at her hands, which were balled into fists, and taking a deep breath, made an effort to unclench them.

55

December 31, 1999

Crystal snored on the floor, Jesse asleep on her chest. When the little guy started to whimper, Crystal startled and passed him to Grace. She lifted up her shirt and fidgeted with her bra.

Grace had grown accustomed to Crystal's naked breasts and Jesse's eager sucking. At first, she was jealous, sad that her own baby girl had been handed off to another mother, leaving her with nothing but a mushy post-partum body, aching breasts full of useless milk, and an ocean of salty sorrow. But tonight, she found it comforting to watch Crystal nourish her baby.

Brian walked into the newly renovated living room. A week after their first fight, he asked if he could knock down the walls and convert the first floor into a single home for all of them. He adored her, he said, and wanted to live with her forever.

She agreed. For the first time in her life, she knew that the man she'd chosen to share herself with could be trusted. Like the piles of rubble left by the demolished walls, she'd felt her defenses crumble.

"Ready?" Brian asked, kissing Grace's forehead. "I've got everything set up."

The crew picked themselves up and trundled toward the kitchen, which Brian had decorated for the holiday. He'd spent all afternoon baking, shooing Grace and Crystal away.

"I've concocted a special surprise for my special ladies on this special day of the year!"

Grace and Crystal giggled. They walked into the kitchen, their arms around each other's shoulders.

He'd been teasing for the past week that if, indeed, the apocalypse was coming, the end days were near, and all the systems were about to crash, they might as well stockpile cookies and go out in style.

Grace gasped. He'd hung white Christmas lights around the windows and set her mother's manger and its ramshackle inhabitants in the center of the table. Behind it, he'd placed a huge silver menorah jammed with candles, all lit and dripping. Piles of hot latkes steamed on a platter; next to them was a plate of homemade cut-out Christmas cookies slathered with green and red frosting.

"Wow! This is awesome, Brian!" Crystal squealed. She looked down at Jesse cradled in her arms. "This is your first New Year's, baby!" She tucked herself and the wide-eyed child into a chair, grabbed a latke, and took an oily bite. She bounced Jesse on her knee and put a tiny morsel of pancake to his lips. They all watched him as he nibbled it.

"I'm floored," Grace said. She hugged Brian tight, inhaling his scent of sugar and hot grease. "Wow. Thank you. You are so sweet to do this."

On New Year's Eve at the end of the millennium, Grace couldn't know that she and Brian would grow old together, learn to laugh openly and talk with great tenderness, their lovemaking generous and honest. They'd live as a family with Crystal and Jesse in their conjoined four-bedroom apartment thanks to Brian's enthusiastic renovations. Grace would continue to learn how to balance her canoe. When her hips ached from carrying their growing boy, or when she needed to quell the occasional panic that arose from allowing a man's energy into the well-worn grooves of her life, Grace would retreat to the Warrior Room to write or stretch or draw.

Jesse would grow up to be a whip-smart young man, funny and kind and protective of roughed-up cats and torn-winged birds. He'd make some dumb mistakes, but the preponderance of his choices would be thoughtful and smart. His strikingly handsome face and thick spray of curly black hair would garner him more favors than even he thought he deserved.

He'd learn to fix everything and ask a zillion questions, accompanied by Brian's eagerness to explore and explain the material world. Grace would teach him to read and paint and swim and ride a bike. Thanks to Crystal's constancy and good humor, it was easy for him to love and forgive.

What Grace could not yet imagine at the end of the turbulent century was that in 2002, reporters at the Boston Globe would blow wide open the story of pervasive priest abuse cover-up, motivating her once and for all to enroll at the University of Buffalo and study journalism. For years after the exposé, newspapers in cities across the country would regularly roll out allegations of molestation and rape of young people by priests, along with conspiracies to buy off victims and hide the abuse. A cavalcade of reports would follow from around the world, from Canada, Ireland, the United Kingdom, Mexico, Belgium, France, Germany, Australia, Chile, Peru, New Zealand, Tanzania, Guam.

In 2003, Grace would have a show at the Pintura Gallery called Victims of a Loving Church. She'd paint impressionistic watercolor portraits of children on enlarged newspaper articles about the priest abuse scandal and ask the museum director if she could display them. *The Free Press* would review the exhibit, calling it "moving and important" and "a radical reminder of a horror that hasn't gone away." Very few people would attend the show, but letters to the paper would complain it was "polemical" and "vindictive" and that she should "let bygones be bygones."

Genevieve and Alma would reunite and live out their old age together in a freewheeling community of ex-communicated nuns, former addicts, and abused women. They would become Roman Catholic Womenpriests, avowing that they were rightly ordained in Apostolic Succession and called by the Holy Spirit to carry out the gospel message. Their marriage, along with twenty-five other same-sex couples, by Mayor Jason West of New Paltz, New York in February, 2004, would get front page coverage in the *Buffalo News*. In response to a continued groundswell of rebellious Catholics who insisted on ordaining women, the Vatican would determine in 2010 that the attempted ordination of women should be placed in the same category as clerical sexual abuse of minors and considered a "grave crime."

Victoria's eventual settlement would come five years after her visit with Grace and Marisol to Halpern's office. She would be awarded enough cash to open a small café in South Central LA called Frankie's Place. The menu would offer "comfort food with attitude," and only people with felonies would be hired. Gloria's frequent visits and bookkeeping advice would help the business run smoothly for many years.

In 2013, the Los Angeles Archbishop José Horacio Gómez would bar the retired Cardinal Roger Mahony from any public ministry. After reading a stockpile of documents about LA priests' abuse of minors, Gomez, one of the few shepherds who would choose to safeguard the flock instead of the wolves, would write, "The behavior described in these files is terribly sad and evil. There is no excuse, no explaining away what happened to these children. The priests involved had the duty to be their spiritual fathers, and they failed."

In 2018, a grand jury in Pennsylvania would make public internal documents from six Catholic dioceses proving that over three hundred "predator priests" abused more than 1,000 teens and pre-pubescent children. One by one, other states would follow suit. Irish Catholics would discover that thousands of children had been sexually and physically abused in parochial schools for decades, and that Irish bishops had methodically concealed the crimes. Silently and steadily, Catholics by the droves would quit the Church. Thanks to the brave testimonies of victims, social scientists would undertake extensive research into the origins and crippling long-term consequences of sexual violence by priests, including suicide, drug abuse, depression, lost wages, and the inability to have healthy sexual relationships.

By 2020, U.S. bishops would report having received allegations of abuse by over 6,500 priests from more than 17,600 victims, though advocates would show evidence that the numbers were much higher. The Church would pay over $3 billion in settlements to victims. The wildly popular humanitarian Pope Francis would eventually apologize for the "irreparable damage" caused by sexual predator priests, but victim advocates would protest that it was not enough. They'd criticize him for his do-nothing conferences, his insistence on handling problems internally, and his contempt for accusers.

Twenty years after Grace's world got turned upside down, Brother Luke would still be kneading monk's bread and tending the lush gardens at the Abbey of the Blessed Virgin. St. Laurence House would continue on, more dilapidated than ever, under the direction of an aging Alvin, a middle-aged Sage, and a handful of alternating volunteers. The neighborhood would become more bleak and boarded up; the number of people sleeping on the streets and needing shelter would quadruple.

Of course, Grace couldn't know any of this on New Year's Eve in 1999, sitting with her adopted family around Brian's candle-lit kitchen table, her Jewish mother's nativity scene in the center. She just reveled in the surprise and delight of it all as they sang *The First Noel* and *The Dreidel Song*, gorged on cookies and potato pancakes, and passed nine-month-old Jesse from lap to lap.

Icy wind slapped the black trees and frost painted crystallized stained glass scenes on the windows. Maybe, Grace thought as she looked out at the treacherous night, she would always have to work toward realizing her ideals, to being more compassionate and less selfish. Maybe she would always wrestle with religion and its hold on her, always question its attempts to explain the unexplainable. But maybe that was okay. Perhaps it was enough to accept uncertainty, embrace the questions, and lean toward the light. She couldn't know that they'd all survive, even flourish a little, but she wasn't worried. What else was there to do but wait and watch in wonder?

Note to the Reader

"The system of the Catholic clergy, for which I have great respect and to which I have given many years of my life, selects, cultivates, protects, defends, and produces sexual abusers."
—Richard Sipes

Long Time Gone is a work of fiction, but it is inspired by true events and characters. The following public figures and organizations, and their actions, are real and searchable:

Boston Globe Investigative Staff
Buffalo Nine
Rev. Daniel Berrigan
Rev. Phillip Berrigan
Rev. Joseph Bissonette
Rev. William R. Callahan
Rev. James Callan
Catholic Worker
Catonsville Nine
Sister Maura Clark
Bishop Matthew Clark
President Bill Clinton
Dorothy Day
Sister Jean Donovan
Sister Ita Ford

Pope Francis
Father John Geoghan
Pope John XXIII
Pope John Paul II
Archbishop José Horacio Gómez
Bishop Edward D. Head
Monsignor David Herlihy
Sister Dorothy Kazel
James Kopp
Cardinal Bernard Law
Monica Lewinsky
Cardinal Roger Mahony
Peter Maurin
Thomas Merton
Mother Angelica
Mother Theresa
Father Lawrence Murphy
Quixote Center
Mary Ramerman
Archbishop Oscar Romero
Servants of the Paraclete (identified as Servants of the Lamb)
Dr. Bernard Slepian
Survivors Network of those Abused by Priests / SNAP (identified as PAIN)
Linda Tripp
Mayor Jason West

Acknowledgements

It takes a village to write a book, and this one could never have been written without the intelligent and generous contributions of many wonderful people.

Eight or ten years ago, over vegetable samosas, when this book was just the kernel of an idea, Penny Alsop and Julie Ferris listened, asked shrewd questions, and encouraged me to dive in.

Mary Jane Ryals and Jane Terrell, fellow writers, took early drafts and patiently chiseled them down into something manageable. Over many months of coffee, wine, and meals, and especially on our golden writers' retreat on Dog Island, they helped me transform ideas into words. Getting that old van stuck in the sand at sunset was so worth it.

The gifted writer and editor Adrian Fogelin used a fine-tooth comb to patiently untangle a multitude of sentences and plot points. I don't think the manuscript would have evolved into any kind of shape without her incisive suggestions.

I am deeply grateful to the many friends and fellow writers who offered insightful comments, suggestions for reworking, and perhaps most importantly, encouragement. Heartfelt thanks and hugs to Emily Wheeler, Sharon Kant-Rauch, Brenda Mills, Jayme Harping, Linda Service, Lynne Knight, Laura Newton, Christine Poreba, Donna Decker, Debbie Hall, Elaine Roberts, David Greene, Janet Greene, Katya Taylor, Leigh Edwards, Lynn Peterson, Gloria Colvin, Margaret Clark, Amy Tobol, Shaari Neretin, Rebecca Miles, and my spirited cheerleader Corine Samwel. My writing teachers Barbara Hamby and Elizabeth Stuckey-French mentored and inspired me early on. Ben Green's comical and hard-nosed critique made the first sections better. Beth Nichols generously read the book twice, and offered thoughtful and helpful comments. Tandy Seery, editor extraordinaire, suggested smart last-minute revisions.

When I had no idea how to begin, Julianna Baggott's advice got me going down the publishing road. Years later, my gem of an agent John Sibley Williams, ever patient and resourceful, connected me to TouchPoint Press.

I was able to go on a fascinating journey into the heart of radical Catholicism thanks to the work of many excellent writers. Paul Elie's *The Life You Save May Be Your Own,* Jim Wallis's *All is Grace,* and *Dorothy Day: The World Will be Saved by Beauty* by Kate Hennessy provided me with an in-depth look at the life of Catholic activists who work for peace and non-violent social change. Harry Murray's *Do Not Neglect Hospitality* paints a surprising and richly detailed portrait of the inner workings of Catholic Worker houses. Mary Johnson's *An Unquenchable Thirst* is an eye-opening and fascinating account of life inside the Missionaries of Charity. Rev. Chava Redonnet's *Standing in the Light* celebrates the visionary Catholics in Rochester, NY who are trying to forge a new way. Father Gregory Boyle runs Homeboy Industries in Los Angeles; his memoir *The Tattooed Heart*, and his work with former gang members, are an inspiration.

Staff and volunteers at St. Joseph's House of Hospitality in Rochester, NY were generous with their time, touring this stranger through their home so she could better portray the daily workings of a thriving Catholic Worker House. Thanks to George McVey, James Murphy, Jasmin Reggler, Don Skillman, and Fog Ruiz for their very necessary and important work. Rev. Chava Redonnet welcomed my sister and me and answered many personal and perhaps impertinent questions about women in the priesthood. I admire her bravery and sincerity.

Many tireless and dedicated journalists pressed against the stubborn resistance of the Catholic hierarchy to expose the truth about the priest abuse scandal. I am indebted to their informative reporting. For anyone interested in learning more about the long, sad history of this travesty, I recommend the following books: *Betrayal: The Crisis in the Catholic Church* by the Investigative Staff of the Boston Globe, *Lead Us Not into Temptation* by Jason Berry, *A Gospel of Shame* by Frank Bruni and Elinor Burkett, *Vows: The Story of a Priest, a Nun, and Their Son* by Peter Manseau, and *Sex, Priests and Secret Codes* by Thomas P. Doyle, A.W.R. Sipe, and Patrick J. Wall.

My nephew Ty Hammond offered tough and considered insights early on; our talks about the Catholic Church of our childhoods helped hone my perspective. My sister Chris Quinlan kept me honest about the weather in upstate New York, went to Mass with me, and cheered me on all the way. My beloved in-laws Friedel Bailar and Dick Bailar exemplify the role religion can play in a life of good work; I'm sorry they passed away before I could share the finished product with them. Their support was unwavering. My daughter Erin Meisenzahl-Peace has a gift for sharp critical insights, and I am so grateful for her very useful feedback, artistic vision, and non-stop support. Over the many years it took to conceive, write, and revise this book, my life companion and fellow writer Roger Peace read many iterations, and, on an uncountable number of long walks and late-night talks, discussed with me every single plot point and the development of each character. His enthusiasm and generous feedback have been immeasurably helpful.

Both my mother and father have died, but writing this book has given me a chance to reflect deeply on their life experiences. My Protestant mother's patience, steadfast support, and kind heart profoundly influenced my world view. My Roman Catholic father made me laugh, and inadvertently helped me develop critical thinking skills by giving me someone very conservative and opinionated to spar with. I appreciate all they taught me.

Made in the USA
Columbia, SC
27 January 2020